D0651417

SOMETHING IN COMMON

SOMETHING IN COMMON

Contemporary Louisiana Stories

EDITED BY
ANN BREWSTER DOBIE

WITH AN INTRODUCTION BY
LEWIS P. SIMPSON

LOUISIANA STATE UNIVERSITY PRESS BATON ROUGE AND LONDON
1991

Manufactured in the United States of America
First printing
00 99 98 97 96 95 94 93 92 91 5 4 3 2 1

Designer: Laura Roubique Gleason
Typeface: Palatino
Typesetter: G&S Typesetters, Inc.
Printer and binder: Thomson-Shore, Inc.

This book supported in part by a grant from the Louisiana Endowment for the Humanities, a state affiliate of the National Endowment for the Humanities. Supported by a grant from the National Endowment for the Arts, the Louisiana State Arts Council, and the Louisiana Division of the Arts, Office of Cultural Development, Department of Culture, Recreation and Tourism.

Library of Congress Cataloging-in-Publication Data

Something in common : contemporary Louisiana stories / edited by Ann Brewster Dobie : with an introduction by Lewis P. Simpson.
p. cm.
ISBN 0-8071-1644-0 (cloth)
1. Short stories, American—Louisiana. 2. Louisiana—Fiction. I. Dobie, Ann. B.
PS558.L8S66 1991
813'.01089763—dc20 90-20232
CIP

The paper in this book meets the guidelines for permanence and durability of the Committee on Production Guidelines for Book Longevity of the Council on Library Resources. ∞

CONTENTS

PREFACE

The title of this collection of fiction by Louisiana writers may initially raise more questions than it answers. And so it was intended to do, because *Something in Common* grew out of musings about our storytellers. Who are they? Where do they live? What do they write about? Do they have a distinctive voice? In what proportions are they old and young? professionals and hobbyists? male and female? Do they have anything in common with one another? with the rest of us who read? Do the strong ethnic groups of the state still exercise their presence as cultural forces, creating for it a unique personality and identity? Or has the twentieth century blurred the distinctions that have always set Louisiana apart? The answers, of course, are for the reader to discover from the stories presented here, but some explanation of the process by which the stories were found and selected may be helpful.

Questions about the writers of Louisiana active today subtly reflect an unspoken belief in the continuing vitality of our literary tradition. The state's sense of itself has from its earliest history been expressed in its literature. Our storytellers have always helped us discover ourselves and understand what it means to live in Louisiana. *Something in Common* began with the assumption that today's writers continue to tell us who we are. They catch the sounds and movements of people, the rhythm of our daily lives. But they give us more than simple recognition; as always, they offer us a sense of self and time and place.

If *Something in Common* was to be comprehensive in the contemporary Louisiana fiction it exhibited, the invitation to be part of it had to take several forms. In the case of established writers with national reputations, the previously published works to be included were suggested sometimes by the author, sometimes by the editor. Shirley Ann Grau, for example, submitted a single work, "The Man Outside," and William Mills offered several stories, leaving the final choice to the editor. In the case of "The Turtles," a short story by Ernest Gaines, serendipity intervened. Despite Gaines's plans to see the story in print again someday, he had lost track of it, and it had not been republished since its appearance some years ago in the Stanford University literary magazine. Discovered in the files of a Gaines biographer, it is here presented for the first time to a general audience.

A special attempt was made to reach writers who publish in journals that have limited circulation although they print fiction of admirable quality, many of them sponsored by colleges and universities. The works that were submitted in answer to this effort came from many states besides Louisiana and were often sent by professors or other professionals who are pursuing their careers elsewhere. Finally, an open invitation to all who by self-definition consider themselves Louisiana writers was mailed to public libraries, universities, arts councils, and school systems across the state. Newspaper and radio releases called for manuscripts, and announcements posted where writers are likely to assemble urged them to participate. The goal was to find works of genuine distinction by active writers, known and unknown.

The response was overwhelming. It left no doubt that the state's tradition of storytelling is alive and well. In a period of four months, more than a thousand manuscripts arrived from over four hundred writers. They came from people living in cities and on farms, from teachers, insurance salesmen, and refinery workers, from senior citizens and high-school students. They were written in French and English, on notebook pages and computer paper, in pencil and pen. Though most of the manuscripts were from writers living in Louisiana, they also came from thirteen other states, ranging from Massachusetts to California.

The submissions were as varied as the people who wrote them. Some used complex literary forms; some followed an organic development. They differed in quality as well as subject, some showing the polish of experienced authorship, others aspiring to improve. Many were set in Louisiana, or in a recognizable South, but others depicted experiences beyond native borders—from Italy to Oregon. Although there was a pronounced southern strain in the depiction of character, especially evident in the idioms of speech, many of the narratives could have taken place anywhere, the characters and situations transcending regionalism.

If the quantity of material submitted came as a surprise, its quality was no less gratifying. Despite economic downturns, shifting demographics, unfavorable sociological statistics, and negative environmental studies, it seems that Louisiana's writers keep writing, and their work is good. Each manuscript was evaluated by a panel of readers who, in the end, had problems not of finding enough material for an anthology but of choosing from the many worthy works those few that could be included. Although the panel selected only one piece per writer, many authors that deserved publication still could not be published.

What, then, did *Something in Common* discover about today's Louisiana writers? It revealed that they are people of all ages, male and female, engaged in a variety of professions, though a sizable number are associated with universities either as students or teachers. They write, in French and English, about their lives and those of people around them, often in search of their own understanding, sometimes for the audience beyond themselves. In short, they seem, except that some are bilingual, much like writers anywhere.

What do they have in common? The nineteen stories published here are typical of the rest in their authors' shared fundamental belief in the power and worth of using words to depict reality, to name experience in an effort at understanding it and possessing it. Dealing in their different ways with the timeless themes of good, evil, identity, freedom, and reality, the writers constitute a community carrying on the tradition of setting down what it is like to be living at a particular place and time. Together they testify to the rich cultural heritage from when Louisiana's differences set it apart, and to a present pulling it to be part of social forces once foreign to its ways.

And what do we see in the mirror our writers hold up to us? We find no single image of ourselves, no single statement of shared values. The old stereotypes do not hold, for in these stories we are not the same people who settled New Orleans, fought the Civil War, or voted for Huey Long. We have absorbed people from other areas of our country, moved from the farms to the cities, and changed the size of our families. What only a few years ago was a segregated society has become a mixed one, and an agrarian economy has been touched by technology. Our stories today speak of a society made up of several races and many histories, with fading definitions of sexual roles and changing family patterns.

Reading the selections in *Something in Common,* one is nevertheless struck that in the midst of variety and change a vision, a distinctive way of looking at things, persists. Even writers from Louisiana now living in other states return home in imagination and memory, depicting in words that resonate with the echoes of their culture's history the struggle of today's society to shape the future. The persistent vision suggests that although Louisiana's cultural distinctions have been modified by interchange with other regions, they have not disappeared. Instead, they give this state, as they always have, an identity all its own, a contemporary identity enriched but not subsumed by cultures beyond its borders. These stories speak of a Louisiana that is discovering, in the act of reaching out to the rest of the country and world, new points of commonality within itself and something in common with others as well. In the end, the vision that shines through the stories that compose *Something in Common* makes itself known not as a simplistic view but as a mature depiction of contemporary culture in all its contrasts, rich and varied, differing and complex, a whole that mystifies and intrigues because it is no single entity but a union that possesses an uncommon strength born of diversity.

ACKNOWLEDGMENTS

The editor must express gratitude to the Louisiana Division of the Arts and to the Louisiana Endowment for the Humanities for their generous financial support of *Something in Common*. Grants from the two agencies provided honoraria for each contributor. No less important was support of a different kind, that of the confidence of Tom Boozer, Director of the Acadiana Arts Council, Derek Gordon, Director of the DOA, and Michael Sartisky, Executive Director of LEH, in the significance of the project. Their encouragement from inception to completion was invaluable.

I am also indebted to the readers who conscientiously studied the formidable stack of submitted manuscripts. Delores Harbuck, of Shreveport, and Professors John Wood, of McNeese State University, and Timothy Gautreaux, of Southeastern Louisiana University, employed their expertise with diligence and good humor, arriving, in the end, at a remarkable consensus. Professor Fred Hobson, of the *Southern Review*, provided the difficult service of advising the panel when it was indecisive.

My thanks also go to Bruce Dobie, who introduced the idea of a collection of works by active Louisiana writers. Without his suggestions and prodding, the project would never have been undertaken.

Finally, I must express appreciation to Claire McVay, whose hours of typing the manuscript were helpful beyond measure.

LEWIS P. SIMPSON

INTRODUCTION

The issue of "state's rights" having been basic to the federal structure of the American republic, political and economic historians have made a great deal of the relationship between individual states of the nation and the national identity. Literary historians have made less of that connection, subordinating it to the American impulse, on the one hand, to create a national letters as an indispensable part of a national culture and to the inclination, on the other hand, to create distinctively regional, and even subregional, literatures. At the same time, the regional motive has been recognized as bearing a decided relation to the tendency on the part of the states of the American federation—or as we would invariably put it today, the states of the American union—to become identified with one of three large sections: North, South, and West. Representing roughly geographical and climatic areas of the continental nation, these sectional entities, which in the case of the northern and southern sections began to evolve as political and economic entities in the colonial period, have often displayed a markedly self-conscious awareness of their existence. At times complementary, at times contrary, to the nationalistic compulsion, the phenomenon of sectionalism—a politicized and more intense form of regionalism—together with an often distinctive subsectionalism, may in fact be reckoned as more important in our literary history than either nationalism or mere regionalism. In the last century a self-conscious, highly articulate New England literary culture, inspired by a desire for autonomy rooted in the original Puritan migration, dominated American letters; in the present century a self-conscious, highly articulate southern literary culture, although it has hardly dominated a now multifaceted American letters, has—as a complex fulfillment of antebellum southern nationalism—played a focal role in shaping the American literary character.

Yet, in spite of the nationalistic, sectional, and regional motives in the evolvement of the general literary character of the United States, the self-conscious identification of literary aspiration with individual states has been, and is, significant as still another aspect of our persistent cultural pluralism. We cannot, for example, read such prominent writers of the nineteenth century as Ralph Waldo Emerson, Henry David Thoreau, and Nathaniel Hawthorne without being aware of their deep attachment to Massachusetts; nor can we read their southern contemporary William Gilmore Simms without realizing his attachment to South Carolina. Similarly, in this century we cannot read Robert Frost without recognizing his fundamental connection with New Hampshire, nor William Faulkner without comprehending his close relation to Mississippi. Nor, to turn to the West, with its less firmly established literary history, can we read Willa Cather without appreciating her sense of Nebraska, nor Robinson Jeffers without entering into his sense of California.

In all these instances, however, the writer's vision of his or her purpose is larger than an affinity with the merely scenic and atmospheric—the "local color" particularities—of a limited, specific setting. When, as often happens, the poet, the storyteller, or the dramatist seeks out only the unique elements of the state scene, the power of the imagination is inevitably diminished. That holds equally true, of course, when the focus is narrowly on a region or on the nation, but it appears to be a special difficulty of the American writer who is self-consciously devoted to the state of his nativity or, it may be, of his adoption. This is notably so if the state has a somewhat intricate and perhaps glamorous history, as to varying degrees do all the states representing the original thirteen colonies and as do all the states, whether of colonial origin or not, that became a part of what southerners nostalgically began to call, even in the immediate aftermath of the Civil War, the Old Confederacy. Paradoxically, a rich historical heritage can be more an impediment to the literary artist than a help, carrying with it, as it inevitably does, a heavy freight of romantic clichés. In no case is the deleterious effect of this burden—that is to say, of the tyranny of local color—more apparent than in the instance of Louisiana.

The simple mention of Louisiana—a name honoring the Sun King of France—evokes images of the exotic. Yet the evocation is largely a reflection of the culture of the southern half of the state. Of French and, to a lesser but an important extent, of Spanish origin, southern Louisiana, together with the city of New Orleans—a world in itself and to itself—still shows its descent from settlement by the largest single migration of Roman Catholics to what is now the continental United States prior to the great Irish migration in the nineteenth century. A Catholic enclave in a nation that has been dominated by Protestants, a multilingual, mixed society—composed originally of French, Spanish, Anglo-Saxon, African, West Indian, and native Indian elements and now far more heterogeneous—the world from New Orleans to Lake Charles and as far north as Alexandria is (if not so much today as formerly) in the basic meaning of the Greek word from which the term is derived, "exotic." It is an "outside" culture, one that may be described as foreign both to the American colonial world and to the world of the later American nation, despite the nation's ever-increasing diversity. Yet in the condition of statehood—ratified by the Congress of the United States after the entity we know as Louisiana had been carved from the vast territory acquired by the Louisiana Purchase in 1803—south Louisiana, with its foreignness except for its enclave within an enclave, the Anglo-Saxon community of the Feliciana parishes, was yoked politically and economically to the northern part of the state, which was Protestant and predominantly Anglo-Saxon save for the Creole community of Natchitoches and the Cane River country. The tensions inherent in the forced bonding have never been resolved. Indeed, much of the history of Louisiana as a state has centered in the varied struggle to discover the basis of community in a state so divided that when A. J. Liebling came to Louisiana in the 1960s during the last gubernatorial term of Earl Long, he found it to be an "American Lebanon" (a more precise characterization perhaps than the one we frequently hear of it as a "banana republic"). At the time of Liebling's visit, however, there was still the strong unifying appeal of the state's compelling populist image created by Huey Long and perpetuated by Earl Long through a politics that, it is to be said, exploited rather than attempted to transcend the state's cultural duality. In spite of the fact that the cultural dualism of the state has been modified by the influx of Protestants into south Louisiana—with the startling result that the capital of Louisiana has become a world center of Pentecostal fundamentalism—the dualistic character not only has remained strong but has, ironically, been incorporated into the exotic picture. But at the present juncture of Louisiana's history—when its economic identity as a major petroleum center has faded, apparently beyond recovery—the question of whether or not the state can any longer afford to project an image of its cultural and political exoticism has arisen. Such an image—one that paradoxically seems to reflect a historical heritage Louisianians have in common—will not willingly be surrended by the travel industry. In fact, the proponents of this industry argue that the flow of tourists—lured to the "sportsman's paradise" or the "dream state"—will replace the revenue formerly derived from the flow of liquid gold.

Yet, if there is anything to the concept that serious poets, storytellers, and playwrights are a deeper indication of what is happening in history than writers who are publicists, it would appear that the exploitation of Louisiana exoticism in advertisements, brochures, and film is not effectively supported by the literary sense of the state's cultural identity. To suggest the extent to which the exotic image of Louisiana once was sustained by its serious writers would require more than can be undertaken here: a review in some detail of the literary history of the state, with special attention to the way the local-color movement that arose in postbellum America was a kind of special literary damnation for Louisiana writers from George Washington Cable, Lafcadio Hearn, and Grace King to Lyle Saxon, Roark Bradford, and Harris Downey. They could not escape the limitations imposed by the assumption, unconscious at times no doubt, of being immured in a community of the exotic. That is not to say that writers like Cable did not try hard to modify the impulse to exotic vision—in moments with signal success as in Cable's *The Grandissimes.* But the persistence of the association of Louisiana with the exotic until the time of the Second World War is notable. One wonders what would have happened to William Faulkner if he had stayed in New Orleans instead of heeding Sherwood Anderson's wise advice to return to Mississippi. His early novel *Mosquitoes,* in spite of its intention to satirize the life of the writer and artist in New Orleans, is pervaded by his entranced vision of life. Had he remained in New Orleans, become immured there, it is unlikely that he would have transformed the world of Orleans Parish into a complex mythical image of the modern world, but he did accomplish that feat in his treatment of his obscure native Lafayette County, Mississippi.

Ann Dobie's collection entitled *Something in Common* suggests, I think, that if we seek to define the quest of the writers we at present associate with Louisiana by something they may be said to have in common, we may well come to the conclusion that in a significant way they are linked by a negation of the image of the exotic Louisiana. As the selections in the volume show, it has become possible for writers—for those who have been stamped with the experience of living in Louisiana either as natives or as migrants—to write imaginative works depicting certain times and places in the state, in the past or present, without subscribing to the conventions of local color. It has become possible, moreover, even though writers may be imprinted by the inalienable quality of the Louisiana experience, for them to distance themselves from it, and this to the advantage of their work. Among the authors in Ann Dobie's collection, certain ones stand out as examples. André Dubus, a native Louisianian now living in Haverhill, Massachusetts, sets his stories in the country north of Boston, a place far different from south Louisiana, and yet in his fictional world displays a sensitivity to family and faith that is a refraction of his experience of growing up in Lake Charles and Lafayette. To cite a somewhat contrary example, the late Walker Percy, who was a native of Alabama but who descended from a family long and intimately associated with Mississippi, moved from Mississippi to south Louisiana—a move farther than the miles it covered—and so solidly identified his novels with the Louisiana setting that the reader who does not happen to know better assumes that for Percy it was indigenous. Unlike Faulkner, who returned from New Orleans to his "little patch up there in Mississippi" where he "started from," to discover there a microcosm of the modern world, Percy stayed in south Louisiana, living initially in the New Orleans French Quarter and later across Lake Pontchartrain, in Covington, and discovered a world-historical microcosm. Meanwhile, the late John William Corrington, born in Tennessee but reared in Shreveport, found in his first novel, *And Wait for the Night,* the literary possibilities of Shreveport and north Louisiana in the realistic utilization of their setting; and in his second novel, *The Upper Hand,* he very effectively explored those possibilities further by bringing the protagonist to New Orleans, to yield to the Crescent City's fabled and seductive difference. At about the same time, Ernest Gaines, a native of the black community of the False River country who as a youth had moved to California, began a literary transformation of the "picturesque" world of his nativity into a multidimensional drama of a world in the historical process of a traumatic transition from an agricultural to an agribusiness economy, and, still more fatefully, from a society officially segregated by race to one officially unsegregated.

I make these bare-boned generalizations about four of the more prominent writers in *Something in Common* only as a gloss on the purpose of this volume as it is cogently set forth in the editor's preface. If the writers we associate with Louisiana today tell us, as Ann Dobie says, who Louisianians are at this moment in history, those writers present, I have meant to say, a different sense of life in Louisiana from the one dominantly conveyed by the Louisiana literary sensibility down to the 1950s. Yet, I must add, I have not wished to say that, in offering us, in the editor's phrase, a "sense of self and time and place" (p. viii), contemporary writers have destroyed the earlier sensibility. The writers who record the shift from the exotic image of the state also record the inner drama of that change. The appeal of the exotic image has continued to assert its claim not only on tourism promoters but also on substantial writers, who, it would seem, reject the claim of an exotic Louisiana not by ignoring it but by subtly incorporating it into their vision of the historical reality of the state. The result is that the element of local color—in, say, Percy's depiction of the Feliciana country in *The Thanatos Syndrome* or in Gaines's depiction of the False River country in *Bloodline* or *The Autobiography of Miss Jane Pittman*—blends with the total impression the story makes. The nature of the blending is elusive, but its success is measured by the fact that the exotic seldom intrudes as ornament. I find myself thinking of Robert Penn Warren and that extraordinarily famous novel about Louisiana in which Louisiana is never mentioned, *All the King's Men.* Written after he had been in Louisiana in the 1930s and early 1940s, this work, published in 1946, may be said to signify the first literary victory over Louisiana exoticism. There were various reasons that Warren did not want to make an explicit identification of Louisiana with the setting of *All the King's Men,* but one reason must have been that he wanted to keep a tight rein on a feeling about Louisiana he expressed twenty years subsequent to his departure from the state: "After Louisiana," he said, "nothing has been real." In the tension toward the exotic expressed in Warren's retrospective summation of his experience in Louisiana, we glimpse the elusive something that animates the sense of commonality we detect in the writings gathered in this book.

SOMETHING IN COMMON

STELLA NESANOVICH

THE PEARL

Sophie liked to see familiar names in print. Her breakfast half eaten, she skimmed the obituary page of the *Times-Picayune,* her buttery fingers smearing the print and making dark splotches on the gray, pulpy pages.

> MURPHY, Mary Katherine. Sunday, June 13. Funeral 10 A.M., June 15, Our Lady of Lourdes Church. Interment in St. Roch Cemetery No. 3. Friends and relatives are invited . . .

Temporarily satisfied, Sophie glanced away to scan the alphabetized list for the name of some other New Orleanian she'd known. Seeing none, she thought over her plans for the day. She and Giselle would meet at the church. They'd attended the wake the night before and were surprised by the strangers there. A Father Albert said the rosary. Dark and olive-skinned women, some with accents, reminisced about Mary Katherine's work with the parish altar society and the women's sodality. In the mellow light of the funeral parlor, Sophie hid her surprise and said nothing, only occasionally elbowing Giselle and hissing softly under her breath at the impudence of the strangers.

She and Giselle had known Mary Katherine since St. Mary's High School, worked together for years at the D. H. Holmes de-

From *Southern Review,* XX (1984), 934–50. Reprinted by permission of the author.

partment store, attended the same class reunions. They'd been a threesome always. In school, Mary Katherine dreamed up exciting adventures. Giselle and Sophie followed along, accepting the blame for their friend when one of them got caught. Glancing at the still, serene face of her dead friend at the wake, Sophie felt an old resentment rise and mingle with her new anger. A mantilla draped from the crown of her head, a Cuban woman talked familiarly of "Mary." Mary Katherine had gotten away with this too, these dark friends she'd never mentioned to Sophie or Giselle.

Sophie found the classified section and located the announcement for the estate sale, to be held Friday and, "if necessary," the ad read, "through Saturday."

"Poor Mary Katherine! No relatives, no husband, only that wretch, that cousin who's happy to get rid of her things as quickly as possible," she said aloud now, anxiously crumbling a crust of buttered toast on her tray. She debated relieving her sudden sadness with cream cheese. Breakfast in bed had become ritual—three or four buttered pieces of toast with marmalade, tea, and that wonderful Creole cream cheese from the Goldseal Dairy. Surely Dr. Johnson didn't expect her to give up both butter and that wonderful cream cheese.

"It's one of my few pleasures in life," Sophie had told him. "I've been a careful girl, Doctor. Only take a small drink now and then. I gave up driving, you know. A lady my age can afford so few indulgences . . ."

"I hope Friday's soon enough for him. That renegade cousin! What does he care?"

Her company was a chocolate-point Siamese. Hearing her words addressed to the air, he leaped quickly to the bed and began rubbing his soft fur against Sophie's leg.

"Get down, Charlemagne."

She swallowed part of the crust and carefully licked a trace of butter and cream cheese from under her darkened fingernails. In her mind's eye she watched Mary Katherine place a small silver tray of mints on the side table, smile, then offer a cup of tea to her company. It was the first time Sophie had seen her since her retirement. Nothing was different, not Mary Katherine, not the Coliseum Street house her mother had left. It was untouched from the time they were St. Mary's girls. Now all of her possessions would be gone. The Whitney Bank, Mr. Pursell, they'd be the last there, overseeing the estate sale.

Sophie's shoulders drooped, the newspaper page rested against her breakfast tray. Giselle would reassure her. Mary Katherine hadn't changed that much, and surely Sophie's own things would never be sold off at auction. Then, as she watched Charlemagne slide gracefully around the half-opened bedroom door, she realized she was hungry again. She'd remembered Mary Katherine's brandy alexander pie.

With the funeral at ten, Sophie had time to dress slowly, then get the St. Charles streetcar the short distance from her house to Napoleon Avenue. Only the bus ride to Our Lady of Lourdes would be unpleasant. It was hot in New Orleans, a high of ninety or ninety-two was predicted, and Sophie dreaded the prospect of riding an unairconditioned bus. She'd have to prepare for the sour odor of unwashed blacks, the sickeningly sweet smell of gum the teenagers chewed, the popping sound of bubble gum wadded thickly in their mouths. Tucking a perfumed handkerchief in the jacket of her black dress to cover her nose from the smell, Sophie paused to straighten the veil of her hat before a hallway mirror. Securing the hat against the wind with a slender, pearl-tipped pin, she looked blandly at the small lines, the dark spots, and the broken veins on her face.

Mary Katherine was dead. She'd gone quickly following a stroke. "It's more merciful that way," Sophie told a sobbing Giselle Monday morning when they commiserated over the loss of their friend. Sophie kept her composure. She'd be strong now for Giselle's sake. Still, why did Mary Katherine die? They were young after all. Sixty or so. Active. As much as they'd ever been.

None of them needed to work very hard now. Just keep busy, pass the time. Had their lives been self-indulgent, there might be reason . . .

Mary Katherine gave too much of herself. That was it. True, none of them had married, no aging husbands to care for, thank goodness. Didn't galavant with men. Stayed close always and fulfilled their religious obligations just as they'd been taught at St. Mary's. But Mary Katherine went too far, wanted everyone to think she was perfect. Oversaw the firemen's Christmas toy collection, kept everyone informed when there'd been a reunion, even a casual one. Worked horribly hard at that church. Still, why would God take her before me, Sophie thought. Why would she be first to die?

Sophie's cheeks were rosy now, her eyes narrow. She resented Mary Katherine's adventurous going before her friends, even in death. But she would show them, Sophie thought, as she proudly examined her profile in the mirror. She envisioned herself telling Dr. Johnson how she'd given up her luncheon martini, was living better than ever.

Gathering her gloves and the coins for her carfare, Sophie checked to see that her purse was orderly. Best to have change in hand lest a mugger or some street thug take advantage of an open pocketbook and a woman alone. Carry little in the purse itself. Oh, she knew these criminal types. The missal with its pearlized cover, the one she'd held on to since confirmation, wouldn't deter them.

Opening a small drawer in her carved mahogany table beneath the mirror, Sophie removed the book carefully and opened it to a place marked by her own calling card. The elaborate gothic script of the card contrasted sharply with the bold red Latin print and the black English translations of the mass. A red ribbon already marked the mass for the dead.

Slowly Sophie ran her fingers across the raised lettering on the yellowed card, one of a lot she'd had printed for her high-school graduation invitations. The cool white corridors and the black-and-white marbled floors of St. Mary's rose before her mind's eye. A young man stepped forward, smiling, a corsage in his hand.

Sophie remembered being surprised to discover it was for her. She could feel even now the roughness of his hands against her arm and shoulder as he pinned the flower in place. Her first date, someone Mary Katherine knew.

Then, Sister Cecilia was sternly addressing her. Giselle and Mary Katherine, slight and frightened, slumped in a corner of their homeroom while Sophie grew red-faced during the scolding, accepting the blame for her friends, their giggles making the nun color and speak more harshly.

"Stand up, Sophie Smithson, and take that gum out of your mouth. Ladies do not chew gum, *especially* when they are being addressed by their elders and teachers. Now tell me what you and Giselle were doing with your dates outside the gymnasium during the prom. I saw you there. There's no point lying. I know you were up to something."

Mary Katherine giggled again. Her name hadn't been mentioned. Sophie remembered the mock surprise in her eyes, her hand over her mouth as Sister Cecilia continued her scolding.

"Silence over there! Speak up, Sophie. Are you going to confess? Were you drinking? My, what will become of you girls, St. Mary's girls at that? Boy crazy, wild at times. Well, sit straight in your chair, and don't let me see your legs crossed at the knee again. Cross your legs at the ankle only. That is the only proper way for ladies to sit."

At church Sophie disliked pressing her full weight on her knees as she knelt. She would lean back, resting her wide hips on the pew behind her. Her attention wandered about the church until she spotted Giselle four rows up across the aisle. Her tightly curled gray hair was tinted blue, making it a deeper gray in the semilight of the church. Sophie longed to whisper to her, to get her attention so they could sit together. It was an act Sister Cecilia would disapprove of.

Behind her a choir of children's voices intoned the *Dies Irae*. Sophie straightened up. Then, forgiving herself her age and her painful back, she rested the edge of her buttocks once again on the pew. Sister Cecilia glowered at her.

"Ladies do not lean on the pews, Sophie. The little Lord Jesus looks down and sees you slouching. He'll remember your disrespect."

Sophie shifted forward again. Her weight was making her knees ache. She knew they'd be red when she got up. She was perspiring too, and her taffeta slip stuck to the backs of her thighs. A solitary fan whirred overhead, partly drowning out the choir.

What had happened to Sister Cecilia, Sophie thought. She seemed so real, yet was she dead also?

Sophie dismissed the thought as she mopped perspiration from her cheeks. These poor parishes, taken over by blacks and Hispanics, couldn't afford to run the airconditioning or light the church properly, especially for weekday mass. How had Mary Katherine continued to live in such a neighborhood, attend this church? St. Stephen's was so much closer.

Annoyed, Sophie slipped her hand behind her, tugged at the girdle that cut into her thigh, and released the slip from the back of her legs. She glanced about, but apparently no one had watched her.

On the streetcar ride to the church, Sophie had noticed high-school girls in shorts and sleeveless blouses, their arms and legs exposed, their laughter loud enough to disturb the other passengers and catch the attention of passing motorists. One was dark, Spanish-looking, though she might be what Sophie called a "Negress." She was the one to fling open the long streetcar window and let the wind stream through while Sophie turned her head angrily to the thin glass. She ignored them. She did not open her window to let the wind muss her hair and hat.

In the hot, sticky church she remembered how she wanted to tell the girls to be quiet, to have some respect for other people. There were people reading and praying on the streetcar. The girls would wake the dead with their noise. She swallowed her words and anger then. She swallowed again now. The prayer book lay open in her lap, and the nausea and headache she experienced on the streetcar ride momentarily returned.

When the girls rose, Sophie noticed their lean, golden legs. (A bell jingled. The communion service was beginning.) Hearing the bell on the trolley, Sophie had looked back through the window as the streetcar wobbled down the St. Charles track. The three girls stood in the neutral ground, laughing and waving at the conductor, who smiled back at them as he turned a lever and opened the car to full speed.

The mass was ending, and Sophie could see that there were strangers in the church, the unidentified poor and the elderly who pray perpetually and offer candles for the welfare of others and the dead. Maybe some were Mary Katherine's friends.

The priest descended from the altar now and stood before the coffin. He'd forsaken his purple vestments and was dressed entirely in white, like a virgin bride, except for the black stole that draped about his neck and hung from each shoulder. A small black book rested in his hand.

"Let us pray for the dead, for Mary Katherine Murphy." He raised his free hand to his forehead. "In the name of the Father and of the Son . . ."

Those girls were young, Sophie thought. They'd left the streetcar at Broadway. Perhaps they were St. Mary's girls.

"Our Father, who art in heaven, hallowed be thy name . . ."

Sophie wondered how Mary Katherine could have been a regular at such a church. Why befriend the poor of the parish? This priest? An unknown? She stared angrily at the young priest whose last name was unpronounceable. Father Albert was all anyone called him. How could Mary Katherine let him hear her confession? Know her intimately?

Sophie's legs throbbed and moisture gathered in the small of her back and between her legs, causing her slip to stick once again to her body.

"Hail, Mary, full of grace . . ."

"I wonder if Mary Katherine was a virgin."

The words were spoken aloud. Instantly, Sophie ducked her head so no one in church would know she'd said them. A stooped woman with a kerchief over her head nodded momentarily in Sophie's direction, smiled, then turned back to her prayers. Perhaps she thought Sophie was asking the Virgin Mary to intercede in Mary Katherine's behalf.

The priest was speaking of the shortness of life now, the pain of eternity in hell, and of his certainty that Mary Katherine would join her Maker.

"I knew this good woman, her failings and her virtues," he said in a high Latin voice.

But knew how? Sophie distrusted the loose familiarity of these Spaniards. That dark girl on the streetcar, the women at the wake.

Two small boys, miniature priests in dwarfs' vestments, had appeared at Father Albert's side. They held a silver pail. From it the priest carefully extracted a long slender rod filled with holy water. His wrist flicked skillfully over the coffin, bathing it with the cool, blessed substance.

Quickly and without warning, six strangers appeared and took posts at intervals alongside the coffin. They lifted the casket slowly and in unison, as if on the count of some unspoken number, then carried the remains of Mary Katherine from the church. Father Albert and the altar boys followed. The heavy cross they carried swayed and tilted above their heads.

Sophie bowed her head as the priest passed. When she looked up, she saw only the last of Mary Katherine's final callers staring awkwardly about themselves. A few were still kneeling. Others were mumbling about rides to the cemetery. Then she saw Giselle. She was smiling and beginning to laugh at the way Sophie's hat tipped forward on her head.

As agents of the Whitney Bank, Yesterday's Treasures scheduled the estate sale for nine o'clock Friday. Sophie and Giselle were there early. Since the doors weren't open, they waited at the entrance, first in line.

Outside Mary Katherine's uptown cottage, the air was oppressive. A hot, humid breeze carried the smell of molasses and coffee from the southeast. At 8:30 it was already eighty-six degrees. Only a small group of people waited. Two elderly black women, one in a checked shirt and a plaid blouse, talked of their aches and troubles in a rhythmic speech Sophie couldn't fully understand. A tall, gray-haired woman accompanied by a man in dingy coveralls tapped a pointy-toed shoe against the sidewalk. A Spanish girl, dark and silent, with black half-moons under her eyes, waited with her arms folded. Sophie sniffed the air. The girl was wearing dime-store talc. Lilac or Pond's. Something McCrory's would sell.

Sophie and Giselle planned on eating out for lunch, so they'd both worn hats and gloves. Sophie had chosen a large summer hat, veilless but bordered with multicolored flowers. Giselle's was simpler, a small black straw fitted to her head. Their linen summer dresses were limp.

"Well, I'm glad Mary Katherine's laid to rest, Giselle," Sophie whispered, eyeing the Spanish girl and two black women. "She'd be *so* disturbed."

"Oh, I don't know, Sophie."

Giselle was so dreamy and accepting. Didn't get angry. Tolerant and forgiving, like Mary Katherine. She lacked Sophie's curiosity and imagination, that was it. Otherwise, she too, Sophie was convinced, would care who got what first at the sale, what sort of people bought Mary Katherine's fine things.

When the doors of the house opened, Sophie, her hand firmly clasped around Giselle's forearm, pushed her way through the entrance, hauling her friend behind her.

"Excuse me!" a curly-headed woman in an apron said, stepping back quickly to open the door wide and avoid being trampled by the eager shoppers.

The furniture in the narrow entrance hall was bare, but Sophie could see small white price stickers on almost every piece. Her throat tightened but she kept silent.

In the joint living and dining room to the right, another aproned worker—a dark, smiling woman of middle age—sat with a small metal box, an adding machine, pencil, and tablet. Mr. Pursell from the Whitney Bank was nowhere in sight.

"Good morning," the woman with the metal box addressed Sophie, who merely lifted her head and turned to glance at Mary Katherine's things haphazardly placed on windowsills and tables, crowding one another, each with a price tag slapped noticeably across its front.

"Oh, Giselle, the nerve! I mean, how could they?"

Giselle had freed herself in the hallway and was busy talking with someone else. They pointed to the silver service and porcelain cups. Seeing Sophie, Giselle smiled and moved toward her.

"Sophie, she says the silver service's only plate. We could have it cheap."

"Giselle!"

"Well, Sophie, Mary Katherine knew we liked it. I mean, it's not as though . . ."

"Giselle, I won't hear of it. These are all Mary Katherine's things."

"But I thought you wanted to get here early to buy. Remember what you said about protecting her stuff, Sophie? We can buy things we like and keep 'em safe, sort of like reminders. I mean, we don't have to use it, you know, if, uh, it upsets you."

The house was crowded now. With the doors of the cottage opened, a mixture of people—black and white, elderly and young—wandered in. Sophie's attention diverted to them. Her eyes narrowed as she watched some of them greedily fondling items that defined the life of her friend.

"Look," Sophie said, pointing to a blue-beaded dress being carried into the room by a teenage girl. Her carrot-colored hair was loose and fell to the end of her spine.

"Mary Katherine's Mardi Gras dress, Sophie. She must have worn that dress every year to the Venus ball, remember?"

Sophie wasn't listening. "Young lady," she said, stepping toward the girl and touching one gloved hand to the young woman's arm.

The girl looked openly into Sophie's face. She was pretty but wore no makeup. She'd thrown the dress across her left shoulder in order to look at a small vase.

"Ma'am?"

"What's the price on that dress?"

"Oh, um, five dollars, I think. There's a whole bunch of other clothes in back."

"Five dollars? Can you believe?"

"Good buy, huh? That's why I'm getting it. I can sell it for more at the French Quarter flea market. If I don't like it after a while, I mean."

Sophie crinkled her forehead and glared at the girl.

"Well, there's lots more in back there, lady."

A giant of a woman with her hair piled on her head in a knot pushed past to see the vase the girl held. She was coming from the rear of the house but carried nothing with her. The dining room appeared to be her last stop.

"Nothing here either," she pronounced loudly, replacing the vase. Then, seeing a group of silver demitasse spoons, she stepped closer, picked one up, turned it quickly in her palm, then replaced it on the table. "Old stuff," she mumbled.

Two small women in plain brown skirt dresses moved through the room, animately discussing something. They carefully lifted each piece that caught their eye, read the price, then placed each item in its original spot, making certain it touched nothing else.

"Those pictures shouldn't be for sale, you know," one said clearly.

"Indecent. Too expensive too."

The other nodded her head loosely as her companion talked. She reminded Sophie of a puppet whose head had been struck with a wand. Giselle held her breath, waited for the women to leave, then grinned.

"Sophie, can you imagine? They're talking about Mary Katherine's nudes."

"Her *what*, Giselle?"

"You know. Remember when Mary Katherine was in the Book-of-the-Month Club way back when and they offered those prints?

Famous masters or something. Mary Katherine had two framed and put them in the back room last year or so."

"Giselle, are the women naked?"

"Sophie, they're Metropolitan Museum stuff. You know. The women are . . . Well, you've seen them. They've got some kind of drape or something on them."

"I could fill a book, Giselle, with what I didn't know about Mary Katherine!"

"Sophie, you knew that . . ."

"Let's go, Giselle. I've had enough. Mary Katherine's things are being pawed by all kinds of trashy, ungrateful people. Besides, I don't want to buy anything anyway now. I've got a headache."

At that moment two giggling young men moved quickly through the dining room, glancing at Sophie and Giselle as the two women talked. One hissed, then broke into a loud laugh as he passed.

"Lawd, girl," he said, tilting his head in Sophie's direction.

"Hey, Charlie!" the other called from the kitchen door. "Look at the booze!"

They had spotted a half dozen or so partially filled bottles of wine and liqueurs Mary Katherine kept mostly for cooking and guests.

"The old lady was a tippler, Van, a genuine tippler."

Sprinting through the doorway, they giggled and bumped sideways into each other. In the hallway, one of them crashed full face into Sophie. She'd followed them to the kitchen. Bracing himself, the young man quickly put one palm against each of Sophie's breasts, drawing his fingers away with a slight pinch.

"Oh, excuse me, madame."

The other guffawed. "Lawd, girl, ain't you something."

Sophie's mouth hung open, her face flushed. Her nipples tingled and hardened. Stunned, she watched Giselle stare after the boys as they swayed their hips widely from side to side in an exaggerated walk Sophie feared a mockery of herself.

"Any dresses in the rear for us, girl?"

"Nah, let's go."

Giselle held Sophie's arm.

"Sophie, you okay? I mean . . . have you ever?"

"Giselle, please let's go. I'm . . ."

On the porch, the two men jumped on and off the railing that held back an overgrowth of palmetto and fern around Mary Katherine's cottage. Together they leaped from the porch to the sidewalk, brushing against a bearded man with blond hair to his shoulders. He pushed a Negro woman before him, his hand at the small of her back. She was braless and barefoot, and her stomach rose before her to form an immense ball. Sophie's eyes moved over them as they approached. Neither wore a wedding band.

"Giselle, I think I need a drink."

On the streetcar ride to Canal Street, Sophie stared blankly out of the window. Occasionally Giselle tried to comfort her with a pat on the arm.

"Sophie, you okay?"

She wasn't okay. She felt sick—queasy and headachy. The car was hot and wobbled to and fro on the tracks, starting and stopping too often and lurching forward each time the conductor restarted the engine. She hated the Negro man who took their bus transfers.

"Napoleon," he had chanted, beaming at them.

"Giselle, where do they come from?"

"Who do you mean, Sophie?"

Sophie didn't explain. She wanted to rest in the seat, lay her head against the windowpane.

When they reached the Pearl Restaurant, it was only 11 A.M. The lunch crowd was still light, so Sophie took the time to stop at the Russell Stover store at Canal and St. Charles. She wanted the Little Ambassador chocolates with soft centers to comfort herself.

"I know it's not a month with an *r* in it, Giselle, but I want oysters too, raw oysters," she said, walking the few steps up St. Charles Street toward the Pearl.

A large oyster on the half shell was etched in tiles on the sidewalk directly outside the restaurant's doors. A half-carved roast weighing at least twenty pounds lay in the window, its center pink, its exterior crusty and hard. For years Sophie wondered if the roast could be real, if it was the same one that stayed in the window for weeks, even years.

Giselle shrugged. "Sophie, you know what you want to eat, but remember Dr. Johnson told you . . ."

"Listen, 'Selle. Look what happened to Mary Katherine, diet or not. Stroke, at what was she? Fifty-eight?"

"Sixty-two, I think, Sophie."

"Anyway, look what happened? Died and had all those people pawing over her things. Then those boys there, Giselle . . ."

"Sophie, I think you ought to forget that, you know."

But Sophie didn't hear. She pushed her way through the Pearl's front doors and seated herself at a small table close to the oyster bar where she could watch the oyster openers work. They, at least, belonged there, as familiar as the roast in the front window, repeatedly doing their job, always friendly and polite.

"I wonder if that roast ever changes. It's been like that since I can remember."

"Jesus, Giselle! Do you think they serve old roast here?"

"But, Sophie, I thought you always said you wondered about it too . . ."

Sophie shooed her with her hand, then pointed in the direction of the oyster bar with her chin. There they could see the powerful arms of the shuckers as they worked. The salty, muddy smell of the oysters blended with the frying oil from the kitchen. Sophie watched one gray-haired man behind the oyster bar wipe his callused hands against his apron, pause, then plunge his right hand into a bed of ice to retrieve an unopened oyster. Shaking water and ice from his weathered hand first, he placed the hard, encrusted shell on edge before him, slipped his steel-bladed knife into one corner, penetrating the oyster's core, then drew the blade lengthwise across the slit. The shell fell open. With another rapid, flowing movement, the man cut loose the moist membrane that linked oyster and shell. The very center looked bruised.

"I want oysters, Giselle. Lots of them."

Sophie's eyes were large as she watched the man work. She'd forgotten her headache and nausea. A diner near her speared an oyster with a tiny fork, dipped it in sauce, and swallowed quickly without chewing. He mashed a cracker in his mouth.

A waitress appeared now to take their orders. Menus were tucked between chrome prongs on either side of the napkin holder, but Sophie didn't need to look at one.

"Y'all decided?"

"A double martini," Sophie said. "And, oh, a half dozen raw oysters."

"Erstahs on the shell. Martuni," the waitress repeated in a short chant, her accent typical of many New Orleanians. "Fries? Slaw?"

"No."

"I just want a tuna-salad sandwich on toast. And, uh, a Dixie beer," Giselle added. "We just buried one of our friends. Good friend. A girl we went to school with, worked with too."

"How she go, honey? Cancer? Seems like everybody's got cancer these days."

"Stroke," Giselle answered.

"Oh, yeah, a shock, huh, honey? But thank gawd she went quick. Know what I mean?" She looked down at her pad. "That's one tuna on toast, Dixie, double martuni, half dozen raw erstahs. Make ya own sauce at the bar," she said to Sophie. "Half dozen on the shell, Joe," she called to the oyster opener.

In a second she headed toward two swinging doors at the rear of the restaurant, stopping once to hand a check to a man spooning gumbo from a small cup.

"Giselle, you don't have to tell everybody about Mary Katherine. That's what's wrong now. Too many strangers know all about Mary Katherine. All those trashy people going through her things, and here you are telling anybody about her."

"Well, Sophie . . . See, she understands. The waitress."

The woman had already returned and placed a large frosted glass and a bottle of Dixie beer before Giselle. A small, chunkier glass held Sophie's martini.

"Order comin' up."

Sophie drank quickly, downing a fourth of her drink before Giselle could angle the beer bottle in such a way that the foam wouldn't spill over the top of the glass as she poured.

"Something else, Giselle. What did we know about Mary Katherine really?"

"What do you mean, Sophie?"

"I mean Mary Katherine didn't tell us much. Look at all those strangers at the wake and the church. I just don't know about her."

"Remember how we always ate grilled cheese sandwiches for lunch, Sophie? I thought I'd turn into a grilled cheese sandwich."

"Giselle, are you listening to what I'm saying? This is serious. Mary Katherine never really told us what she did most of the time after she retired. She was too damned quiet about herself."

"Sophie, don't cuss."

"Too private, you know what I mean?"

"But you just said she was too familiar with strangers. I don't know, Sophie. Sometimes you're hard to understand."

"Don't tell me what I said, Giselle. I know what I said. Now listen."

But the waitress interrupted with Giselle's order from the kitchen. "Tuna salad," she said, placing the plate before Giselle. "Hey, Joe, where's my erstahs?"

The gray-haired oyster opener nodded and pointed to the counter. Wiping his hands on his soiled apron, he walked to the end of the oyster bar and pushed a tray toward the waitress. Horseradish sauce and catsup in small paper cups sat in the center surrounded by cellophane-wrapped crackers and a bed of oysters on the half shell. A special effort. Sophie felt pleased.

"Another martuni, hon?" the waitress asked as she laid the tray on the table.

Sophie nodded. "A single this time." She'd remembered her resolve earlier in the week to give up drinking.

The lunch crowd was pouring through the front doors now. Businessmen squeezed shoulder to shoulder at the lunch counter ordering po' boy sandwiches. Orders for fried oysters were shouted across to the shuckers. They worked faster, counting half shells to get a tab for those customers who'd finished eating. Up front a man stood behind the window carving rare and well-done pieces of roast beef to fill the sandwich makers' orders.

"Sophie, don't get too upset, okay? I miss Mary Katherine too, you know."

The waitress had returned with another drink for Sophie, slamming it on the table. She removed the empty glass Sophie left floating in a small ring of water on the formica tabletop.

"But, Giselle, didn't she ever just make you plain damn . . . darned mad? Always keeping to herself like that? Starting things, then keeping herself out of trouble?" As she spoke, Sophie watched the waitress, who now leaned at the oyster bar, smiling and laughing briefly with the men while she placed new orders. Her loose, easy manner annoyed Sophie.

"Sophie, I don't know if I understand. You're talking about things that happened way back when."

"I'll tell you what I mean, Giselle. Sophie Smithson got the blame for Mary Katherine all the time. She'd start something, at school, at reunions, then, poof, she was gone. You remember. She talked about this or that, wanted to know all kinds of personal stuff about us, but it was like she was hiding or playing innocent about herself."

Sophie's gloves rested on an empty chair next to her, but her hat remained on her head, wobbling as she talked.

"Sophie, now you're getting mad about all that old stuff again."

"You're not listening to me, Giselle. Mary Katherine was mean. Playing games to get out of trouble. And another thing. It irritated me no end how she kept going to that cheap church. Just left us out of her life."

She picked up her glass and gulped. Then, spearing another oyster, she dipped it in pure horseradish sauce without mixing in any catsup. Her eyes were already watery, her throat tight.

"That sauce's gonna hurt your throat, Sophie."

"It's my throat."

The waitress approached again. "You ladies want anything else?" she asked, tallying the checks. She placed Giselle's down in a small pool of water. It was clear she wanted them gone, Sophie thought. At least six or eight men accompanied by leggy, loose-looking girls stood in the doorway waiting to be seated.

Sophie glanced once again at the gray-haired oyster opener. He still wielded his knife, drawing it in and out of the oysters with precision, laying each opened oyster naked and raw before his customers, occasionally laughing and showing his shiny white teeth.

A man was asking about finding pearls.

"What do you think, Mac?" the oyster opener responded.

"I want to eat up there," Sophie said. "And I think I want another half dozen oysters. I'm starved."

"Okay, lady," the waitress told her. "Pay this tab later at the front. Joe'll give ya another one."

When she got up, Sophie felt dizzy again. The cool air-conditioned air rushed between her thighs. Her skirt stuck to her legs, but she didn't bother to loosen it. Wobbly, remembering how she felt on the streetcar, she moved forward with tiny steps, holding her glass like a sacred vessel before her. As she did, she focused on the oyster opener, her attention drawn to the way he dipped his hand into the ice, drew forth another encrusted shell, then skillfully slit it open. She wanted to stand close to him, to watch his hands work, to see if he would discover a pearl at the core of the oyster.

Once she reached the bar, Sophie rested her weight against the counter. She felt better and could eat more oysters, now. All those years of abstinence she had missed their salty taste, their slippery texture inside her mouth.

"Aw, Sophie, sometimes . . ." But Giselle didn't finish. She continued to talk with the friendly oyster shucker. "We all went to the same school and worked together for a while. You know St. Mary's?"

"Happens all the time," the man said. "People come in here one day, then I hear they died the next." His hands continued to invade the cloistered world of the oyster.

"To think they're still alive!" Giselle exclaimed.

"Don't feel a thing," the man answered, winking.

Giselle was so easy, Sophie thought, like Mary Katherine, that waitress. Momentarily she saw herself closed off from the worlds of people she'd known all her life. There was this tightness in her chest, a panicky feeling she couldn't quite place. Quickly she gulped another oyster, then reached for the empty shell. Lifting it, she let the liquid slide into her mouth. A trickle dribbled down her lip onto her chin.

"Ah," she said, loudly, deliberately.

"You like that juice, huh, Sophie?"

"You damned right I do, Giselle."

Sophie reared back on her heels, stumbling slightly into a businessman passing behind her. She felt his hands grasp her two arms to steady her. Her hat had slipped sideways. Only the elastic band held it to her head.

"You all right, miss?" the businessman asked.

"I . . . I just need my bill," she said. "Yes, uh, thank you. I better get my check."

When Sophie and Giselle walked into the hot afternoon air, the traffic on St. Charles was heavy, and the sun glared off the crawling cars. Sophie felt nauseated, and her headache had returned.

"Sophie, your gloves. You forgot your gloves."

"Oh, Giselle. I made a fool of myself, and I think I'm going to be sick."

"Sophie, you can't be sick here. We're on the street."

Sophie leaned momentarily against the cool marble facade of the building abutting the Pearl.

"I'll be okay, Giselle. Just stay with me, will you? Get me on the streetcar home, please?"

She was crying now, the first time since Mary Katherine's death. A few passersby looked at her, shrugged, and moved to the outer edge of the sidewalk. Others hurried by, ignoring her.

"Any spare change, lady? Huh? Any spare change?"

The voice was close. The breath reeked of wine. With her eyes closed, Sophie swayed, moving away from the smell. Her head whirled.

"Leave my friend alone, buddy."

It was Giselle. She was going to help.

Outside the gymnasium they sat with their dates in a parked car passing a bottle wrapped in paper. They were drinking wine, that was it. Sophie's date had brought it, a blind date Mary Katherine got her for the prom. Then Sophie was kneeling in the bushes by the gym. Her face was wet with tears. She was vomiting, too. The boy was laughing. She knew God wouldn't forgive her. It had all gone too far, and it was Mary Katherine's fault. Now Sophie'd have to confess to Father and Sister Cecilia.

"Let's go, Sophie. The streetcar's coming. We got to get across the street to get on."

"But Mary Katherine, she dared me to do it. She *told* me to do it, and then Sister . . ."

"Mary Katherine's gone, Sophie. She's dead. So's Sister. They won't bother you anymore."

DAVID MADDEN

THE NEW ORLEANS OF POSSIBILITIES

Rind mist prickling his nostrils, he crushed the orange slice against his palate, constricted his gullet to keep from swallowing too much of the surging juice at once, enjoyed even the sting where his new pipe had burned the tip of his tongue.

"Where did you get this orange?" Kenneth asked the woman at the next table whose smile as she had offered him the fruit had enhanced the shockingly sudden deliciousness of the juice.

"At the produce market down the street," said the man, realizing the woman had not heard Kenneth, enrapt as she obviously was in the first hour of the Sunday morning of lovers.

"I haven't had a real orange in years," Kenneth said to the woman, who turned toward him, the breeze blowing her hair across her eyes. She smiled again, for him now.

Eating the orange, section by section, Kenneth glanced at the lovers, who, in their felicity, had chosen more strawberries, bananas, black cherries, peaches, and oranges than their stomachs could hold, whose overflow of felicity and fruit had touched him. So it was not only in balmy breeze and Sunday morning sunlight that they basked.

New Orleans, the most romantic city of his imagination, the

From *The New Orleans of Possibilities*, by David Madden (Louisiana State University Press, 1982); reprinted in *New Orleans Review*, IX (1982), 21–28. Reprinted by permission of the author.

city in which he had once expected to realize so many possibilities, had become so routine, he had awakened in the Royal Sonesta this morning to a palpable, almost urgent impulse to do something slightly unusual. Having supper along at Begue's last night, on the occasion of his thirty-sixth birthday, he had realized that except for Charleston he had seen—though only as a salesman can see—every American city he had ever wanted to see. Doubting there would ever be a necessity to go to Charleston and failing to imagine it as a vacation attraction for Helen and John made him sad. But up in the room, looking down on Bourbon Street, where he no longer felt safe walking at night, he had realized too that New Orleans, his favorite city even over San Francisco, had in his routine become almost as bland as an airport layover. And when the morning light woke him, he knew he had not felt merely the blues of a man away from home on his mid-passage birthday. He had projected his life to live in cities, and the cities were gone. Sipping café au lait with fifty tourists outside the Café du Monde and eating beignets had not quite met his criterion for something slightly unusual. The gift of the orange, the woman's smile, had.

The lovers left their table littered with fruit peelings, seeds, rinds, pits. Unable to sustain the shared moment in the breeze and sunlight, Kenneth walked toward the produce market, his system so unused to juice straight from the rind that he felt nauseated.

The second time he had come to New Orleans the heat, humidity, and pollution had been so intense he had seen the market from an air-conditioned touring bus with Helen and John. The first time, he had come alone to handle a new account and had confined his walking to Bourbon Street.

The mingled odors of fruits and vegetables were so intense that he tasted the market before he smelled it.

Walking under the long open-sided shed, down the narrow aisle between the stalls, Kenneth felt as if the bodies, faces, hands, and the fruit and vegetables were a palpitating morass that excited and delighted him, reminding him of his childhood birthday parties in Indiana. He bought pears, apples, peaches, bananas, a pineapple, strawberries, oranges, and tomatoes, and wondered what he would do with them. Appointments in Houston and Dallas lay between New Orleans and home. I may never see stuff like this again in my lifetime, he thought, smiling condescendingly at his isolated gesture.

Entering the lower end of the shed, he saw that this section was given over to a flea market. He wished Helen, who loved garage sales, could be there. The intriguingly slummy atmosphere of this part of the French Quarter, of the market, drew him among the tables, some of which were set up in the parking spaces. Bright old clothes hung from the barred windows of a discarded streetcar with Desire as its destination. Inside a high iron fence, tourists were being guided through the vast Old Mint building, recently restored after decades as a prison.

His mood fluctuated between revulsion at the sleaziness and excitement at possibilities. Looking at objects that ranged from cheap new pseudocraft products to genuine antiques, from trash to bizarre oddities of some value to collectors, he forgot the queasiness that café au lait, powdered-sugar-sprinkled beignets, and orange juice had induced. Realizing that he had fully acted on impulse to break routine and open himself to possibilities made him feel a sense of adventure, and a little anxiety—made him reach for objects he had never imagined he would ever want to look at, much less buy and use and enjoy.

"For the man who has everything," Helen had said, presenting the pipe three days before his birthday. Now he had twelve pipes, only one of which got the use and care a pipe demands. And here, too, among the disgorgings of New Orleans attics were discarded pipes that perhaps someone here would be glad to smoke.

That a buyer had been imagined for each likely and unlikely object on disarrayed display intrigued him as much as the objects themselves. The snaggle-toothed old woman, who looked like a caricature of a witch, had sat in a foul-smelling room somewhere in this sprawling city and imagined a buyer for those rusty iron pots. Kenneth paid her three-fifty for the cast-iron corn-stick mold, so heavy it almost balanced the load of fruit in his other hand.

And that bearded man, whose underarm stench, palpable as flesh, reached across the table, and stooped among those coils of barbed wire and anchors and canoe paddles, seeing buyers clearly enough to load it all into the back of his VW van and haul it down here at daybreak. Kenneth passed on by the barbed wire.

And this spaced-out girl, dark circles under her eyes, veinless smooth hands trembling more visibly than the old woman's, had squatted in some chairless, mattress-strewn, windowless slave quarters off a courtyard as sump-smelling as a Venice canal, convincing herself someone would buy one or two or three of the old photographs she had foraged out of attics and basements and rooms of abandoned houses, old houses torn down, and trash cans where she had hoped perhaps to find edibles. Too flummoxed by such incomprehensible assumptions to move on, Kenneth stopped, stared down into the lopsided cardboard box into which the girl had dumped thousands of photographs, mostly snapshots muted in time's sepia tone.

The moist fruit had dampened the bag. He lifted and hugged it, damp side against his coat, and walked on among the 78-rpm records, the fabrics and shirts and blouses and dresses, the rings and buttons, the glass insulators, the Mississippi driftwood and cypress knees, the old comic books, the tables of unfocusable clutter, the neater displays of antique toys, the moldy books and National Geographics dating from the twenties, that Kenneth was too burdened to leaf through.

He made the rounds, continuing long after fatigue and nausea and the increasing heat and humidity had made him sluggish, as if to miss even scanning sight of any of this stuff would wake him in the middle of the night in Houston or Dallas or home in Chicago, regretful, with that gnawing sense of unfinished business. The peculiarness of such a premonition making him feel a need to assert his own control over his behavior, he turned away from the flimsier tables lined up alongside the streetcar named Desire, and with the phrase, he retraced his steps, consciously in his mind, went back the way he came.

Kenneth waited for a young man in overalls and wide-brimmed leather hat to pay for the photographs he had stuffed into his pockets.

"May I set these down a moment?" Kenneth looked at the dark circles around the girl's eyes. She nodded rapidly, unblinking.

He reached into the bulging box, asking, "How much are these?" to make conversation, for the girl made him uneasy. He picked one of the photographs gently from the clutter, as if handling someone's personal effects.

"Fifty cents a handful."

"You don't sell them one by one?"

"Fifty cents a handful."

Imagining the young man in overalls grabbing two fistfuls, cramming his pockets, crushing some of the photos, shocked Kenneth.

"Get out the pictures, Granny." His grandmother used to imitate the way he had said that when he was a boy. Then she would honor his new request and take the hatbox down off the shelf in her closet and sit beside him on the couch and gently pick them one by one from the loose pile. He felt an urge to tell this girl what his grandmother said, to imitate her voice imitating his own, but even had she not stared at him, seeing nothing, he knew he wouldn't have told anybody.

His fingers webbed together to cradle his head, a man leans back in a high-backed straight chair, his foot braced on a white railing that runs blurred out of the edge of the photograph toward the end of the porch, getting thinner as it reaches his foot, the toe of the other foot touching the floor almost delicately. Someone caught his semicandid pose at the turn of the century. The locale was possibly the Garden District. Smiling, imagining his grandmother's response, Kenneth placed the photograph back on top, trying to put it where he found it.

He picked up a raw recruit of the forties, saluting, mock-serious, his billed cap resting on his ears. On V-J Day was he in Times Square or beneath a white headstone in France? He laid it down.

Propped up in a hospital bed, a young woman in a lace-trimmed nightgown holds her newborn baby. The kind of shot Kenneth had once snapped himself.

A plump man in suspenders sits in his favorite chair under a fringed lamp on a stand, his delicately smoking cigar held between the fingers of his upraised hand, at the ready.

An old man changes a tire on a road in arid hills, a little boy sitting on the running board. The man's wife probably took this one. Out West, on vacation.

An elementary-school class against a freshly washed blackboard, half of the children smiling, half tight-lipped. Losing their baby teeth?

A child sits on a table, a birthday cake with three candles between its legs, presents heaped on both sides. Kenneth had one of himself at four, a similar pose.

A young man in a jogging outfit, his arms full of old record albums, stopped to glance over Kenneth's shoulder at a family in their backyard under a mimosa tree, a man in hammock, a child in diapers wearing a sailor hat, lifting the long handle of a lawn mower, a woman taking a bite from a piece of cake, an old man reaching for an apple from a tree, smiling for the camera.

"You want that one, sir?"

"I'm just looking."

"Mind if I take it?"

"No, go ahead."

"Fifty cents a handful," the girl said, with no more response to the young man than to Kenneth, who was feeling older than thirty-six the longer he stood there.

The young man obediently grabbed "a handful" and carefully slipped them into the pocket where he had found the fifty-cent piece.

Kenneth wondered whether older people had bought any of the pictures. As he picked them up at an increasingly fast tempo, his assumption that they came from many sources was confirmed. The faces from picture to picture bore no resemblance to each other, although a few that turned up in succession were in a sequence. They seemed to span decades, with many settings beyond New Orleans. Kenneth looked at her. Maybe she wanders in a trance like a gypsy from city to city, rummaging in trash cans. A free romantic life, for which he felt a fleeting envy, irrational not only because she looked like death warmed over, but because "wandering from city to city" described his own life.

A young man and his date pose in formals at a prom. Kenneth wondered whether the slim young man now had a potbelly.

A telephone operator of the forties, surprised, ruins a candid shot, shouting no, her hand thrust out to blot the camera eye.

Children, perhaps a Sunday-school class, at a picnic, one boy in a swimsuit, looking straight up into the sky. Kenneth imagined an airplane.

A grinning young man opens the door of his new, perhaps his first, car, early-fifties model.

A man behind a soda fountain, his hand on the nozzle, two girls having turned from their sodas to smile at—good ol' George, Kenneth imagined. I can remember cool soda fountains, said Kenneth, almost aloud. Helen would get a kick out of this one. They were just going out when we came in.

"I'd like to buy this one."

"Fifty cents a handful."

"No, just this one. Glad to pay fifty cents for this one."

"Look, man, I'd like to dump all of this, save me the hassle of lugging it back to the room. Take a handful, will you?"

"Why not?" He pushed together, like strewn bridge cards, enough to stack on his right palm.

As he slipped the stack into his coat pocket, she said, still not looking at him, not seeing him, "Take two—no extra charge."

That would be greedy, he started to say, but the comment seemed inappropriate even for her benumbed ears. He started aligning another stack.

"Look, man, like they aren't going to bite you."

"No, I just . . ." He wondered how, in such situations, such marginal people manage to make one feel inept, inferior.

Digging down with a kind of venal abandon, Kenneth dredged up an overflowing handful, noticing that one of those that spilled was a snapshot of a young man sucking in his belly, flexing his muscles, letting his pants drop over his hips below his navel, clenching teeth and bugging eyes that were the spitting image of his own. He smiled self-consciously, as if the girl, her hand still held out for the fifty cents, had discerned the resemblance in the same instant of surprise.

Now what do you know about that? Amazing. He'd always heard that by the law of averages there must be somewhere on the earth someone who exactly resembles yourself, and in all time and all the universe, someone who is your exact duplicate, or your doppelgänger, a scary concept that had universal appeal. And once, he had picked up the newspaper, startled at the face of a bush pilot who had crashed in the Alaskan wilds, survived subzero weather for five weeks, and lay in the hospital. Even with a tube up the nose, the frostbitten face against the white pillow was so obviously his own, he called Helen out of the shower, dripping, to look at it. "That's Kenneth Howard all right," she corroborated.

Picking it up, recalling the girl's assurance it wouldn't bite, Kenneth started to slide it beneath the deck as a novelty item to startle Helen and John and party guests. Within the magnifying range of his first pair of glasses, the face proved to be Kenneth's own.

The exhilarating moment of discovering a wild coincidence faded quickly into reasonable doubt. He put the second deck in his other coat pocket and looked closely at the face. Holding his breath, his teeth clenched in a jack-o'-lantern grin, his eyes bulging like Peter Lorre. Who could—could even he?—say whether the face was his. When? When he was about seventeen. Where? Against the side of a garage, the white paint peeling badly. He remembered his severe sunburn peeling that summer. But that was not his father's garage. Perhaps a neighbor's. He tried to remember, and couldn't. He looked for a scar or some revealing mark on his naked chest. All his scars dated from college football. Was that black spot the size of a nickel his navel? How does one recognize one's own navel? He laughed. But it didn't seem as funny as on the surface it ought to have. Well, it's not me.

Imagining the girl scrutinizing him for his strange behavior, Kenneth looked up. Still, she saw nothing—catatonic—her palm open, not impatiently. Indifferently.

Not possible. Not possible? Hadn't he always thought of New Orleans as the city of possibilities? In New Orleans, what was not possible? Uneasily, he smiled, shrugged it off as a wild coincidence, the kind of experience you come to New Orleans for, even if you're coming anyway for routine reasons, and slipped the photo into his coat pocket with the others, wondering who had snapped this shot.

Idly, as he felt in his pocket for a fifty-cent piece, he pushed his fingers through the box, stirring up images. He handed her two quarters and picked up the corn-stick mold. As he lifted it, the bag broke, and he had to chase the fruit down the aisle among shuffling feet. People helped him. It's the business suit. He remembered reading an article that answered the question, Who gets helped, where and when, if somebody drops something in a public place? Noticing that the oranges rolled the greater distance gave him a comforting sense of workaday reality. And there were the bananas lying where they had landed. None of the fruit was ruined except for several squashed peaches; rising imperceptibly, bruises would show hours later.

He eased his armload onto the table and walked briskly to the fruit and vegetable stalls and paid a dime for a paper bag. Walking back, the possibility struck him that if there was one, there could be another, perhaps others, in the bulging shapeless box, and he hurried to her table, afraid his fifty cents added to the day's take might have given her enough for a fix and she would be gone.

The girl, the box, the fruit were still there. He offered her an orange. She shook her head in revulsion.

The back of a man's head, severely barbered, as he leans away from the camera to kiss a woman, blotting out her face.

A woman smells a rose on a bush, wearing a flared hat of the forties.

A girl wearing a Keystone Kop hat and coat, a moustache pasted under her nose, thrusts herself toward a boy behind bars in a gag shot at an amusement park.

A formal gathering at an outdoor celebration of some sort—no, a funeral. Photographs are deceptive, Kenneth thought decisively.

Practicing, a majorette twirls her baton, fractioning her face.

A man washing his car. I think I know that guy. Kenneth set it aside.

A man working at his desk, looks up, smiles quizzically at the camera.

A sober-faced little girl pushes a toy, no, a regular baby carriage down a cracked sidewalk. Empty, or occupied?

His head turned, his eyes half-closed, his mouth oddly ajar, Kenneth, in an ambiguous setting, caught in a Polaroid shot, the surface poorly prepared by the chemical substance he almost smelled now. Cracking, scratched, perhaps by fingernails pawing over the contents of the box. Kenneth licked his lips. The eyes blurred, closing. Perhaps another—no, not another coincidence. He rejected the possibility that some submerged need in him was looking for resemblances. Letting the picture drop on the cast-iron corn-stick mold, he dug farther.

Firemen pose in front of a fire hall, standing, hanging all over a new engine, perhaps only freshly washed—yes, water sparkles, drips from the fenders.

A man, leering, pretends to sneak into an outhouse marked Women.

A businessman, perhaps a government official, presents a check and a handshake to a well-dressed middle-aged woman.

A man strides down a crowded sidewalk, caught unaware in a shot obviously snapped by a sidewalk photographer.

A young man poses with his parents at a high-school graduation ceremony, the mother blurring herself as she moves toward her son, as if to kiss him.

A young woman sits in a swing, empty swings on each side, blowing cigarette smoke toward the camera.

If I find one more, just one more, then . . . The third was clear, his face quite natural, the suit his first-job suit, the setting unmistakably the front of the building, at the curb, beside the red, white, and blue mailbox and the Keep Chicago Clean courtesy trash receptacle. What was the occasion? Probably not his first day because he stood there (waiting for the light to turn green) with such aplomb, one hand in his pocket, the other casually holding a cigarette at ease—obviously between puffs, not in a hurry, looking straight into Kenneth's New Orleans stare, but not into the camera's lens. Looking, like the girl, at nothing in particular, but unlike the girl, so young and vibrantly alive and receptive, he struck Kenneth as a charming, likable young man in his early twenties. He couldn't see the street sign, but he knew it was Halstead and Grand. When was it taken? Who took it? The questions drew such total blanks, he didn't start going over the possibilities. He wanted to dig for more.

One impression held his attention on the picture already in his hand—he didn't seem to realize he was being photographed. He looked at the Polaroid. Obviously candid. He pulled out the muscle-flexing shot—even around this classic exhibitionist pose hovered a sense of privacy violated. The show-off eyes were introspective. He set the three aside, neatly together.

A man driving a tractor looks up as if responding reluctantly to a request.

A stiffly posed, badly retouched color shot of a married couple.

An infant wearing a knitted tam manages a brilliant smile with only a single tooth. The brilliance in the eyes. Was it still there?

A teenage boy strains to pose for a self-portrait as he presses the shutter release lever on the camera, seen in the lower right-hand corner of a bathroom mirror.

People in tennis togs crowd around as a man in a suit presents a trophy to a man dressed for tennis. Kenneth thought one of the spectators resembled a man he knew years ago.

Through glass from the rear, a shot of himself standing in an empty room, his back to the camera, looking out a tall window in an old house, wearing his football jersey, number 8. The stance, one foot cocked back, his body leaning, his elbow propping it against the window frame, his arm bent back so he could palm the back of his head, the other hand in his pocket, was obviously not a conscious pose for a photograph. He seemed to have been shot through a side window at an angle that caught him looking out a front window.

The possibility that anyone he knew had taken these pictures without his knowledge as a joke—they were not, except for the muscle-flexing pose, gag pictures, and he remembered none of the situations or occasions—was so remote, he left himself open to a joking assumption the CIA had had him under surveillance since he was seventeen, or maybe younger. He looked for younger shots.

A teenage girl in shorts strikes a pinup pose against sheets on a clothesline.

A man sets his face in a mindless expression for a passport or an ID photo that has turned yellow.

Kenneth looked for someone he might know, even vaguely, in a family-reunion grouping on steep front-porch steps.

A woman and a boy pose in front of a monument, looking so intimately at the photographer, Kenneth lucidly imagined the photographer himself.

A woman has turned from the trunk of a car, a sandwich held up to her open mouth, four other people bent over, their backs toward Kenneth, who, unable to see their faces, feels uneasy.

A double-exposed shot of Kenneth reading a newspaper on a train, so intent upon a particular article he holds the paper and thus his body at an awkward angle, giving the photographer an opening. On the train window, as if it were a reflection, a child sits on a Shetland pony. A Chicago train? Nothing showed to answer his question. He had ridden hundreds of trains, perhaps thousands.

He looked at the girl, wondering whether she might not suddenly recognize him as a recurrent image in her scavenged collection. She was still in a hypnotic world of her own making or of some chemical's conjuring. He took off his jacket, lapped it over the bag of fruit, picked his sweat-saturated polyester shirt away from his skin, wiped his hands along the sides of his pants, licked his lips again. His mouth was too dry.

Kenneth began to dig into the box, shuffling quickly past the little brown studio portraits of the 1860s whose edges crumbled, leaving his fingertips gritty, past the baby pictures—in his mother's collection, he had never recognized himself—past the group pictures that obviously excluded him, past the ones with Spanish-moss backgrounds, New Orleans settings, nothing specific to look for, his breathing fitful against the expectation that each movement of his hand would turn up out of this deep box his face. The savage's fear that cameras snatched, photographs held the soul captive made Kenneth laugh at his own fearfulness.

A young man of the seventies sits on the grass on the levee playing a guitar, a barge passing behind him.

The rim of a pale shadow in bright sunlight smokes on a stucco wall, the partial outline of a camera looking as if it is attached to the photographer's hip.

A couple sit on a New Orleans streetcar, having exchanged hats, exhibiting beer cans.

A company picnic. Kenneth looked anxiously for someone he may have known at some phase of his life.

A man sleeps, perhaps pretends to sleep, in a fishnet hammock.

Kenneth is having lunch with a man whose fork obscures his face. Kenneth sits before his own plate as if wondering whether he can eat it all. Between himself and the man—he tried to recognize the ornate cuff links—communication has visibly ceased or not yet really begun, perhaps was never resumed. What restaurant was that? His memory responded to nothing in the decor. "November, 1972" printed in the white margin stimulated nothing. It did not appear to be one of those restaurants where girls come around taking pictures of moments to be treasured forever. No third party had said, "Hold it! Smile! That's terrific!"

"Say, miss . . . say, miss?"

"Fifty cents a handful."

"I know, but I just wanted to—I just wondered—could you tell me where you collected these photographs?"

"I don't remember."

He showed her one of the pictures."Do you have any more of this fellow here?"

He showed her the one of his back in the empty room.

"I don't know."

He showed her the one on the street corner. "Him. Recognize him?"

"No."

"Him?"

"No."

"How about him?"

"No."

"They're me. They're all me." He looked into her lackluster eyes. "See? Each one of them resembles me to a T. I mean, they are of me. Somebody . . . Do they look like me?"

She nodded, expressionless.

"Then do you remember where you first found them?"

"No."

Pigeons perch on a woman's arm, tourists feeding pigeons behind her, a European cathedral in the background.

A boy stands at attention to show off his new scout uniform.

An elderly couple stands in front of a tour bus, the letters spelling its destination backwards.

A religious ceremony, ambiguous.

A man shows a string of fish, a river flowing in the background.

A young man and a young woman sit on a diving board, in profile, looking away from the camera, squinting into the sun.

A little boy sits on a plank placed across the arms of a barber chair, obviously captured on the occasion of his first haircut.

Kenneth stands in line at an airport, the destination on the board unclear. He is lighting his pipe, his lips pursed on the stem.

Another Polaroid. Between himself and the woman in front of him, a fat boy in shorts takes snapshots with a minicamera. In the picture the boy snapped—of his mother, his father, his sister, his aunt, his teacher, his friend, a stranger who caught his eye—one could see perhaps the person who had taken Kenneth's. The combination of images—in hand and imagined—made him aware of the nausea again. He had to make it to a bathroom quick.

He riffled through the box, thinking, I'm missing some, I must be missing some—there's no system to what I'm doing. The pictures, too quickly scanned, spilled from his hands back into the shifting clutter out of which he had fished them. The sun, the nausea, the eyestrain in the bright polluted air made him too weak for the task of sorting them all out on the cramped table.

"Will you be here all day?"

The girl shrugged her shoulders, "Man, how do I know?"

"Here, I'll pay for these—I'm—I'll come back right away—here, let me take some more handfuls." He shoved a handful into his right pants pocket, spilling, another into his left pants pocket, spilling, into both his back pockets, his inside breast pockets, his shirt, worrying about the effect of his sweat on them, stuffed some into the bag with the fruit, picked up the ones he had spilled, and give her five dollars.

"Keep the change and try to stay around awhile, I'll come right back." He turned, hugging the bag of fruit, carrying the corn-stick mold out through the stalls, the parking spaces, and went back to her. "Well, did you get them all in the same place?"

"No, man."

"The same town? New Orleans?"

"Yeah. Maybe. Take another handful at a discount. Only a quarter."

"I just hope you're still here. I want to go through them one by one, systematically."

He made a final effort to see a glimmer of recognition in her eyes, and failing, turned away again, feeling distance increase between himself and the box hunched on the table.

In the dirty, narrow street he flagged a taxi.

Lying stripped to his briefs, on his bed in the Royal Sonesta, the nausea ebbing, the photographs spread around him, he said over and over, Who took these pictures?

As he named his brother, his sister, his mother, his father, his other relatives, Helen, John, and a combination of them to account for the variety, each possibility struck him as so absurd, the rapidity with which he rejected them made him pant in exasperation with himself for even considering them.

He scanned the pictures slowly, hoping to stop short at the face of someone who might have become somehow obsessed, a creepy childhood friend, a spurned sweetheart, an oddball relative, or a deranged business associate.

Looking up at the ceiling, he saw himself in many places, at many periods in his life, all past his seventeenth year, but he saw no faces of likely secret photographers.

What happened to the people who had taken them, causing the pictures to end up in the New Orleans flea market?

Was this person or persons male or female? Young or old? A contemporary? Known to him? Known well? A mere acquaintance? A business rival? Or a stranger? Friend or stranger, loved one or enemy, his frustration, his helpless astonishment had a quality of zero that he felt in his bones.

In the batches he had snatched up at the last moment, he had found other shots of himself. He is gassing up the car at a self-service island. Sitting on the bench as a player. Having a drink, sitting on the patio. Waiting for his bags to show up at a carrousel in an airport. Walking the dog. Looking at stills outside a movie theater. Sitting in a lobby, his face hidden by a newspaper, as if he were a private eye, but obviously himself. Caught taking trash down a driveway to the curb. Lighting a cigarette in a stadium with friends, their faces turned away from the camera. Doing what people in the other photographs did. Sometimes strangers in the frame with him, but most often alone. As if he were being contemplated.

Each of the snapshots declared at a glance that he had not posed the image he held in his hand. Several types of cameras had taken the pictures, a range of paper sizes, shapes, stocks had been used. The quality of the photography ranged from awful to professional. A few were dated by the processors, a few had been dated in pencil, perhaps by the same hand but not one he recognized. Age or neglect had yellowed some. The negatives of some had been scratched. Some were soiled, damaged. A few had tabs of fuzzy black paper or smears of rubber cement on the backs as if they had been preserved in a scrapbook, then ripped out and put away or discarded.

Some of the places he recognized but couldn't fix in time. For some, he determined a time, but was at a loss to name the place. Perhaps he, she, they had kept a record of the dates and the places. Sometimes, he even remembered generally how he had felt, once specifically (melancholy), but not the context.

Lying on the double bed as if on a rubber raft at sea, he tried to go over every possibility again, imposing a kind of system. But each sequence to which he tried to adhere was besieged by so many unaccounted-for possibilities and sheer impossibilities, he abandoned them and gave himself up to chance. If a photo was worth a thousand words, he needed the words for these, because, as a neutral voice told him, "the camera never lies."

He scrutinized each picture of himself for the third time, straining his eyes to detect ghost images such as spiritualists and UFO enthusiasts claim to see, or as religious fervor discerns Christ's visage in commonplace photographs. He remembered reading about a news photographer who happened upon a wreck on the highway and who shot the scene too fast to distinguish faces until his own seventeen-year-old son's face became more and more distinct in the developing tray.

The bounce of the springs as he jumped off the bed spilled some of the pictures onto the carpet. As he picked them up, he realized that the almost reverent care he used came not from narcissism but from respect for the feelings of the person or group who, he was inclined to conclude, had pursued through the years an obsession to chronicle his life.

Returning to the Market, he caught a glimpse of the Sunday-morning lovers, hoped they would wave to him, but more than a hundred people milling about the flea-market tables distracted them.

The girl was gone, but behind the box a little black boy's head was visible from the eyes up, his hands clutching the top, as if he were guarding.

"Where's the lady?"

"You the man?"

"Yes, where did she go?"

"She split, man. Said, give me a dollar for this box of pictures and a man come in a business suit give you a million dollars for this ol' box of trash."

"Here's two tens. Okay?"

"Man, that trash belong to you." He took the two tens and shoved the box toward Kenneth.

Kenneth picked up the box, looked around for any strays, and turned, lifting his knee to balance, as he embraced the shifting, bulky sides of the torn cardboard box, feeling mingled awe and anxiety, remembering the two men who had bought pictures, feeling an impulse to track them down, wondering whether and from what angle sudden light was for a fraction of an instant flooding a dark chamber, etching his struggle on sensitized paper.

ELTON GLASER

BLUE CAT CLUB

His first thought was, The air smells fried. Nine years old, his knees weak as weeds, he was marooned in the crowded middle of the dance floor, leather gliding over grit. The rasp of a saxophone made his eardrums hum.

"Who this white boy belong to?" The voice came from somewhere beyond the dancers, bullhorn loud.

The band stopped playing, all of them shut down except the lean black man on saxophone who was far too high in the spirals of his solo to find his way down at once. He weaved slowly back to his starting point, shook three golden grunts out of the horn, and swung it away from his purpling mouth.

"That Crookneck," said a woman in a deep-green dress. "He don't stop if the club catch fire. He don't stop if the Mississippi roll in the windows. He don't stop if the po-*leece* come in the door, cracking heads."

Before the boy could find his way out of the milling dancers, the loud voice boomed again, sounding in that close room like the wrath of Moses when he found his people bowed down and drunk before false idols.

"What this white boy doing in my Blue Cat Club?" A huge face

From *Louisiana Literature*, III (1986), 22–27. Reprinted by permission.

under a houndstooth porkpie hat leaned down to look at the boy, the black jowls stubbly and alive with hard tremors.

"He listening to the music, Alabama, just like the rest of us." It was that woman in the green dress again. She put a dark arm over the boy's shoulders. Golden hoops the size of handcuffs pulled down on her ears.

"Well, shit then," Alabama said. "Git the music going again. You take care of him now, Camille, till we figures this thing out. Don't want no trouble over no white boy."

"No trouble," she said. "You come with me, honey."

The boy followed her to a table in the rear of the big room, a dim corner away from the hubbub of dancers. Out of the window, he could see the railroad tracks not fifty yards away and beyond them the great tan-and-white warehouses on the Mississippi docks. A thin rain was still falling. He was trembling again, not sure what would happen to him now.

"You like a Co-Cola?" Before he could answer, she yelled over the band that was just kicking into a new tune, "Two Co-Colas, one with something in it." Her eyes were the brightest black the boy had ever seen, the color midnight ought to be if it lived up to its reputation, and they were looking right down at him.

"Now what you doing here, boy?" she asked. "Your mama know where you at?"

And he wanted to answer but how could he when the saxophone just then slid into something smoky and the drummer rapped out five rimshots like a firing squad, then put down his scarred sticks and let the brushes work out, a sound like moonlight over a tin roof? He wanted to tell her how every night since his father had trucked in the family two weeks ago from Opelousas, he had left that unfamiliar house and walked through the strange neighborhood, past the wholesale oyster shops and the small shuttered groceries and the steel-grilled windows of the late-night bars, down to the gravel of the railroad tracks, where he stood in the shadows watching the old blue house slipping to its knees in the mud and the three wooden steps that led into the music burning fiercely inside. He started to tell her how much he needed to hear that saxophone break a blue note high in the air and let the cornet swoop down to catch it and put it back together—but a woman with dangerous red hair was suddenly standing at the table and saying to Camille,

"You finally got yourself a white man, honey? After all them years, I feels so happy for you."

"Help yourself to a chair," Camille said, the golden hoops clinking as she threw back the hair from her face. "You know I always share my men with you, Thelma."

Thelma slipped in between the boy and the woman in the green dress, the glass in her hand spilling something amber and sticky on the wooden table. Her dress, one shade redder than the heavy curls springing loose like greased corkscrews, was cut low enough for the boy to see the tops of her breasts mounding there. They looked gray where the sweat had damped the powder that she smelled so strongly of.

"You still harping on Jimmy Lee?" Thelma said. "That buzzard sucked me clean and took off three, four weeks ago. You lucky you lost him when you did, honey."

"I *lost* Jimmy Lee the way I lost a big blue crab at the lake early this summer," Camille said. "He just crawled over to the stronger smell of old meat somebody was using as bait."

Wide-eyed, getting as low in his seat as he could, the boy was waiting to hear what Thelma could say back to that, when a skinny baldheaded man barely an eyebrow taller than the bar top brought over a tray with four drinks, sniffing three before he set the right one down in front of the boy.

"Compliments of Alabama," he said to them. "Say he be right by. Say to drink up and don't wait none on him."

Thelma drained the glass she had carried over with her and started on the new one. On the other side of the room, the horns were silent now, and over the swishpad of the brushes, the stand-up bass was popping out fat tones that filled the air. The boy felt he could get up and leave without a voice halting in conversation, without the big bass losing its way in the mounting solo that slowed down the higher it rose, as if every note counted more in the rarer atmosphere. But he sat still.

"How come Alabama so generous tonight?" Camille asked.

"He always be like that when he drinking with a lady," Thelma said. "I expect we leave here soon for something to eat, maybe some oysters down on Dumaine. That man can jazz, honey. He could be *needing* some oysters tonight."

"If he taking you out," Camille said, "he could be needing a lot more *whiskey* than I seen him drink already. Beside, he never leave before Crookneck go home. You know that fathead nigger *love* to hear that saxophone."

Thelma looked over at the boy, her brown face drawn up in a scowl. Without turning her head, she said to Camille, "Watch what you say here, honey. They's white folks at the table. No sense running up yourself when they do it so much better."

And now the boy knew it was too late to leave. Thelma had him pinned down with her eyes, turning away only when the big man in the porkpie hat lowered himself slowly into the last chair. His hands rested on the table; they looked as if they had been carved from solid stumps of bayou cypress.

"You got a name, boy?" he boomed, and the boy's tongue flapped up and stuck to the roof of his mouth. He struggled a few moments to coax it down, then said,

"Luther. My name's Luther Thibodeaux."

"Coonass!" The big man laughed, his little porkpie hat bouncing like a washtub on an ocean swell.

"But he's a sweet one," Thelma said, pulling the boy over to her overflowing bosom, as full as a moon now reflecting the glow of the big man. Kisses beating on a trapped cheek. Hair the sheen of wet pillows.

"A sweet coonass with a taste for colored music!" Alabama rocked the shaky table with his laugh. "Well, Luther, you can't stay here, you know. The Blue Cat Club be out of business before you can say Jackie Robinson if the po-leece catch you round this place. Now where you live, boy? Somewhere about here?"

And suddenly he heard the little cornet, alert and glistening, bray over the popping bass, and then the drummer unloaded with both sticks while Crookneck stormed down from that high place he kept his music, and the boy knew he did not want to go, he wanted to listen to this band until the club closed down, so he told the big man across from him,

"I don't live nowhere."

"Oh, that's terrible," Camille moaned, and the boy thought she meant it, and he could not bear to see her hurting for him. But Alabama cut her off quickly:

"Shush now! This boy ain't telling the absolute truth. He mean he don't live nowhere he want to be right now. Now am I right or am I wrong, Luther?"

The boy did not want to worry Camille any more, so he said, "That's right. I got a home but I just want to stay here and listen to that band. I never heard nothing like them back in Opelousas. I was standing outside but it started up to rain and so I come in."

"Oh, let him stay longer," Camille pleaded. "I watch him good." Her hands reached out to cup one of Alabama's, but that black stump of a fist was too large for her to circle all the way around.

And the boy felt Thelma ruffle beside him, about to say something before she changed her mind and sank back in the chair, bored now, or perhaps sullenly recalling the kisses that had made her his ally only a few thoughtless minutes ago. She turned her back to the table and used the rain-smeared window to touch up her face with something from the plastic tortoiseshell compact in her purse. Luther felt as if a whole damp hour had passed before Alabama spoke again.

"Hmmm," he said, pulling at the scrabbly beard on his jowls. "I suppose he can stay this one time. But I don't ever want to see you round here again, you hear me, Luther? After tonight, you find some white music you can listen to—if they is any such thing."

And the boy, relieved, leaned back in the chair and sucked up a piece of sweet ice from his glass. He closed his eyes, shutting out all the other sounds in the room, concentrating hard on Crookneck and that cornet battling it out for three or four notes they were tossing back and forth. Behind the saxophone, Crookneck seemed much thinner than before, as if the music were wearing him away. Cheeks straining out tight, he whipped the big horn up and down, pushing out a three-figured riff, bearing down on it until it was all his, and then it was the band's too, and then everyone in the long room of the Blue Cat Club was picking up those same three notes and moving to them, and just when the boy felt the ache of those three notes too, Crookneck broke free from the spell he had cast on himself and on the whole room, and he climbed up a crazy staircase and fell off before he reached the top, and tried it again and this time almost made it but could not quite go all the way, and voices were screaming some hot encouragement so he gave it one more try, nearly losing it at the very top before he was over and free and there were no more stairs underneath him, no net to catch him, and he was flying in an air purer than anything the boy had ever imagined before that night. Now everyone in the Blue Cat Club was silent, except Thelma, who rattled her drink and said to Alabama,

"Let's go. I got the hungries."

"What?" the big man said. "What you say?" His gaze was lost in the golden bell of the saxophone.

"I want to go, Alabama," she repeated. "I want to go eat me some oysters. *Right now.*"

"*Eat it, woman,*" he roared at her, immense in his chair, his eyes snapping back from the bandstand. "I don't go nowhere till Crookneck gets done. You knows that. Now hang up your mouth and let me be."

"Crookneck, Crookneck, Crookneck," she mocked him. "He some kind of god? You niggers rather listen to some music don't make no sense than go do something re-*spon*-sible with your life."

"Like buying you dinner?" the big man said, loud enough so the boy could hear the threat lying on top of the syllables. "Listen, woman, this white boy sitting here got more sense than you do.

He got ears anyway, and something inside to stop the music from going clean through!"

Now it was impossible to listen to anything but the hard voice of Alabama, and Luther felt his heart thudding like the pounded hide of the bass drum. The rain suddenly sounded very sharp against the window, manic as ricochets in a blind alley.

"Well, well, well," said Thelma, trying to catch her breath. "White boys! Well, well. We see about that."

She scraped back her chair and soon disappeared among the jostling bodies on the dance floor. The boy looked closely at Alabama and tried to make himself smaller in his seat.

"She be back," Camille said, and rubbed a soothing hand against the big man's rough cheek. "You know how Thelma can get when things don't fall her way all the time."

"Course she be back!" Alabama said, laughing so hard the porkpie trembled. "She forgot to take her whiskey with her!"

And the band was vamping steady and easy now, the floor in front of them hypnotic with dancers. Luther turned his attention once more to the music, glad the squall had swept off for now. How late was it, he wondered, hoping his father, come back from his shift at the creosote plant, would not think to look into the boy's room, would not discover the bed with the pink chenille bedspread still pulled taut over the pillow, would not stalk out looking for him with the belt he cut from the studded hide of an alligator he had killed with one shot through its yellow eye.

"Don't you worry none, boy," Camille said, petting his hand. "It weren't none of your fault. She be back soon, blowing on about nothing, just as she always do."

Luther did not relax, though, until Thelma returned five minutes later, twitching her lace-edged hanky at her neck as if to dry up the sweat before it could run down and streak her heavy bosom again. On her face, there was a superior, a satisfied smile. Alabama took one look at her and said,

"I once seen a bluejay look like that just after he sucked out every egg in a blackbird's nest. You got what you want, baby?"

"I always do," she said, tucking the hanky between her breasts until only a scallop of soiled lace showed there.

Camille picked up her highball and set it down again without drinking. Her forehead was ridged with wrinkles. And the boy realized that he too did not trust Thelma. He did not understand what had been happening; he wanted only to leave but knew now that he could not, that both he and Thelma had to stay until Alabama said go, and he would not say that until the music stopped. Luther thought he might as well get lost in those sounds again, and he moved his chair back to find a better view of what was taking place on the distant bandstand.

Crookneck had shifted now to the piano, an ugly upright the boy had not noticed before at the rear of the platform, trying out some chords that went sour against the sweet grain of the cornet. The golden saxophone still hung from his neck, and Luther wanted him to stop undermining the horn's solo and pick up his own instrument, blowing into it his reviving breath. Strangely, the cornet did not seem to mind the sabotage, even pointing sometimes at the piano and nodding with a little flourish of sweet notes. Maybe, Luther thought, I don't understand this music either; maybe there is nothing in this world I understand. Still, he was happy when the saxophone once more rose to those shining lips and a soft twining melody threaded through the solo of the cornet.

"Hear that man," said Alabama. "He could bring down the governor weeping to his knees. He could make the harps of the angels sound like a bunch of washtubs racketing on a sad Monday. But I be *damned* if he can take the chill off Thelma's heart when she freezes up like tonight. I don't like when you jazz me, woman!"

"Now that ain't fair, Alabama," the redhead said, and the boy could not tell if the catch in her voice was because she was hurt by his words or because she was scared she had pushed him too far. "I just want you to do what you said you was going to."

"Well, now then," he said, "I am going to do it. But you got to listen to that man blow. You got to open up sometime, Thelma, and give up to the music."

"I got nothing against Crookneck, I love that . . ." But before she could finish, the door at the front of the club slammed open and shuddered against the wall, and two men in blue uniforms rushed in, large blue revolvers sweeping the dancers back.

"What the hell going on here?" Alabama said, starting to lift his bulk out of the chair, when the taller man in blue yelled, "Everybody stay where you are! First nigger I see moving is fishbait. You got that?"

The dancers froze into position, as in a child's game, but the band continued to play, ignoring the two men with guns.

The shorter policeman, his bull chest and thick neck thrust forward, pushed through three or four couples, looking around the room packed with people in the dim light.

"Now, we got a report a white boy is in here," he said, "and that's against the law. You can't have no boy in a place that sells liquor. That's the law and you can look it up." He stared out again into the crowd. The boy, who was tucked down in his chair, could feel how nervous the room had become. There was a small quaver in the policeman's voice when he spoke again. "Now, where you got that boy? Bring him out and we can maybe leave here with no more than a couple of arrests."

The band had stopped playing now, but Crookneck was caught again high in a solo and was working his way slowly down. His horn tore through the sudden silence of the room. Luther started to feel prickly at the back of his neck and his breath came short.

"Get under that table, Luther," Alabama said softly, "and don't say nothing to nobody."

The thickset policeman had backed up a few steps and was waving his revolver at the bandstand. "Somebody tell that nigger to shut up," he said. But Crookneck went on oblivious, his tones coming out as sharp and clear as photographs.

"He can't stop," Alabama said, his voice rolling out from the back of the room. He stood up and began walking toward the open door, speaking calmly. "Leastways, he can't stop *yet*. He got caught in his pattern and the music won't let him stop till he come out the other end."

The two policemen glanced at each other, and the thickset one said, "This place is full of crazy niggers tonight. We hit the goddamned jackpot, Charlie."

Alabama was still coming, the small hat on his head like a bird's nest on a mountain top. He stopped only when the taller policeman shouted, "You stop right there and identify yourself!"

The boy, hunched up in the dark circle the table made, could see nothing but the legs of the chairs and of the two women. But he could tell that the two policemen, in spite of their guns, were not at all sure of themselves now. And over the music still bristling from the saxophone, he could hear Alabama say in a rumbling voice, "My name is Alabama Brown and I *own* this club. Now what you want here with them big guns? You spooking all my customers."

The crowd said nothing, did nothing. All Luther heard now was Crookneck blowing his horn as if he were not in the same room as the rest of them, not even in the same world. Then the boy jumped, rapping his head on the underside of the table, as a rush of dark hair came down over the edge, followed by a woman's face.

"It be okay soon, honey," Camille whispered to him. "Alabama paying off them cops now. They won't be back, not tonight anyways. You hush till I tell you when to come out."

He nodded as her head lifted out of view again. O good Jesus, he thought, what have I done now? All I did was come in out the rain and now I'm going to get some nigger killed. And in his cramped position, he thought he would pee in his jeans if he had to stay hunkered up a minute longer.

Then he could feel the room relax and the noises start up around him. Suddenly a door slammed, and he grabbed his heart, for a moment mistaking that door's explosive closing for a pistol shot. Trembling, without waiting for Camille to call him out, he eased upward into the scattered light and took his chair again. Alabama was parting the crowd, heading straight for him and looking mean.

"Boy," he said to Luther, "you could maybe got somebody shot here tonight with your foolishness. Your daddy must have called the po-leece to come get you—come get me too, for that matter. You told somebody you was coming here?"

And the boy, his eyes hot and on the point of watering, blurted out, "My daddy don't know about this place. He'd *kill me* if he knew where I was. I swear to the risen Jesus, I didn't tell nobody. I didn't say nothing to nobody, Alabama. I just came out of the rain to hear some music."

"Then how the shitfire hell they know you was here, boy?" He drove his fist downward on the table top so hard that it leaped off the floor and the boy's glass of melted ice tilted over, spilling water over the surface toward the people seated around it.

Thelma scooted back her chair. "You watch out now, Alabama! This is a new-cleaned dress I put on tonight just to go out with you, and now you trying to mess it up. I got all pretty to *dine* with you, if you can ever leave this place to get along without you!"

Slowly, the big man moved his head to look at her. Luther felt frightened at the strange, grim smile starting across those lips. He watched the big man's eyes lock on the redhead.

"Where you go a little ways back, Thelma? You come back all sassy and satisfied with yourself."

Thelma pulled out her hanky and blotted the water that had sprinkled the front of her dress. She's trying to act calm, the boy thought, but she's having a hard time of it, just like those policemen.

Alabama asked her again, "What you did when you was gone, Thelma?"

"Well," she said, folding the hanky neatly, avoiding the big man's stare. "Well, I was just out in the lady's room, fixing myself up pretty for you."

"That all you was fixing?" Alabama asked, his voice quiet enough to make Luther fidget in his seat.

"What you mean by that?" Thelma said. "You making some accusations about me?"

Alabama slowly lifted the porkpie hat from his head and placed it carefully on the table in front of him. Luther found himself staring at the bald, dark brown dome, lines of sweat furrowing the glossy skin. Then the boy jumped quickly back as Alabama whipped the cap across Thelma's surprised face.

"Alabama!" Camille screamed, and rushed over to comfort the sobbing woman.

"Huh," he grunted. He dropped his eyes to the cap crushed in his hands and began talking, his voice throaty and powerful as a tractor in low gear,

"I certainly does accuse you. I accuse you of getting uppity, whereas you ain't had no business to do so. I accuse you of the everlasting grumbles—can't nothing satisfy you except it be done your way, *as* you want it and *how* you want it and *when* you want it. I accuse you of calling the po-leece to come pick up this white boy and close down my club, just so's you could haul me away to buy you some dinner, and get whatever dessert might be coming your way. Now, woman, is I right or is I wrong?"

And again the boy was leaping out of the way, this time as Thelma's chair screeched back over the hardwood floor. And as he ducked to the side, he heard her yells cut through the smoke:

"Tell that nigger to shut up! I hate you! I hate that ugly low-life noise don't stop no night for nothing! Stop it! Stop!"

But her jagged cries could not divert the saxophone that bobbed over the flow of music. And before Alabama could reach out to grab her arm, she had unsnapped her purse, jerked out a small snub-nosed revolver, and sprayed three wild shots at the bandstand, the gun's roar for once overwhelming the blowtorch tones of the saxophone.

And at the sound of the first explosion, Luther broke cover like a flushed bobwhite, slipping past Camille's outstretched arms, somehow squirming his way through the crowd of stunned dancers and racing up to the bank platform. He snorted the stench of gunpowder out of his nostrils and looked up wildly to see Crookneck still standing, lean as a lightning rod, his lips cut where the mouthpiece had been yanked violently away, blood dripping down his chin. He still held in his hands the saxophone that one of the aimless bullets had burst open, a barbed hole in its gleaming flank. And Luther cried up to him,

"I'm sorry! I'm sorry! I'm sorry!"

No one stirred. The silence in the club seemed louder than the sharp reports of the revolver. Then Crookneck lifted the saxophone strap over his head and laid it gently down at the foot of the platform. Taking a lavender handkerchief from his breast pocket, he dabbed at the blood, pasty on his mouth. For the first time that night, he seemed to notice the faces massed below him in the hot room. And in a low tone, to no one in particular, he said,

"No call to do that, man."

Luther looked up, confused, unable to speak again or to walk away, as Crookneck turned his back and moved to the piano at the rear of the bandstand. He sat down on the bench disfigured from a thousand damp glasses, from forgotten cigarettes that left their scars like the names of lovers knifed into the skin of live oak. And over the sound of the white boy's sobbing, Crookneck began a long slow blues, his left hand rolling like thunder on the black keys.

WILLIAM MILLS

MR. BO

His wife had gone in the rickety old Ford to Bayou Goulas to see her old man and her mama and had taken those smart-aleck kids with her—those goddam hybrids only a coonass and a redneck could throw. Like a horse and a jenny—throwing a dead end. Some people fancied the old woman might keep the kids and not come back, but it was too much to wish for. And anyway, Bo Simmons was still around. Like rounding up a herd of wild hogs only to find you have left the boar still in the bushes.

He had been on the island in the middle of Tickfaw River all afternoon trying to drive a few cows that always found their way across the river when it was low. But when the hot weather came—and it was hot—the mosquitoes would eat them up. He chose this time because he did not want to have to see the family off. Saying good-bye made him uncomfortable.

The greeting, the salute, this was something else.

It would have been easier to move the cows if he had brought several men. But Bo decided to work alone except for his two Catahoula curs. He had traded for the two dogs in the upper part of the state when they were only puppies. Black and brown patches mottled their white hides. That was striking enough, but it was

From *New Orleans Review,* I (1969), 230–33.

their eyes caught hold of you—they were ghostly—glass eyes, or a pale, pale blue, almost like an albino's. They were close to the shade of Bo's eyes: startling; you felt Bo could look inside you and know exactly what you were thinking. Well, he must have seen something inside those young puppies. Grown, they had the look of crazies in the asylum. But they knew what Bo wanted when it came to working cows. It was just as well they did.

During the summer the island steamed with heat and moisture. The cypress trees trapped the air and there was little breeze. The cows moved the way they should and the dogs were in the right places at the right time. This eased the muscles in Bo's stomach and made him forget the weather. The world seemed to function smoother when he was free of people. Not because he could not handle them. Lord knows, he could. But people were fools, the old and the young. Bo had thought it many times. Mainly because they lied to themselves. Not just to other people. This Bo would have understood. But they were hypocrites before themselves. Fools.

As the last Brahma cow moved to the ford in the river, Bo eased his horse down the steep embankment through a small cut, blocking the way in case one of the cows bolted. As the tall sorrel crossed the narrow strip of sandbar, Bo took his feet from the stirrups and brought his knees high above the saddle, his feet resting on the saddlebow. The swift, muddy water rose to the horse's belly, and a good feeling, almost exhilaration, rose up in Bo Simmons, rose from his legs to his head and gave him a shiver. The horse clambered up the dirt bank, and in a few minutes the cattle were shuttled to a nearby pasture. After he got down to close the gap, Bo took off his tattered straw hat and wiped his face and neck with a red handkerchief. The sun had started below the tops of the trees now, and a brief, cool breeze fanned the quietness. Simmons watched the humped, gray cattle move to join the herd in the distance. The sorrel shook his bridle—not a jingle, closer to a rattle. Bo saw a horsefly on the sorrel, crushed it in his hand and threw it to the ground. His horse and his dogs gave him the highest, the purest pleasure he was capable of accepting. He could cut a dog's throat if it did not do what dogs are supposed to do. But he took very good care of his animals.

The heat had warmed the thousands of honeysuckles to a disconcerting fragrance, and the sudden, cold wind of late evening carried the scent at a time when Bo could think of his own pleasure or think of his own will not so much in conflict with the earth, the weather, or people. He got back into the saddle, the horse still dripping from the ford, picked up the rope reins, and headed down the long lane to his house.

Wagons carrying hay to the barn and sleds with two-by-four runners had worn lines in the mud, and they had been baked there. Simmons rode in the middle of the ruts, his horse clopping along easily. The lane was lined with wild blackberry bushes, and this was the time for picking.

As Bo drew close to several small shotgun houses, he remembered that he would have no one to cook for him and that he was already hungry. He rode past the first two houses, and he was greeted by those sitting on the porch. The hands were in from plowing and were cooling off.

"Howdy, Cap'n." And he would nod.

When he came to the third house, his right eye crinkled a moment in decision, and then he pulled up to the wooden gate.

"Mary!" he hollered. There was no man, no one rocking on the porch at this house. A skillet clanged against a wood stove inside. A woman of maybe forty came onto the porch. She was hefty, with strong, thick arms and big hams of hips, thighs, and calves.

"Suh?"

"You might send one of your girls down to cook supper for me. Miz Simmons's gone for a while."

"I kin come down if you want," she answered.

"No. You go on with what you're doing and send one of your girls." He spoke flatly and decisively.

"Yessuh."

Bo clucked to his horse and rode on down the lane. He had allowed Mary to stay on the place even after her husband had one day up and left. It was unusual for Bo to do this, because he needed the man for the fields, but he had left everything sort of hanging, telling his wife that Mary could help her at the house. He never told Mary flatly that she would be able to stay. This made her feel even more the unsubstantiality of her place, made her a better worker.

When Bo came to the big, dingy farmhouse, he took his horse to the lot and unsaddled him. He gripped the heavy work saddle with one of his powerful arms and stepped into a room next to the crib. Several ropes dangled from the ceiling, each with a loop at the end. He threaded the one free rope through a hole in the saddle and up and over the horn. The room lent itself to fancy in the dusty gloom—the dark-tanned, textured hide of animals, fashioned into something that related to humankind but hanging static or swinging gently in the thick, powdery silence.

A thick rat scooted off as Bo stepped heavily on the wooden floor. Briefly it scared him. He leaned his head out the door and called, "Kitty, kitty, kitty." The high, almost falsetto of the call sounded strange, coming from the stern and masculine face of the man. A white cat bounded across the lot and stopped silently, anticipatory, with uplifted face, looking with one blue eye and one gold eye.

"Ppsst, ppsst," Bo hissed, and turned back into the saddle-room. The cat leaped inside and stalked around the sacks and cans cluttering the floor.

"Ppsst—catch 'em!" Bo urged. Suddenly the cat hit—thunk—and a rush of little bones swatting the floor. Her teeth had cracked the base of the neck, gripped, and the huge rat was slung from left to right in a furious, primeval rage.

Satisfied, Bo went to the corncrib and gathered ten or twelve ears of corn and dumped them in a box for the sorrel.

He swung the backyard gate open and treaded up the brick walk. From the gate to the house the character of the land and foliage changed. This one thing, all the shrubbery and flowers, undertaken by his wife and grumbled about by Bo himself, was in fact a secret pleasure. He had growled about having to plant and cultivate the whole thousand acres and keep up fifteen miles of fence, but he liked it all. Once in a while it was quiet enough to sit on the long back gallery, and especially then he liked it. But most of the time the damn children were screaming and yelling. He wished he had never had the first one. But you needed one to pass the place on.

Now it was quiet. He did not realize the new freedom at first until he got to the back door. A family man expected, was inured to, noise and commotion. Sanctuary had to be found somewhere else, away from home.

He went to the bathroom and washed the dust and grit from his hairy arms and his face, exulting in the freshness. Then he went to the icebox and took out a bottle of home brew and poured it into a clay mug until the frothy head looked over the side.

The sun was setting as he went out again to the back gallery and propped his feet up on the railing and leaned his chair back. This last batch of home brew had come off good. A light amber, not the darkness of the last crock.

As he drank the cold beer he thought about what he had to do the next day. More corn had to be laid by. Had to get one of the hands up with a mule in the morning to plow the garden. His wife had been after him about that. Damn woman. These two acres around this house caused him more trouble than the whole place.

He got up to get another beer and noticed that one of Mary's girls was coming down the lane. By the time she got the back gate opened, he was already seated again. It was the one called Gloria. She was maybe fifteen.

"Evenin', Mista Bo." She approaching him.

"Hey, girl," looking at her.

"Mama says you want me cook some dinner. Says Miz Simmons gone," she said, just saying anything.

"See what you can find in the icebox and go ahead and start. I'm going to take a bath."

"Yessuh." Gloria walked up the steps of the gallery and past Bo. She trailed a thick smell behind her, and it pricked the flow of Bo's thoughts. He watched her walk through the screen door and noticed her buttocks jut out. He remembered how Louis, a field hand, had remarked about it one day when Gloria had shuffled by them on a dusty lane.

On his way to take a bath, he got another home brew from the icebox, poured it into his mug, and started the water. He thought how much easier it was now that there was water from the cistern piped into the house. And he thought how much he enjoyed—when he was in the mood—lying in the tub and sipping a home brew. It was not often that he felt relaxed enough. As he was washing off, he realized there was no towel.

"Dammit," he muttered. "Gloria!" He bellowed the name. A couple of rooms away she yelled back, "Suh?"

"Bring me a towel."

Soon she knocked and said, "Here it is," not moving the door.

"Well, throw it in here, girl."

She opened the door just enough to throw in the towel, but she saw in a wink Bo Simmons as few had ever seen him. But there was a studied lack of recognition by both of them—a dark immobility on the girl's part, a feigned otherworldliness on his part. But the recognition was there. Bo dried off and went to his room where he found a loose-fitting shirt and a pair of khakis. He didn't bother to put a belt around him but got into some slippers.

When he came to the dining room there was a plate full of sliced cucumbers and tomatoes waiting, which he promptly set to. The scratching of his knife and fork brought Gloria to the door. After she confirmed that the boss man was there, she went back to the kitchen and came out with a big slice of fried ham in one plate and a bowl of black-eyed peas. She moved close to Bo and set them down near his salad.

"Mista Bo, did you want another home brew, or some milk, or jest what?" she asked, looking down at him.

He thought a second and turned his face to speak, and he was confronted with the looming bulk of her breasts. His eyes fastened on them, and he spoke as if he was directing his request there.

"I reckon you can bring me another home brew."

"Yessuh, hit sure do make you feel good on a hot night." But she said it with an insinuative lilt to her voice, a prerogative gainsaid now by the image in the bathroom and her cognition of Bo's last glance, a glance he had not in fact directed but rather halted.

"You can pour yourself one if you think you can handle it"—not looking at her.

"Yessuh. I think I can"—assuming her womanhood by the challenge, the awakened forces freed of anything servile, obedient.

The sound of caps popping on two bottles stirred Bo now to the point where there was little question whether, but only when. The problems it might bring crossed his consciousness slightly, but the alcohol quietly dismissed the future. Anyway, he was Bo Simmons.

Gloria came back to the table with a plate of french fries and a mug of home brew. When she had placed them on the table, Bo Simmons whacked her on her butt.

"Mista Bo!" she yelled, and ran out to the kitchen, leaving Bo grinning at the table.

They sure have hard rear ends, he thought. That's what field work will do.

Before he had finished the meal, he heard the cap pop on another bottle.

"All right," he yelled, "you better go easy on that stuff!"

A quiet grunt from the kitchen. Finally she came into the dining room to clear away some of the dishes, this time from the other side of the table. Then she sat herself down in a hide-covered chair just inside the kitchen door. He ate slowly and stole glances while he chewed his food. She sat knowing he was looking, and he sat and ate knowing that she knew.

She wet her lips with her tongue, moved it in that learned way, left her lips open. Then, as if it was part of the ritual, she began to move her crossed leg up and down gently, undulating her body in the way schoolgirls do on the front row. Gloria had never been to school.

The flirting was easy. Perhaps for someone who had fallen into a world of tease, this would be like any other happening. But these were not lovers, tired of the world. Her world was limited by the dirt road which she had walked coming from her cabin, the fields where she sometimes worked, the river, and now and then the house of the Simmons family. Several years ago she had been awakened to her sex by the frantic caress of a grown field hand, a friend of her father's. This had pushed back the boundaries of her world more than anything else that had ever happened to her.

And Bo. Living in a circle of work made for his own diversion, working himself away from some place inside him that was too complicated for him to understand.

The slap across the rear did not altogether make clear to Gloria where she stood. The evening had been beyond any foretelling, that was certain. The recognition in the bathroom had been clear, and an awful excitement had engulfed her; that was substantial. But men had taken the license Bo Simmons had taken before and meant nothing, except to make clear what was theirs or could be if they wanted it.

It was time. Bo finished his supper, and she picked up the few remaining dishes and went to the sink. Bo followed her, and as he came up behind her, held on to her hips.

"Mista Bo, you gotta stop now"—looking straight ahead, not confident, a little afraid.

"Never mind 'bout all that, girl. Forget them dishes and get on in here with me." He started out of the kitchen.

She didn't move, only moistened her lips that kept drying. He turned, looked at her strangely, then grabbed her wrist and pulled her along with him. She did not pull back; neither did she move forward on her own but kept her feet dragging under her, so he would know it was all his doing.

"Take your clothes off, girl," he said and sat down heavily on the side of the mammoth tester bed. There were solid oak posts ten inches at the base and a brownness that spoke of permanence and stability. It had come from a prominent home when the family failed. His back to her, he undressed, threw his clothes on the nearby stand, and finally stood there naked. He started out of the room, said, "You better have that dress off before I get back or I'll tan your hide. I'm gonna git us some more home brew."

When he came back, her plain dress was on the floor, and she was sitting in the rocking chair next to the fireplace, the ashes gun-barrel gray, cold, the fires long out. She had settled there out of habit, as if being there was a comfort to her. He handed her a clay mug, and she got up and followed him to the bed.

After he had possessed her and she had exhausted him, he napped with his head on her chest beneath her big breasts. His knees were pulled up close to him in a position unseemly for a man so big. She did not sleep but remained staring at the designs of stars and new moons in the canopy above her. The face was young, and her cheeks had the fullness of a young woman, but something about her reflected knowledge that had been beaten to shape and tempered long before this small fire had been lit. In the midst of her dark, shadowy lap lay his callused hand, the digits slightly curved to the grip of an ax, or a gun.

For a while the young woman did not think of much beyond the bed. With her head propped on the pillow, she could study his head, the long, brown hair with silver sides like the silver-sided fox she had heard his dogs hunt, his neck reddened by years in the sun. She stared almost uncomprehendingly at the sudden change to the alabaster skin of a child covering his torso, an awful whiteness, sharp against her own dark body.

But the heat and their half-dried, perspiring bodies soon forced her to other thoughts. How she had cleaned and swept this room and made this bed for Mrs. Simmons, never seeing the room like this. For some reason the thought of chores reminded her of her mother, and she reflexively moved one of her legs. Bo stirred and pulled his whiskered face across her chest, straightened out his legs, and lay on his back. His eyes were open, but he didn't say anything for a while.

When he ran his hands along the lines of her body, she didn't move. Something in his touch reassured her. She waited, knew now that he was awake, that the next move had to be his. She did not think what it would be and did not want to care.

"You better get on home now," he said, and his words were

heavy in the thick air of the room. She rolled out of bed, the shape of her naked body barely visible against the papered wall. She got dressed in the dark.

She didn't look at him again and went out of the room quickly, not bothering to close the door. On the back steps she could hear the Brahmas lowing across the fields. The man's voice reached out to her where she stood.

"Don't you tell anybody 'bout this."

"Nosuh, Mista Bo," she said. "I ain' gone tell nobody." And she moved from the darkness of the house to the darkness of the road, where she knew her way.

DEV HATHAWAY

THE GOOSE AND THE THORN

I wish the Judge was still here. I could ask him again, How does someone get caught up in mixed feelings so much? It doesn't seem right.

Here's one for you, Judge, I'd say. One moment I'm heading home from your place, but only get as far as the front porch, with a warm jar of tomato pickle from Queen Mary in one hand and holding the screen door open with the other. My family's expecting me any time now, and you know it's a long walk. The lids of the jars I've set out on the woodbox are popping down tight, cooling off. The jar I'm holding grows warmer. The sun has already set, and now just the trees on the top of the ridge show a line of orange light, narrow like a back fire. Everything below there has a purple look, except the river is silvery. The hill beside the house is all in blue shadows . . .

Besides having to go, it's sad to see something I know the Judge would like. That's another kind of mixed feelings.

Oh, says Queen Mary. She steps out on the porch and pulls her shawl around her. She's looking out at the last light on the river and up on the ridge. I think she knows my thoughts.

She picks a bobby pin and holds it in her lips, pulling her hair

From *Carolina Quarterly*, XXXVI (1984), 38–44. Reprinted by permission of the author.

back. The skin goes smooth under her chin and her throat glistens, touched by the light.

So hot by the stove, she says, shaking her hair out. I didn't mean to keep you this late, Geoffrey.

It's no trouble, I say. The sound of my voice surprises me, the grown-up tone, and I feel a little better. But also there's a pinch inside somewhere. Partly it's when you try just talking and being serious at the same time, the words don't say half what you're feeling, so it feels like you're telling a lie. Isn't that the way it is, Judge?

Then, instead of saying good-bye, Queen Mary keeps looking off and calls out in her high voice for the Judge's goose. The sort of trembly call embarrasses me, being close.

Lu-lu-lu-lu-lu-lu-lu-luu, she calls. Her voice wavers and stops.

Then it's quiet except for the river breaking at the bend in a long shush, and another jar lid popping. The goose doesn't answer.

Queen Mary—I mean, Mrs. Hines—looks tired and sad now, watching the river. From the side, with her mouth puckered to call again, I see the lip wrinkles and tiny hairs of an old woman. But when she calls, longer this time and more like yodeling, I feel it down the back of my neck as the ridge echoes Lulu's name. Then she turns her head toward me, the little light that's left drawing into her eyes. She's almost nodding. Her lips are almost touching. And I think if the Judge was still here he would kiss her.

Why don't I check on her, I say.

I'm guessing because it's getting dark Queen Mary will say, No, Geoffrey, you get on home—and let me go. Besides, the goose, Lulu, doesn't come to just anyone calling. Only the Judge could do that.

No, she sighs, you should be going. I'll get the egg basket and walk down by myself.

The next moment, I'm the one heading down the river bank with the egg basket, in the shadowy part, the catbriers and blackberry canes raking me over, shale and clay slipping loose each step. I slip, and the earthslides catch up to my sneaker heels. I can feel the crumbles inside around my ankles. I have to jerk the basket free of a brier.

And there's the goose.

Her head is showing above the flap of aluminum roofing where she has her nest. When I lay a foot on the metal it makes a buckling noise and she rises up. She beats her wings on her sides and points her head in the air. She's coming across the roof, hissing, with her head low. I jump past her, but she nabs me two quick bites in the calf before I grab her egg.

Queen Mary's voice comes over the top of the bank, Don't get her too worked up, Geoffrey.

Already I'm scrambling back. But not with much luck. Pulling up on a clump of grass one-handed and slipping in the clay, I go down on a knee. It's all dim in the weeds, and something feels wrong. Lulu is hissing herself crazy a few feet behind me, and the egg feels heavy.

Queen Mary calls out, Don't take the laying egg.

The egg is smooth and cold and doesn't have the shifting feel inside a real one does. It's the laying egg, it's solid soapstone.

Ho-back, ho-back ho-back, I wave at Lulu. Those are the words that used to work for the Judge. He had her eating out of his hand. I'm shooing her best I can and edging down so I can put back the fake egg. Her eyes are shiny black and she stabs at my arm with nub teeth. I wave again and she nips my wrist hard.

Then it happens. I backhand her. It's not just a shoo-away swat but a strong one with feeling in it, and surprises me. It undercuts her hard before she can try to dodge. Her head clicks and jerks and I can feel it in my stomach as she lies out all at once. Her neck looks crooked like it's broken.

How's that for one, Judge? You're not a year gone and here's your old white goose laid out on her roof, and I'm the one who did it.

I lie there a moment, holding the cold egg, trying to warm it. Then I lean up and pull Lulu against my chest. She leaves a dark skid of gooseshit on the roofing, and I'm sure she's done for. But she's still warm and soft to hold, and I stroke her neck. It's like she's peaceful being dead. I even kiss the top of her bill.

Geoff? Queen Mary's voice is seeking me out again. Are you all right?

Then there's twitches jumping in the goose's body. She stiffs up and gives a squeaky cough and starts flopping to get to her feet. I let go and watch the down fly as she flaps onto the roofing.

White spots are floating everywhere.

Finally I call back, There isn't any other eggs, Mrs. Hines.

Well, she says, maybe she's taken to another place. Look around a bit.

I look for a minute at Lulu, who's squatting quietly and blinking at me. She makes a soft cluck. A goose. I think, How is the Judge's ornery keep-to-itself goose going to lay eggs anyway? Queen Mary's crazy.

Mrs. Hines, I don't see anything.

Well, it's gotten pretty dark, she says.

Lulu is still sitting quietly. Back up the bank I can hardly make out the briers and weeds, so I just scooch down the rest of the way on my seat to the mud flat beside the water. It isn't as easy as I thought, picking my way along the marshy part of the bank. It's hard to keep my balance. My sneakers scoop and fill with water and muck, making a sickly sound, and I realize I'm feeling a little queasy. Like I have what the Judge calls a thorn, a pinching that's heavy in your stomach. Judge says by the time you feel a thorn there's no telling where you picked it up.

Then I look around behind me.

Here's another one, Judge. It's your goose. She's paddling along a little ways back, stretching her neck out to drink when she sees I see her. She's staying pretty near the edge. Then I see she's keeping up, that she's really following along, and it gives me a fluttery feeling and I can't tell if it's like something sinking or floating.

When I climb the bank and walk back, Queen Mary holds out the jar of tomato pickle, with her arm straight, like it's a trophy. It's still warm.

I just know she'll be laying somewhere soon, she says.

She squints and reaches to pick the down off my jacket. Hold still, she says. She's smiling to herself in a strange way, looking through me at the same time.

I step back and brush myself off.

Well, you'll find where another time. Now you better be going. And Geoff, she says, I'm very proud of you. She's smiling funny again, like the Judge himself is standing there in the grass just behind me.

But I'm afraid to look back. I find my way to the end of Queen Mary's garden, my shoes squishing in the dirt, under the last rows of bent-over sunflower heads and beside the cornstalks. I feel their sandpapery leaves reaching in the dark for the brier welts and teeth marks on my arms. They're starting to sting.

I go past the Judge's apple tree, with the limbs wired to each other, and past the toolshed, and head up the fire trail that cuts over the hill home. At Indian Rock I hear the spring pipe dribbling steady in the bathtub I helped the Judge put there, end of last winter. We ran a hose from the overflow to the garden so Queen Mary can water everything. That should take care of her, he said.

The Judge says the rock spring always flows because there's another hill trapped inside the one we see, and all it can do is ooze water.

Up close, the bottom of the tub shimmers white, and some black leaves are turning in a circle on the surface. I have a lot of thinking to do. My head is full of hitting Lulu and Queen Mary's knowing things and everything the Judge used to say and how they found him cold and gone in the river. How I end up over here so much since then. Splitting wood after school, tilling, picking tomatoes and snaps, taking full buckets into the kitchen. Queen Mary canning and singing in a soft, humming voice. I know she misses him, they were together so many years, but she doesn't really talk about him. She fixes hot turnovers and ice tea, and we eat in the living room where it's cool in the daytime with the curtains closed. The couch the Judge used to take his long naps on is stacked high with Ball-jar boxes, so I sit at his desk. The broken arrowheads he's found in the garden fill the 4-H glass his ninth-grade science gave him, with Best Teacher in red slanted script. According to him, all the arrowheads are from the same spot in the garden where this old Indian chief chips every one he tries to make. The Judge and his stories. That's another one.

Sometimes I stay late, like tonight, with Queen Mary somehow pulling on me. My mom will say something about it after supper, not directly to me, but to my dad. He doesn't mind as long as I do my work and don't stay out at the Hines' too often. Then Mom changes the subject and says she's going to clear the dishes.

But all this isn't the thorn I'm feeling, exactly.

It's the Judge, and I bet he would tell me. He'd say something like thorns are funny and get buried down deep before you know it.

I can hear him: Say, like the time I borrowed somebody's parked car with the keys in it, Geoff, to take the Whitten girl to her appointment. Someone had to, poor thing. Then ran the light, so telling the officer we were afraid it was the appendix, and her winking at me, as he sped ahead of us. Not one in a hundred hold a candle to that girl. Why they sent her away . . . And just bringing the car back, not a scratch on it, to the same parking place, getting out, when one of the mothers of my general-science kids is coming out of the post office and sees me. I say amazing how people forever leave their car lights on and she just stares and walks off. One thing gets passed to another, Geoffrey, and you never know where the twist'll pop up next. Few days it comes back in a wisecrack Coach makes about maybe letting Hines take the driver-ed course, and I know the boy whose mother must have told him. Comes out next week in class when the kid's sniggering about something. I make a mean dig about his low grades, and right then I know I've picked up a thorn somewhere. Gave myself hard labor for that one, Geoffrey, weed all of Queen Mary's garden. And you know, it was that last weed I went back to, hardest one to get. Top broke off and made me about punch myself in the face, and I had to gouge for it—split a fingernail. And what was that last weed, Geoffrey, what was that thorn?

I always feel like I know and don't know. It's right there in what the Judge says, but I can't say.

Judge give you hard labor you would know, Geoffrey. That thorn was the nasty old coach. This time.

Maybe I do know after all, but it's like he tells things in a way to trick me and then I'm not sure how much he means.

I wish I could tell the Judge a couple of thorns.

I told Miss Maye, my new history teacher at the county school, all about the Judge. Except how he died. We were doing My Most Unforgettable Character in History and I was so swelled up with everything, but I didn't lie. Some of my friends looked at each other, then kept their eyes down. I pulled that little thorn, I thought, going on with my story. Besides, Miss Maye held her beautiful face in her hand and was smiling. So, let them tease, a little anyway.

But I want to tell you a real one, Judge.

Judge, see I'm crazy about Miss Maye. And one night I stay late to help Queen Mary, so I don't have my history report to hand in next day. What can I say to Miss Maye? What will she think? Then when my best friend, Jerry Zoeller, rushes in late from gym I make a snorting noise for the other guys to hear and pull his chair out on him when he sits down. Jerry goes falling back hard on his seat bone and everyone laughs. Then he's crying and says he can't move his legs. When Mr. Price closes the office door he asks me do I know what he's having second thoughts about. My Good Citizen Award. My dad says I'm a lucky young man because Jerry is all right, it's just a bad bruise. I don't get to go to Scouts that night, so I can think about it. Angela—Miss Maye—doesn't say anything about my apology letter signed Love, but she phones my mom about the P.S. that I won't accept the award. Your dad would be very disappointed, says my mom. Jerry says we're still friends, if I let him sock me in the boys' room. Miss Maye gives me a special essay to write, What Is a Friend? After awards assembly I try to give Jerry my certificate in the boys' room. He won't even hit me then and walks out. Now I'm including my Good Citizen for the

Courier article on making Life Scout. It feels like a part of me now, Judge, like my stupid letter to Miss Maye.

Judge, where's the thorn? Can you tell me that? Can you? You want a worse one?

Meantime, I'm throwing rocks at the trees along the fire trail and mostly missing. I feel like throwing the damn pickle jar.

The moon is up by the time I get to the top of the hill. I leave the trail and cut across the pasture to the Hines family cemetery and sit down on the rock wall. It's almost bright enough in the moonlight to see colors. My red jacket sleeve and brier scratches look bluish, like they aren't mine. The cattle pasture is chewed down to bare rocks like it's on the moon itself.

Below the slope of the hill shines the roof of the Judge and Queen Mary's house. The river bends white and looks like it's running backwards up into the hollow. There isn't a sound at first except a late cricket and the hush coming from the interstate down the other slope, on my family's side. They seem far away. Then the cedar over the gravestones creaks, and a dog barks seven faint times in the distance. There's another sound, like a car door slamming somewhere. It makes me catch my breath like after you've been crying. Then I'm looking at the Judge's stone.

It's gray-white and smooth, like the goose's laying egg, and looks different from the others. They're worn and leaning crooked. One of them, Raymond Shay Hines, is so thin and loose it rocks back and forth and feels shallow in the ground. I bet I could pull this one out easy, but that wouldn't do me any good. The last date is only 1902.

The Judge's real name is on his. Oliver Markel Hines, Jr., not the Judge. And the dates. The stone is straight and thick. It would probably take both of us to move it, dragging it off like the tub for the spring. I can hear his voice: Easy now, let's rest for a minute.

I set the jar of tomato pickle on top and leave it there. The glass is cold now, and the speckles held inside show in the moonlight.

He can't be here, not in this place.

But he isn't at the river either. Purple on one side, and white on the other. His mouth and nose all scrinched up with his gums showing like the way he pushes his glasses back up without using his hands. But no glasses. Just his pajama bottoms, and the water dripping off them when they carry him out. Over the rush the river makes I can hardly hear the men get in the car after they lay him in back, when they slam the doors. They drive away without a sound.

I stayed home sick, Judge. Everyone went up the hill to the service. Then I walked around by the road to your place, and took the string peg out of the toolshed door and got the tiller and set the throttle and choke and started her on the first pull. It chugged the blue smoke for a second until I pushed the choke wire back in. The tines were tangled with white roots from last year, but it dug along pretty good down the rows. It threw up some winter-over orchard-grass chunks nice and clean. No arrowheads. Queen Mary saw me when she came back but didn't say anything. But I could hear you, Judge, in the garden.

I'll be out here, Geoffrey, first thing each spring. Dancing all over this garden with the crazy tiller. And just about you know where the chief chucks his arrowheads, the blame tiller squeals and coughs up the drive belt. Then I see the old chief winking at me, Geoff. If he and the Judge aren't one of a kind, don't you know. There's me with the wrenches and I've just about got the drive belt back when one last snug snaps another bolt head. And my knuckles, Geoffrey, my knuckles are so numb it's like I'm looking down on somebody else's skinned hand. So I call in to Queen Mary for another beer, and one for the chief while she's at it. I see he's just tossed another cracked arrowhead over his shoulder and I give him the nod. Say it's time we call it quits, and he says, Thanks, Judge, I've been waiting a long time for somebody to tell me that. Then you know what he says to me, Geoffrey? Chief puts his hand out all trembly like this, says in his time he's seen the river wiggle over every inch of this valley like a piece of thread dancing inside the movie projector at school. Then he says if I don't mind he really feels like lying down now, you understand.

Well, what kind of lousy reason is that, Judge? Tell me that.

He doesn't answer. I'm still sitting on the rock wall in the pasture, looking down at the house roof and the garden. The moon has risen higher and I can make out the rows I've been turning under for Queen Mary, all dusty like a blackboard eraser. And the toolshed. Then I think, They could have seen me tilling when they had the funeral up here. She must have heard me the whole time, and she didn't say a thing.

I can see the piece of roofing on the bank shine, too, where the goose's nest is, and there's white dots moving on the river in the moonlight. It looks like the moon trying to drown itself, but it must be the goose, drinking or treading water. I can't believe now I hit her.

I stand up and start across the pasture, watching the place moving on the river. It gets like a blind spot, black instead of white, but every time I look away I see it again. The goose. I start hurrying and stumble, catching myself. Then I'm going back down the fire trail. I think I hear Queen Mary calling, yodeling for the goose and echoing through me, all along the ridge and up and down the river. The rocks along the trail are jumping and I've been running the whole way down, by the bathtub, the shed, the apple tree, and running along the garden, the corn leaves crowding and slapping my hands, Here, Here.

Here's the real one, Judge. Me with the moon in my eyes and the sting on my hands. The house is dark, and Queen Mary is wrapped in her shawl, in the sharp shadow. And I can feel the goose nearby. But whether she's paddling on your river or drowning or dead or following close behind when I climb the porch steps, I can't tell.

Queen Mary? I call out.

I tap on the window. Then I see the lamp turned up. She passes in front of it and comes to the door.

Is that you, Geoffrey? Come in, come in.

It feels warm and bright inside. She looks at my scratched hands and then my eyes. She's turning my chin slowly side to side in the light. Her fingers are hot.

Geoff, Geoff, Geoff. Here. Sit by the stove.

Her shadow moves along the wall toward the door. Wood

rattles in the box out on the porch. Then she's opening the stove door, feeding in the sticks. The glow touches her face beautifully, her hair flaming for a second.

There, she says.

I try to speak to her—

Let me get you some tea, she says. She ladles water from the big steaming pot and busies at the deep sink, steeping the tea through a straining cloth. I can smell the pinch of basil she grinds between her fingers. The wood is catching and rushing, flickering through the seams on the stovetop, making shadows from the hanging pans dance on the ceiling.

I tell her I went up to the cemetery.

She's leaning over me close. Here, just sip it, she says.

I went up to the cemetery and it's like the Judge isn't there.

I know, she says. She's looking at me steadily now, and I can see every flick in her eyes.

It just says Oliver Markel Hines, Jr.

I wanted it that way, Geoff. What would you want it to say? Her calm voice is making me start to cry.

But I don't understand. All that made-up stuff, that Judge crap. And you know exactly what I mean—Queen Mary.

Wood's popping and she's looking down at her teacup, almost smiling sadly, that smile. The pot starts to spit bubbles and she stands and takes two hotpads from the hooks to slide it a little to the side. A slap of water bounces out on the stove and goes up in steam.

I'm sorry, Mrs. Hines. I don't want to hate him. And I'm sorry about the goose. I hit the goose.

Yes, she says, I thought so.

She opens the stove door and shakes down the burning wood with a larger stick that she lays in slowly, holding her hair back. For a second her hand disappears all the way inside, and now she closes the door and sits down.

I start to ask, but she reaches and holds her fingers against my lips. They feel soft and smell of the basil and smoke, and somehow the two go together.

I mean we've both had some things to do, she says. Yes, the goose is one.

She's smiling her smile again and squeezes my hands. Then she leans and her lips close on mine. The smoke and basil take my breath away.

Queen Mary.

Then she's holding me in her eyes, holding me.

Why don't you go out and call her, she says. You know she's yours.

PATRICK ANDREWS

WHEN THE BANG COMES, SHE'LL BE LYING IN BED DREAMING

I'm packing my bags 'cause I figure it doesn't matter anymore. Sherry stands by the sink, alternating between fury and terror. Fury at the thought of wasted years and terror of an uncertain future.

"You son of a bitch, get the hell out!" she rages, followed by an angry silence. Her, leaning against the refrigerator, hugging herself and looking small and miserable.

Domestic fucking bliss.

Now she's standing over the sink, puking and muttering, "Son of a bitch, son of a bitch," over and over like a mantra. I try to ignore her as I steadily rummage through the house collecting the things I consider mine and mine alone. There's no pattern to my work; I just grab whatever I see. It would be interesting to see what other people would save from a burning house.

I'm leaving a burning house.

I walk past her and climb into my car, the one that's paid up, and drive off. I drive around aimlessly, looking for a direction, but there isn't any. So I pull up to the Best Western just off the interstate exit, and sit in the parking lot. I just sit, trying to think about this thing that just happened to me, but I can't concentrate. I don't feel anything and that might be the problem.

So I stare at this motel, idly wondering if anyone's fucking in there and feeling glad that I don't know.

Glad I don't know.

Six years were now behind me. Six years and it didn't amount to anything more than a car filled with things I thought I cared about and an empty spot in my brain. Empty . . . I decide I need a drink.

Inside the motel bar I choose a seat that faces the door. The place is pretty empty, but then again, it's a Tuesday night. Motel bars . . . they all look the same, with the same plastic sheen to all the surfaces and the same glazed look in everyone's eyes. People don't come to motel bars to have fun; they come to drink.

Not thinking about it, I order two drinks.

"Why you want *two* screwdrivers, dear?"

The barmaid has an air of bored familiarity about her. She could be a machine.

"Why you want to *know,* dear?"

She seems used to pissed-off drunks and is immune to this. She stares at me for a second, head cocked to one side and shrugs. "Have it your way."

I think I will. For once, I think I will.

As she walks down the length of the bar to get my drink, I casually appraise her ass. It's large compared to the rest of her body, which is lean but soft-looking. My impression of her is one of softness, not in the gentle way but a spongy quality. I imagine poking my finger into the cheek of her ass and watching it sink in, deeper and deeper.

For a moment I feel bad about the way I snapped at the barmaid, but this soon passes. I've spent my entire life doing the right thing, and right about now I'm pretty tired of it. I show up at work every day, I go to the in-laws on Sundays, I mow the lawn and go to church. I put up with an awful lot of shit, all in the name of civility. Now all of that is replaced with an emptiness that begs to be filled with something else. All that's available is anger, so I indulge myself. I reach into my pocket and pull out a cigarette and light one.

Six drinks later I am loose, my feelings blurred to a dull edge of unfocused anger. I have found a comrade in a businessman who has come to the bar to pass an evening in a strange town. He talks of his life on the road, but I hear very little of it. I am somewhere else.

"That's when the bitch left me," he says.

This catches my attention. "Why?"

"Something about wanting a full-time husband. I dunno, she just got tired of waiting for me to come home." He leans over toward me, his breath heavy with alcohol, and continues, "How was I to know, huh? I come home one night and all she left was a note. A note, can ya imagine that? That's supposed to explain walking out on ten years together. She never told me anything. Not a thing."

My head is throbbing, and I need another drink. "There's no reward for doing things right. You expect to be treated fairly?"

"I just wish she'd let me know."

"Yeah. I think she did, pal." I signal for the barmaid and order another round. I smile weakly at her, but she's having none of it. She's seen my type before.

The sunlight streaming through the windshield of my car wakes me and I find I am still behind the wheel. I'm really *under* the wheel in a position that's hard to describe and even harder to get out of.

The tape deck is playing; it must have played all night. Graham Parker is singing,

> I'm just a tick in a box on a crushing mill
> . . . another moment that passes into nowhere
> . . . a brand name on a pill that gets you there.
> I'm getting nowhere and expecting oblivion
> and the past aint even worth living in
> . . . it's a nail that keeps being driven in.

I'm cold blooded and completely relaxed,
on the up escalator, going down the cracks

His voice is full of rage. I don't remember putting that tape in.

The night slowly comes back to me. I left the bar and started driving. Eastbound. I figure I went about one hundred miles, judging from the road sign I have conveniently parked in front of. It seems I did a decent job of pulling off the road, and I suppose I'm lucky to be alive. Lucky.

I've been told that I'm lucky. Lucky to have held the same job for six years and have the same faithful wife for just as long. Lucky to be the owner of a comfortable home and a comfortable mortgage. Lucky to be living my life with no accidents and no catastrophes. Lucky to be on the road to a quiet retirement complete with no worries and no danger. Fucking lucky.

And now I'm lucky again. With a pounding head and empty stomach, I find a packet of aspirin in the glove compartment, a pack of cigarettes in my front pocket, and I see a Perkins restaurant on the highway up ahead. I pull into the parking lot and kill the engine. Perkins looks like Denny's, which looks like Sambo's, which all look like the most godawful sanitized places imaginable. You don't need to be too soulful in a Perkins. You just have to be breathing and not too interested in where you are. The place minimizes any emotional pain; it's just *so* safe.

I pick a booth near the rest room just in case last night catches up with me. Here I am, faced with another serving machine.

"Good morning! Can I get you some coffee?"

Her sunny, good mood annoys me, but I know it's me and not her.

"Yeah, coffee, that sounds fine."

She brings my coffee, and I order eggs and toast even though I'm certain I won't be able to get them down. It now occurs to me that today is Wednesday and it's 9:30 and I'm supposed to be at work. I'd like to call Mike and tell him to stuff it; I'm not coming in and I'm not sure when I'm gonna come in again. That's what I'd *like* to do. Instead, I go to the pay phone near the rest-room entrance.

"Can I speak to Mike?"

He's out in the back warehouse. I try to stop her and say, "No, don't page him. Look, I'll leave a message."

Too late. She's already called him.

"This is Mike."

"Mike, it's Randy. I won't be in today. I'm not feeling too good. I think I might have something. The flu or something, you know?"

He sighs. "Inventory's today, Randy. But if you're sick then you're sick."

Yeah, if you're sick then you're sick. Brilliant. But he's right, I am sick. There is some pleasure in the thought of Mike stuck with the inventory and me not there to do all the things he really hates doing. I don't know why I didn't just quit.

It's hard to imagine not going to work and not doing the same things over and over. Mike's pissed off and that's all right. Pissing anyone off right now is all right. That makes me think of Sherry.

Last night . . . We stood there, tired of glimpses of the truth, tired of the distance we'd traveled only to find *this* at the end. How many times had I tried to walk out that door, after all?

Images: Scenes from a movie run out of sequence . . . Pretending everything was all right . . . She said, "If any of this *mattered,* then maybe we'd be able to go another night—another year."

I said, "Things matter, baby. You better believe things matter. I matter and *we* matter."

"Yes . . . but not that much." She never raised her voice. "Not that very much, anymore."

I'd left then. I should have told her all the things I'd never been able to say. The longing for something that was just out of reach. I should have shaken her and made her listen to *me* for once. Just once, listen to my problems and not have to hear her whining self-pity.

I should have put my fist in her face.

The waitress returns with my order. The eggs run into the toast and it makes me sick just to look at it. I light a cigarette and use the plate for an ashtray. So this is my new life.

I go to the counter to pay the bill feeling light-headed. Last night's revenge. Three dollars and fifteen cents, and I'm gone. The car has a rancid smell due, no doubt, to spilled beer. There are several bottles rolling around the floor as I make the turn onto the highway. The clinking is annoying, so I look for a tape to drown the noise out.

I choose another Graham Parker tape and shove it in. He's singing, "When I pretend to touch you, you pretend to feel." That sounds like something I can relate to. The day is sunny, and there aren't many other cars out.

Up until now, I haven't been sure where I'm going, but now a vague plan starts to develop. I have a cousin in Atlanta. I can drop in on him and sort things out. Atlanta is about a six-hour drive from here, so I have plenty of time. I decide to take the scenic route along the Florida Panhandle. It's really out of the way, but there's no shortage of time.

After about an hour, I notice the sky has turned gray. It begins to rain, at first just occasional large drops and then a steady stream of smaller raindrops. I'm entranced by the hypnotic rhythm of the rain and the steady slap of the windshield wipers. The rain sounds like the shower at home, and I'm reminded of my first year with Sherry. Young love. She would step into the shower with me, uninvited. The stall was too small for two people so we would be pressed against each other. She'd kiss me under the shower spray, long and slow. Her light brown hair, weighted down by the water, would hang down just above her breasts. Perfect bliss. The memories flood back, and I find I'm getting hard.

As the years passed, things slowly changed. We asked fewer questions and didn't wait for the answers. There's a quiet in many homes that once invited, never leaves. A contentment bred of lost desire. A sameness. It's that tired feeling you get when you walk into a room for the thousandth time. It's the unbearable knowledge that this day will be like the one before, and it won't really matter.

I can see Sherry's face in my mind. Six years is long enough to memorize every wrinkle, each acne scar—which she *thought* she disguised so well—and to see her teeth, slightly crooked and like everything else about her, not quite perfect but supremely adequate.

She will carry on. The clothes will be washed, the groceries bought, and the bills paid. Her life won't stop for love or lack of it. She will draw on her endless supply of strength, that well of common sense and social grace, she always had. She'll assure everyone that everything is fine.

How will I tell my parents? Then again, I suppose that's unimportant. I can picture them, rigid in their assumed positions, their attitudes molded by years of little variation. They are beyond concern.

It occurs to me that what's kept Sherry sane all along were her dreams. Up until last night, she still made plans and still believed things would change. I desperately wanted to believe her. She was waiting for passion . . . waiting for things that had passed us by. All that had been replaced by a mannequin dance passing for passion.

I can still see Sherry . . . curled up on her side in our bed, hugging a pillow between her legs and dreaming. Just dreaming.

It's raining harder now. I slow down to forty-five and notice what looks like a young girl hitching up ahead. I stop a few yards past her and light another cigarette while she grabs her bag and runs up to the car.

She gets in. "Hey, thanks. How far you going?"

"Atlanta." The decision is made.

"Great. I'm trying to get to Chamblee. It's right outside of Atlanta."

I pull back onto the highway. "Been out there long?"

"About an hour. I figured it'd be easier to catch a ride when it's raining, but no such luck." She turns toward me and smiles. I'm not good at guessing ages, but I put her around twenty. It turns out she's seventeen. Her name is Stacy.

"So what are you doing out here all alone?"

"Going to meet a friend." She turns back to facing forward. Water is dripping down the side of her face, so I hand her a towel I keep to wipe the window with. From what I can tell, she's a pretty girl. Her face is lean with pale blue eyes that attract my attention. Her hair is tucked into a baseball cap which is also dripping water. I can't tell much else about her since she's wearing an oversized army jacket. It's the kind that has a dozen zippered pockets that are never used by the suburban men who buy them. Hers are bulging.

I toss my cigarette butt out the window and pull out my pack and offer her one. She pulls one out, lights it and hands the pack back to me.

"Thanks." She leans back, takes a drag and puts her feet up on the dashboard. Yesterday, this would have really pissed me off, but today I don't care.

"Look, it's none of my business, but aren't you afraid to travel like this? I mean, it's not safe for a girl catching rides with strangers." She seems amused by my pedestrian concern.

"I can handle myself." She turns to me and smiles. It's a winning smile. "What's the worst that can happen, right? I ain't spending my time worrying 'bout what *might* go down. I'll handle it. Nobody fucks with me and gets away with it."

I don't believe it. She talks tough, but I'm sure that she'd look for a safe way out of trouble if she stumbled into a tough situation. She'd find a compromise just as I always have.

"Okay. You're tough," I say. She's still smiling.

She turns away and in an offhand manner says, "We can make it if you want to."

This takes me by surprise, but my answer comes quickly. "I don't think so. I'm married, but thanks anyway." I say this like I just turned down a drink.

The idea of screwing this young girl attracts and repels me. There's a certain excitement about the casualness of it, but Sherry is in my mind and that's much stronger. It occurs to me that I miss Sherry.

"I've got a wife. She's at home."

"Hey, it's no big deal, man." She continues to stare straight ahead.

Stacy interrupts the silence, telling me it's stopped raining. We're driving along the highway near Pensacola, along the beaches. She wants to stop and dry off and stretch her legs. So we do.

We climb over the dune that runs along the highway and walk down to the water. The sand is wet from the rain but the sun is out and it feels good. Stacy takes off her bulky jacket and lays it on the sand. She's wearing a plain white T-shirt, which she proceeds to take off and place on top of the jacket. She's not wearing a bra. Her breasts are small with light pink nipples.

I realize I'm staring at her chest, and this amuses her.

"You sure you don't want to come over here?" She rubs a hand over one breast.

"Please put your shirt on." I feel my face heating up. I'm embarrassed. This young girl with no shirt on has the advantage on me. "You can wear one of my shirts. They're dry."

"Hey, man, don't lose it. I won't rape you." She's laughing now. "I think I'll go for a swim."

She unzips her jeans, and I turn and walk away. I quit being married last night, so what's the big deal? I climb back into the car and wait for Stacy, who returns about an hour later. I'm under someone else's control now. Great.

I sense a subtle shift in Stacy's attitude. She seems tougher and more confident than before. All that stuff about taking care of herself seems more believable right now. Why be afraid of a man who can't even take advantage of a free fuck? It's as if she knows it isn't a *moral* choice I've made. It's a reflex. I'm still living by design and not choice, even here.

We drive in silence for an hour, listening to an INXS tape Stacy has in one of her pockets. I pull off into a large truckstop. The place is deserted with the exception of one pickup truck parked at a pump. I pull in to the next pump over from the truck and get out of the car. Stacy is already headed for the restaurant, walking with her head bowed down, holding her cap on with one hand. It's quite windy.

I start to follow her but decide to gas the car up first. It's a simple job which is just fine for my present state of mind. I thrust the nozzle into the filler hole and idly watch the digital counter register the sale. I wonder about the way things happen. I mean, what random series of events have led me into this absurd situation? I decide that as soon as I finish with the car, I'll tell Stacy that this is the end of the ride. I don't need that bullshit.

I look over at the truckstop office, and I can see Stacy talking to a short, stoutly built man. Even though I'm at least twenty yards away I can tell what's on this guy's mind by the way he's leaning toward Stacy. He hovers about her, following her to the back, where I lose sight of them.

It occurs to me that there is a catch on the nozzle and I can let the thing go. It'll continue to pump until the gas backs up the nozzle a bit and trips the shutoff. I leave it pumping by itself and walk into the wind, headed to the relative shelter of the truckstop. Shelter from the storm on a fairly sunny day. There are several puddles on the cement, but outside of that I wouldn't know it had rained.

I push the glass door open and look around. I can't see Stacy or the short man at first. It isn't until I've paid for the gas that I hear Stacy's voice behind me. She's saying something, but I can't make out the words although I detect urgency in her tone.

I turn and can see Stacy step back from behind a display of Quaker State oil, but an arm reaches out, grabs her and yanks her back. As I run down the aisle, I can now make out what the man is saying.

"Come on . . . ya said ya was friendly . . ."

I'm in back of Stacy watching this short, muscular man hold on to her with one hand while he slides the other inside her T-shirt. Stacy's struggling seems to excite the man even more.

Without thinking, I step up to the man and shove him in the side. Startled, he releases Stacy, who scrambles away and watches from a safe distance. Time seems to stand still as the man decides just what he's going to do about me. I have time to size the situation up, and I realize the odds aren't in my favor.

This all takes less than five seconds but it seems much longer. I stand about three feet from the man, who begins to smile and slowly rub his hands on the sides of his legs. He's about four inches shorter than me but looks solidly built. He looks down at the floor and without warning swings his right fist at me. I see it coming but I don't have time to react. He catches me on the side of my nose and I immediately know that it's broken.

Blood flows out of my nose as I lie on the floor looking up at this cretin who's standing over me, daring me to get up and fight. Stacy looks on from the corner. I could be wrong, but I detect an expression of contempt on her face. She walks up to the man and without saying anything, kisses him. It's a scene right out of a bad movie.

The cashier is yelling, "I'm calling the cops . . . you hear? I'm calling the cops."

Stacy lets him put his arm around her, and he speaks to me for the first time. "You like to go 'round again?" He's grinning and rubbing Stacy's ass while he continues. "Come on faggot. Let's play . . ."

I pull myself up, and he pokes me in the chest. We begin a dance, me backing up and him poking and taunting me. I back up until I hit the oil display and topple over, bringing the display down with me. The cashier starts yelling again.

This time, I get up and the redneck doesn't follow me. Stacy just watches me and smiles. I walk out into the cool wind and go to the island to get a paper towel. I tear off a piece and attempt to stop the blood which continues to slowly drip out of my nose. I'm a mess.

Suddenly, everything catches up with me. Leaving Sherry, last night's drinking, and the fight. I fall to my knees and heave, but there's nothing in me. I wait until the nausea passes and get up.

I take one look back at the three of them inside and then start toward my car. I pass the man's pickup on the way and after a few steps turn around and look at it. It's a Ford, and it looks pretty expensive. It's got all sorts of crap on it . . . things like fog lights, chrome running boards, and stainless steel rims. I look inside the open window and see he's also invested pretty heavily in stereo and CB equipment. It would serve the son of a bitch right if I bled all over the goddam thing.

I start to walk to my car, thinking about all the shit that's been heaped upon me. For some reason, all I can think of is Stacy in there letting that guy grope her. I get in my car, start the engine, and light a cigarette. Blood has now soaked the upper half of my shirt, and when I wipe my upper lip, I get blood smeared on my hands, which I then accidentally rub on my new seat cover. Suddenly a rage overtakes me. *Why have I let these assholes control me?*

I get out of the car and walk quickly to his truck. There's no hammer around, so I settle on the gas nozzle. I unhook the nozzle from its cradle and change my mind. Instead of smashing the window in, I squeeze the trigger and set it on automatic. Then I toss the nozzle in the open truck window. Gas flows out of those things pretty quickly and the truck soon has puddles forming on the floorboard and in the buckets of the custom seats.

I've gotten his attention now. The redneck comes running out of the truckstop, followed by Stacy and the cashier, who starts to come, starts to go back in, and finally settles on watching from a safe distance.

"You motherfucker . . . You're dead, man . . . fucking dead." He's out of breath as he gets within ten feet of me. I smile and take a drag off my cigarette. Then I hold the butt inside the window. He stops dead in his tracks.

"Come kill me, asshole." I take another drag and hold it inside the window again. "Come on . . . I thought you wanted to play?"

The expression on his face is comical. It's a mixture of horror and anger. Gas is now dripping out from the seam at the bottom of the doors. Stacy yells, "You're gonna kill us all, you shit."

For a few long seconds, we all stand around in silence. They start to edge away. "Stacy, get in the car," I say in a low voice. I must look grotesque standing here with a lit cigarette in a gasoline filled truck cab, with blood dripping down my face. Stacy doesn't move.

"Get in the fucking car!" She looks dazed but starts over to the car and gets in. She sits in the car, which is still idling.

I look at the driver and ask, "Want to save this piece of shit? Huh?" He wants to rip my heart out but says nothing.

I take one last drag off the smoke and tell him, "Run asshole." When he realizes what I mean, he starts to run, stumbling then righting himself as he makes a breakneck effort to get away. He's convinced I've lost my mind as I toss the butt in the window.

I get in my car and take off. Stacy leans over, waiting for the blast that doesn't come. "What happened?" she asks as she gets up and turns around to look back at the truckstop we're pulling away from.

"Nothing," I reply. "I expect he'll call the cops, but besides a ruined interior, nothing's going to happen."

Stacy doesn't understand, and I don't bother to tell her what she wants to know. I used to work at a refinery, and I remember how the older guys would get off on scaring new men by pitching lit cigarette butts into the open gas tanks in the tank farm. The thing is, gasoline won't ignite that way. It's the vapors which will catch if they're concentrated enough. It's not fail-safe but it's a pretty safe bet.

"What are you gonna do with me?" Stacy's voice has a plaintive whine about it. She seems more like a scared young girl now.

"I'm going to take you to Chamblee," I say more to myself than to her. And after that . . . I think I'll go home.

I put in a Springsteen tape and listen as the miles fall away. Springsteen sings in a subdued voice, "God help the man who doubts what he's sure of." Yeah . . . God help him.

ERNEST GAINES

THE TURTLES

When we got to Mr. James's house, my old man leaned the fishing poles against the fence and he went into the yard. Mr. James and Benny were sitting on the porch. Mr. James was fanning his face with his straw hat.

"It's coming down," my old man said. He put his foot on the step and leaned upon one knee. "You and Benny about ready?"

"Aren't you and Max going to rest awhile?" Mr. James asked.

"Better not stop too long," my old man said. "You don't feel like starting again."

"I see what you mean," Mr. James said. "Get the poles, Benny."

"You want me to wake up ma and tell her we're going?" Benny asked.

"She knows we're going," Mr. James said.

Benny went inside and got his hat, then he got the fishing poles from beside the house. He got the can of worms from under the steps, where he kept them cool and moist, and we started out for Gillman's lake. Gillman's lake was about two miles from Mr. James's house, and we made it over there 'way inside of an hour.

It was quiet and cool around the lake, and the lake was as smooth and shiny as a clean mirror. Looked like you could lay on

From *Transfer*, I (1956), published by the Associated Students Press of San Francisco State College.

top of it, or walk on it, and not go under and get wet. There wasn't a bubble or a ripple on it, and a few leaves from the trees slept on top of it like cocoons on a twig. I felt like diving in with all my clothes on and swimming from one side to the other.

"Find yourself a can and bring me half of the worms, Max" my old man said.

I found a can down at the water where somebody had left it, and put about half of the worms in it. I gave my old man the other half, then I got my line. Benny and Mr. James divided their bait; then Benny and I moved down the lake to find a good spot to fish. We moved about a hundred yards from where my old man and Mr. James were, to a dead tree that had fallen out on the lake. We walked out on the tree—that is, I walked out on the tree. Benny crawled out on it, like he was afraid he might fall and get his clothes wet. I was hoping my feet might slip so I could fall in.

Benny and I sat sideways on the tree, and I could see my old man and Mr. James sitting down on the bank farther up the lake. They were talking and looking out in the lake.

"There's no fishes out here," Benny said.

"Give them time," I said.

Benny had a big stopper on his line because he didn't know how to fish too good, and the stopper laid on top of the water, leaning a little to the back, like it was waiting for something to grab the hook and pull on the line so it could dip right under.

"We're going to the baseball game next Sunday," I told Benny.

Benny didn't say anything.

"Why don't you ask Mr. James?"

"Ma'll never let me go," Benny said.

"Church, huh?"

"That's every Sunday," Benny said.

"Why don't you ask Mr. James?"

Benny looked at his old man down the lake.

"Shucks," Benny said.

Then something struck Benny's line and Benny jerked the line up in the air.

"You can't catch anything like that," I said.

"Something was on it," Benny said.

"He was just playing around with the bait," I said. "You didn't give him enough time."

Benny drew in the line and looked at the hook. He covered the hook well with the bait; then he dropped the line into the water again.

"You have to let them run with it awhile," I told Benny.

Benny nodded his head, and about a minute later something struck his line again. The stopper dipped under the water a little; then it was still. It set still for a moment; then it began to move a little.

"Let him play with it for a while," I whispered.

Benny held the pole with both hands.

"Must be a little one," he said.

"Not too much noise," I told Benny.

The stopper went all the way under, and whatever was on the hook started to move toward the tree.

"Better pull it up," I said.

Benny jerked the line up out of the water and a little turtle was hanging on the end of the line. Benny dropped the line back into the water.

"Pull him up," I said. "He'll tangle your line on the tree."

"I don't like to catch these things on my line," Benny said.

"Pull it up," I told Benny.

Benny pulled the turtle up out of water again, and tried to shake him off the line.

"He's swallowed the hook," I said. "You can't shake him off."

"You want to take him off for me?" Benny asked me.

"Benny, you're not afraid of a little turtle, are you?"

"I just don't like to mess with them," Benny said.

I looked at the little turtle hanging on the end of Benny's line. "Here," I said, handing Benny my line. "Hold mine. I'll get him off."

I took the line on the bank and took the turtle off and killed it. I brought the line back to Benny.

"Did I have a bite?" I said.

"A little one," Benny said. "But he left."

"Did you pull up the line?"

"No," Benny said.

I drew in the line and saw that something had cleaned the hook. I baited the hook again, and threw it out toward the other side of the tree.

"I just don't like to mess with turtles," Benny said.

I didn't answer Benny and we didn't talk any more. We sat there about fifteen minutes. Then Benny caught another turtle. I took that one off the line and killed it; then we moved from the tree. We found another spot farther down the lake, but we didn't have any luck there either. Even the turtles weren't biting there.

"They just aren't biting today," Benny said.

"I guess not," I said.

We moved down about fifty yards and threw our lines out into the lake; then we sat down on the bank. We figured that nothing was going to bite, and we made ourselves comfortable. Soon we were lying down on our backs and looking up at the trees overhead.

"Hey there," Mr. James said, standing over us. "You boys come out here to fish or sleep?"

We sat up and I pulled in my line. Nothing was on it, and the hook was clean.

"Where's mine?" Benny said.

"Something must've taken it," Mr. James said. "Why didn't you stick the pole in the ground like Max did?"

"I stuck it," Benny said.

"Well, no use crying over spilled milk," Mr. James said. "Come on, let's go."

"Must've been another turtle," Benny said.

"You all caught many?" I asked Mr. James.

"About a dozen, each," Mr. James said. "Maybe more. Your pa caught a nice trout farther up the lake."

I wound up my line and threw the rest of the worms out into the lake. Benny did the same thing with his cup of worms.

When we got down where my old man was, he was standing beside a tree with the pole in one hand and the fishes in the other. He had about twelve or fifteen perches on one string, and the trout on a stick. The trout looked like it was about two feet long.

My old man looked at me and Benny; then he started up the bank.

"Want me to carry the trout, pa?" I asked my old man.

"You don't like to carry fishes," my old man said, without looking around.

I knew my old man was mad because I had gone to sleep and not caught anything. I wanted to say I was sorry, but my old man didn't like for me to say I was sorry about anything. So I dropped back and walked along with Benny.

"Here," my old man said. "Take it."

I ran up beside him and took the trout, then I dropped back and walked alongside Benny. Benny didn't like the way I was grinning and feeling proud.

My old man and Mr. James walked in front of me and Benny when we were going back home, and nobody was doing much talking. When we got to Mrs. Diana Brown's place, the sun was still about two hours up in the sky.

"We might as well stop in and have a drink of water," my old man said. "I'm a bit thirsty. Aren't you, George?"

"I can stand a drink," Mr. James said.

"Me and Max'll stay out here," Benny said. "I'm not thirsty."

"Come on in," Mr. James said.

"I'm not thirsty," Benny said.

"Come on in anyhow," Mr. James said. "Might as well be sociable."

We leaned our fishing poles against the picket fence and went into the yard. Benny walked in back of us.

Mrs. Diana Brown was a widow who lived back in the fields with her grown-up niece, Amy. There wasn't another house within two miles of Mrs. Diana Brown's place, and none of the other womenfolks associated too much with her or Amy. They said that no woman with a grown-up niece like that was worth anything, if neither one of them were married. But that never bothered Mrs. Diana Brown. She came out to the store every Saturday and made grocery and came back to her place without saying anything to anybody. Mrs. Diana Brown walked more prouder than any other lady that I had ever seen.

Amy was sitting on the porch when we went into the yard.

"Diana home, Amy?" my old asked.

"She went to town," Amy said.

My old man looked at Amy.

"Well, we just want a drink of water," my old man said.

Amy smiled.

"Well's in the back," she said. "Help yourself."

My old man and Mr. James went around the house, and Benny and I stood out in the yard next to the porch. Amy looked at us, then she went inside of the house. My old man and Mr. James came from in back of the house and sat on the end of the porch.

"It's been hot today," my old man said.

"Yes," Mr. James said.

Then they didn't say anything else, and my old man took out his pocket handkerchief and wiped his face and neck. They didn't look like they were going to be moving soon, so I leaned against the steps to rest awhile. Benny moved over to the big mulberry tree that Mrs. Diana Brown had in her front yard.

"Max," my old man said. "I want you to go into the house, and go into the first room on your right. Just push the door open and go in there."

"What for?" I asked.

"Because I said so," my old man said.

"Yes sir."

I went upon the porch and into the house. I pushed the door open like my old man had told me to do, and I saw Amy lying in the bed under the spread. She was covered up all the way up to her neck.

"Hi, Max," she said.

I looked at Amy but I didn't say anything. The window right in back of the bed was opened, but the two curtains were very still. It had been a hot day, and no wind was blowing. I looked at Amy grinning at me; then I backed out of the room and went back on the porch.

"Pa—," I started to say.

My old jumped like something unexpectedly had hit him.

"What are you doing out here, Max?" he said.

"Amy is in there."

"I know she's in there," my old man said.

"She's in the bed," I said.

"I know that too," my old man said. "Go back in there like I told you."

I went back to the door, and thought maybe my old man had made a mistake about the room. I went back out on the porch.

"Pa, is that the right room?" I said.

My old man looked at me like he knew I was going to come back out there.

"Max," he said, looking at me. "If you come back out here one more time without going into that room and staying in there awhile, I'm going to take my belt off to you."

"Yes sir."

I went back to the room where Amy was and stood just inside of the door.

"Max is afraid of girls," Amy sang. "You're afraid of me, Max?"

"I'm not afraid of anybody," I said.

"Then come here," Amy said.

"I rather stand here where I'm at," I said.

"Your pa want you to come where I'm at," she said, grinning.

I looked at Amy, and I wanted to leave the room again, but I thought about my old man. Not that he would whip me. I knew he had been bluffing out on the porch. He had never whipped me, and I doubted if he ever would. But that wasn't what I thought about. I thought about our friendship and our partnership. I had been his partner since mom had died, and that had been a long time. And nothing had broken it up, because I had always obeyed him. And I knew as long as I obeyed him the partnership would last. When I didn't, it would end. I wasn't ready for that to happen. So I went where she was, like he wanted me to do.

When I went back on the porch, my old man was sitting with his back against the post. He had one leg drawn up on the porch. He gave me a glance as I passed by him, going to the end of the porch to sit down, but he didn't tell me anything. I looked at Benny sitting down on the ground against the tree. He had a little stick in his hand, and he was poking in the ground. Mr. James was sitting next to my old man, looking down at his feet.

"Benny," Mr. James said.

And just like that, Benny started crying.

"Cut that out," Mr. James said. "Look at that. Look at that boy."

My old man looked at Benny but didn't say anything.

"Fifteen years old," Mr. James said. "And look at him."

Benny cried and poked in the ground with the little stick.

"Look at Max," Mr. James said. "Isn't he still breathing? Isn't he still alive? Did she eat him up?"

The tears and snot began to run out of Benny's eyes and nose. He kept jabbing the little stick down in the ground. He didn't bother to wipe his face.

"When you get tired crying, just get up from there and go inside the house," Mr. James said. "I've got all night."

My old man was looking at Benny, and I knew my old man felt like walking over there and butting Benny's head against the tree two or three times. Benny was about a year older than I was, and I knew if he was my old man's son, my old man would have butt his head against that tree and then picked him up and threw him in the room where Amy was. But Benny was not my old man's son, and Mr. James was not like my old man, and so Benny just sat against the tree and cried and jabbed in the ground with the little stick.

I stood up to go around the house to get some water from the well.

"Where're you going, Max?" my old man asked.

"Just to get some water," I said.

I went around the house and drew some water from the well and drank. When I came back to the porch, Benny was still sitting against the tree. He had stopped crying.

"You're ready to go in there, now?" Mr. James asked.

Benny started crying again. He still had the little stick in his hand.

My old man looked at Benny, then he looked at me.

"Well, we might as well move along," he said picking up the string of fishes. "You're taking off now, George?"

"Might as well," Mr. James said, and stood up.

Mr. James looked at Benny sitting against the tree with his head down, then picked up his string of fishes. He and my old man started out of the yard. I went to the tree where Benny was.

"You're going now, Benny?" I asked him.

Benny didn't look up. I stood there about a minute, looking down at him, and he didn't look up once.

"Well, I'd better be going," I said. "I'll have to clean the fishes for supper."

I caught up with my old man and Mr. James and we walked down the road without saying anything.

When we had gone about a half of a mile, Mr. James looked over his shoulder and saw Benny following us.

"Damn it," Mr. James said. "This is one day that boy is going to do what I say."

Mr. James turned around and started up the road toward Benny. Benny saw him coming and stopped. Mr. James walked up to Benny and grabbed him by the arm and turned him around. We were too far to hear if Benny was crying or not, but within myself I knew he was crying.

My old man and I started walking again.

"I guess you think you're a man now?" my old man said.

"Sir?"

"You heard me," my old man said.

"No sir," I said. "I didn't think I'm a man."

"Well, you are," my old man said.

I didn't say anything and my old man didn't say any more. The sun was going down, and the cool dust felt good under my bare feet.

WALKER PERCY

SIEUR IBERVILLE

Sure enough, three hours later we are rocking along an uneven roadbed through the heart of the Ponchatoula swamp.

No sooner do we open the heavy door of Sieur Iberville and enter the steel corridor with its gelid hush and the stray voices from open compartments and the dark smell of going high in the nostrils—than the last ten years of my life take on the shadowy aspect of a sojourn between train rides. It was ten years ago that I last rode a train, from San Francisco to New Orleans, and so ten years since I last enjoyed the peculiar gnosis of trains, stood on the eminence from which there is revealed both the sorry litter of the past and the future bright and simple as can be, and the going itself, one's privileged progress through the world. But trains have changed. Gone are the uppers and lowers, partitions and cranks, and the green velour; only the porter remains, the same man, I think, a black man with palms the color of shrimp and a neck swollen with dislike. Our roomettes turn out to be little coffins for a single person. From time to time, I notice, people in roomettes stick their heads out into the corridor for some sight of humankind.

Kate is affected by the peculiar dispensation of trains. Her gray jacket comes just short of her wide hips and the tight skirt curves under her in a nice play on vulgarity. On the way to the observation car she pulls me into the platform of the vestibule and gives me a kiss, grabbing me under the coat like a waitress. In celebration of Mardi Gras, she has made up her eyes with a sparkle of mascara and now she looks up at me with a black spiky look.

"Are we going to live in Modesto?"

"Sure," I say, uneasy at her playfulness. She is not as well as she makes out. She is not safe on a train after all; it is rather that by a kind of bravado she can skim along in the very face of danger.

The observation car is crowded, but we find seats together on a sofa where I am jammed against a fellow reading a newspaper. We glide through the cottages of Carrollton cutting off backyards in odd trapezoids, then through the country clubs and cemeteries of Metairie. In the gathering dusk the cemeteries look at first like cities, with their rows of white vaults, some two- and three-storied and forming flats and tenements, and the tiny streets and corners and curbs and even plots of lawn, all of such a proportion that in the very instant of being mistaken and from the eye's own necessity, they set themselves off into the distance like a city seen from far away. Now in the suburbs we ride at a witch's level above the gravelly roofs.

It gradually forces itself upon me that a man across the aisle is looking at me with a strange insistence. Kate nudges me. It is Sidney Gross and his wife, beyond a doubt bound also for the convention. The son of Sidney Gross of Danziger and Gross, Sidney is a short freshfaced crinkle-haired boy with the bright beamish look southern Jews sometimes have. There has always been a special cordiality between us. He married a pretty Mississippi girl; she, unlike Sidney, is wary of such encounters—she would know which of us spoke first at our last encounter—so she casts sleepy looks right past us, pausing, despite herself, on Kate's white face and black spiky eyes. But Sidney hunches over toward us, beaming, a stalwart little pony back with his head well set on his shoulders and his small ears lying flat.

"Well well well. Trader Jack. So you slipped up on your plane reservations too."

"Hello, Sidney, Margot. This is Kate Cutrer."

Margot becomes very friendly, in the gossipy style of the Mississippi Delta.

"So you forgot about it being Mardi Gras and couldn't get a plane."

"No, we like the train."

Sidney is excited, not by the trip as I am, but by the convention. Leaning across the aisle with a program rolled up in his hand, he explains that he is scheduled for a panel on tax relief for bond funds. "What about you?"

"I think I am taking part in something called a Cracker Barrel Session."

"You'll like it. Everybody talks right off the top of their head. You can take your coat off, get up and stretch. Anything. Last year we had this comical character from Georgia." Sidney casts about for some way of conveying just how comical and failing, passes on without minding. "What a character. Extremely comical. What's the topic?"

"Competing with the variable endowments."

"Oh yass," says Sidney with a wry look of our trade. "I don't worry about it." He slides the cylinder of paper to and fro. "Do you?"

"No."

Sidney suggests a bridge game, but Kate begs off. The Grosses move to a table in the corner and start playing gin rummy.

Kate, who has been fumbling in her purse, becomes still. I feel her eyes on my face.

"Do you have my capsules?"

"What?"

"My capsules."

"Why yes, I do. I forgot I had them."

Not taking her eyes from my face, she receives the bottle, puts it in her purse, snaps it.

"That's not like you."

"I didn't take them."

"Who did?"

"Sam gave them to me. It was while I was in the hammock. I hardly remember it."

"He took them from my purse?"

"I don't know."

For a long time she sits, hands in her lap, fingers curling up and stirring a little. Then abruptly she rises and leaves. When she returns, her face is scrubbed and pale, the moisture still dark at the roots of her hair. What has upset her is not the incident of the capsules but meeting the Grosses. It spoils everything, this prospect of making pleasant talk, of having a delightful time, as Sidney would put it ("There we were moping over missing the plane, when Jack Bolling shows up and we have ourselves a ball")—when we might have gone rocking up through dark old Mississippi alone together in the midst of strangers. Still she is better. Perhaps it is her reviving hope of losing the Grosses to gin rummy or perhaps it is the first secret promise of the chemicals entering her blood.

Now, picking up speed, we gain the swamp. Kate and I sway against each other and watch the headlights of the cars on the swamp road, winking through the moss like big yellow lightning bugs.

The drowsiness returns. It is unwelcome. I recognize it as the sort of fitful twilight which has come over me of late, a twilight where waking dreams are dreamed and sleep never comes.

The man next to me is getting off in St. Louis. When the conductor comes to collect our tickets, he surrenders a stub: he is going home. His suit is good. He sits with legs crossed, one well-clad haunch riding up like a ham, his top leg held out at an obtuse angle by the muscle of his calf. His brown hair is youthful (he himself is thirty-eight or forty) and makes a cowlick in front. With the cowlick and the black eyeglasses he looks quite a bit like the actor Gary Merrill and has the same certified permission to occupy pleasant space with his pleasant self. In ruddy good health, he muffles a hearty belch in a handkerchief. This very evening, no doubt, he has had an excellent meal at Galatoire's, and the blood of his portal vein bears away a golden harvest of nutrient globules.

When he first goes through his paper, he opens it like a book and I have no choice but to read the left page with him. We pause at an advertisement of a Bourbon Street nightclub which is the picture of a dancer with an oiled body. Her triceps arch forward like a mare's. For a second we gaze heavy-lidded and pass on. Now he finds what he wants and folds his paper once, twice, and again, into a neat packet exactly two columns wide, like a subway rider in New York. Propping it against his knee, he takes out a slender gold pencil, makes a deft one-handed adjustment, and underlines several sentences with straight black lines (he is used to underlining). Dreaming at his shoulder, I can make out no more than

> In order to deepen and enrich the marital—

It is a counseling column which I too read faithfully.

The train sways through the swamp. The St. Louisan, breathing powerfully through the stiff hairs of his nose, succeeds in sitting in such a manner, tilted over on his right hip and propped against himself, that his thigh forms a secure writing platform for the packet.

The voices in the car become fretful. It begins to seem that the passengers have ridden together for a long time and have developed secret understandings and old grudges. They speak crossly and elliptically to each other.

Staying awake is a kind of sickness and sleep is forever guarded against by a dizzy dutiful alertness. Waking wide-eyed dreams come as fitfully as swampfire.

Dr. and Mrs. Bob Dean autograph copies of their book *Technique in Marriage* in a Canal Street department store. A pair of beauties. I must have come in all the way from Gentilly, for I stand jammed against a table which supports a pyramid of books. I cannot take my eyes from the Deans: an oldish couple but still handsome and both, rather strangely, heavily freckled. As they wait for the starting time, they are jolly with each other and swap banter in the professional style of show people (I believe these preliminaries are called the warm-up). "No, we never argue," says Bob Dean. "Because whenever an argument starts, we consult the chapter I wrote on arguments." "No, dear," says Jackie Dean. "It was I who wrote the chapter—," etc. Everyone laughs. I notice that nearly all the crowd jamming against me are women, firm middle-aged one-fifty pounders. Under drooping lids I watch the Deans, peculiarly affected by their routine which is staged so effortlessly that during the exchange of quips, they are free to cast businesslike looks about them as if no one were present. But when they get down to business, they become as sober as Doukhobors and effuse an air of dedicated almost evangelical helpfulness. A copy of the book lies open on the table. I read: "Now with a tender regard for your partner remove your hand from the nipple and gently manipulate—" It is impossible not to imagine them at their researches, as solemn as a pair of brontosauruses, their heavy old freckled limbs twined about each other, hands probing skillfully for sensitive zones, pigmented areolas, out-of-the-way mucous glands, dormant vascular nexuses. A wave of prickling passes over me such as I have never experienced before.

My head, nodding like a daffodil, falls a good three inches toward the St. Louisan before it jerks itself up. Kate sits shivering against me, but the St. Louisan is as warm and solid as roast beef. As the train rocks along on its unique voyage through space-time, thousands of tiny thing-events bombard us like cosmic particles. Lying in a ditch outside is a scrap of newspaper with the date May 3, 1954. My Geiger counter clicks away like a teletype. But no one else seems to notice. Everyone is buried in his magazine. Kate is shaking like a leaf because she longs to be an anyone who is anywhere and she cannot.

The St. Louisan reads a headline

SCIENTIST PREDICTS FUTURE IF NUCLEAR ENERGY IS NOT MISUSED

Out comes the gold pencil to make a neat black box. After reading for a moment he comes back to the beginning and is about to make a second concentric box, thinks better of it, takes from his pocket a silver knife, undoes the scissors and clips the whole article, folds it and places it in his wallet. It is impossible to make out any of the underlined passages except the phrase "the gradual convergence of physical science and social science."

A very good phrase. I have to admire the St. Louisan for his neat and well-ordered life, his gold pencil and his scissors-knife and his way of clipping articles on the convergence of the physical sciences and the social sciences; it comes over me that in the past few days my own life has gone to seed. I no longer eat and sleep regularly or write philosophical notes in my notebook and my fingernails are dirty. The search has spoiled the pleasure of my tidy and ingenious life in Gentilly. As late as a week ago, such a phrase as "hopefully awaiting the gradual convergence of the physical sciences and the social sciences" would have provoked no more than an ironic tingle or two at the back of my neck. Now it howls through the Ponchatoula Swamp, the very sound and soul of despair.

Kate has stopped shivering and when she lights up and starts smoking, I am certain she is better. But I am mistaken. "Oooh," she says in a perfunctory workaday voice and starts forward again. The car lurches and throws her against Sidney's chair; there the train holds her fast: for three seconds she might be taken for a rapt onlooker of the gin-rummy game. Sidney rocks the deck against the polished wood until the cards are perfectly aligned. The gold ring on his little finger seems to serve as a device, a neat little fastening by means of which his hand movements are harnessed and made trim.

Half an hour passes and Kate does not return. I find her in her roomette, arms folded and face turned to the dark glass. We sit knee to knee.

"Are you all right?"

She nods slowly to the window, but her cheek is against me. Outside a square of yellow light flees along an embankment, falls away to the woods and fields, comes roaring back good as new. Suddenly a perky head pops up. Kate is leaning forward hugging herself.

"I am all right. I am never too bad with you."

"Why?"

"No thanks to you. On the contrary. The others are much more sympathetic than you, especially Mother and Sam."

"What about Merle?"

"Merle! Listen, with Merle I could break wind and he would give me that same quick congratulatory look. But you. You're nuttier than I am. One look at you and I have to laugh. Do you think that is sufficient ground for marriage?"

"As good as any. Better than love."

"Love! What do you know about love?"

"I didn't say I knew anything about it."

She is back at her window, moving her hand to see it move in the flying yellow square. We hunch up knee to knee and nose to nose like the two devils on the Rorschach card. Something glitters in the corner of her eye. Surely not a tear.

"Quite a Carnival. Two proposals in one Mardi Gras."

"Who else?"

"Sam."

"No kidding."

"No kidding. And I'll tell you something else. Sam is quite a person behind that facade. An essentially lonely person."

"I know."

"You're worse than Sam." She is angry.

"How?"

"Sam is a schemer. He also likes me. He knows that someday I will be quite rich. But he also likes me. That isn't so bad. Scheming is human. You have to be human to be a schemer. Whenever I see through one of Sam's little schemes, I feel a sensation of warmth. Aha, think I to myself, so it must have been in the world once—men and women wanting something badly and scheming away like beavers. But you—"

"Yes?"

"You're like me. So let us not deceive one another."

Her voice is steadier. Perhaps it is the gentle motion of the train with which we nod ever so slightly, yes, yes, yes.

She says: "Can't you see that for us it is much too late for such ingenious little schemes?"

"As marrying?"

"The only way you could carry it off is as another one of your ingenious little researches. Admit it."

"Then why not do it?"

"You remind me of a prisoner in the death house who takes a wry pleasure in doing things like registering to vote. Come to think of it, all your gaiety and good spirits have the same death-house quality. No thanks, I've had enough of your death-house pranks."

"What is there to lose?"

"Can't you see that after what happened last night, it is no use. I can't play games now. But don't you worry. I'm not going to swallow all the pills at once. Losing hope is not so bad. There's something worse: losing hope and hiding it from yourself."

"Very well. Lose hope or not. Be afraid or not. But marry me anyhow, and we can still walk abroad on a summer night, hope or no hope, shivering or not, and see a show and eat some oysters down on Magazine."

"No no."

"I don't understand—"

"You're right. You don't understand. It is not some one thing, as you think. It is everything. It is all so monstrous."

"What is monstrous?"

"I told you," she says irritably. "Everything. I'm not up to it. Having a little hubby—you would be hubby, dearest Binx, and that is ridiculous—did I hurt your feelings? Seeing hubby off in the morning, having lunch with the girls, getting tight at Eddie's and Nell's house and having a little humbug with somebody else's hubby, wearing my little diaphragm and raising two lovely boys and worrying for the next twenty years about whether they will make Princeton."

"I told you we would live in Gentilly. Or Modesto."

"I was being ingenious like you."

"Do you want to live like Sam and Joel?"

"Binx Binx. You're just like your aunt. When I told her how I felt, she said to me: Katherine, you're perfectly right. Don't ever lose your ideals and your enthusiasm for ideas—she thought I was talking about something literary or political or Great Books, for God's sake. I thought to myself: is that what I'm doing?—and ran out and took four pills. Incidentally, they're all wrong about that. They all think any minute I'm going to commit suicide. What a joke. The truth of course is the exact opposite: suicide is the only thing that keeps me alive. Whenever everything else fails, all I have to do is consider suicide and in two seconds I'm as cheerful as a nitwit. But if I could not kill myself—ah then. I would. I can do without nembutal or murder mysteries but not without suicide. And that reminds me." And off she goes down the steel corridor, one hand held palm out to the wall.

None of this is new, of course. I do not, to tell the truth, pay too much attention to what she says. It is her voice that tells me how she is. Now she speaks in her "bold" tone and since she appears more composed, to the point of being cheerful, than her words might indicate, I am not seriously concerned about her.

But the roomette soon becomes suffocating and, not feeling up to talking business with Sidney Gross, I head in the opposite direction, stop in the first vestibule, and have a long drink from my Mardi Gras bottle. We must be pulling into Jackson. The train screeches slowly around a curve and through the back of town. Kate comes out and stands beside me without a word. She smells of soap and seems in vaulting good spirits.

"Have a drink?"

"Do you remember going up to Baton Rouge on the train to see the football game?"

"Sure." Balancing there, her oval face aglow in the dark vestibule, hair combed flat on her head and down into the collar of her suit, she looks like a college girl. She drinks, pressing fingers to her throat. "Lord, how beautiful."

The train has stopped and our car stands high in the air, squarely above a city street. The nearly full moon swims through streaming ragtags of cloud and sheds a brilliant light on the capitol dome and the spanking new glass-and-steel office buildings and the empty street with its glittering streetcar track. Not a soul is in sight. Far away, beyond the wings of the capitol building stretch the dark tree-covered hills and the twinkling lights of the town. By some trick of moonlight the city seems white as snow and never-tainted; it sleeps away on its hilltop like the holy city of Zion.

Kate shakes her head slowly in the rapt way she got from her stepmother. I try to steer away from beauty. Beauty is a whore.

"You see that building yonder? That's Southern Life and Accident. If you had invested a hundred dollars in 1942, you'd now be worth twenty-five thousand. Your father bought a good deal of the original stock." Money is a better god than beauty.

"You don't know what I mean," she cries in the same soft rapture.

I know what she means all right. But I know something she doesn't know. Money is a good counterpoise to beauty. Beauty, the quest of beauty alone, is a whoredom. Ten years ago I pursued beauty and gave no thought to money. I listened to the lovely tunes of Mahler and felt a sickness in my very soul. Now I pursue money and on the whole feel better.

"I see how I could live in a city!" Kate cries. She turns to face me and clasps her hands behind my waist.

"How?"

"Only one way. By your telling me what to do. It is as simple as that. Why didn't I see it before?"

"That I should tell you what to do?"

"Yes. It may not be the noblest way of living, but it is one way. It is my way! Oh dear sweet old Binx, what a joy it is to discover at last what one is. It doesn't matter what you are as long as you know!"

"What are you?"

"I'll gladly tell you because I just found out and I never want to forget. Please don't let me forget. I am a religious person."

"How is that?"

"Don't you see? What I want is to believe in someone completely and then do what he wants me to do. If God were to tell me: Kate, here is what I want you to do; you get off this train right now and go over there to that corner by the Southern Life and Accident Insurance Company and stand there for the rest of your life and speak kindly to people—you think I would not do it? You think I would not be the happiest girl in Jackson, Mississippi? I would."

I have a drink and look at her corner. The moonlight seems palpable, a dense pure matrix in which is embedded curbstone and building alike.

She takes the bottle. "Will you tell me what to do?"

"Sure."

"You can do it because you are not religious. God is not religious. You are the unmoved mover. You don't need God or anyone else—no credit to you, unless it is a credit to be the most self-centered person alive. I don't know whether I love you, but I believe in you and I will do what you tell me. Now if I marry you, will you tell me: Kate, this morning do such and such, and if we have to go to a party, will you tell me: Kate, stand right there and have three drinks and talk to so and so? Will you?"

"Sure."

Kate locks her arm around my chest, wrist in hand, and gives me a passionate kiss.

Later, just as I knew it would, her precious beauty leaves her flat and she is frightened. Another trip to the washroom and now she stands swaying against me as Sieur Iberville rocks along through north Mississippi. We leave spring behind. The moon hangs westering and yellow over winter fields as blackened and ancient and haunted as battlegrounds.

"Oh oh oh," Kate moans and clings to me. "I feel awful. Let's go to your roomette."

"It's been made up."

"Then we'll lie down."

We have to lie down: the door opens onto the bed. Feeling tender toward her, I embrace her and tell her that I love her.

"Oh no," says Kate and takes hold of me coarsely. "None of that, bucko."

"None of what?"

I misunderstand her and pull away.

"No no. Don't leave me either," she says, holding me and watching me still.

"All right."

"Just don't speak to me of love, bucko."

"All right, but don't call me bucko."

Her black spiky eyes fall full upon me, but not quite seeing, I think. Propped on one hand, she bites her lip and lets the other fall on me heavily, as if I were an old buddy. "I'll tell you something."

"What."

"The other day I said to Merle." Again the hand falls heavily and takes hold of me. "What would you say to me having a little fling? He misunderstood me and gave me the business about a mature and tender relation between adults etcetera etcetera—you know. I said, no no, Merle, you got it wrong. I'm talking about some plain old monkey business—" she gives me a shake, "—like a comic book one of your aunt's maids showed me last week in which Tillie the Toiler and Mac—not the real Tillie, you understand, but a Frenchy version of Tillie—go to an office party and Tillie has a little set-to with Mac in the stockroom and gets caught by Whipple. I told Merle about it and said: that's what I mean, Merle, how about that?"

"What did Merle say?"

Kate doesn't seem to hear. She drums her fingers on the sill and gazes out at the rushing treetops.

"So—when all is said and done, that is the real thing, isn't it? Admit it. You and the little Hondurian on the second floor with her little book, in the morning, in the midmorning, and there in the linen closet with the mops and pails—"

"It is your Hondurian and your comic book—"

"Now I'll tell you what you can do, Whipple. You get out of

here and come back in exactly five minutes. Oh you're a big nasty Whipple and you're only fit for one thing."

I'll have to tell you the truth, Rory, painful though it is. Nothing would please me more than to say that I had done one of two things. Either that I did what you do: tuck Debbie in your bed and, with a show of virtue so victorious as to be ferocious, grab pillow and blanket and take to the living-room sofa, there to lie in the dark, hands clasped behind head, gaze at the ceiling, and talk through the open door of your hopes and dreams. Or—do what a hero in a novel would do: he too is a seeker and a pilgrim of sorts and he is just in from Guanajuato or Sambuco where he has found the Real Right Thing or from the East where he apprenticed himself to a wise man and became proficient in the seventh path to the seventh happiness. Yet he does not disdain this world either and when it happens that a maid comes to his bed with a heart full of longing for him, he puts down his book in a good and cheerful spirit and gives her as merry a time as she could possibly wish for. Whereupon, with her dispatched into as sweet a sleep as ever Scarlett enjoyed the morning of Rhett's return, he takes up his book again and is in an instant ten miles high and on the Way.

No, Rory, I did neither. We did neither. We did very badly and almost did not do at all. Flesh poor flesh failed us. The burden was too great and flesh poor flesh, neither hallowed by sacrament nor despised by spirit (for despising is not the worst fate to overtake the flesh), but until this moment seen through and canceled, rendered null by the cold and fishy eye of the malaise—flesh poor flesh now at this moment summoned all at once to be all and everything, end all and be all, the last and only hope—quails and fails. The truth is I was frightened half to death by her bold (not really bold, not whorish bold but theorish bold) carrying on. I reckon I am used to my blushing little Lindas from Gentilly. Kate too was scared. We shook like leaves. Kate was scared because it seemed now that even Tillie the Toiler must fail her. I never worked so hard in my life, Rory. I had no choice: the alternative was unspeakable. Christians talk about the horror of sin, but they have overlooked something. They keep talking as if everyone were a great sinner, when the truth is that nowadays one is hardly up to it. There is very little sin in the depths of the malaise. The highest moment of a malaisian's life can be that moment when he manages to sin like a proper human (Look at us, Binx—my vagabond friends as good as cried out to me—we're sinning! We're succeeding! We're human after all!).

"Good night, sweet Whipple. Now you tuck Kate in. Poor Kate." She turns the pillow over for the cool of the underside. "Good night, sweet Whipple, good night, good night, good night."

ANDRÉ DUBUS

A FATHER'S STORY

My name is Luke Ripley, and here is what I call my life: I own a stable of thirty horses, and I have young people who teach riding, and we board some horses too. This is in northeastern Massachusetts. I have a barn with an indoor ring, and outside I've got two fenced-in rings and a pasture that ends at a woods with trails. I call it my life because it looks like it is, and people I know call it that, but it's a life I can get away from when I hunt and fish, and some nights after dinner when I sit in the dark in the front room and listen to opera. The room faces the lawn and the road, a two-lane country road. When cars come around the curve northwest of the house, they light up the lawn for an instant, the leaves of the maple out by the road and the hemlock closer to the window. Then I'm alone again, or I'd appear to be if someone crept up to the house and looked through a window: a big-gutted gray-haired guy, drinking tea and smoking cigarettes, starting out at the dark woods across the road, listening to a grieving soprano.

My real life is the one nobody talks about anymore, except Father Paul LeBoeuf, another old buck. He has a decade on me: he's sixty-four, a big man, bald on top with grey at the sides; when he had hair, it was black. His face is ruddy, and he jokes about being

---

a whiskey priest, though he's not. He gets outdoors as much as he can, goes for a long walk every morning, and hunts and fishes with me. But I can't get him on a horse anymore. Ten years ago I could badger him into a trail ride; I had to give him a western saddle and he'd hold the pommel and bounce through the woods with me, and be sore for days. He's looking at seventy with eyes that are younger than many I've seen in people in their twenties. I do not remember ever feeling the way they seem to; but I was lucky, because even as a child I knew that life would try me, and I must be strong to endure, though in those early days I expected to be tortured and killed for my faith, like the saints I learned about in school.

Father Paul's family came down from Canada, and he grew up speaking more French than English, so he is different from the Irish priests who abound up here. I do not like to make general statements, or even to hold general beliefs, about people's blood, but the Irish do seem happiest when they're dealing with misfortune or guilt, either their own or somebody else's and if you think you're not a victim of either one, you can count on certain Irish priests to try to change your mind. On Wednesday nights Father Paul comes to dinner. Often he comes on other nights too, and once, in the old days when we couldn't eat meat on Fridays, we bagged our first ducks of the season on a Friday, and as we drove home from the marsh, he said: For the purposes of Holy Mother Church, I believe a duck is more a creature of water than land, and is not rightly meat. Sometimes he teases me about never putting anything in his Sunday collection, which he would not know about if I hadn't told him years ago. I would like to believe I told him so we could have philosophical talk at dinner, but probably the truth is I suspected he knew, and I did not want him to think I so loved money that I would not even give his church a coin on Sunday. Certainly the ushers who pass the baskets know me as a miser.

I don't feel right about giving money for buildings, places. This starts with the pope, and I cannot respect one of them till he sells his house and everything in it, and that church too, and uses the money to feed the poor. I have rarely, and maybe never, come across saintliness, but I feel certain it cannot exist in such a place. But I admit, also, that I know very little, and maybe the popes live on a different plane and are tried in ways I don't know about. Father Paul says his own church, St. John's, is hardly the Vatican. I like his church: it is made of wood, and has a simple altar and crucifix, and no padding on the kneelers. He does not have to lock its doors at night. Still it is a place. He could say mass in my barn. I know this is stubborn, but I can find no mention by Christ of maintaining buildings, much less erecting them of stone or brick, and decorating them with pieces of metal and mineral and elements that people still fight over like barbarians. We had a Maltese woman taking riding lessons; she came over on the boat when she was ten, and once she told me how the nuns in Malta used to tell the little girls that if they wore jewelry, rings and bracelets and necklaces, in purgatory snakes would coil around their fingers and wrists and throats. I do not believe in frightening children or telling them lies, but if those nuns saved a few girls from devotion to things, maybe they were right. That Maltese woman laughed about it, but I noticed she wore only a watch, and that with a leather strap.

The money I give to the church goes in people's stomachs, and on their backs, down in New York City. I have no delusions about the worth of what I do, but I feel it's better to feed somebody than not. There's a priest in Times Square giving shelter to runaway kids, and some Franciscans who run a breadline; actually it's a morning line for coffee and a roll, and Father Paul calls it the continental breakfast for winos and bag ladies. He is curious about how much I am sending, and I know why: he guesses I send a lot, he has said probably more than tithing, and he is right; he wants to know how much because he believes I'm generous and good, and he is wrong about that; he has never had much money and does not know how easy it is to write a check when you have everything you will ever need, and the figures are mere numbers, and represent no sacrifice at all. Being a real Catholic is too hard; if I were one, I would do with my house and barn what I want the pope to do with his. So I do not want to impress Father Paul, and when he asks me how much, I say I can't let my left hand know what my right is doing.

He came on Wednesday nights when Gloria and I were married, and the kids were young; Gloria was a very good cook (I assume she still is, but it is difficult to think of her in the present), and I liked sitting at the table with a friend who was also a priest. I was proud of my handsome and healthy children. This was long ago, and they were all very young and cheerful and often funny, and the three boys took care of their baby sister, and did not bully or tease her. Of course they did sometimes, with that excited cruelty children are prone to, but not enough so that it was part of her days. On the Wednesday after Gloria left with the kids and a U-Haul trailer, I was sitting on the front steps, it was summer, and I was watching cars go by on the road, when Father Paul drove around the curve and into the driveway. I was ashamed to see him because he is a priest and my family was gone, but I was relieved too. I went to the car to greet him. He got out smiling, with a bottle of wine, and shook my hand, then pulled me to him, gave me a quick hug, and said: "It's Wednesday, isn't it? Let's open some cans."

With arms about each other we walked to the house, and it was good to know he was doing his work but coming as a friend too, and I thought what good work he had. I have no calling. It is for me to keep horses.

In that other life, anyway. In my real one I go to bed early and sleep well and wake at four forty-five, for an hour of silence. I never want to get out of bed then, and every morning I know I can sleep for another four hours, and still not fail at any of my duties. But I get up, so have come to believe my life can be seen in miniature in that struggle in the dark of morning. While making the bed and boiling water for coffee, I talk to God: I offer Him my day, every act of my body and spirit, my thoughts and moods, as a prayer of thanksgiving, and for Gloria and my children and my friends and two women I made love with after Gloria left. This morning offertory is a habit from my boyhood in a Catholic school; or then it was a habit, but as I kept it and grew older it became a ritual. Then I say the Lord's Prayer, trying not to recite it, and one morning it occurred to me that a prayer, whether recited or said with concentration, is always an act of faith.

I sit in the kitchen at the rear of the house and drink coffee and smoke and watch the sky growing light before sunrise, the trees of the woods near the barn taking shape, becoming single pines and elms and oaks and maples. Sometimes a rabbit comes out of the tree line, or is already sitting there, invisible till the light finds him. The birds are awake in the trees and feeding on the ground, and the little ones, the purple finches and titmice and chickadees, are at thc feeder I rigged outside the kitchen window; it is too small for pigeons to get a purchase. I sit and give myself to coffee and tobacco, that get me brisk again, and I watch and listen. In the first year or so after I lost my family, I played the radio in the mornings. But I overcame that, and now I rarely play it at all. Once in the mail I received a questionnaire asking me to write down everything I watched on television during the week they had chosen. At the end of those seven days I wrote in *The Wizard of Oz* and returned it. That was in winter and was actually a busy week for my television, which normally sits out the cold months without once warming up. Had they sent the questionnaire during baseball season, they would have found me at my set. People at the stables talk about shows and performers I have never heard of, but I cannot get interested; when I am in the mood to watch television, I go to a movie or read a detective novel. There are always good detective novels to be found, and I like remembering them next morning with my coffee.

I also think of baseball and hunting and fishing, and of my children. It is not painful to think about them anymore, because even if we had lived together, they would be gone now, grown into their own lives, except Jennifer. I think of death too, not sadly, or with fear, though something like excitement does run through me, something more quickening than the coffee and tobacco. I suppose it is an intense interest, and an outright distrust: I never feel certain that I'll be here watching birds eating at tomorrow's daylight. Sometimes I try to think of other things, like the rabbit that is warm and breathing but not there till twilight. I feel on the brink of something about the life of the senses, but either am not equipped to go further or am not interested enough to concentrate. I have called all of this thinking, but it is not, because it is unintentional; what I'm really doing is feeling the day, in silence, and that is what Father Paul is doing too on his five-to-ten-mile walks.

When the hour ends I take an apple or carrot and I go to the stable and tack up a horse. We take good care of these horses, and no one rides them but students, instructors, and me, and nobody rides the horses we board unless an owner asks me to. The barn is dark and I turn on lights and take some deep breaths, smelling the hay and horses and their manure, both fresh and dried, a combined odor that you either like or you don't. I walk down the wide space of dirt between stalls, greeting the horses, joking with them about their quirks, and choose one for no reason at all other than the way it looks at me that morning. I get my old English saddle that has smoothed and darkened through the years, and go into the stall, talking to this beautiful creature who'll swerve out of a canter if a piece of paper blows in front of him, and if the barn catches fire and you manage to get him out he will, if he can get away from you, run back into the fire, to his stall. Like the smells that surround them, you either like them or you don't. I love them, so am spared having to try to explain why. I feed one the carrot or apple and tack up and lead him outside, where I mount, and we go down the driveway to the road and cross it and turn northwest and walk then trot then canter to St. John's.

A few cars are on the road, their drivers looking serious about going to work. It is always strange for me to see a woman dressed for work so early in the morning. You know how long it takes them, with the makeup and hair and clothes, and I think of them waking in the dark of winter or early light of other seasons, and dressing as they might for an evening's entertainment. Probably this strikes me because I grew up seeing my father put on those suits he never wore on weekends or his two weeks off, and so am accustomed to the men, but when I see these women I think something went wrong, to send all those dressed-up people out on the road when the dew hasn't dried yet. Maybe it's because I so dislike getting up early, but am also doing what I choose to do, while they have no choice. At heart I am lazy, yet I find such peace and delight in it that I believe it is a natural state, and in what looks like my laziest periods I am closest to my center. The ride to St. John's is fifteen minutes. The horses and I do it in all weather; the road is well plowed in winter, and there are only a few days a year when ice makes me drive the pickup. People always look at someone on horseback, and for a moment their faces change and many drivers and I wave to each other. Then at St. John's, Father Paul and five or six regulars and I celebrate the mass.

Do not think of me as a spiritual man whose every thought during those twenty-five minutes is at one with the words of the mass. Each morning I try, each morning I fail, and know that always I will be a creature who, looking at Father Paul and the altar, and uttering prayers, will be distracted by scrambled eggs, horses, the weather, and memories and daydreams that have nothing to do with the sacrament I am about to receive. I can receive, though: the Eucharist, and also, at mass and at other times, moments and even minutes of contemplation. But I cannot achieve contemplation, as some can; and so, having to face and forgive my own failures, I have learned from them both the necessity and wonder of ritual. For ritual allows those who cannot will themselves out of the secular to perform the spiritual, as dancing allows the tongue-tied man a ceremony of love. And, while my mind dwells on breakfast, or Major or Duchess tethered under the church eave, there is, as I take the Host from Father Paul and place it on my tongue and return to the pew, a feeling that I am thankful I have not lost in the forty-eight years since my first Communion. At its center is excitement; spreading out from it is the peace of certainty. Or the certainty of peace. One night Father Paul and I talked about faith. It was long ago, and all I remember is him saying: Belief is believing in God; faith is believing that God believes in you. That is the excitement, and the peace; then the mass is over, and I go into the sacristy and we have a cigarette and chat, the mystery ends, we are two men talking like any two men on a morning in America, about baseball, plane crashes, presidents, governors, murders, the sun, the clouds. Then I go to the horse and ride back to the life people see, the one in which I move and talk, and most days I enjoy it.

It is late summer now, the time between fishing and hunting, but a good time for baseball. It has been two weeks since Jennifer left, to drive home to Gloria's after her summer visit. She is the only one who still visits; the boys are married and have children, and sometimes fly up for a holiday, or I fly down or west to visit one of them. Jennifer is twenty, and I worry about her the way fathers worry about daughters but not sons. I want to know what she's up to, and at the same time I don't. She looks athletic, and she is: she swims and runs and of course rides. All my children do. When she comes for six weeks in summer, the house is loud with girls, friends of hers since childhood, and new ones. I am glad she kept the girlfriends. They have been young company for me and, being with them, I have been able to gauge her growth between summers. On their riding days, I'd take them back to the house when their lessons were over and they had walked the horses and put them back in the stalls, and we'd have lemonade or Coke, and cookies if I had some, and talk until their parents came to drive them home. One year their breasts grew, so I wasn't startled when I saw Jennifer in July. Then they were driving cars to the stable, and beginning to look like young women, and I was passing out beer and ashtrays and they were talking about college.

When Jennifer was here in summer, they were at the house

most days. I would say generally that as they got older they became quieter, and though I enjoyed both, I sometimes missed the giggles and shouts. The quiet voices, just low enough for me not to hear from wherever I was, rising and falling in proportion to my distance from them, frightened me. Not that I believed they were planning or recounting anything really wicked, but there was a female seriousness about them, and it was secretive, and of course I thought: love, sex. But it was more than that: it was womanhood they were entering, the deep forest of it, and no matter how many women and men too are saying these days that there is little difference between us, the truth is that men find their way into that forest only on clearly marked trails, while women move about in it like birds. So hearing Jennifer and her friends talking so quietly, yet intensely, I wanted very much to have a wife.

But not as much as in the old days, when Gloria had left but her presence was still in the house as strongly as if she had only gone to visit her folks for a week. There were no clothes or cosmetics, but potted plants endured my neglectful care as long as they could, and slowly died; I did not kill them on purpose, to exorcise the house of her, but I could not remember to water them. For weeks, because I did not use it much, the house was as neat as she had kept it, though dust layered the order she had made. The kitchen went first: I got the dishes in and out of the dishwasher and wiped the top of the stove but did not return cooking spoons and potholders to their hooks on the wall, and soon the burners and oven were caked with spillings, the refrigerator had more space and was spotted with juices. The living room and my bedroom went next; I did not go into the children's rooms except on bad nights when I went from room to room and I looked and touched and smelled, so they did not lose their order until a year later when the kids came for six weeks. It was three months before I ate the last of the food Gloria had cooked and frozen: I remember it was a beef stew, and very good. By then I had four cookbooks, and was boasting a bit, and talking about recipes with the women at the stables, and looking forward to cooking for Father Paul. But I never looked forward to cooking at night only for myself, though I made myself do it; on some nights I gave in to my daily temptation, and took a newspaper or detective novel to a restaurant. By the end of the second year, though, I had stopped turning on the radio as soon as I woke in the morning, and was able to be silent and alone in the evening too, and then I enjoyed my dinners.

It is not hard to live through a day, if you can live through a moment. What creates despair is the imagination, which pretends there is a future, and insists on predicting millions of moments, thousands of days, and so drains you that you cannot live the moment at hand. That is what Father Paul told me in those first two years, on some of the bad nights when I believed I could not bear what I had to: the most painful loss was my children, then the loss of Gloria, whom I still loved despite or maybe because of our long periods of sadness that rendered us helpless, so neither of us could break out of it to give a hand to the other. Twelve years later I believe ritual would have healed us more quickly than the repetitious talks we had, perhaps even kept us healed. Marriages have lost that, and I wish I had known then what I know now, and we had performed certain acts together every day, no matter how we felt, and perhaps then we could have subordinated feeling to action, for surely that is the essence of love. I know this from my distractions during mass, and during everything else I do, so that my actions and feelings are seldom one. It does happen every day, but in proportion to everything else in a day, it is rare, like joy. The third most painful loss, which became second and sometimes first as months passed, was the knowledge that I could never marry again, and so dared not even keep company with a woman.

On some of the bad nights I was bitter about this with Father Paul, and I so pitied myself that I cried, or nearly did, speaking with damp eyes and breaking voice. I believe that celibacy is for him the same trial it is for me, not of the flesh, but the spirit: the heart longing to love. But the difference is he chose it, and did not wake one day to a life with thirty horses. In my anger I said I had done my service to love and chastity, and I told him of the actual physical and spiritual pain of practicing rhythm: nights of striking the mattress with a fist, two young animals lying side by side in heat, leaving the bed to pace, to smoke, to curse, and too passionate to question, for we were so angered and oppressed by our passion that we could see no further than our loins. So now I understand how people can be enslaved for generations before they throw down their tools or use them as weapons, the form of their slavery—the cotton fields, the shacks and puny cupboards and untended illnesses—absorbing their emotions and thoughts until finally they have little or none at all to direct with clarity and energy at the owners and legislators. And I told him of the trick of passion and its slaking: how during what we had to believe were safe periods, though all four children were conceived at those times, we were able with some coherence to question the tradition and reason and justice of the law against birth control, but not with enough conviction to soberly act against it, as though regular satisfaction in bed tempered our revolutionary as well as our erotic desires. Only when abstinence drove us hotly away from each other did we receive an urge so strong it lasted all the way to the drugstore and back; but always, after release, we threw away the remaining condoms; and after going through this a few times, we knew what would happen, and from then on we submitted to the calendar she so precisely marked on the bedroom wall. I told him that living two lives each month, one as celibates, one as lovers, made us tense and short-tempered, so we snapped at each other like dogs.

To have endured that, to have reached a time when we burned slowly and could gain from bed the comfort of lying down at night with one who loves you and whom you love, could for weeks on end go to bed tired and peacefully sleep after a kiss, a touch of the hands, and then to be thrown out of the marriage like a bundle from a moving freight car, was unjust, was intolerable, and I could not or would not muster the strength to endure it. But I did, a moment at a time, a day, a night, except twice, each time with a different woman and more than a year apart, and this was so long ago that I clearly see their faces in my memory, can hear the pitch of their voices, and the way they pronounced words, one with a Massachusetts accent, one midwestern, but I feel as though I only heard about them from someone else. Each rode at the stables and was with me for part of an evening; one was badly married, one divorced, so none of us was free. They did not understand this Catholic view, but they were understanding about my having it, and I remained friends with both of them until the married one left her husband and went to Boston, and the divorced one moved to Maine. After both those evenings, those good women, I went to mass early while Father Paul was still in the confessional, and received his absolution. I did not tell him who I was, but of course he knew, though I never saw it in his eyes. Now my longing for a wife comes only once in a while, like a cold: on some late afternoons when I am alone in the barn, then I lock up and walk to the house, daydreaming, then suddenly look at it and see it empty, as though for the first time, and all at once I'm weary and feel I do not have the energy to broil meat, and I think of driving to a restaurant, then shake my head and go on to the house, the refrigerator, the oven; and some mornings when I wake in the dark and listen to the silence and run my hand over the cold sheet beside me; and some days in summer when Jennifer is here.

Gloria left first me, then the Church, and that was the end of religion for the children, though on visits they went to Sunday mass with me, and still do, out of a respect for my life that they manage to keep free of patronage. Jennifer is an agnostic, though I doubt she would call herself that, any more than she would call herself any other name that implied she had made a decision, a choice, about existence, death, and God. In truth she tends to pantheism, a good sign, I think; but not wanting to be a father who tells his children what they ought to believe, I do not say to her that Catholicism includes pantheism, like onions in a stew. Besides, I have no missionary instincts and do not believe everyone should or even could live with the Catholic faith. It is Jennifer's womanhood that renders me awkward. And womanhood now is frank, not like when Gloria was twenty and there were symbols: high heels and cosmetics and dresses, a cigarette, a cocktail. I am glad that women are free now of false modesty and all its attention paid the flesh; but, still, it is difficult to see so much of your daughter, to hear her talk as only men and bawdy women used to, and most of all to see in her face the deep and unabashed sensuality of women, with no tricks of the eyes and mouth to hide the pleasure she feels at having a strong young body. I am certain, with the way things are now, that she has very happily not been a virgin for years. That does not bother me. What bothers me is my certainty about it, just from watching her walk across a room or light a cigarette or pour milk on cereal.

She told me all of it, waking me that night when I had gone to sleep listening to the wind in the trees and against the house, a wind so strong that I had to shut all but the lee windows, and still the house cooled; told it to me in such detail and so clearly that now, when she has driven the car to Florida, I remember it all as though I had been a passenger in the front seat, or even at the wheel. It started with a movie, then beer and driving to the sea to look at the waves in the night and the wind, Jennifer and Betsy and Liz. They drank a beer on the beach and wanted to go in naked but were afraid they would drown in the high surf. They bought another six-pack at a grocery store in New Hampshire, and drove home. I can see it now, feel it: the three girls and the beer and the ride on country roads where pines curved in the wind and the big deciduous trees swayed and shook as if they might leap from the earth. They would have some windows partly open so they could feel the wind; Jennifer would be playing a cassette, the music stirring them, as it does the young, to memories of another time, other people and places in what is for them the past.

She took Betsy home, then Liz, and sang with her cassette as she left the town west of us and started home, a twenty-minute drive on the road that passes my house. They had each had four beers, but now there were twelve empty bottles in the bag on the floor at the passenger seat, and I keep focusing on their sound against each other when the car shifted speeds or changed directions. For I want to understand that one moment out of all her heart's on earth, and whether her history had any bearing on it, or whether her heart was then isolated from all it had known, and the sound of those bottles urged it. She was just leaving the town, accelerating past a nightclub on the right, gaining speed to climb a long, gradual hill; then she went up it, singing, patting the beat on the steering wheel, the wind loud through her few inches of open window, blowing her hair as it did the high branches alongside the road, and she looked up at them and watched the top of the hill for someone drunk or heedless coming over it in part of her lane. She crested to an open black road, and there he was: a bulk, a blur, a thing running across her headlights, and she swerved left and her foot went for the brake and was stomping air above its pedal when she hit him, saw his legs and body in the air, flying out of her light, into the dark. Her brakes were screaming into the wind, bottles clinking in the fallen bag, and with the music and wind inside the car was his sound, already a memory but as real as an echo, that car-shuddering thump as though she had struck a tree. Her foot was back on the accelerator. Then she shifted gears and pushed it. She ejected the cassette and closed the window. She did not start to cry until she knocked on my bedroom door, then called: "Dad?"

Her voice, her tears, broke through my dream and the wind I heard in my sleep, and I stepped into jeans and hurried to the door, thinking harm, rape, death. All were in her face, and I hugged her and pressed her cheek to my chest and smoothed her blown hair, then led her, weeping, to the kitchen and sat her at the table where still she could not speak, nor look at me; when she raised her face it fell forward again, as of its own weight, into her palms. I offered tea and she shook her head, so I offered beer twice, then she shook her head, so I offered whiskey and she nodded. I had some rye that Father Paul and I had not finished last hunting season, and I poured some over ice and set it in front of her and was putting away the ice but stopped and got another glass and poured one for myself too, and brought the ice and bottle to the table where she was trying to get one of her long menthols out of the pack, but her fingers jerked like severed snakes, and I took the pack and lit one for her and took one for myself. I watched her shudder with her first swallow of rye, and push hair back from her face—it is auburn and gleamed in the overhead light—and I remembered how beautiful she looked riding a sorrel; she was smoking fast, then the sobs in her throat stopped, and she looked at me and said it, the words coming out with smoke: "I hit somebody. With the car."

Then she was crying and I was on my feet, moving back and forth, looking down at her, asking, Who? Where? Where? She was pointing at the wall over the stove, jabbing her fingers and cigarette at it, her other hand at her eyes, and twice in horror I actually looked at the wall. She finished the whiskey in a swallow and I stopped pacing and asking and poured another, and either the drink or the exhaustion of tears quieted her, even the dry sobs, and she told me; not as I tell it now, for that was later as again and again we relived it in the kitchen or living room, and, if in daylight, fled it on horseback out on the trails through the woods and, if at night, walked quietly around in the moonlit pasture, walked around and around it, sweating through our clothes. She told it in bursts, like she was a child again, running to me, injured from play. I put on boots and a shirt and left her with the bottle and her streaked face and a cigarette twitching between her fingers, pushed the door open against the wind, and eased it shut. The wind squinted and watered my eyes as I leaned into it and went to the pickup.

When I passed St. John's I looked at it, and Father Paul's little white rectory in the rear, and wanted to stop, wished I could as I could if he were simply a friend who sold hardware or something. I had forgotten my watch but I always know the time within minutes, even when a sound or dream or my bladder wakes me in the night. It was nearly two; we had been in the kitchen about twenty minutes; she had hit him around one-fifteen. Or her. The road was empty and I drove between blowing trees; caught for an instant in my lights, they seemed to be in panic. I smoked and let hope play its tricks on me: it was neither man nor woman but an animal, a goat or calf or deer on the road; it was a man who had jumped away in time, the collision of metal and body glancing, not direct, and he had limped home to nurse bruises and cuts. Then I threw the cigarette and hope both out the window and prayed that he was alive, while beneath that prayer, a reserve deeper in my heart, another one stirred: that if he were dead, they would not get Jennifer.

From our direction, east and a bit south, the road to that hill and the nightclub beyond it and finally the town is, for its last four or five miles, straight through farming country. When I reached that stretch I slowed the truck and opened my window for the fierce air; on both sides were scattered farmhouses and barns and sometimes a silo, looking not like shelters but like unsheltered things the wind would flatten. Corn bent toward the road from a field on my right, and always something blew in front of me: paper, leaves, dried weeds, branches. I slowed approaching the hill, and went up it in second, staring through my open window at the ditch on the left side of the road, its weeds alive, whipping, a mad dance with the trees above them. I went over the hill and down and, opposite the club, turned right onto a side street of houses, and parked there, in the leaping shadows of trees. I walked back across the road to the club's parking lot, the wind behind me, lifting me as I strode, and I could not hear my boots on pavement. I walked up the hill, on the shoulder, watching the branches above me, hearing their leaves and the creaking trunks and the wind. Then I was at the top, looking down the road and at the farms and fields; the night was clear, and I could see a long way; clouds scudded past the half-moon and stars, blown out to sea.

I started down, watching the tall grass under the trees to my right, glancing into the dark of the ditch, listening for cars behind me; but as soon as I cleared one tree, its sound was gone, its flapping leaves and rattling branches far behind me, as though the greatest distance I had at my back was a matter of feet, while ahead of me I could see a barn two miles off. Then I saw her skid marks: short, and going left and downhill, into the other lane. I stood at the ditch, its weeds blowing; across it were trees and their moving shadows, like the other clouds. I stepped onto its slope, and it took me sliding on my feet, then rump, to the bottom, where I sat still, my body gathered to itself, lest a part of me should touch him. But there was only tall grass, and I stood, my shoulders reaching the sides of the ditch, and I walked uphill, wishing for the flashlight in the pickup, walking slowly, and down in the ditch I could hear my feet in the grass and on the earth, and kicking cans and bottles. At the top of the hill I turned and went down, watching the ground above the ditch on my right, praying my prayer from the truck again, the first one, the one I would admit, that he was not dead, was in fact home, and began to hope again, memory telling me of lost pheasants and grouse I had shot, but they were small and the colors of their home, while a man was either there or not; and from that memory I left where I was and while walking in the ditch under the wind was in the deceit of imagination with Jennifer in the kitchen, telling her she had hit no one, or at least had not badly hurt anyone, when I realized he could be in the hospital now and I would have to think of a way to check there, something to say on the phone. I see now that, once hope returned, I should have been certain what it prepared me for: ahead of me, in high grass and the shadows of trees, I saw his shirt. Or that is all my mind would allow itself: a shirt, and I stood looking at it for the moments it took my mind to admit the arm and head and the dark length covered by pants. He lay face down, the arm I could see near his side, his head turned from me, on its cheek.

"Fella?" I said. I had meant to call, but it came out quiet and high, lost inches from my face in the wind. Then I said, "Oh God," and felt Him in the wind and the sky moving past the stars and moon and the fields around me, but only watching me as He might have watched Cain or Job, I did not know which, and I said it again, and wanted to sink to the earth and weep till I slept there in the weeds. I climbed, scrambling up the side of the ditch, pulling at clutched grass, gained the top on hands and knees, and went to him like that, panting, moving through the grass as high as and higher than my face, crawling under that sky, making sounds too, like some animal, there being no words to let him know I was here with him now. He was long; that is the word that came to me, not tall. I kneeled beside him, my hands on my legs. His right arm was by his side, his left arm straight out from the shoulder, but turned, so his palm was open to the tree above us. His left cheek was clean-shaven, his eye closed, and there was no blood. I leaned forward to look at his open mouth and saw the blood on it, going down into the grass. I straightened and looked ahead at the wind blowing past me through grass and trees to a distant light, and I stared at the light, imagining someone awake out there, wanting someone to be, a gathering of old friends, or someone alone listening to music or painting a picture; then I figured it was a night-light at a farmyard whose house I couldn't see. Going, I thought. Still going. I leaned over again and looked at dripping blood.

So I had to touch his wrist, a thick one with a watch and expansion band that I pushed up his arm, thinking he's left-handed, my three fingers pressing his wrist, and all I felt was my tough fingertips on that smooth underside flesh and small bones, then relief, then certainty. But against my will, or only because of it, I still don't know, I touched his neck, ran my fingers down it as if petting, then pressed, and my hand sprang back as from fire. I lowered it again, held it there until it felt faint beating that I could not believe. There was too much wind. Nothing could make a sound in it. A pulse could not be felt in it, nor could mere fingers in that wind feel the absolute silence of a dead man's artery. I was making sounds again; I grabbed his left arm and his waist, and pulled him toward me, and that side of him rose, turned, and I lowered him to his back, his face tilted up toward the tree that was groaning, the tree and I the only sounds in the wind. Turning my face from his, looking down the length of him at his sneakers, I placed my ear on his heart, and heard not that but something else, and I clamped a hand over my exposed ear, heard something liquid and alive, like when you pump a well and after a few strokes you hear air and water moving in the pipe, and I knew I must raise his legs and cover him and run to a phone, while still I listened to his chest, thinking raise with what? cover with what? and amid the liquid sound I heard the heart, then lost it, and pressed my ear against bone, but his chest was quiet, and I did not know when the liquid had stopped, and do not know now when I heard air, a faint rush of it, and whether under my ear or at his mouth or whether I heard it at all. I straightened and looked at the light, dim and yellow. Then I touched his throat, looking him full in the face. He was blond and young. He could have been sleeping in the shade of a tree, but for the smear of blood from his mouth to his hair, and the night sky, and the weeds blowing against his head, and the leaves shaking in the dark above us.

I stood. Then I kneeled again and prayed for his soul to join in peace and joy all the dead and living, and doing so, confronted my first sin against him, not stopping for Father Paul, who could have given him the last rites, and immediately then my second one, or I saw then, my first, not calling an ambulance to meet me there, and I stood and turned into the wind, slid down the ditch and crawled out of it, and went up the hill and down it, across the road to the street of houses whose people I had left behind forever, so that I moved with stealth in the shadows to my truck.

When I came around the bend near my house, I saw the kitchen light at the rear. She sat as I had left her, the ashtray filled, and I looked at the bottle, felt her eyes on me, felt what she was seeing too: the dirt from my crawling. She had not drunk much of the rye. I poured some in my glass, with the water from melted ice, and sat down and swallowed some and looked at her and swallowed some more, and said: "He's dead."

She rubbed her eyes with the heels of her hands, rubbed the cheeks under them, but she was dry now.

"He was probably dead when he hit the ground. I mean, that's probably what killed—"

"Where was he?"

"Across the ditch, under a tree."

"Was he—did you see his face?"

"No. Not really. I just felt. For life, pulse. I'm going out to the car."

"What for? Oh."

I finished the rye, and pushed back the chair, then she was standing too.

"I'll go with you."

"There's no need."

"I'll go."

I took a flashlight from a drawer and pushed open the door and held it while she went out. We turned our faces from the wind. It was like on the hill, when I was walking, and the wind closed the distance behind me: after three or four steps I felt there was no house back there. She took my hand, as I was reaching for hers. In the garage we let go, and squeezed between the pickup and her little car, to the front of it, where we had more room, and we stepped back from the grille and I shone the light on the fender, the smashed headlight turned into it, the concave chrome staring to the right, at the garage wall.

"We ought to get the bottles," I said.

She moved between the garage and the car, on the passenger side, and had room to open the door and lift the bag. I reached out, and she gave me the bag and backed up and shut the door and came around the car. We sidled to the doorway, and she put her arm around my waist and I hugged her shoulders.

"I thought you'd call the police," she said.

We crossed the yard, and in the kitchen I put the bag of bottles in the garbage basket. She was working at the table: capping the rye and putting it away, filling the ice tray, washing the glasses, emptying the ashtray, sponging the table.

"Try to sleep now," I said.

She nodded at the sponge circling under her hand, gathering ashes. Then she dropped it in the sink and, looking me full in the face, as I had never seen her look, as perhaps she never had, being for so long a daughter on visits (or so it seemed to me and still does: that until then our eyes had never seriously met), she crossed to me from the sink and kissed my lips, then held me so tightly I lost balance and would have stumbled forward had she not held me so hard.

I sat in the living room, the house darkened, and watched the maple and the hemlock. When I believed she was asleep I put on *La Bohème,* and kept it at the same volume as the wind so it would not wake her. Then I listened to *Madame Butterfly,* and in the third act had to rise quickly to lower the sound: the wind was gone. I looked at the still maple near the window, and thought of the wind leaving farms and towns and the coast, going out over the sea to die on the waves. I smoked and gazed out the window. The sky was darker, and at daybreak the rain came. I listened to *Tosca,* and at six-fifteen went to the kitchen where Jennifer's purse lay on the table, a leather shoulder purse crammed with the things of an adult woman, things she had begun accumulating only a few years back, and I nearly wept, thinking of what sandy foundations they were: driver's license, credit card, disposable lighter, cigarettes, checkbook, ball-point pen, cash, cosmetics, comb, brush, Kleenex, these the rite of passage from childhood, and I took one of them—her keys—and went out, remembering a jacket and hat when the rain struck me, but I kept going to the car, and squeezed and lowered myself into it, pulled the seat belt over my shoulder and fastened it and backed out, turning in the drive, going forward into the road, toward St. John's and Father Paul.

Cars were on the road, the workers, and I did not worry about any of them noticing the fender and light. Only a horse distracted them from what they drove to. In front of St. John's is a parking lot; at its far side, past the church and at the edge of the lawn, is an old pine, taller than the steeple now. I shifted to third, left the road, and aiming the right headlight at the tree, accelerated past the white blur of church, into the black trunk growing bigger till it was all I could see, then I rocked in that resonant thump she had heard, had felt, and when I turned off the ignition it was still in my ears, my blood, and I saw the boy flying in the wind. I lowered my forehead to the wheel. Father Paul opened the door, his face white in the rain.

"I'm all right."

"What happened?"

"I don't know. I fainted."

I got out and went around to the front of the car, looked at the smashed light, the crumpled and torn fender.

"Come to the house and lie down."

"I'm all right."

"When was your last physical?"

"I'm due for one. Let's get out of this rain."

"You'd better lie down."

"No. I want to receive."

That was the time to say I want to confess, but I have not and will not. Though I could now, for Jennifer is in Florida, and weeks have passed, and perhaps now Father Paul would not feel that he must tell me to go to the police. And, for that very reason, to confess now would be unfair. It is a world of secrets, and now I have one from my best, in truth my only, friend. I have one from Jennifer too, but that is the nature of fatherhood.

Most of that day it rained, so it was only in early evening, when the sky cleared, with a setting sun, that two little boys, leaving their confinement for some play before dinner, found him. Jennifer and I got that on the local news, which we listened to every hour, meeting at the radio, standing with cigarettes, until the one at eight o'clock; when she stopped crying, we went out and walked on the wet grass, around the pasture, the last of sunlight still in the air and trees. His name was Patrick Mitchell, he was nineteen years old, was employed by CETA, lived at home with his parents and brother and sister. The paper next day said he had been at a friend's house and was walking home, and I thought of that light I had seen, then knew it was not for him; he lived on one of the streets behind the club. The paper did not say then, or in the next few days, anything to make Jennifer think he was alive while she was with me in the kitchen. Nor do I know if we—I—could have saved him.

In keeping her secret from her friends, Jennifer had to perform so often, as I did with Father Paul and at the stables, that I believe the acting, which took more of her than our daylight trail rides and our night walks in the pasture, was her healing. Her friends teased me about wrecking her car. When I carried her luggage out to the car on that last morning, we spoke only of the weather for her trip—the day was clear, with a dry cool breeze—and hugged and kissed, and I stood watching as she started the car and turned it around. But then she shifted to neutral and put on the parking brake and unclasped the belt, looking at me all the while, then she was coming to me, as she had that night in the kitchen, and I opened my arms.

I have said I talk with God in the mornings, as I start my day, and sometimes as I sit with coffee, looking at the birds, and the woods. Of course He has never spoken to me, but that is not something I require. Nor does He need to. I know Him, as I know the part of myself that knows Him, that felt Him watching from the wind and the night as I kneeled over the dying boy. Lately I have taken to arguing with Him, as I can't with Father Paul, who, when he hears my monthly confession, has not heard and will not hear anything of failure to do all that one can to save an anonymous life, of injustice to a family in their grief, of deepening their pain at the chance and mystery of death by giving them nothing—no one—to hate. With Father Paul I feel lonely about this, but not with God. When I received the Eucharist while Jennifer's car sat twice-damaged, so redeemed, in the rain, I felt neither loneliness nor shame, but as though He were watching me, even from my tongue, intestines, blood, as I have watched my sons at times in their young lives when I was able to judge but without anger, and so keep silent while they, in the agony of their youth, decided how they must act; or found reasons, after their actions, for what they had done. Their reasons were never as good or as bad as their actions, but they needed to find them, to believe they were living by them, instead of the awful solitude of the heart.

I do not feel the peace I once did: not with God, nor the earth, or anyone on it. I have begun to prefer this state, to remember with fondness the other one as a period of peace I neither earned nor deserved. Now in the mornings while I watch purple finches driving larger titmice from the feeder, I say to Him: I would do it again. For when she knocked on my door, then called me, she woke what had flowed dormant in my blood since her birth, so that what rose from the bed was not a stable owner or a Catholic or any other Luke Ripley I had lived with for a long time, but the father of a girl.

And He says: I am a Father too.

Yes, I say, as You are a Son Whom this morning I will receive; unless You kill me on the way to church, then I trust You will receive me. And as a Son You made Your plea.

Yes, He says, but I would not lift the cup.

True, and I don't want You to lift it from me either. And if one of my sons had come to me that night, I would have phoned the police and told them to meet us with an ambulance at the top of the hill.

Why? Do you love them less?

I tell Him no, it is not that I love them less but that I could bear the pain of watching and knowing my sons' pain, could bear it with pride as they took the whip and nails. But You never had a daughter and, if You had, You could not have borne her passion.

So, He says, you love her more than you love Me.

I love her more than I love truth.

Then you love in weakness, He says.

As You love me, I say, and I go with an apple or carrot out to the barn.

JOHN S. TARLTON

PICCADILLY

"*Life*, Jules, is a fast joyride down a dark road on a summer night. Sit back, lower your window, let the cool breezes blow over your face, and taste it. It'll be over before you blink."

That's Cecil talking. Cecil just turned eighty-one years old, and he's told me life's a fast joyride about two thousand times. He also says the best is yet to come.

"So leave the child to his own joyrides, and *taste* your food, you old fool."

That's Billie—Cecil's girlfriend. Billie's only sixty-eight, and she zaps Cecil a good one every chance she gets. Cecil just flashes me a little smile like he hasn't heard a word (maybe he hasn't?) and plunges into his stewed cabbage. What a pair.

"It's being too old to sleep, Jules, too old and worn-out to even sleep," says Billie. "It's lying wide-awake in the middle of the black night, listening to the clock. It's having death for a houseguest. You understand what I'm saying, child?"

What Billie means is she's getting old and afraid and obsessed with dying, and she wants to know what I've got to say on the subject. She wants me to talk about it. Instead I pack away the

From *Louisiana Literature*, IV (1987), 66–74. Reprinted by permission.

Jello—one wiggly green cube at a time—and nod and listen and watch.

"Let *me* tell you about a night," says Cecil. "It was a black winter night on the back of a hay wagon. I was about your age. It was cold. And the stars were big as your fist. We were hauling my old granddad into town to see the doctor. Only he never made it. He lay on his back in the bed of the wagon and croaked with his eyes open. I watched it. He didn't moan or groan or even move, he went with his eyes *open*."

I used to avoid old people. Let's face it, most of the old-timers shuffling into the Piccadilly here are just barely hanging on. If you got into a rush and slammed into one of them in the serving line, you might kill him. Send him crashing to the floor like a stack of plates. It would be murder.

"It's watery!" says Cecil, meaning the cabbage.

"You said that yesterday," says Billie. "You say it *everyday*. What's wrong with you?"

"Nothing's wrong with *me*," says Cecil. "It's the cabbage! They've soaked it again. I never felt better."

"It's the blood vessels in his brain, Jules," sighs Billie. "Stiff as copper pipe."

"Whose brain she talking about?"

Truth is, I never knew so many old-timers were still running loose. I thought they'd all been rounded up in nursing homes someplace out of the way. Or bought the ranch. Don't you believe it. Stop by the Piccadilly for lunch sometime and see for yourself.

"It's a fact, Jules, proven fact!" says Billie. "Your hair and fingernails keep growing after you're dead. Right there in your grave! Imagine that."

"Good God!" moans Cecil. "All the way to heaven and your first stop is your barber's."

I try picturing my old man's ghost slinking around at night with long hair and fingernails, howling, scaring the socks off his victims. It would be just like him. At his funeral, while all the relatives stood around looking like they'd been shot, trying to say the right things, the old man just looked bored. Like he was ready to be up and out of there.

"So tell me, Mr. Wise Guy, how did you do on your history test?" asks Cecil.

I made a B.

"A B? *B*. What did he say? Speak up."

"A B is real nice, Jules," says Billie.

"A B!" says Cecil. "When I was your age I got nothing but A's. Great strings of A's running down the page. *History* was my best subject. I got a mind for history."

"He don't know history from hemorrhoids," cracks Billie.

I got to know Billie and Cecil one day standing in the serving line. Cecil—he has dizzy spells—Cecil fainted and I grabbed him. It was like catching a sack full of paper matches. I just grabbed him and stood him up in line till he got his balance back. Nothing to it. Only Cecil made this big deal out of it, called the manager over, told every single person standing in the serving line, acted like I'd saved his life or something. I could have killed him. He tried to give me a dollar! When I wouldn't take the money, he demanded I join them for lunch. That was the beginning of it.

"I've been living so long, Jules," says Cecil, "I've been alive so long, I've forgotten where it was I came *from*. Now I ask you, Mr. Too Big For His Own Britches, if we go on living *after* we're dead, then where in blazes were we before we got here? Answer that one."

The first thing you notice about old people is they don't sit around waiting for you to *ask* them what's on their mind, what's bothering them. They give it to you straight.

After his fainting spell in the serving line, I followed Cecil and Billie out into the dining room, where they couldn't agree on a table. A whole room full of empty white tables and they couldn't agree. This one was too near the main aisle, that one sat in a draft, this one was not clean enough, that one had a wobble.

But you can't hurry the old ones. You put a little pressure on them and they get nervous, jumpy. They start to drop things, they forget what it is they're doing, where they are, what it is they're after in the first place.

Billie and Cecil finally agreed on a table up at the front of the cafeteria near the cash register—the worst seat in the house. I was so hungry I was drooling. Then the show really got rolling: each of them had to unload his tray *just so,* with the little bowl of carrots here, and the scoop of green peas there, the glass of tea up on top, the cornbread stick down here on this side . . . I almost went berserk. My roast beef had turned grey.

"You go to school, young man?" Cecil asks me after we're finally seated.

High school.

"Playing hooky, are you?"

"Kids today say skipping," says Billie.

"Skipping? *Skip?* What's this skipping?" asks Cecil.

"It's hooky I told you," says Billie

"Skipping," says Cecil, popping a carrot into his old mouth. "I don't like it."

I considered taking off right then, but the idea of bagging groceries all afternoon on an empty stomach stopped me. Humor them, I told myself, they're just old and probably don't know any better.

"You go to school, young man?" Cecil asks me again in a few minutes.

Is he kidding?

"He goes to high school, you old hoot owl!"

Cecil just nods his head and blinks, looking like a hoot owl.

At lunch the next day—I swear I'd forgotten all about them—Cecil and Billie strolled up to where I was sitting in a booth in the corner and started unloading their trays. Just said hello and started setting out their peas and corn and carrots like I'd been holding the table for them. Like we'd all agreed to start meeting every day for lunch.

My husband, Jim, poor man," says Billie, "died without a stitch, *naked* as the day he was born. He was toweling down after his bath when it happened. One second he was living—I remember he was singing to himself—and the next he was stone dead. I heard his body hit the bathroom floor. It was just like *that*. Like he stepped off in a hole in the earth. He never knew what hit him."

After they pulled my old man out from under the Oldsmobile, they dressed him up in a new blue suit and tie, slicked his hair down, and stuck him in his coffin. My mother kept saying how good he looked. Like a dead president, she said. It was a lie. I remember staring at him for hours and finally deciding whoever it was lying there in the box, whoever people said it looked like, it wasn't the old man. My father was a big man full of long funny stories who had ghosts. Screaming blue demons, he called them. The wax dummy in the blue suit was somebody else. They'd made a mistake.

"Your father is dead, child," says Billie. "You loved him and now he's gone and you must face it. If you want, you can talk to Cecil and me about it. It'll do you good."

"It won't be long now," says Cecil. "I'm all set. I got my tickets, my dancing shoes, my party hat! My bags are packed. Where I'm going next, you don't need money and the music is free."

"Next stop Disneyland!" says Billie.

I get a real blast out of Billie. So does Cecil, even if she is dropping a bomb on him every minute or two. It's just her sense of humor. She can't stop it any more than she can stop yakking about dying. Try to imagine talking about death every day for lunch. It'll test your appetite.

"Some nights, Jules," says Billie, "some nights I lie awake for hours and just listen. It's so quiet, so terribly still, I can't bear it. Only my mind is present. A mixed-up jumble of memories fixed on itself. Words and bits of old conversations. I feel I'm lying in my grave."

I guess all old people lie awake at night wondering what's going to happen to them. What happens after the lights go out. Everyone except Cecil.

"When my head hits the pillow, I'm a goner," says Cecil. "Shut my eyes and good night! Out like a light. I never move. I don't even dream."

"Everybody dreams," says Billie.

"I don't," says Cecil.

"Everybody dreams," says Billie. "Woodpeckers dream. Kangaroos dream. *Everybody*."

"Not me," says Cecil. "In the bed and out like a light."

Sometimes I dream about dragging the old man out from under the exhaust pipe of the Oldsmobile before he's had the chance to gas himself. I just grab him by the ankles and pull him free. Then I talk him out of doing it. It's a terrific dream. We sit there in the wet, green grass and laugh off his voodoo spirits. We send them packing. Then we turn the car off and go back inside the house where we belong.

"That reminds me," says Cecil. "Reminds me of a time in St. Louis. I was young, had no job, it was bad times. I'm standing on the back of a streetcar next to a guy in a new black suit. He asked me for a cigarette. A *cigarette?* There I am with holes in my shoes and hungry and no pot to pee in, and this yahoo wearing a two-hundred-dollar suit wants a cigarette. I told him no. When we cross the bridge over the railroad yard, this fellow jumps. Doesn't scream, doesn't holler, just throws himself headfirst over the railing like a bird. It killed him. Now I ask you, if I'd given him the cigarette, you think he would have jumped?"

"It's as if the past, Jules," says Billie, "were some fantastic dream you had long ago and now mostly forgotten. Only snatches of it are clear, flashes of a color or a feeling or a smell, and the rest is dark. Pieces of bright ribbon hanging in a closet."

Next time you're backed up in a line waiting for your tray at the Piccadilly, keep an eye out for the old ladies. I mean the old biddies who trot in breathless from the parking lot and break in line ahead of you. Watch out for them. The other day I caught one old girl trying to slip past me but I trapped her up against the babies' high chairs.

Going someplace? I asked her.

"What? Yes? Oh, my goodness, I didn't see you there," she said, turning a blast of old-lady charm on me. She looked like a parakeet. Then she dug this Kleenex out of her sleeve and honked her old nose. As if that explained everything. Some of these birds think they own the joint.

But it's the tottering old men who take the cake. I mean I've never once stood next to some old pirate in the serving line who didn't start griping about the weather. Rain or sleet or shine, these old boys are never satisfied. They must spend half their lives talking about it. Who cares? What can you do about it anyway?

"We never once discussed it," says Billie. "We were married forty-seven *years* and never discussed it. I suppose Jim and I thought we would live forever. Or that death was just something else we would go through together. Arm and arm, whenever we decided we were ready. It was wrong of us. And now he's gone and I don't even know what he thought about it. If he was afraid. What he believed. What he thought might be waiting for him. We should have discussed it. Do you want to talk about it, child?"

If you ask me, old people ought to know plenty about dying. They've been around the block. They've seen what there is to see. And death is where they're headed next. You can see it in the way they move. It's on their breath.

"There will be great parades, Jules," says Cecil, "great parades stretching out in all directions. Far as the eye can see. Marching bands. Fire-eaters. Dancing girls. It's like nothing you've ever seen. And everybody's there! Gypsies, movie stars, kings and queens! You got something you want to ask somebody—Lincoln, Marco Polo, *Houdini*—you just walk right up and ask him. He'll be glad to talk to you. We'll parade around all day and into the night! Then we'll get up early the next morning and do it all again!"

"*That* is ridiculous," says Billie.

"It's what I believe," says Cecil. "Death is a lot like living, only more fun and it lasts forever."

"Then I hope to go straight to hell!" says Billie.

"No such thing," says Cecil, biting off half his cornbread stick.

Heaven or hell. So what's the difference? And what's the big rush to get there anyway? The point, if you ask me, the only point of dying, is being dead. And dead people vanish. They do. They're here one day talking on the phone, making jokes at the table, *alive*, and the next thing you know they've crawled up the tailpipe of the family car. They don't even leave a note.

"So how's your mother?" asks Billie.

Mother? Same as always. She's fine.

My mother worries too much. She spends most of her time keeping the peace between me and my stepfather, and the rest worrying over my future. She's afraid if I don't go to college I'll become a bum. It's her word: *bum*. In her mind all the kids who don't go to college end up wearing overcoats and drinking wine on the streets. They're bums.

"Don't be so hard on your mother, child," says Billie. "She loves you."

"Good God, look at her today, will you!" moans Cecil. "Look at her, will you! Good God!"

Her is one of the old ladies who eats at the Piccadilly. She must have had a stroke or something because her mouth keeps dropping open every other second or so like it was on springs. No kidding, her mouth flops open, *wide* open, then snaps shut. Like a gate. To eat, she has to pop a spoonful of food in her mouth at just the right instant or it flies across the table. Some days the gate flops open and shut faster than others. It gives Cecil fits.

"How can I eat looking at something like that?" asks Cecil. "It's sickening! Why don't she wear a hat? Or a sack over her head? Good God!"

"So don't talk with your mouth full," snaps Billie. "*That's* sickening."

Warning: you'll see all kinds of sick and crippled people eating at the Piccadilly. Some of them are wheeled in, some use walkers, and some are led in by the arm. Some of them are blind. Two or three of them act insane. The main thing is they're almost always old. We've even got two real live midgets! Old midgets I mean. A couple. Everybody's got to eat.

"At eighty-one, life is done. Lookout, heaven, here I come!"

It's Cecil again. Who else? He says that all the time. How he believes an old coot his age ought to be winding down.

"Shuffling off to Buffalo," Cecil calls it.

"Creeping senility," says Billie.

I think he means it.

"Sooner or later, Jules, we've all got to die," says Cecil. "Rockafella's millions couldn't stop it. Caesar's armies couldn't conquer it. Soon it'll be my time."

So Cecil's an old man who says he's not afraid of dying. For him death is going on some long holiday. It's his reward. He believes he'll be with all the people who matter to him. Not that he's in a hurry. He's not fixing to toss himself off a bridge or anything. He's just ready when the time comes. For Billie it's different.

"I'm so frightened," says Billie. "I can't help it. Maybe I haven't lived long enough. Maybe I'm just not smart enough. But it's no use. I can't explain it. Sometimes I can't breathe. Some nights I can't even sleep."

The exhaust fumes filled the old man's body like a balloon. He lay there on his back under the Oldsmobile and took them deep into his lungs. They filtered in and out of his organs and bones and killed everything that was there. They left his blood a thick, black poison. And when it was over, he was stiff as a broom. We could have stood him up in a corner of the garage and left him there. We could have brought him inside and used him for a hat rack. But we didn't. Instead we stuck him in the ground and agreed not to talk about it. Nobody said a word.

"It's been three years since your father's death, child. It's time you stopped brooding about it," says Billie. "Stop holding it inside. Tell us what you feel."

"Death," says Cecil, "is just like California. Only more so. Sun's always shining. Nights are cool. And everybody's smiling. You do only what you want, *when* you want to do it! There's no snow. No religion. And free money! Just like California. I can see it, Jules, I can see it when I shut my eyes. And your father's smiling with them."

Says who?

"Says *me!*" says Cecil. "Says me and anybody else who knows the score."

Is it true, Billie? Is the old man free of his demons? Do you believe he's smiling?

"Child, the devil himself smiles down on you."

"And when I join up with him," says Cecil, "when I join up with your father, Jules, I'll tell him he's got a son who's going to college someday. And that you miss him. What else?"

What do you mean?

"What else do you want me to tell him?"

"Go on, child, say something if you want," says Billie. "Believe what you want to believe. If you want Cecil to carry a message to your father, believe it."

"Something short, Jules, short and sweet," says Cecil. "My mind ain't what it used to be."

"Just say whatever comes into your head," says Billie. "If you had one last chance to speak to your father, one last chance to talk to him, what would you say? What would you tell him?"

I would tell him not to do it.

"You can't stop him from doing it, child. It's already done. You can't change it. But what would you tell him?"

"I'm waiting, Mr. Smarty Pants," says Cecil. "Just keep it simple."

"Hush, old man, he's going to talk."

"If the boy wants to talk, let him talk."

"*Hush.*"

I would tell him it was wrong.

"Go on, child."

I would say it was wrong. I would tell him it was gutless and ugly and I'll never forgive him for it. *Never.* That's what I would tell him! I would ask him if he ever stopped to think about any of *us?* The ones he walked out on. The ones he left holding the bag.

What about us? I would tell him I hate him for what he did! I would tell him as long as I live I'll never stop seeing him under the Oldsmobile with his feet sticking out! I would tell him that's what I see when I think about him! A dead man with his feet sticking out from under the Oldsmobile! *That's* what I would tell him!

Don't tell him I said that.

"That's enough for today, child," says Billie. "It's good to get it out. It's good for you to talk about it. Next time it won't be so hard. Next time you can give Cecil a real message for your father. Now wipe your face."

Don't tell him I said that, Cecil.

"Said what?"

"At eighty-one—"

"Pipe down, old man, I was awake half the night."

"—life is done. Lookout, heaven, *here I come!*"

"Eat your cabbage, you old fool. You'll live to be a million."

"Not *me,*" says Cecil. "My bags are packed. The clock's running. I'll soon be gone!"

"You're not going anywhere. *None* of us is going."

Of course Billie is always saying that—about the three of us never going anywhere—because she wants to believe it herself. It's what she tells herself in the middle of the black night. It's her only weapon.

In the meantime, the three of us meet every day at the Piccadilly and, in between mouthfuls, discuss the dead and dying, who we think is next in line to get it, where it is they'll likely be going, how much we miss the ones that have already gone.

Billie's nuts on the subject, and Cecil's just nuts.

JAMES H. WILSON

BECAUSE I WAS NAKED

And the Lord God called unto Adam, and said unto him, Where *art* thou?
And he said, I heard thy voice in the garden, and I was afraid, because I *was* naked; and I hid myself.
—Gen. 3:9–10 KJV

Oh, to be lost, never to be found! Never to be found again! That's just the way Ben felt earlier that morning as he sat on the edge of his bed. It was not a depressing feeling but one which brought to him a warmth and a feeling of security. Never to be found again. Never to have to go back to squadron, never to have the airdrome officer shake him awake in the darkness from behind his probing, blinding shaft of light.

"Hey, Whiskey—Whiskey—come on, Whiskey. You're flying with Solomon today. Casey's sick. Come on."

"Jesus! Huh? What time is it? Casey's sick? Damn! What the hell time is it?"

"After three. Come on—get up. Don't go back to sleep. Breakfast in about twenty-five minutes. Briefing at four-thirty. Come on."

"Okay, I'm awake. What's for breakfast, or should I ask?"

"What else? Horse cock and dehydrated eggs. Yum, yum. Come on."

"Okay, okay. After the war I'm gonna trace down the son of a bitch who got himself the Spam concession for this godforgotten heroic struggle and make him eat it the rest of his unnatural life."

"Whiskey, you got yourself a reason to survive. Now, come on. I'm running behind. Still got five crews to call."

The tent door would slam in the darkness, the light retreat outside and disappear. Ben would wriggle out of his sleeping bag, put his stocking feet on the cold brick floor that he, Mayo, Collie, and Skip had so carefully laid, and search in the darkness for the little lamp at the head of his cot. They had rigged one for each of themselves by tapping into the main power line to Cerignola. The others in the tent would bury their heads deeper into their bags, mumbling.

Oh, to be lost, never to be found again! But, hell, they'd find him. He knew that. They knew where he was all along. What was today? Tuesday. He and Mayo had arrived on Capri Sunday afternoon. On Friday the motor launch would pick them up at Marina Grande and take them back across the Bay of Naples, back to the airport where the B-24 would be waiting to take them back to squadron. It would be over; he would be found again. Oh, God, to be lost, lost, lost.

That's the way he had felt as he sat in his skivvies on the edge of the bed in the room where he and Mayo were billeted for the week of rest leave, a week which had turned out to be only six days, because weather had canceled their flight from squadron to Naples by twenty-four hours. Ben had slept late and Mayo was gone. The room seemed empty without Mayo's booming voice and laughter. But they had arranged to meet later at the Quisisana Bar. Then they would go to the little bar overlooking the sea that Ben had stumbled upon the afternoon before as he explored some of the passageways around the island above the village and which served real Pinch Bottle for seventy-five cents a shot. He had told Mayo about it. He walked over to the window which opened out onto a tiny balcony and pulled aside the curtain before it. In the saddleback just below were the rooftops of the village of Capri; across the saddleback towered Monte Salaro, with Anacapri hidden at its top. He and Mayo would go there, too. To his left, hidden below the steep declivity, he knew was Marina Piccola, the little pebble-and-stone beach where he and Mayo the morning before had rented kayaks and had flirted with the dark, pretty Capri girls who made fun of them when they tipped the kayaks over and dunked themselves beneath the surface of the water and struggled, sputtering, back to upright. The Mediterranean had sparkled with a lush green in the shallows near the beach and become an unbelievable cobalt blue in the distance. He and Mayo had whooped in the fierce joy of their freedom, in the desperate anguish of their happiness. Ben burned with the brotherhood of the blind, fated commitment that bound him and Mayo, and in moments like these wanted to reach out to him in an offering of the love, the friendship he knew they shared, shared with all of their lost brothers who would learn the true meaning of love in the blood and the rage and the fury of hate and helplessness and hope. To the right, down the hill, past the clock tower of the Piazza Primo Umberto he caught a glimpse of the Bay of Naples in the sun, and across the bay in the haze of distance the dimly etched hump of hills of the ageless city itself. The sun was warm for October, but the air was heavy. It would rain later in the day. He looked at his Air Corps–issue watch. Ten-fifteen. The morning was quiet. There was a woman's laughter far away and the sound of someone walking unseen in the narrow passageway below that led circuitously down the hill to the piazza. He dressed quickly.

Down in the piazza he had purchased one of the gaudy nonreg Fifteenth Air Force shoulder patches for his blouse; he had searched for and found a shop which sold the little silver bells of San Michele which airmen wore suspended around their necks instead of dogtags when they were on leave. Their tiny tinkling seemed to be everywhere on the island, distant but invisible reminders of distances, of escape, of freedom. Ben bought ten bells on their intricately woven silver strands. Presents for when he got back home. Back home. Oh, to be lost, never to be found.

He bought some food to satisfy his nonhunger and then began to make his way westward from the piazza down a narrow passageway between shops in the direction of the Quisisana Hotel. The passageway made a right turn and the white facade of the hotel was in front of him. He entered the lobby and went directly to the bar. The bartender recognized him and before he had seated himself on a stool had served him the sweet Italian brandy which he found so distasteful until at least the third one, but which was the best drink the bar served. The other little bar he had found yesterday was different—real Pinch Bottle. It was expensive, but it was worth it. When Mayo came they would go and have some. He had made a habit in the first two days they had been on the island of stopping by the Quisisana Bar. It gave a regimen to his afternoon. And the bartender recognized him. There was a turntable and some V-discs that were pretty good. A copilot from New Jersey who they had met the first night had some fine jazz records. And there was a recording of "Lili Marlene," which they all sang very loudly when they had got drunk.

Ben sipped his second brandy slowly. It was improving, and he was beginning to feel isolated and closed in from the war that was going on somewhere. It all began to feel like a dream, a dream of something distant and out of reach, something lost, eradicated, smothered in the sweet taste of the brandy. A dream of the northeast marshaling yard at Vienna when the lead bombardier flew drunker than usual and forgot to lock his bombsight switch in up position and the bombs failed to release and he ordered a 360 over the target at the same heading, altitude, and airspeed and the German antiaircraft gunners with their triangulations all figured from the first pass and never expecting such an opportunity shot B-24s out of the sky almost at will and as the first bombs appeared from the bomb bay of the lead plane hearing over his headset as he hunched down into the protection of his helmet and flak suit, "Jesus God! Lookit the formation below us . . . they just blew up! Goddam! There's two more up 'head on fire . . . Christ damn! They're in a vertical spin . . . look over there, bailing out . . . oh, shit! Their chutes are on fire . . . oh, my God! Lutcher's hit, he's going down, oh, my God! Get the hell offa the command channel . . . Let's get outta here . . ." and seeing the black blossoms of flak against the white puffs of cloud below and the whacking of the shrapnel into the aluminum fuselage and wondering if today would be the day. A dream of the scared-shitless little brand-new major who flew his first combat mission as squadron leader with their crew the day he forgot to crack bomb-bay doors at twenty thousand feet and who ordered him to read aloud over the command channel to the whole wing the entire reg stating that bomb-bay doors were to be cracked every five thousand feet beginning at ten thousand and how, with the lead commanders trying to get the channel to order lowering of ball turrets and the wing already over the German fighter line at Lake Balaton, he tried to read fast but the major made him read slow "so every goddamned word of that reg will be burned into your memory, lieutenant, and you'll never again forget to crack your bomb-bay doors." A dream of Goldsmith and his crew with whom they had been ever since staging at Biggs Field in El Paso shot down over the bridge across the Po at Ferrara and forgetting the next morning at breakfast before briefing and asking where the hell Goldsmith was and the silence in the mess hall. A dream of the day they broke formation and flew home off Schmidt's wing on the way back from Wiener Neustadt, Schmidt with number-four engine feathered and number-three smoking, with Jake Kobalevski sitting dead in the right seat with three pieces of flak in his brain, Jake who like every B-24 co-pilot who ever lived had dreamed of flying a P-38, Jake with three pieces of flak in his brain, and how they unloaded Jake's body and put it into what the men called in some strange and fearful euphemism the meat wagon and the next afternoon Captain Hennessey, flight surgeon, told Ben that he was taking Jake's body to the morgue in Bari for burial in the Allied cemetery and that an English orchestra was playing the Brahms First at a local hall and did he want to go and after they had driven the coast road through Barletta, Trani, Bisceli, and Molfetta to Bari and had taken Jake to the morgue they found the hall but the orchestra didn't play the Brahms but played the Beethoven Seventh which infuriated Captain Hennessey but not Ben who preferred the Beethoven anyway, especially the vast slow second movement with its massive chords which embraced him and gave him the feeling of being lost, oh, lost, never to be found again, and on the way back to Cerignola Captain Hennessey said the orchestra did a lousy job of the Beethoven. A dream.

Ben was on his third brandy and the afternoon was passing, and still no Mayo. Brandy in hand, he walked back across the lobby toward the hotel entrance to where he could see some people, mostly in service uniforms, in the passageway outside and could hear their voices in the afternoon light on the white building blocks and plaster. Looking up and beyond the walls, he could see that clouds were beginning to gather. It would rain. He walked back toward the bar. Only two other people were in the lobby, a soldier and a pretty Italian girl, sitting at a small table across from the bar. The girl was smiling at something the soldier was saying. Ben felt a loneliness as he watched them, and he knew that he would leave and walk before he began to lose the good loneliness he so wanted.

He started to order another brandy but decided against it. He needed the air and the sky and the light and the voices of the people. He left the bar and crossed the lobby toward the exit. The young couple at the table were holding hands. Oh, lost. The passageway outside was empty. He stood still, listening for the voices from the direction of the piazza, for the cries and laughter in the briefness of the afternoon. Then he turned away from the sounds and walked to his right in the general direction, he thought, of the heights above Marina Piccola. He walked slowly, between shop windows, past lights glowing in the darkened interiors, past little closed entrances to he knew not where. The numbness the brandy had created suited his mood. He walked. Soon a fine mist distracted him. It did not fall but descended and settled on everything. He walked. He began again to notice his surroundings. He was no longer between shops or other entrances. He did not know how long he had walked. The passageway guided him around to his left and suddenly there occurred an emptiness on his right hand which he recognized as the distance above the sea below. The mist made a fine veil through which he could not make out if Marina Piccola was there below with the sounds of its waves upon the rocks, but through which he could gradually visualize the dark waters stretching away in the distance. He paused as if to listen to the silence. An instant in the stillness, the silent passing of a camera shutter, and whatever it was was gone, lost, and there remained only the sea and the mist. A little stone parapet on his right excluded him and in so doing sharpened the memory.

He heard the sounds of his shoes against the stones of the walk. He was alone. No one else was out in the dampness, the dampness which brought upon him a cool, soothing comfort. The clouds had grown heavier, the mist was coagulating into drops, the afternoon was becoming unreally dark. The waters below began to grow more obscure, to take on a countenance dark, brooding, menacing. The *faraglioni* were out there somewhere shrouded in nothingness. Ben shivered. It had not occurred to him until that moment that he might be losing his way. Was this the way he had taken when he found the little bar that served the Pinch Bottle? He wasn't sure. He looked ahead into the settling shadows and saw the passageway continuing before him. He followed it. It turned gently to his left, the parapet on his right giving way to an ascending face of rock. He had left the sea behind. Here and there on the face of rock he could make out sharp hands of aloe or palmetto or a clump of cactus, and above these up in the gloom a lone umbrella pine. The passageway continued to turn gradually to his left, guiding him along with a strange fascination. There was now a stone height on his left hand, also. He began to wonder if he had wandered into a dead end. He shivered again.

The dusk was deeper between the walls of rock. He continued more slowly. Suddenly the rock face on his right dropped away to a man-made stone wall a little more than shoulder-high. He looked toward his left again and there, also, the wall of rock had begun to drop back toward ground level, although on that side it still stood well above his head and was covered with what seemed a kind of ivy and other forms indistinguishable in the dusk. When he turned his attention back toward the wall on his right he was passing before an open entrance that seemed to have appeared out of nowhere.

He stopped and stood in the dusky, wet passageway staring into the darkness beyond the entrance into . . . whatever it was. There was a fragile trellis arching over the entrance with what seemed creepers or ivy hugging to and hanging from it. Ben wanted to move on up the passageway, but it was almost as if he dared not. He looked up the passageway in the direction he had been walking and then down it in the direction from which he had come. Some boughs overhead in the dusk that protruded over the passageway and also over the wall above the enclosure gave momentary shelter from the raindrops. He stood still, cold, and stared again into the darkness beyond the trellised entrance.

It occurred to him that the entrance to the little bar where he had found the Pinch Bottle also had a vine-covered entrance, almost the effect of the trellis above the entrance before him. At the bar there were three steps up from the floor of the passageway, then the vine-covered entrance into the room. There were three small cloth-covered tables in the center of the room and, to his right, the length of the room, a bar with two bar stools. A man in a white apron looked up when he came in. Ben hesitated, then said, "Buon giorno."

The man answered, "Hi, Joe. You walk long way? You thirsty?"

"You betcha."

The man smiled. "What you wanna drink, Joe? Wine? Brandy? Champagne?"

Ben thought he would take a long shot.

"You got any Scotch?

The man reached beneath the bar and brought out the Pinch Bottle and set it before Ben. It was nearly full.

"Boy! Where'd you get that?"

"Special for American friends."

Ben knew that he had got it through the black market in the Peninsular Base Section in Naples and that it was probably easier for him to get it than for the combat troops, but right now he didn't care.

"I'll have one," he said.

The man poured a generous portion into a small glass.

"Water on the side," Ben said.

He sipped the Scotch. God, it was good. It warmed his throat, deeper and deeper. He closed his eyes. The warmth began slowly to diffuse through his body. He ordered another. Glass in hand, he got off the stool and walked back toward the vine-framed doorway. The sun was bright. He had been tired but refreshed the day before by the morning at the beach with Mayo. He had not noticed when he entered that from the doorway he could look down directly to an inlet of the sea about three hundred feet below. The water was a vibrant green in close and deep blue farther out. He stood for a long time, sipping the Scotch. The beauty of the sea and the afternoon burned into his eyes and into memory, glowing around the edges of darkness into forever. He asked for a third.

"Boy, wait till I tell Mayo," he said, as though the man knew Mayo.

"Mayo your friend, Joe?"

"Yes."

"He G.I. too?"

"Yes."

"You fly-boys?"

Ben knew that he could tell from his uniform and wings and was just making conversation. He felt a sudden sympathy with the man. He smiled and answered,

"Yeah."

"You whip the Germans, huh?"

Suddenly he felt uneasy, angered, compromised, betrayed, like a child who has just been caught doing something ugly. The feeling of sympathy faded. He wondered how many German soldiers the man had asked the same question about Yanks or Limeys. He muttered,

"Sure."

"You bring your friend back, Joe?"

The question seemed so innocent, almost wistful, that Ben was jarred out of his resentment. He looked at the man and realized that his anger had really nothing to do with the man but with himself. Hell, this guy had to survive the war just like everyone else, the best way he knew how.

"Sure. You betcha," Ben smiled. "He likes Scotch, too. He's the best B-24 pilot in the whole damned war." He laughed. That was better.

But now Ben stood in the dusky passageway looking into the darkness of the strangely beckoning trellised entrance. He felt himself step toward it. He hesitated, but a growing, sinking fear dared him. Quickly he stepped under and past the hanging vines and found himself in what seemed a small enclosure. His eyes slowly became accustomed to the darkness within, and he began to make out shapes, at first an amorphous clump of shadow within shadow, and then there began to appear a profusion of too lush undergrowth, of kinds indistinguishable in the darkness but charged with a ghostly presence that astonished him with a momentary loss of orientation. Gradually he could see, just in front of his feet, long uncut grass crawling from beneath the undergrowth. To left and right, remains of stone walks led away into farther darkness. He would see that there was a wall on his right about the same height as the one bordering the outside passageway, about shoulder high. The boughs which had covered him in the passageway extended above the portion of the enclosure to his right. Pushing and hanging over the wall were heavy, hanging festoons, like wisteria, in rank funereal fertility. Farther back, in the gloom beyond the wall, he could see the top of an umbrella pine. Against the wall, a few feet from where he stood, he could make out under the boughs a small stone bench. He was suddenly tired, but he did not move toward the bench. He moved, instead, a couple of steps along the stones to his left and peered down the walk to a darkness of bushes and vines into which the stones disappeared. He turned and made his way back down the other walk, past the bench. It seemed less cluttered, but he couldn't be sure. He took a few steps along it gingerly, but saw that it, too, disappeared, seeming to turn to the left into the embrace of the undergrowth. He felt possessed by an uncontrollable desire to walk farther along the stones. He slipped his feet along slowly, one after the other. The grass reaching up from between the decomposing stones cushioned the sound of his shoes. A memory jumped out at him of the vandalized and lost rot of the old Girod Street Cemetery he had wandered into on an afternoon long ago in New Orleans, its gaping tombs which hobos had emptied of their tenants to make places to sleep, its broken stones of obliterated names and numbers, the stagnating dust of death and eternity. And the distant humming of the streets. He suddenly realized that he was almost at the end of the visible walk, almost within reach of the tangle of vines and deep growth. He stopped. A cold fear gripped him. He shivered. How far in was he? He stifled a sound in his throat. He knew he had to go back, but he couldn't make up his mind whether to turn away from the darkness and run back toward the bench or to back up toward the bench keeping his eyes on the darkness before him. If he backed away, he might stumble and fall, and if he did he wasn't sure he could crawl fast enough to get to the bench. The longer he stood the more real the terror became. He finally forced himself to turn sideways; then he began to sidle along the walk back toward the bench, looking carefully in both directions. When he was at last seated on the bench with his back against the wall he felt safer. He became aware again of the light drizzle; he could feel it on his face and hear it sizzling in the leaves above his head. He relaxed. He could hear again the great chords of the Beethoven Seventh and the roaring of the engine of the ambulance along the road back to Cerignola, with Jake lying dead in the morgue in Bari, the roaring which deafened and blotted out the highway over which they sped to squadron at Cerignola and the mission board which would tell him if he was scheduled to fly the next day. Oh, to be lost, never to be found! If only he could re-create the roaring of the engine of the ambulance, it might never stop and they never get to Cerignola. Never get to Cerignola. But Jake was lying dead in Bari and the mission board was on the wall outside operations.

Ben looked at the Air Corps watch on his wrist, but he could not make out the time. He knew that it was getting late. Maybe Mayo was looking for him at the Quisisana. Maybe he was looking for him along the passageway. He had told him how to get to the bar in case they didn't meet at the Quisisana. Suddenly a new, raw fear pinched his heart. If Mayo found him, he would have to go back. The idea turned like a worm inside him, deeper and deeper. Before him was the obscurity of the lush, rotting growth, the vines weaving across the crumbling stones of the walk, the festoons suspended above his head, reaching out, waiting. He looked again at the entrance. Mayo, passing by, might see him. For the first time he noticed that there was a double gate which closed the entrance. He stared at it for a long time. The half of the gate closer to him stood out into the enclosure at a right angle to the wall; the other half was opened completely and rested against the passageway wall on the other side of the entrance. If the gate were closed, Mayo would never notice him. Suddenly he was on his feet. He reached the half of the gate closer to him, standing out into the enclosure. He pushed to move the gate into closed position. The gate would not budge. He pushed harder. Still it would not move. He leaned against it with all his weight. It remained fixed. The word *damn* occurred to him, and he knew that he had spoken aloud. He looked about self-consciously. Then he slipped noiselessly across to where the other half of the gate rested against the wall. He pulled. It did not move. He leaned back with all his weight pulling against the gate, tugging hard and evenly, holding his breath for more strength to move it toward closed position. It remained silently frozen against the wall. Maybe if there were something to pry it away from the wall with, but he knew he would not be able to find anything firm enough for that in the enclosure. He wouldn't be able to budge the gate. He felt frustrated, and anger began to rise within him. He tore at the gate with both hands until his breathing frightened him in the darkness. Finally, he stood erect, turned and walked back to the bench, and sat down. He took off his Bancroft Flighter and placed it on the bench beside him, and as he did so a piece of the hanging wisteria softly fingered the top of his hair and he put the cap back on. He watched the interwoven vines in the undergrowth, the sharp green swords of aloe, the fat cacti within the shadowy rich depth of the dark. Some vines lay across the walk between him and the gate. He sat silent. Then he heard it,

"Whiskey! Whiskey!"

Mayo.

"Hey, Whiskey!"

He didn't answer. The voice came nearer. Mayo was coming along the passageway just as he had.

"Whiskey!"

He was closer. Ben sat still.

"Whiskey!"

He was approaching the entrance.

"Whiskey!"

He was at the entrance.

Ben spoke suddenly as though without willing it,

"In here."

"Where?"

"In here."

"Where? Where the hell are you?"

"Right here."

"Whiskey, what the hell are you doing in there?"

He knew Mayo could see him.

"Whiskey, what the hell are you doing in there?" Mayo repeated.

Silence. Then,

"Hiding."

"Hiding? Whiskey, you crazy son of a bitch!"

Then Mayo laughed a joyous booming laughter that reverberated through the darkness of the enclosure with a shattering resplendency. Ben jumped to his feet.

"Let's get the hell out of here," he shouted.

He lunged toward Mayo, grabbing his arm and spinning him around and shoving him roughly back through the entrance.

"Come on, Mayo!"

As he passed through the exit into the passageway Ben started to look back into the enclosure, into the darkness, but he did not. He pulled Mayo along, forcing him, the two of them side-by-side, into a gallop and then into a skipping along the passageway up the hill.

"Whiskey, you crazy bastard, take it easy!"

"Come on, Mayo, run, run!"

"Jesus! Hiding! Jesus!"

"Come on, Mayo!"

"Goddamit, Whiskey, hold up!" Mayo was laughing again in spite of himself.

Suddenly Ben knew where he was. The rain had stopped. The air had become cool and fresh, exciting with soft, sensuous invitation.

"Come on, Mayo! I know where the bar is. Up here and to the left."

He broke loose from Mayo and ran ahead up toward a wall which appeared to cross athwart their path but indicated instead another passageway into which theirs entered and which branched out at ninety-degree angles in both directions.

"Come on, Mayo! Come on! You can make it! I have faith in you, Mayo! You're the best big-assed-bird pilot in the whole goddamned Fifteenth Air Force—in the whole goddamned war! Come on!"

Mayo was running behind him, trying to keep up, yelling and laughing at the same time,

"Whiskey, you crazy bastard!"

"You can make that big-assed bird do the Charleston if you want it to!"

He could hear Mayo running behind him. They were almost to the other passageway. Suddenly there came from Ben's throat a whoop, a shout, an inhuman bellow that rose uncalled and unnamed into the coming night above Capri.

"Whiskey! Whiskey! What the hell's the matter with you?"

Ben darted into the passageway to their left, Mayo just behind him. The sea suddenly appeared below on their left. No longer was it menacing, brooding, dark. It glowed softly, sensually in the coming night, like the velvet voice of a woman, low, exciting, promising. The clouds had broken and a moon was beginning to appear fitfully, creating a broken trail of sparks across the water, catching a hint of the luminous green close to shore and the darker blue-black in the distance of the night where the sea was and was not.

Everything was going to be all right. Mayo was there, wonderful, beautiful, wonderful Mayo, his friend Mayo forever in a love of brother, a love of the lost and the found that would endure forever, that would outlast even death itself. Mayo was there, and he and Mayo were going to the little bar in the night above the lost lights of Capri, the little bar with the trellised entrance overlooking the sea where the Pinch Bottle was seventy-five cents a shot.

"Come on, Mayo! Come on!"

"I'm coming! I'm right behind you, you crazy bastard!"

He and Mayo were together, and the little bar was just around the turn in the passageway to the right. The night was fresh and free. Ben whooped again. Everything was going to be all right.

And it was still only Tuesday.

MARTHA LACY HALL

THE PEACEFUL EYE

The pecan leaves didn't crackle under her saddle oxfords as they might have on a warm, clear October morning. The rain last night had made them soggy. She felt a need for a crisp response beneath her shoes, and the little corner of her mind that was aware of these things told her that the magnolia leaves up in front of the Gatchells' would be crunchy. It took more than a night's rain to soften them, and this gave her a half-conscious comfort. They would jigsaw into little brown geometrics and lie there until barely larger than grit. She kicked a pecan, still in its bright green outer shell. It smacked sharply against a tree and glanced off into the gutter, where it lay bruised and immature on the concrete.

I promised myself I'd never go to Miss Emma's again. I wish I could turn back. But Miss Scott would wonder why. And I'm the only one in the class who knows where her rooms are. She'd think I was crazy.

It was just after morning recess when Miss Scott asked her to run an errand. Civics class was about to begin, and Mary had spent recess memorizing the names of the president's cabinet: John Nance Garner, Henry Wallace, James Farley . . . Mary gave no thought to what the errand might be. Miss Scott knew she liked to get out of class to do almost anything except dust erasers.

From *Southern Review,* XXVI (1970, 1171–84. Reprinted by permission of the author.

She laid her yellow Mikado pencil in the long narrow slot on her desk with the point right at the J. of J.V.B. that someone had carved there long ago. Then she walked up to the teacher's desk with the envious eyes of twenty sixth-graders on her back.

"Mary, I forgot my grade book. Would you mind walking up to Miss Emma's to get it?"

"Yes ma'am. I mean no ma'am. I'll go. Where'll I find it?"

"Just look in my room on the bed or the dresser. I'm sure it's out where you'll see it. I'll appreciate it, honey." She smiled.

Mary knew all about Miss Scott's apartment. Miss Emma Lamar's house was across the street from her own, and Mary knew where Miss Scott kept most of her things. She knew what books were in the bookshelf, where the alarm clock sat beside the yellow breadbox on the oilcloth-covered table in the tiny kitchen, and how the three little fringed pillows were lined up on Miss Scott's bed, which was covered with the white chenille bedspread. Mary's favorite thing in the whole apartment was a perfume bottle of delicate pink frosted glass that sat on the white linen, lace-edged dresser scarf. Miss Scott had once pulled out the long glass stopper and touched her white wrists, where the veins were blue. She assured Mary her beating pulse forced the scent into the air about her. Mary tried this with some of her mother's perfumes, and she felt that it worked, but she couldn't find a scent on her mother's crowded dressing table that was as heavenly as Apple-blossom.

Miss Scott wasn't Miss Scott at all. She was Mrs. Fite. Last year she had married Billy Fite, a fat little meatcutter who had no education, and who cried and called his mother when it lightninged. Everyone in town knew about that. Billy was a butcher—a butcher! Everyone called him a meatcutter. It somehow sounded better—almost artistic. Billy wore a bloody apron, and Mary had watched him cleave the largest joint of a cow with one blow of that great axlike knife. It was a splendid and terrifying performance, and Mary knew that Billy put his heart and soul into that blow. Afterward he would strike the surface of the huge square block of a tree that was his table and leave his meat-ax vibrating while he wiped his hands on his blood-browned apron. He had a sweet, shy smile.

Now Mary zigzagged so she could step on the big magnolia leaves and at the same time avoid the lines of the sidewalk.

"I hope Miss Emma's not at home, so I won't have to see her." Realizing she had spoken out loud, she looked around to see if anyone might have heard her, but no one was near. For a moment she walked straight, heedless of crackling leaves or the lines that would make her a rotten egg if she stepped on them.

Miss Scott had asked her why she never came to see her anymore. But Mary couldn't tell her why—that something too terrible to describe had happened between her and Miss Emma—that she felt she never could look at Miss Emma again, much less run the risk of talking to her.

Miss Scott was tall and looked like a Spanish queen. She wore her dark hair parted in the middle and pulled back into a low full bun on her neck. Not one bit of her ears showed, and her hair shone like Sunday shoes. She had a jawline like Joan Crawford—square with sort of hollow cheeks. Her eyes were large and dark with thick, strangely straight black lashes that looked like starched fringe. Mary had studied them, and she'd decided that they were too stiff to yield to the eyelash curler that her sister used to turn up her light brown lashes. The most fascinating thing about Miss Scott's face was her dark moustache, which could fill Mary with a mixture of revulsion and awe. Once, Miss Scott had bleached it only to have the most horrible yellow moustache glowing like a Mardi Gras joke on her proud face. But the moustache didn't really bother Mary.

Miss Scott had married Billy because she was thirty and figured he was her only chance. How many grown people had Mary heard say that? He was a foot shorter than she was, and he was a mama's boy, but he did come from a nice family, and Miss Scott seemed happy with him. Mary wondered if Miss Scott had ever seen Billy at work at McGraw's Market, where he hacked and sawed and sliced his way through cow after cow and pig after pig.

Miss Emma's house was only four blocks from school, and Mary could have made the trip blindfolded because she walked to and from school twice every day—she went home for lunch. Everybody went home for lunch in Sweet Bay, only it was dinner in the middle of the day. Myrt cooked a big dinner every day, and at night Mary had a light supper. It was only when they stayed in a hotel in New Orleans that Mamma called the night meal dinner. And that was because it was dinner. In New Orleans all meals were dinners, and Mamma and Daddy would try to be polite with their belching on the way home while Mary sat on the back seat of the car counting turtles on floating logs in the canal. Between La Place and Ponchatoula she would sometimes count over a hundred. After dark she counted one-eyed cars. The swamp road was wavy, and Daddy drove fast. She would stare ahead at the road lighted by the headlights, trying not to think of the deep black water on either side of the highway.

Mary ran her hand along the tops of the fence pickets as she walked past Mrs. Gatchell's. Mrs. Gatchell was sitting on her front porch with a large blue-and-white enameled bowl on her lap. She was picking over mustard greens and rocking. Her heels came down rhythmically as she discarded the tough ends of the greens on a newspaper beside her chair. "Morning, Mary. Playing hooky?" Mary said no.

The Gatchells had a concrete platform in front of their gate on the edge of the street. It was made for stepping into a carriage or mounting a horse. Now it was just something to scratch the paint off a car door. It had a slab of white marble in the top of it with GATCHELL set in blue tile letters. Last Halloween some high-school boys had painted out the GATC with green paint, leaving HELL. Mrs. Gatchell was outraged, and she found out that Bud Carnes and Mickey Beaumont did it and made them clean the paint off. Mary looked at it now. Faint traces of green paint showed in the concrete around the marble. Mary looked at Mrs. Gatchell and her blue bowl of greens and her funny, skinny ankles that showed below her cotton print housedress. She liked to think of her out there standing over Bud and Mickey, threatening to call their parents if they didn't scrub and scrape harder. Mrs. Gatchell was tough, but she wasn't crazy. Miss Emma was. Mary liked a lot of old people in Sweet Bay whom she regarded as a little odd. Old Mr. Dickerson really believed his house was haunted by the man who built it before the Civil War. That was fun. But Miss Emma was something else.

Once, Mary had thought Miss Emma was merely a little mysterious, and she liked her. *My friend Miss Emma.* For one thing she was a Yankee, and the way she pronounced her *r*s made Mary think of biting hard candy that had been in the refrigerator. Mary used to spend hours in Miss Emma's porch swing, her toes barely scraping the clean gray-painted floor. As she swung gently back and forth, her fingers traveled up and down the links of chain and she and Miss Emma talked about all sorts of things. The porch faced east and was lovely and shaded in the afternoons. In the spring it was fragrant with wisteria and magnolia fuscatas humming with bumblebees, and in the fall the air changed so mysteriously and the smell was of burning leaves and acorns; and the grassless spots under the big oak in front of the porch were traced with the finely combed trails of the leaf rake. She remembered the good croquet games they used to have. But all of this ended for Mary months ago.

Miss Emma's house was a quaint old two-story cottage with banistered porches upstairs and down. Her house sat to one side of the property, and she had a big side lawn that was flat enough for croquet. It sloped off near the street corner, where there was a great cedar with the ground underneath covered with ivy and fern, and to Mary it had been a wonderful place. Miss Emma's yard was surrounded by a hedge—low boxwood up near the house but eight-foot-tall privet down by the cedar, to screen off Negro town, which started right across the street.

The first Negro house belonged to Jim Cannon. Jim had a wooden leg and a moustache. He smoked a corncob pipe, and he was an expert at trimming hedges. He once told Mary that his shears were his "living." Mary had never forgotten, and after that she noticed he always carried his shears under his arm. His empty pants leg was packed in neat folds between the wooden leg and his stump. Jim's own hedge was as high on Miss Emma's side as hers was on his. His was very fancy in places, with higher squares at the corners and at his gate. In one side he had sculptured a bench with arms, but you couldn't sit in it. Mary had tried. The sharp, stubby branches had pierced and scratched her when she sat on the soft looking green foliage. It was like jumping into a big pile of leaves expecting to plop down on a cushiony heap and landing with a shocking thud on the hard ground beneath. You couldn't tell how soft something was by looking at it.

Miss Emma was a Methodist and a widow. She walked to church every Sunday in good weather. When it rained she rode with Mary's family or with Miss Phaedra Mullins, another neighbor. Miss Emma was thin as a slat, with a pale little face, and she wore only white powder for makeup—no lipstick even. Mary always noticed that. She wore beige or brown, and in the summer she sometimes wore white. Now she reminded Mary of a dead mouse that she had seen in a trap, especially when she sang in the choir. Her mouth dropped open just like the mouse's had, chin receding. She was so like that mouse that lay dead on the storeroom floor. But Miss Emma hadn't been to church lately.

She used to play bridge almost every night except Sunday, which would have been a sin. She played with her two upstairs roomers, whom Mary, to her puzzlement, had heard called "those two pansies." She had pictured the bridge foursome in Miss Emma's sitting room as Miss Emma and two large gold-and-purple velvet pansies and somebody else for a fourth—Miss Phaedra sometimes. Miss Scott used to play with them before she married. Now she and Billy spent every night in their rooms with the shades down, and the mouse and the two pansies had to call someone—when they played, which was hardly ever now. Silky playing bridge didn't sound any sillier than two pansies. Silky was Miss Emma's golden spaniel.

Mary stopped and put her foot up on the red fire hydrant and tied her shoe. Silky was dead. She walked on.

When Miss Emma sang in the choir her lips never changed

shape. Her jaw just worked up and down. She looked out over the congregation as though they weren't there, and she patted her foot, impatiently, to speed up the slow hymns. Her foot was the only one that moved in the row of shoes that showed under the short brown curtain that hung in front of the choir.

One day Silky had followed her into church; she went right up into the choir, and Miss Emma held her on her lap until the service was over. When it came time to stand and sing the offertory, Miss Emma stayed in her seat and patted her foot a little faster than the organ and sang with Silky on her lap.

Miss Emma had loved Silky better than anyone or anything. She brushed her and fussed over her and never let her run with the other dogs in the neighborhood. Last spring when it was discovered that Silky was going to have puppies, Mary thought Miss Emma might go crazy over it, she was so upset.

"I just don't know how this happened." Her mouth would clop, over and over, and tears would come in her eyes, and her little face would twitch. Then she quit mentioning it, and nobody else seemed to think much about it except Mary, who was excited and wanted one of the puppies.

One day she went over to Miss Emma's. She walked along the driveway on the narrow side of the yard, under the camphor trees that were planted too close to the house and had to lean out over the graveled paths.

At the back porch steps she called through the screened door, "Miss Emma." There was no answer, so she opened the door and started in. Silky lay on her side on the rag rug that Miss Emma used to wipe her shoes when she came in from the yard. Mary knew at once that Silky was dead. There was something brown on her back legs, and her sides were strangely flat and empty-looking.

Mary backed down the wood steps. She heard a faint chipping sound down near the cedar. She ran down and found Miss Emma under the tree trying to spade the hard ground.

"What happened? I saw her. What happened?"

"She's dead."

"I know. But what happened? What happened to the puppies?"

"They're dead."

"Oh." Mary pressed her fists to her cheeks.

"Can't I go get someone to come help you? Can't I do something? Where are the puppies?" Mary held a drooping cedar bough away from her face.

Miss Emma's face glistened with sweat. She was making little headway. Her small mouth hung open, and she pressed her foot on the shovel.

Mary turned and pushed through the high privet hedge. Jim was watering his flower beds. His shears lay on the porch.

"Jim! Come help Miss Emma dig a grave for Silky. She's dead from childbirth."

"Gawd. Limmie git a box." He turned the water off at the nozzle, and the hose writhed in the grass like a snake that refused to die. Mary turned the water off at the hydrant, and the hose lay down and began to relax.

Jim looked around for a moment, then picked up a large pasteboard Grande Dame coffee box with a label on the top.

"What do you want?" asked Miss Emma. "I can do this."

"No'm," said Jim. "You gimme that shovel, now." And he began to dig. He was a powerful man and soon had a deep hole dug. He fitted the box into it, then took it out. "Now that'll jist about do it," he said. "Where the dog at, Miz Emma?"

Miss Emma said, "Show him, Mary. Wrap her in that rag rug."

Mary and Jim soon returned. The box was closed, but Miss Emma didn't even look at it. She just sat on the cold stone bench. The Grande Dame lady on top of the box looked straight ahead, her wavy hair parted in the middle and her little pink mouth prim. She had a peaceful eye. Jim threw the first spade of dirt into her blank, pretty face. Miss Emma rose. "Thank you, both." The cedar raked her hair. Mary heard the back porch door slam.

Jim beat the back of the spade down hard on Silky's grave, and then he stamped heavily on it with his big feet, to tamp the earth. Mary thought of the picture of the Grande Dame coffee lady staring out forever, with her peaceful eye. And Silky—

Mary's eyes filled with tears.

"Ain't nothing but a dog, Miss Mary."

"I know it. Thanks a lot, Jim." And they left.

Later Mary found Miss Emma on her front porch. Mary leaned against the banister, feeling sorry for her.

"What happened to the puppies? How many were there?" She had to know.

"There were six," said Miss Emma. "They are all dead. They had slick short hair—black and white—terrible looking mongrels just like that beast that belongs to those nigras over there." She indicated the other end of the block by cutting her eyes to her left.

"What did you do with them?"

"I buried them behind the shed after you and the nigra left. The ground is softer back there. They were all born dead."

"Oh . . ."

"I'll go in now. You be careful crossing the street." Miss Emma left Mary, and Mary swung around the post and stepped off the front porch.

She found the fresh mound of earth just beyond the black pot where Sadie did Miss Emma's wash. On the bench under the shed was a galvanized tub half filled with water. Mary put her hand on the clothesline and leaned forward. A white puppy with black spots floated there. Puppy hair floated on the water.

Mary heard her own breath sucked in. *She's drowned them. She lied. Drowned them—with her own hands—and she forgot to bury one.*

The spade leaned against the tub. Mary was about to reach for it when she heard a sound—a faint squeak. She froze. The squeak became a chorus. No! Oh, no, no, no. Dim baby cries came from the mound. She felt ill, as though she might faint or vomit. She dropped the spade, fell on her knees, and began clawing the damp earth. But she had barely felt the dirt under her nails when Miss Emma's voice, strange and harsh, rasped, "What do you think you are doing?"

"Please, Miss Emma! They aren't dead! I hear the puppies. Maybe we can save them." She lifted her hands from the dirt.

Miss Emma grasped Mary's arms roughly. "Go home immediately, young lady! This is none of your business."

In her own room Mary took a pillow and hid under her bed. She shut her eyes and beat her ears with her palms to try to destroy the awful thing. She felt buried alive with the dying puppies under the dark, wet earth, squeaking out their last instinctive calls for help. She wrapped the soft pillow around her head and moaned.

It was almost dark when her mother waked her.

"Mary! What are you doing sleeping under the bed? A big girl nearly twelve years old! Come out from under there. Supper's almost ready."

Mary opened her eyes. Mamma had turned on the lamp, and she could see dust thick on the baseboard near her face. She felt the same dust lining her nostrils. She clutched her pillow, and crawled out and went to the front porch to look at Miss Emma's house. It had been no dream. And she was going to hear that terrible sound forever. If she couldn't dig them up, why hadn't she . . . but there was nothing she could do. Maybe . . .

She crossed the street. When she stepped behind Miss Emma's shed, she saw in the half-light that the galvanized tub had been emptied and hung on the wall—the molded rings in its bottom barely visible. She listened, one ear turned to the mound. There was no sound, and she felt some relief to know it was over.

Now she heard a soft rustle. She turned her head enough to know that Miss Emma was close behind her, and though she did not look at her, she knew so well what that face looked like.

"You forgot to bury one, and the others weren't dead."

"They are now. And they are all buried."

"How—why did you do it?"

"I thought they were dead. I held them under a long time—each one—till they quit squirming and were perfectly still and limp. I thought they were dead."

As she turned to look at Miss Emma, a picture of her flashed across Mary's mind—the pale hymn singer patting her foot impatiently in the church choir—Get on with it! Die! Die! I haven't got all day.

"You had done this before you buried Silky."

"This is what I planned to do all along. You forget, Mary, that these were my puppies to do what I please with. They were just mongrel puppies. They might have been cute for a while, but would have grown to be ugly dogs—mockeries of my poor Silky. Don't meddle, Mary, or I'll speak to your mother."

Mary knew she would speak to no one. She went home and sat down at the supper table. She slid her knees under the white cloth and began to push food around on her plate, but she couldn't eat.

As the months passed, she heard remarks about Miss Emma. "Emma was always peculiar. But here lately she seems hardly interested in anything." "Emma used to play bridge regularly, but she never picks up a card now." "Emma's just quit the Missionary Society." Mary found it easy to avoid Miss Emma, and she learned to avoid pondering the things people were saying. *I don't care about Miss Emma one way or the other.* And in her bed at night when she thought of the sad little cries, she would turn on her lamp and read until she fell asleep. School started. She had for her teacher the Spanish queen who moved about in a pulsing mist of Appleblossom perfume, and for the first time in her life, she felt that she might be the favorite pupil in class. And this was a secret too dizzying to dare breathe to a soul. She was less troubled . . .

Miss Emma's apartment was on the right side overlooking the croquet lawn. Miss Scott and Billy lived on the left. She found, to her surprise, that Miss Scott's door was locked so she tried another farther down the hall. It was locked. Like it or not, she would have to ask Miss Emma to let her in.

She knocked at her door and got no answer. She rattled the white china knob and found the door bolted. Then she went into Miss Emma's kitchen from the back porch and called, "Miss Emma," into her bedroom. The room was neat and prim, the bed smoothly made, but there was no Miss Emma. Mary went no farther than the bedroom door; she returned to the kitchen and took Miss Emma's keys off the hook over the gas stove. She quickly found the one to open Miss Scott's apartment. The grade book lay on the bed. She locked up, replaced the keys, and hurried out of the house. This was her lucky day. She walked briskly back to school swinging the thin blue grade book by her side.

Coming home that afternoon, she noticed two cars in Miss Emma's driveway; also her father's car was home, parked in front of Mrs. Judge Griffith's and Mrs. Doctor Hough's cars. She went in the side door to avoid the living room, but her mother heard her and met her in her room. Something was wrong.

"Mary, honey, something very unfortunate has happened. It's Miss Emma." Mary tilted her head upward, and her eyebrows lifted slightly, questioning. Mamma's face had never looked quite like this before. There were fine little lines kind of stretched under her eyes, and there was a little shiver in her voice when she said, "She's dead, Mary."

Mary put her books on her desk. The big geography book fell to the floor, displaying a brown-and-green relief map of South America. Miss Emma was dead. She felt nothing. She tried to feel something. *What do I feel? Nothing.*

"What—when did she die? What happened to her?"

"Well, Miss Phaedra walked over there about eleven-thirty this morning, just to look in on her. She found her—dead."

"Found her? Dead at eleven-thirty? Where was she? What happened to her? Did she have a heart attack?"

"No, Mary. She found her lying on the floor beside her bed. She—darling, she took her own life. Shot herself—Dr. Hough figures she did it about nine this morning."

Nine. Eleven-thirty. "What side of the bed was she on?"

"Why—she was on the side nearest her sitting room. You know—not on the kitchen side, the other side. What makes you ask that?"

"I just wondered—wondered where she—her body was."

"This is such a terrible thing to have to tell a little girl about her friend. I know it's shocking, darling—something awful you've never had to even hear about—you and Miss Emma—friends since you were a baby—poor darling—" Poor Mamma.

She leaned her cheek against her mother's arm, and her mother hugged her close. Poor Mamma. "Poor darling."

"I'm sorry, Mamma—I mean it really is terrible, isn't it? But don't worry—about me, I mean."

Her mother left her abruptly because she heard the two ladies—Mrs. Hough and Mrs. Griffith—leaving.

Mary put on her blue jeans, sneakers, and one of her brother's shirts. Later she looked into her mother's room. "Mamma, there are only about six blooms left in that nasturtium bed under your window. May I pull them up before frost gets them?"

Her mother looked surprised for only a moment. "I wish you would. That's very sweet, Mary." Mary was careful not to slam the screen door.

She dropped to her knees at the bed of annuals and began to pull up the spent summer plants.

"You never can tell about children." Her mother's voice. "Some little girls would have had hysterics." The voice drifted softly from the window. "Of course, I didn't go into the bloody details. My Lord! Poor Phaedra, coming on that gruesome . . ." The rich dark soil was cold. It made black arcs under the end of her nails. She crumbled handfuls and sifted it between her fingers letting it fill holes and depressions.

" . . . why? God knows." Her father's voice. "Don't let it prey on your mind, Katherine. I'll have to help with the arrangements. Phaedra can't do it all."

"I know. I know. She took Emma's best beige silk down to the funeral parlor. And she's talked with the brother in Oklahoma; he'll be in tomorrow night on No. 4. He agreed on the phone that Emma of all people should be buried from her church . . ."

A katydid struck its one-note song—not a song either, just a note with never a hurry or pause for breath. Katydids must not breathe.

The brittle nasturtiums had shallow roots, and they came up as though they'd never had a grip on the earth. An agile, sherry-colored worm writhed frantically in the loose soil, then disappeared underground. She gathered the plants and broke off the bouquet of remaining blossoms—fragile gold and yellow petals. She added a few round green leaves with fine white throbless veins. Unfolding her body, a little stiffly, she knocked moist dirt from the knees of her jeans.

In the kitchen she stood on a chair to reach a glass—the only one left of her grandmother's heavy old goblets with thistles on the sides—and she took it to the sink and filled it with water. Then she sank the pale, translucent stems into the water and walked to her mother's room. She set the flowers on the desk by the window—on an envelope so the glass wouldn't make a ring. She rubbed her hands back and forth on the hard, smooth surface of the desk that warmed with the friction.

Looking out the window, she saw that Miss Emma's porch was shady and beginning to go lilac, as it sometimes did when the sun sank lower in the evening. The swing was empty, and the fern baskets hung motionless over the banisters. The big oak tree laid a transparency of itself across the street and over half of Mary's yard. The croquet lawn was smooth and wicketless. She knew the wickets were stored neatly on the back porch with the mallets and balls, their bright-colored bands faded from years of use. The old house smelled of turkey carpets and mothballs. Silky lay beneath the dark cedar with the Grande Dame coffee lady whose face was so peaceful and unworried.

The nasturtiums glowed alive like sunshine, in the old goblet on the desk, and Mary felt the hotness of tears in her eyes.

JOHN WILLIAM CORRINGTON

REUNION

All the way up from Milledgeville it had rained off and on. It was early July, and when the rain stopped and the sun came out you could see steam rising from the rutted roads in southern Virginia. But by the time the train crossed into Pennsylvania, there was little sun, and water stood in the roads and there was no steam.

There were just the three of us: Grandfather, my brother Bedford, who was nine then, and me. I was almost fifteen. It was the first trip out of Georgia for Bedford and me, and the first time out of the South for anybody in the family for a long time. Grandfather had been north one time before, but it had not been on a train, and he had been only a few years older than me then.

—I don't see how he sleeps like that, Bedford whispered to me.

—When you get old you sleep more, I told him. —It doesn't matter where you are. You could sleep for fifty years, I guess.

Bedford looked out the coach window and squirmed in his seat. He had wanted to come, but he had wanted to stay home, too. It was something to take a train trip all the way to Pennsylvania, but at home the fishing was reaching its peak, the woods were full of birds, and the sun had warmed the water until it felt like part of your skin when you were swimming in it.

From *Southwest Review*, XLVIII (1963), 200–210. Reprinted by permission of Joyce Corrington.

—How much longer? Bedford asked.

—Not long, my grandfather said from the seat opposite. He did not open his eyes or push his hat back from his face.

—Thought you was still asleep, Grampaw, Bedford said.

—I been some. It comes and goes. You sleep more at my age, he said without smiling.

He was sixty-eight years old that summer, and his face was brown and spotted with little discolorations, each one smaller than a dime. His eyebrows were thick and still black, and they made his wrinkled face seem fierce and somehow young under a scattering of pure white hair that was beginning to show some pink scalp through it. The backs of his hands were brown as his face and neck, and tendons showed through the skin almost as if he cupped a powerful light in each palm.

Under his shirt there were three dead-white depressions in his chest. Each one was the size of a quarter, and they were clustered together along his ribs on the right side. In back, there were two white puckered gatherings of flesh, and now we were going back to see the place where he had gotten the marks on his chest and back.

—See those rises, my grandfather said, pointing out the train window. He had opened his eyes. They were large and still bright blue like my father's. —Over there. Those humps.

—Sure, Bedford said. —If it snowed, you could use a sled on 'em.

—No, Grandfather said. —They're too rocky for that. They're called the Roundtops. Little Roundtop and Big Roundtop.

—They look like they'd be fun to climb, I said. Then I remembered and bit my lip. But my grandfather smiled.

—They might be. If it was a cool day and nobody minded you climbing.

Then we saw the station up ahead at the end of a long curve of track. All around the edges of the station there was red, white, and blue bunting, and there was a United States flag above the station. There was a painted sign that read WELCOME VETERANS with roughly drawn cannon and canteens and bayoneted rifles around the border of it. Underneath the eaves of the station on our side, there was a little wooden plaque hanging down. It said Gettysburg.

They registered Grandfather and gave him a kind of medal to wear that said he was a veteran who had fought there, and what his rank and regiment had been.

—I expect I'll be a rarity, he said.

—What do you mean, Grampaw? Bedford asked him.

—A private soldier. You can't hardly find a private anymore. Seems only officers survived.

—That doesn't make any sense, I said. —The officers would have been older to start with.

But he was right. There were all kinds of captains and majors and even a few brigadier generals. My grandfather said the promoting hadn't ended yet, either.

The people in town were nice, mostly. Their voices were funny and harsh, and they moved fast, as if they were all after something about to get away from them, and they seemed to be real careful not to say anything that would slight the southern soldiers. With the Union veterans it was different. They acted as if everybody had been in the same army, fighting for the same thing. We met a man who had been with Sickles' staff.

—It's cooler now, he said to Grandfather. —It's a lot cooler.

—The sun's older, Grandfather said. —We can use all the warmth we can get.

The Union man laughed.—I thought we'd given each other enough heat those three days to last out all the rest of our lives.

—I expect we feel warmer than the ones who paid to stay home or hid under the chicken house when the conscription officer came by.

—That's so, the Union man said lustily. —That's so. Who are these fine boys?

—These are my grandsons. Meet Captain McCleoud. Robert and Bedford.

—I expect the Robert is Robert Edward, the captain said, smiling.

—Yes, sir, I said.

—There wasn't a better name on either side. If I had a grandson, I just might have risked it and named him the same.

Bedford kept looking at the captain with an expression on his face like the one you see on a whiteface calf when you come up on it suddenly.

—You're an honest-to-God Yankee?

—Bedford, Grandfather said mildly, watch what you say to the gentleman.

—I take that title as an honor, Captain McCleoud said, still smiling.

—I expect so, Grandfather said. —It's just that I'm not sure the boy intended it that way.

During all that, Bedford was still staring at the captain's rusty blue uniform with its gold shoulder bars and the wide-brimmed black hat. One side of the brim was turned up against the crown and pinned there.

—I never seen a Yankee before, Bedford said. —Grammaw said the last ones was run out of Georgia a long time ago after the Drunkard was gone from the White House. Grammaw said . . .

—Hush, boy, Grandfather told Bedford. His smile was gone, and I could see the cords in his neck tightening. —Just hush.

Grandfather never raised his voice to either of us, and Bedford was beginning to snuffle because of the tone of voice Grandfather had used.

—I'm sorry for that, he said to the Union captain. —My missus never took to the outcome of the war or what followed it. In her latter days, she talked a lot to the boys. She's over it now, I reckon.

The captain didn't say anything. He ruffled Bedford's hair, bowed to me, and shook hands with Grandfather. —I know. I suppose it will be a while yet.

—I expect, Grandfather said.

After signing up at the encampment office and drinking lemonade, we walked around some. It was hot with the sun standing high above us, and on all sides, as far as we could see, were long rows of army tents set up in orderly streets. In one corner of the tent city, we found the place reserved for us. It had four cots in it, and Bedford and I put the pallets we had brought to sleep on under one of the cots.

—I expected they'd be here, Grandfather said. —They said the second of July for sure.

—Grampaw, Bedford said, how come you didn't wear no uniform up here like that Yankee captain? How come you ain't ever showed us your uniform?

—I had a uniform in 1862, he said, smiling softly. —It was blue. Almost as blue as the captain's.

—Lord, Grampaw, you weren't a Yankee.

—No. It was a militia uniform. It was all we had, and when they mustered us into the regular army we went on wearing it until it wore out. Then we wore whatever we could get hold of.

—I wouldn't have fought if they didn't give me a uniform, Bedford said.

—Yes you would, Grandfather said. —If you had to fight, it wouldn't matter what you had to wear.

—Who are we waiting for? I asked.

—A couple of old friends. They were in Armistead's brigade with me. They were here before.

That afternoon and evening there were speeches welcoming everybody, and a mayor or governor said that the war had been like a great burning sword that had cauterized the soul of America, and from much wrong, much good had come, and that now, North and South, we were united under one flag.

—Huh, Bedford said afterward as we walked in the dark down the torchlit tent-city streets. —That's all he knows. I reckon Grammaw could tell him something.

—Your grandmother is dead, Grandfather said evenly. —She remembered too much. Sometimes a good memory does you no service.

—How can you help remembering? I asked him. —You've got holes in you to help you remember if you were to start forgetting.

—Holes, Grandfather said. —Maybe I fell onto your great-grandfather's picket fence when I was courting your grandmother.

—Maybe not, too, Bedford said darkly. —Maybe it was some of these bastards . . .

—All right, Grandfather said shortly. —Watch your tongue, boy. I remember what your mother told you about coarse talk.

—I don't give a hoot in hell for their flag, Bedford said defiantly.

—Grammaw used to say the red in it was southern blood. That the Union got fat eating its own people when they tried to be free . . .

We reached our tent and went inside. Bedford lighted a kerosene lantern and hung it on the main pole.

—Your grandmother said a lot, Grandfather said wearily. —But her text was always the same.

—But . . . , I began.

—Do you want to carry the graves home from here with you? Do you want to carry the graves inside the house and set them up there?

—What're you talking about, Grampaw? Bedford asked him.

—This is just a celebration, he said, sitting down heavily on his cot. —It's something for a lot of old men who want to remember that they were once young and brave and maybe held the fate of their nations in their hands. They want to remember that they fought well and did all they could, whether they did or not. The other people just want to look at them like they'd read a history book or look at a painting of Waterloo. It doesn't mean anything anymore.

—If it doesn't mean anything anymore, why'd you come back up here? Bedford asked cagily.

Grandfather pulled off his trousers and carefully swung his legs up onto the cot. —If it meant anything, he said, I don't reckon I could have stood to come. It's like a picture in my mind, like photographs in one of those little books Charlie Stokes has—the kind you riffle through and it looks like the pictures move. I see men and horses and cannon, and I see bursts of dark smoke in the air and on the field, and I see men falling. But I can't feel the sun on my back or feel the fear in my belly when we started out. I know my mouth was dry. It was so dry I couldn't move my tongue. And my feet were cut and blistered and wrapped up in pieces of tent cloth.

Grandfather touched the slanting side of the tent with his fingers. —But I can't feel the pain of the grass stubble underfoot. All I can feel is sorry for that boy. I feel sorry he had to get himself hurt and had to hurt in his turn. I guess I feel sorry for all of them, but it doesn't mean anything anymore. I can't get hold of the heat and the sweat. I can't hope for the Confederacy; I can't hate and respect that goat-whiskered terrible proud Jefferson Davis anymore. All of it seems like a picture I saw once. How much can you care about a picture?

—Grammaw cared, Bedford said accusingly.

Grandfather's eyes were closed, and the soft, buttery light of the kerosene lantern played across his face in profile. You could see how the flesh of the jaw and around the chin had melted away and left the sharp outline of the bone. The creases around his eyes and on his forehead and cheeks stood out like elevation markings on a map.

—Your grandmother wasn't here, Bedford. Her imagination wasn't limited by having been subjected to the facts. I expect she was making up for not having been here. I think she believed had she been here it might have been different. She had to keep it going until she felt she'd done her duty. But death caught her short.

I almost blushed, and I was glad he had his eyes shut. Bedford looked at me, not understanding. But I understood. Because I had felt the way he said Grandmother must have felt. I could remember, even when I was younger than Bedford, how I had felt when Grandfather took off his shirt to chop firewood or for a bath. I would see how thin and flat his chest was, and the three milky depressions through his ribs and the ugly drawn-up little mouths in his back, and I would feel a funny cold thing move from my tailbone up into my scalp. I knew when he said it that what I had felt was shame just as if I had been alive then, in the brigade, and had run, or been a staff officer or courier, and had stayed behind.

—All I remember, my grandfather was saying, is a boy just a little older than Robert running across that road filled with fear and thirst and barely aware of his feet being opened again by the stubble. And the smoke and uproar, the artillery and rifle fire, and then him being hit and falling but still holding on to his rifle and crawling on until the smoke closed all around him. But even that doesn't mean much, because when I remember, it seems he was a boy cut out of paper like a doll, and the minié balls only punched through his paper guts, and the paper boy lay down near a lot of other cutouts under a sun painted on a piece of blue canvas sky with the blue maybe overdone some. How can you care about something like that?

—You were that boy, I said as the fatigue of the long day came over me.

—I expect so, he said, his voice blurring, trailing off. —I expect so.

Then, after a minute: —You-all hang up your clothes, turn down the lantern, and sleep on those cots. They won't be in before morning now. Goodnight, boys.

Before the sun was up, I heard voices just outside the tent. Then I heard somebody fooling with the flap.

—All right, I heard Grandfather say without any sign of sleep in his voice. —All right, come on in.

I couldn't get my eyes open right away, but I heard Grandfather move toward the lantern and heard someone else come into the tent.

—I thought maybe he'd caught up with both of you, I heard Grandfather say.

—He ain't none too far off, a strange voice answered.

—Specially in the early morning, a third voice said. —Twilight and first light I feel like one of them Greek heroes on the Happy

Isles. Like my body was gone, and nothing left but what I look and think with.

—How is it up here?

—All right, I guess, my grandfather said over the sounds of his dressing. —We got here yesterday and they had already started the speeches full tilt. I think today is the big day.

—I reckon so. Today was the big day.

I managed to get up finally and open my eyes. The two of them were sitting on either side of Grandfather. The one who had been talking about Greek heroes was short and fleshy without really being fat. His face was red and blotchy, and it showed no feeling at all. He had on a gray uniform with gold braid on the sleeves. The other old man was just under Grandfather's six feet in height. His voice was reedy and pleasant. He was narrow all over. From his long head to his narrow hips he looked as if he had spent all his years standing up in a close room, or as if someone had tied him between horses at intervals in order to force his growth.

—Hello, boy, the smaller one said bluffly when he saw I was awake.

—This is Michael Clinton, Grandfather said. —We were here together.

—This would be Robert Edward Lee, Michael Clinton said, nodding at me.

—That's him, Grandfather said with only a slight smile. —Over there's Nathan Bedford asleep.

—Fine, Michael Clinton said.—Robert, this is John Edgar Turner.

—Sorry, Grandfather said.—I was fixing to do the rest of the honors.

—All right, John Edgar Turner said in that soft, breathless voice that sounded like a clarinet or a flute. —I been looking him over.

—He's all right, Michael Clinton said. —He's just fine.

I was getting embarrassed, but about then we went outside and found the cook tent, where there were a lot of old men, most of them Union veterans, standing in line for coffee and rolls. Up where the food and coffee was, I saw a young man with a fur-collared overcoat on. He was talking to one of the army officers who were trying to make sure everybody was happy and getting to the speeches and fireworks and whatever was going on. The man with the fur collar was gesturing toward the men in line, and the officer, his face set and showing nothing, was listening without seeming to agree or disagree. The young man's face was red, and I thought it was the early-morning chill until we got close enough to see all the pimples and scars of old pimples on it. He had a high celluloid collar and kept talking about spectators and the angle, but the officer looked away, and when another officer came by, he excused himself and walked off as if he had something important to do. The young man with pimples didn't look insulted. He pulled a notebook from his pocket and read something, and then started off in the direction opposite from that the officer had taken.

Later we were walking on the east side of the big Pennsylvania memorial. All around us, people looked at tablets and statues and little pillars with bronze plates. Bedford was with us, and we were waiting for the time when President Wilson would speak.

—None of us ever got this far before, John Edgar Turner was saying. I guess we stopped over there a couple hundred yards.

—That's right, my grandfather said. —If you stand on one of these tablets, you can see the wall.

—Do you want to walk over there? John Edgar Turner asked quietly.

—How about some lemonade? Michael Clinton asked us. —Would you-all like some lemonade?

—Where did you get your uniform, Mr. Clinton? Bedford asked. —Did you wear it here before?

—Lord no, John Edgar Turner laughed. —We didn't any of us have uniforms.

—My sister . . . , Michael Clinton started to say. He was looking gray, and his hard-lipped, expressionless face was covered with moisture.

—His sister in Danville had it made for him. We didn't any of us have uniforms that last time.

—I wouldn't have done no fighting if they hadn't given me a uniform. What's the good of joining an army if they don't give you a uniform? Bedford asked.

—I reckon they gave us a kind of uniform, Grandfather said. —They gave us one that day.

—That's so, John Edgar Turner said.

Bedford shrugged, and Michael Clinton still looked sick. John Edgar Turner looked at him and frowned.

—Don't be silly, he said to Michael Clinton. —Come on. We'll take a look at the angle. We'll take a look at Cemetery Ridge right after we hear the president talk.

—Maybe the boys would . . .

—Like to see where their country died, John Edgar Turner finished. His long narrow face looked hard and naked in the bright sunlight.

Michael Clinton shrugged, and looked as if he had shrunk some. He followed a few steps behind us.

—You'd think . . . , John Edgar Turner began.

My grandfather cut him off. —Hush, John. Maybe it doesn't seem so long to Mike. I expect he's got something to remember.

—It was the worst way to be hurt. I remember he screamed all the way down through Maryland. I remember . . .

—All right, mind the boys.

—Oh, John Edgar Turner said. —I wasn't going to say anything.

All the president had to say was about how close we all were, and how the Boys in Blue and the Boys in Gray were all heroes and brought glory and unity to the country after all.

—Whose country? Bedford snorted right while the president was talking, and some of the old men with Grand Army of the Republic badges stared and frowned at him. My grandfather hushed

Bedford hard, but then he stared back at the other men without blushing any at all.

While the president was getting the good old U.S.A. off his chest, Michael Clinton still looked pasty and sick, and after it was over, we started back to see the angle and the fence which we had been started for when it was time to go hear the president.

We went past the little monument they call the High Water Mark, and there right ahead of us was this little square of field, a few trees, and a broken-down snake-rail fence running along one side of it. What was left of a broken-down stone wall maybe three and a half or four feet high straggled out perpendicular to the fence. Beyond was a long wide field knee-deep in dry summer grass, and down the slope a few hundred yards was a road. That was all there was.

But Grandfather and John Edgar Turner and Michael Clinton all walked slowly, as if the place was full of cannon or big statues. Michael Clinton stopped under a tree and mopped his head with a checkered handkerchief.

—Right out there, he said, I gave 'em my life.

—Sure, John Edgar Turner said, looking over at us kind of nervously. —You gave it all.

—I gave it all, Michael Clinton said after him. —I was only twenty-two. They got as much from me as if I was buried out there. Do you-all know what it's like going through life without . . .

—The boys, Grandfather cautioned him sternly.

Michael Clinton leaned against the tree. His eyes were damp, but he still had no expression. Just that strange bluff red face with a tortured voice coming out of it, and nothing in the face to match the voice. Like one of those wooden puppets they use in shows.

—Reckon I made it about three-quarters of the way, Grandfather said to John Edgar Turner. —I never saw it from this point of view. They say we covered the whole field there as far as you could see.

—I expect we looked like judgment on the way from up here, John Edgar Turner said in his reedy voice.

—I don't see anything, Bedford said. —It's just a pasture. I don't see nothing but a pasture.

—Shut up, I said. —They'll hear you.

— . . . all the way up here to see a pasture and a fence with a couple of trees and a dinky road running through it.

—You want to go back? I said. —I'm going to kick you all the way back to the tent if you don't shut up.

But then a man came walking up and started talking to Grandfather and the others. It was the man with the pimples and the celluloid collar. At first I couldn't make out what he wanted.

— . . . in an hour or so. The Pennsylvania veterans are scheduled to present the Pickett's Division Association folks with an American flag right here.

My grandfather was nodding courteously, and John Edgar Turner was craning his long neck first to one side and then the other like a tall puzzled bird looking down on a hedgehog for the first time. Michael Clinton was still leaning up against the tree and looking over the field.

— . . . lots of folks from all over, the young man was saying earnestly. —From South and North. Lots of good people to celebrate with you, and we thought . . .

Michael Clinton had stopped rubbing his face with the outsize checkered handkerchief. He stepped over to where the others were talking as if he was drawn by a magnet. His eyes widened as the pimple-faced man went on, but he kept listening as if he couldn't help it and couldn't believe what he was hearing either.

— . . . if you fellas would get together and go on down by the Emmetsburg road there, and then kind of run back up toward this wall here, and maybe give us the old rebel yell . . . you know . . .

My grandfather remained placid and showed nothing of what he was thinking. John Edgar Turner's long gentle face was like rubber, passing from a kind of embarrassed horrified smile to a frown, and back again, like the face of someone confronted with a preposterous and unexpected situation that might turn out funny or dangerous or both.

—Lord, John Edgar Turner said slowly, softly.

—What're they going on about? Bedford whined irritably. —I want to go back. I want to go back. I'm tired.

But now it was coming through to Michael Clinton. —O Jesus Christ, he moaned, looking away from the young man who had not stopped talking even then but continued to tell how much the good folks would enjoy it, and how much it would add to the celebration.

—O Jesus Christ in heaven, Michael Clinton crooned, and now his rough scarlet face was no longer bland, no longer even a face, but a collapsing unsorted collection of wide eyes, a twisted mouth, and fresh streams of sweat flowing into both like the catch of a violent spring rain. —Do you know what they . . .

But the pimple-faced young man only stared at Michael Clinton curiously and drew breath to begin his persuasion again.

—Pickett's charge all over again, he said. —This time the Pennsylvania boys will meet you with open arms. Think of how proud . . .

By then John Edgar Turner and Grandfather had turned away from him. They were watching Michael Clinton who had begun staggering back in the direction of the tents. He had gone only a little way when he fell heavily against one of the trees. He held himself up long enough to get turned around. Then he sagged into a sitting position facing us, his back against the tree, his eyes wide and staring past us into that wide grassy field beyond. There was no expression on his face at all.

I started toward him but Grandfather caught my arm.

—No. You take Bedford and go back. If you see one of those boy scouts or army people, send them down here with a stretcher. Tell them to hurry.

As I pulled Bedford along, I could hear the young man with the pimples and high celluloid collar saying to Grandfather:

—After you get the old gentleman taken care of, maybe we could go over it with the others . . .

By that time we were too far away to make out words, but I heard Grandfather say something in a short, vicious tone, and his voice was as strong and deep as a young man's. Then I could hear nothing more.

We had some late lunch, and Bedford fell asleep in the hot, stuffy tent afterward. I sat on a campstool outside for a long time, but Grandfather didn't come. Old men in blue suits and gray suits moved past quietly talking or, once in a while, laughing in that high, womanish shrill of the very old. The sun began slanting downward, and when suppertime was near, I began to worry. Bedford woke up covered with sweat. He was sullen and uncomfortable and kept saying he wished he was home, and how all of this didn't mean anything. —It ain't like all the stories, he said. —All it is, is a lot of old men and ground with the grass all cut and some big places built of marble with iron horses on top. It's not anything.

I sent him on to supper and went to look for Grandfather.

I found him my first try. He was sitting on the low stone wall at the place we had been, the place they called the Bloody Angle. All around the green well-trimmed acre or two, there were pieces of paper scattered, some bread crusts, and what looked like a jam jar. My grandfather was facing west, looking at the long-deserted slope that flowed downward to the Emmetsburg road, and then up again to the bulky shadow of Cemetery Ridge, where the sun stood low and red like a swollen wound.

—I got worried about you, I said as I climbed up and sat on the stone wall beside him.

He turned and looked at me. It seemed at first he didn't recognize me.

—I'm sorry, he said after a moment. —After we left the hospital, I meant to come back to the tent . . .

—How's Mr. Clinton?

—Mr. Clinton is dead, my grandfather said. —Too much heat. Too much excitement.

—No, it wasn't . . . Did you tell them about that man . . .

—I didn't tell them anything. They told us Michael Clinton was dead. There wasn't anything to tell them. So I came here to take another look before time to go.

He stood up and stretched and when he yawned, with his head thrown back, it seemed all the wrinkles in his cheeks dissolved. It may have been some trick of light in the early summer evening, but he looked for a moment, squinting toward the darkening sun, his mouth open as if to cheer invisible friends forward, no older than myself, and just as strong.

—We should have gone right on, he said quietly. —We never should have stopped.

It was twilight. Then it was dark, and we had put our things in the cardboard suitcase and said good-bye to John Edgar Turner, who held my hand and Grandfather's for a long minute, and who embarrassed Bedford by leaning down and kissing him in front of some old men who were shuffling past on their way to a regimental reunion.

—Good-bye, John Edgar Turner called after us. —God bless you-all.

—I'll be seeing you, Grandfather said, waving. —We'll see you again.

—Sure enough, we heard John Edgar Turner call in his soft, reedy voice. —Sure enough.

On the train we split two hot dogs among us, and got the porter to sell us two bags of salted peanuts for a nickel instead of just one. By the time we finished eating, Bedford was beginning to be contrite. He was sorry for letting it show that he wished he had stayed home.

—He was a mighty nice old man, Bedford said. —I'm sorry about it.

—I expect he was ready, Grandfather said. —It gets to be that time, and then you get set for it.

He rolled his coat into a ball and set it in the corner of the seat next to the window.

—It's beginning to rain, I said.

—Yes, my grandfather said. —It would.

Outside we could see the raindrops striking our coach window and shattering into long shivering beads that tracked down and across the glass, and then spun off into the night again. There were blurred yellow lights in town windows and on farm porches as we passed. Once there was an empty crossroads with lamps above it on poles. The roadway was slick and shiny with rain and light, and the lamps had halos of swirling mist around them.

My grandfather had pulled his hat down over his eyes, and his arms were folded across his chest.

We rode for a long time in silence, looking out at the rain. I could feel myself going slack inside. It would be easy to sleep in a little while. Bedford took his Ingraham watch out and looked at it.

—It's almost one o'clock. It's the Fourth of July.

—Shut up, I said. —He's trying to sleep.

Bedford leaned over and tried to look up under Grandfather's hat.

—You asleep, Grampaw? he whispered.

We could see Grandfather's mouth twist into a smile under the battered hat.

—Sure now, he said softly. —I reckon I could sleep for fifty years.

SHIRLEY ANN GRAU

THE MAN OUTSIDE

There were horses on the streets in those days. You could sit on our front porch and listen carefully and you could hear the plop-plop of the hoofs and the rumble of the iron wheels of the carts in town—a mile away.

You might call our place a farm, though it hadn't been worked in years. Not since the time I was three years old and my father moved out of our house and went to live in his shack back in the woods.

It seemed to me once that I could remember when my father was living with us. Seemed I could remember the time when the fields around were full of white blooming cotton, and the east plot had corn growing. Seemed I could remember a hogpen too, lower down, in the bog where the pitcher plants stuck up their green flowers in the spring. And a sow that ate her litter, every one, and my oldest brother getting whipped for his carelessness.

But most likely I was too young to have seen my father. And if I remember my brother Dan yelling and running around the yard, without his pants, screeching with rage and fear, most likely it was my mother on the end of the switch.

(My brother Dan was a grown man when the First World War

---

began, and working on the fishing boats down at Biloxi Bay. He had never much cared for fishing, or farming either, so he volunteered. He married a French girl, whose name I don't remember, and he was killed a couple of months before the Armistice. His wife wrote once to say that she had had a daughter, but didn't send her address. And my mother worried the rest of her life about that little French baby that had her blood and carried her name. It was the only thing I've ever seen disturb her. No . . . it was the second thing . . .)

My mother was what you would call a driving woman. For fifteen years she made a living for herself and her eleven kids off that farm, scratching away at the ground like one of her chickens. Without my father that wasn't easy, but I never heard her complain or say that she was tired. And only once I saw how scared she'd been. But that was later.

We lived in moonshine country, where most people had big fields of corn. Some of the corn went to the hogs and some of it went to the cows, but most went into likker. Practically every low swampy stretch that was wide enough and deep enough and tangled with old clumps of hackberry and poison ivy and swamp oak had one tiny little patch cut into it. The sort you couldn't follow unless you knew where you were going. And at the end there'd always be a little still.

People would come from fifty miles away to buy the likker, and that was a long trip in those days. They came by train, the Smoky Bill it was called, to Plainfield and then they'd rent a carriage or some kind of wagon and drive the rest of the way. Lots of people did it, and corn whiskey was just about the biggest business for three or four counties around. There was even a special firm that came out from New Orleans and sold nothing but sugar—in any amounts, with no questions asked and no records kept. The business was that big.

Every so often there'd come a reform government in the state capitol, and you could see people drifting into town, casually enough. They'd wander around asking innocent questions, and the stills would finish up what they had going and lie idle for a while.

A couple of times those reform people talked to my mother. Once was a Saturday evening when she'd gone into town to deliver the pies she'd baked. She had gone to the drugstore and as she was coming out, with me tagging along at the end of her primly long skirts and high button shoes, a man I'd never seen before stepped up to her, politely tipping his hat.

"Move off, child," my mother said, and I went to the curb and stared up and down the red dusty street, waiting and trying to hear what they were saying. I couldn't. I caught only the last words and those only because my mother lifted her voice, indignant. "I am not a Judas Iscariot!" She stamped off down the streets, her skirts swishing high around her ankles in her haste.

Even so, my mother would have nothing to do with the moonshining business, though there was a nice spot for a still on her property and she had had offers. She needed money the worst way, but she was a Baptist and she took it seriously.

She didn't countenance any hard likker, legal or not. We were all brought up to believe that the devil was a tall red man with a pitchfork in one hand and a bottle of whiskey in the other. And there was quite a to-do when my brother Roger, who must have been about fourteen at the time—a big, strong boy with the beard of a man—came home dead-drunk and passed out in his bed. My mother got the wheelbarrow, the one that still stank of the chicken yard, and dragged or rolled him out of bed (by herself, though she wasn't a big woman) and carried him out to the front gate to the edge of the dirt road where there was a kind of little ditch cut by the rains. She dumped him out there, and left him, though it was a sharp night, with a little mold of frost on the ground.

When he did come up to the house the next morning, so stiff and sore and cold he was limping like a cripple, my mother only glanced up from the pot of mush she was stirring. "Morning, Roger," she said. "You look like you had a bad night."

"Yes, ma'am," he said.

She brought us up carefully. Her girls wore cotton stockings summer and winter if they wore any of the shorter skirts. And if they didn't have stockings they had to have their skirts ankle-length.

When you worked all day with chickens and walked the dirt roads, the hems got thick and crusted and heavy with mud and dragged at your feet. Once my sister Rosalie asked if she couldn't pin them up just for a little while, one wet fall when the mud and bramble burrs were caking and scratching. My mother looked at her—looked right through her—and didn't even bother answering. And that was the last said about that.

Maybe she was a little rough with the children. But maybe there wasn't any other way for her to do without a man working the place and the babies coming, year after year, in early summer, June usually.

It couldn't have been easy for her, after our father had his vision and stopped working and took his dog and went to live in the little shed down by the spring, right on the east side of the swamp. My mother went down each evening carrying his supper on a tin pie plate.

She would always leave us at our supper while she went down. She can't have stayed too long, because I remember hearing her come back, hearing the firm steady unhurrying tread of her heavy shoes.

For all of her energy, she wasn't a thin woman or a gaunt one. She was short, and inclined to be heavy. Her hair changed from light brown to gray, but her face was full and pink. Her mother had been German, and the blood in her showed. Even mud on her looked clean.

Her children were dark, every last one of them; they all took after their father.

I wonder now what she must have thought of him. But she didn't give a sign, nor say a word. She kept on bringing his food and bearing his children.

Not even my oldest brothers, Mark and George, knew exactly what happened. One day they noticed that they had considerably more of the chores to do, and their father didn't seem to be home for supper. Like kids, they weren't really very interested. They grumbled to themselves about the extra work, then they forgot all about it. Next they noticed what was happening to the fields—they filled with dry stalks that rustled in the wind during the winter until even they fell down and blended into the mud and disappeared. And the fields turned into stretches of open ground covered by creepers and grass, the marks of old plow lines showing very faintly.

It was maybe six months, maybe a year, or maybe more, before the boys discovered where their father was living. They found his shack one day in early summer when they were heading for Taylor Pond to see if they could get any green trout. The shack itself had been there for as long as they could remember, only now the walls shone with bright new tar paper. The roof had been patched with sheets of tin and around the whole thing was a fence of chicken wire.

The boys tried to open the gate—they wanted to peep in the windows and see who was there. The gate wasn't a very good fit and it had warped besides; they were struggling with it when a big yellow hound came rushing out.

They recognized the dog. Their father's. It was in worse shape than they had ever seen, ears cut by brambles and coat tangled with burrs, but it was sleek and heavy. As if it'd been lying around for a week and hadn't been cleaned up after the last run.

The boys stopped fooling with the gate, not because they were afraid of the hound, but because they were no longer curious. They knew who was living there.

They backed off and tiptoed away, the hound watching them go, and them not talking until they were a half mile off. It was almost like they'd been to a graveyard.

They didn't go to the pond that day after all. Instead they went over to the Tickfaw River and caught some catfish, though it was a longer walk and they didn't particularly like the taste of cat. So that was that. After a while we children forgot he was there. And things went on just the way they had before.

My mother baked, and we brought the cakes and pies and bread into town every Saturday. She made preserves and we'd comb the country for wild fruit. From the first blossom we'd know where the berry thickets were and we'd start praying for a good dry spring so the berries wouldn't blight and fall off. There was one particular spot, a kind of swampy one, where the bushes had plenty of sun and their roots were always damp—we'd be out before daylight, fighting the birds for every single berry. Poison ivy got in our scratches and we'd cool them by scooping up great handfuls of wet mud and smearing them on the spots until we got home. Then my mother would use a special lotion made of eleven different kinds of leaves and that would stop the itching.

We helped with the preserving, too, watching the long lines of jars stretched out along the kitchen table and over the windowsills. And eating the hulls out of the bottom of the jelly bag.

Usually food wasn't any problem. There were plenty of wild greens and we grew a little garden too. Mark and George were good shots with the old Winchester rifle that hung over the kitchen door. The younger boys used slingshots. So we had deer and rabbit and plenty of birds: dove and pheasant and quail. All of us, boys and girls together, fished the streams for miles around. My sister Marjorie was very clever at spotting honey trees and we always had plenty of the sweet and faintly musky tupelo honey.

But winters were hard, no two ways about that. They were short and very cold, with little skins of ice on the ground and air so damp you felt you were swimming under water. The house was never warm; the walls dripped moisture and the wind blew straight through. We put newspapers under the mattresses and newspapers between the blankets so that the whole night roared with crackling. Even so we went to bed right after supper, two and three together for warmth. Sometimes it seemed that there was a big lump of ice in the middle of my stomach that didn't thaw out until March.

But mornings were worst of all. There were things to be done and we had to be out doing, stumbling over our own feet because we were so sleepy. We all had our different ways of beating the cold. Like my brother John. On Saturday mornings he had to kill and pick and draw the chickens that were going to town to be sold that day. He had to work outside, in a special little fenced yard, where a charcoal burner heated a barrel of water. He was very good at the job and very fast, and he had added some improvements of his own, ones that saved him standing in the cold, stamping his feet and waiting. He had one in particular he was very proud of. When he had slit the throat, instead of throwing the chicken in an empty barrel to bleed, he grabbed it by the feet and swung it around his head like a lariat. The blood drained out faster that way, he said, and he stayed warmer with the exercise. Sixty years later I can still see him—red blood spinning out, splashing like a sort of heavy summer rain on ground that was frozen hard into little ruts and hollows. (He became a car salesman in Pensacola, eventually, and never had chicken in his house.)

Once when my mother noticed him, she said quietly to no one in particular, "That is a great waste of energy." And later on she said to the kitchen sink, "I wonder if you couldn't do something with chicken blood. Seems such a pity to waste it."

That was the way she thought.

One day my father was gone. Really gone this time.

My mother said nothing. You would never think anything had changed. It was my sister Marjorie who came home from hunting honey and whispered to us that the shack was empty, and the door of the yard was standing open.

That evening we were all of us dying to get out. We often did that at night—after my mother had gone to bed, and we could tell by her heavy slow breathing that she was asleep.

But not this night. This night she sat rocking, alone in the kitchen, only moving every now and then to put more wood in the range. We could hear the thump of the sticks as she got them out of the basket behind the door and the clank of iron as she put them in the stove. Then the rocker began its creaking all over again.

We lay waiting, not even daring a whisper to each other, because she had sharp quick ears and could tell in a flash what the first whimper of a child meant. (She was always the first to tell when a fox or a weasel was bothering her chickens too; just the slightest flutter told her that.) We couldn't even creep to the door, because the old boards of the house would groan and sway under our weight. The foundations had needed repairs for years.

So we stayed very quiet and waited, and one by one we fell asleep. We never did know when she went to bed. Or if she did.

That same night the shack burned to the ground leaving only the fence posts. Pretty soon, in the damp and weather, those fell down and the brush covered it all up again. Until we weren't even sure any more just where it had stood.

Days went rolling into weeks and weeks into years. I remember worrying about my clothes, beginning to wonder how I looked. Beginning to fret at the old-fashioned pier glass that was so wavy you could hardly tell if your hair was combed. I was growing too, and I remember my mother adding ruffle after ruffle to the hem of my dress. They were all different materials, and my sisters thought the effect was very gay. I thought it was horrid. I had my heart set on a bright blue cotton in Keating's window.

I can still see the that dress, as plain now as the day I coveted it so much my stomach was shaky. I can see how it was displayed, pinned up against a silver-paper wall. But I can't remember what my littlest sister looked like then.

And I can't remember the name of the boy who made love to me in the cotton shed on the Turner place. (My mother, being a practical woman, did not oppose sex before puberty for her girls.) He was a tall thin boy, with a beginning moustache, though he couldn't have been more than twelve then. I thought the moustache was terribly attractive.

He lived on one of the places close by, and he came every evening. He would circle close around the house, whistling like a night bird, a whippoorwill usually.

Sometimes my mother would look up and say, "Those are the saddest birds." She was too busy to notice that the call had an extra trill that no bird would make. He claimed to have learned it from an old Cherokee on the reservation at Wallace Falls some twenty miles away; he said it was a war signal.

I was impressed. War signals sounded romantic; and so did twenty miles. He might just as well have said ten thousand, like the old songs; I had never been either distance.

They weren't very successful, those early tries, more full of hurt than pleasure. I was kind of glad when I became a woman and stayed in the house and the cries of the whippoorwill stopped.

The next winter was unusually hard. I remember that my brothers couldn't go hunting for weeks on end, because there were no shells for the Winchester. Instead the boys set snares for rabbits. There were always plenty of them, and we had rabbit stew most of that winter. The walk to school was an endless trip of dripping noses and chattering knees. Until we finally gave up and stayed at home.

It seemed long, even to us. But then it was over, and my mother was sending us out to dig sassafras root and making us drink the pink tea. And all of a sudden the sun got hot and the days stretched out and, kid fashion, we forgot that we had ever been cold. We ate the wild watercress that grew around the spring and dug the young dandelion shoots out in the old pasture field and carried them home in our skirts.

That was the summer Albert Benton began coming to the house.

He was the foreman of a lumber mill in town, a short, squat, heavyset man, with almost white hair and a face sunburned a bright red.

He came every Sunday, wearing a suit and tie, with his white hair carefully combed. He always brought something for us kids: a bag of apples, or peppermint candies.

After a time my mother began building a new room on the west side of the house. We were so excited that we just stood around and watched the Negro carpenter from town, until our mother chased us off with not so gentle swats. And every Sunday Mr. Benton inspected the week's work very carefully, plank by plank.

It did look kind of strange, all those new boards hung on to the blackened paint-stripped main house. After all, any sort of addition was unusual in this part of the world. Most people lived in a house until it was ready to fall down with termites and old age before they built another one a few dozen yards away and moved into that.

Finally, one Sunday morning, my mother put on a new dress and gloves and a hat. "Elizabeth," she said to me, "go find the children." I scurried around the yard and yelled out over the closest fields, though I knew before I started that I would find only the littlest ones, because it was fall and the pheasants and quail were in their prime and all my brothers had left before daybreak. My sisters were off hunting for field lettuce, which we called lamb's tongue. They wouldn't be back until evening.

I found only Marilyn and Junine and Jesse and took them into the kitchen.

My mother looked at us. "Where are the others?"

"Out," I said.

She folded her hands in her lap. I saw, all of a sudden, how old and rough and hard they looked against the new shiny material. I couldn't help glancing over to the net gloves that lay next to the little round bag on the kitchen table. And I thought how funny it was that a man's hands should wear lacy gloves.

"Well," my mother said, "they will have to find out later."

"Yes ma'am," I said. "Yes ma'am."

"I am going to get married," she said. "Mr. Benton is coming this morning. Now sweep the mud off the front steps."

Those were the words she used to tell us. Not "You're going to have a new father." No, she was a plainspoken woman. He wasn't our father and he would never be. She had simply found herself another man.

Later that morning, Mr. Benton drove up—in a borrowed carriage this time—and got my mother and handed her in like a lady. We all stayed very quiet and listened to the hoofs on the dirt road. You could hear them for quite a distance, because it was Sunday and everything was very quiet.

He was a hardworking man, Mr. Benton. He'd be up early, as early as we were, joking with us over breakfast. Then off he'd go to town and his job in the lumber mill. He kept his own horse in a lean-to he'd built at the side of the kitchen, a small chestnut mare, a bit on the elderly side and quite a bit slow, but even tempered and quiet.

He was a good, steady man, and things began changing. That spring, first thing I noticed, there was a hired man out with a mule plowing the east field. After that came a couple of Negroes planting.

One by one the fields filled up. Very slowly things got back to what they were when my father had lived with us. No, I guess they were better, a lot better. My father hadn't ever been one to make too much money out of the farm, he just managed to keep things going. With Mr. Benton it was different. He had a paying job and an all-year one, and whatever the farm made was extra. He had plans for that too. "Don't grow for yourself," he was always telling my mother. "Grow for money and buy what you need." That was a strange idea for us, because each of the farms around here always tried to be self-sufficient.

Mr. Benton just laughed at them. "With money," he would say, "nobody ever got hurt yet."

And I can see my mother sitting and looking at him, her full, smooth face coming alight with a kind of liveliness she didn't usually have.

They got the house painted, and my mother even started a little bed of cosmos along the new front porch, the first thing she'd ever done that was for beauty and pleasure and not for practical need. Then there was a young brown-and-white cow in the new pasture lot. My mother milked it herself twice a day and never let anyone else tend it. And each Sunday she and Mr. Benton went off to church, all dressed up, looking smug and fat and altogether satisfied with life. They even had their picture taken. That picture stood in a big gilt frame on the handkerchief table in the corner, the one that my grandfather had made years ago.

Then something happened, along one fall when the rains that bring in winter had started. (I don't remember the date exactly. But Mr. Benton and my mother had been married quite a few years. The three oldest boys had left home to find their own ways: Dan to try his hand at fishing, George to work in a department store at Leesville, and Mark all the way to St. Louis for a job with the telephone company. I was pretty near finished with school myself. So it must have been a good long time.)

This happened one evening, late evening. It had been pouring sheets all day, but along toward the time of sunset it slacked off, leaving just a light drizzle hanging like heavy smoke. The wet air was beginning to turn a funny fishy color, a sort of silver.

I was in the kitchen, helping with supper. I even remember that my mother was wearing a print dress and big freshly starched apron that crackled as she walked. Everybody was inside, too, in that sort of weather. There was a new kitten in the box just inside the door; you could hear it mewing.

My brother Jesse, who would have been nine or so, yelled out from the front room: "There's a man standing outside the fence, right in the road."

Nobody paid attention to him. So he stood in the doorway and repeated: "He's standing still right in the road, looking at the house."

"Well," Mr. Benton said, "maybe he wants to stay out in the rain."

Jesse hopped up and down on one foot. "He's got a big old sack over one shoulder."

"Bogeyman," my sister Marilyn said.

"Tramps," Mr. Benton said. "Must have got thrown off the cars over by Ellenville."

Nobody bothered to look; they were more interested in supper. Marilyn and Junine, feeding the kitten in the corner, giggled softly, their heads close together over some private joke.

I finished the dish of potatoes, scraped clean, and began to quarter them. Then I noticed my mother. She stood in front of the range and her hands held a wooden spoon crosswise in front of her, just the way I'd seen people hold whips when they stood and talked on the main street in town. She was staring straight ahead at the wall, where a line of pots hung. They were mostly new, and some of them were copper, burnished so that they winked at you. And some of them were iron, blackened and greasy, and some were porcelain, mottled like a wild bird's egg.

I watched, the point of my knife digging little holes in the potato I was supposed to be quartering. She didn't so much as move her fingers for the longest time. Then she said very quietly, so that you could hardly hear it over the giggles of the kids and the bubbling of the pots on the range: "Make him go."

Mr. Benton looked up, puzzled, as if he'd heard a far-off sound and was trying to place its direction.

My mother turned around and walked crisply over to her chair, the black painted rocker that stood right by the kitchen table. And she sat down in it.

She didn't look particularly excited. She folded her hands over her stomach and began to rock, tapping her heels on the ground. And everybody stopped. You could hear breathing, and the whimpering of the kitten.

It was like hearing the roof fall, this sort of quiet.

She repeated: "Make him go."

Mr. Benton was on his feet now, scrubbing at the side of his cheek.

"Don't let him stand out there and look, make him go."

For a couple of seconds Mr. Benton figured out what she was

telling him. Then he nodded to her and went out through the front door. My mother stayed in her chair, rocking the same sleepy rhythm. You'd have thought she was perfectly calm, if you hadn't seen her eyes. When we finally collected our wits and thought about going outside, there was just Mr. Benton standing in the front yard, looking off toward the east. The road was empty, what we could see of it in the mist.

Jesse rushed up to Mr. Benton. "Who was that?"

"Nobody," Mr. Benton said. "A tramp."

"Where'd he go?" Jesse said. "Where'd he go?"

He made a quick move to dodge by Mr. Benton and dash out the gate. I suppose he had some idea of following after the man. But Mr. Benton grabbed him by collar and belt and swung him off his feet, carrying him on one side, the way you'd carry a bag of meal. He gave a swing and tossed him up to the porch. Jesse landed like a cat, on all fours.

"Kids," Mr. Benton said, "get on inside."

And we went fast enough.

My mother was still rocking, quietly.

"He's gone," Mr. Benton said.

"Who was that?" I asked.

And Jesse, taking courage from my question, asked, "Did you know him?"

"No," Mr. Benton said.

My mother said nothing.

Mr. Benton said: "There was nothing to get scared about."

"He went away," my mother said.

"You said to send him off."

"Yes," my mother said, and you could see that her eyes were coming back to normal.

Mr. Benton sat down, slumped way down in his chair, solidly, so that he looked a part of it. It seemed to me that he had never looked quite that way before.

All that was a long time ago, of course. It worries me sometimes, comes back to worry me. I suppose we could have asked my mother about that tramp, but none of us did, not even when she was an old lady sitting in a wheelchair, long after Mr. Benton had died. Just an old lady sitting on her front porch looking out across a yard that she had carefully planted in flowers.

We didn't know. And we didn't ask. Sometimes we would think that it was. And sometimes we would think that it wasn't. I guess we liked it that way.

FREDERICK BARTON

BEACH BALLS, GOLD STARS, MAHATMA GANDHI, AND HELL

Memo

From: Richard A. Janus

To: The members of the doctoral committee, Warren J. Burden, chairperson, Jonathan B. Stein, Thomas W. Greene

In re: The dissertation of Richard Albert Janus

Date: July 4, 1976

I realize that when each of you picked up this manuscript you expected to find a doctoral thesis on King Philip's War. You probably became perplexed when you felt its brevity. Perhaps if your busy schedules had allowed you to notice my profoundly long face over the last year you might have suspected that my work was far from completion. But you didn't. I understand.

To remind those of you whose minds it might have slipped, King Philip's War was not an obscure engagement fought on behalf of a sixteenth-century Spanish monarch. Rather, it was an obscure engagement fought in 1675 and 1676 between the Puritans of New England and their Algonkian Indian neighbors. King Philip was an Algonkian Indian chief. But this is largely irrelevant because King Philip's War is the topic of a dissertation that I have decided not to write.

When my wife found me composing this note instead of another thesis chapter, she inquired, "Don't you like Indians anymore?"

"Sure, I still like Indians," I replied. And it was true. Though I hardly know any that are still alive. "Some of my best friends are Indians. It's just that I don't want to spend the rest of my life writing about one."

But my period of studying Indians has not been a waste. I have learned that Indians were not hopeless, helpless savages, who were the passive recipients of the historical course plotted for them by white people. Rather, I learned that Indians were active agents in their own history. Hence, my suspicions that I am not an Indian were confirmed. I am not an Indian because I am a hopeless, helpless recipient of the historical course plotted for me by white people. I have not been an active agent in my history. But then it comes as no real surprise to me that I am not an Indian. I never had the talents to be a good Indian. Only those, I was always told, to be a chief.

I am already twenty-eight years old and have recently been overwhelmed by the realization that in only twelve years I will be forty. My waistline has begun to spread. I occasionally find a gray hair or two. My ankles, which were always weak, now sprain themselves the moment I set foot on a basketball court. Sometimes they sprain themselves when I walk down the street. I've had to buy a pair of glasses, and soon, I guess, I will have to begin to wear them.

Even though I never had any particular ambition to be in the movies, I find it disturbing that men younger than myself are already stars. I can't name a specific actor right offhand, but that's because I seldom go to the movies anymore. I never have the time. Not writing my dissertation has proved very demanding, filling my leisure as thoroughly as it has my work hours.

Was Robert Redford already in the movies when he was younger than twenty-eight? I'm pretty sure that neither Jack Nicholson nor Dustin Hoffman was. Not in any good movies anyway. But there's no solace in that fact. Because without a doubt, long before either turned twenty-eight he was preparing to be in the movies.

I'm preparing to be an historian. Something I'd just as soon not be.

Exactly the same sort of trauma sweeps over me whenever I watch an athletic contest on television. I watch a lot of sports on TV. I have the time since I seldom go to the movies. All the young men shooting jump shots, stealing bases, and making diving one-handed pass receptions are under twenty-eight. Except for those who are older, of course, who are mostly baseball players. But again, there is hardly any solace for me in those who are older, because they all reached the major leagues before they turned twenty-eight. I'm already twenty-eight, and I haven't even reached the minor leagues.

Which is precisely why I am overwhelmed at the thought of being forty in only twelve years. Twelve years is nothing. Twelve years is yesterday when I was sixteen, playing basketball, dating girls, being embarrassed over having to wear braces, getting pimples, and preparing to be in college. And twelve years is tomorrow when I'll commence being old, preparing to die without being a movie star, or a professional baseball player, both of which I was always too mature ever to have planned on being.

Maturity. That, I think, is the nub of my problem. Always my strongest trait, maturity has exerted a powerful influence on my life. I have always had it, even when I was in elementary school. My teachers said I was among their most mature pupils. Usually they said I *was* their most mature pupil. I loved it. I strove for it. I competed with others for having more of it. On my report cards I always got checks in maturity. Of course, I always got checks in finishes what he starts too, but that's another story. If they had given grades, instead of just checks or blanks in maturity, I'm sure I would have gotten A's. I got A's in everything else.

I was so mature as a child that I never said I wanted to be a baseball player when I grew up. That was strange, since the only thing I wanted to be when I grew up was a baseball player. But if you told people that you wanted to be a baseball player when you grew up they never said, "Oh, what a mature young man you are." Instead, they said, "Oh, that's nice," which meant, Boy, that's dumb. So I told everyone I wanted to be a doctor when I grew up. When I told them that, they all said, "Oh, what a mature young man you are." I craved to hear it.

Of course, most everyone I told that I wanted to be a doctor was an adult. Every time I told a kid I wanted to be a doctor, the kid said, "Boy, are you dumb." That's because every kid in my neighborhood wanted to be a baseball player when he grew up.

On the first day of school in first grade my teacher gave each member of the class a dittoed drawing of a multipaneled ball. "Boys and girls," she said, holding one of the sheets neck-high, the top just at the bottom of her chin. "This is a beach ball. How many of you have been to the beach and seen a beach ball before? Raise your hands. Most of you. That's good. What colors are beach balls? Red. Yes. And yellow. Yes. And green. Sometimes they're green. Black? I don't think I've ever seen a black one. Yes and some are blue. Beach balls are lots of colors. They are any color you want to make them. And that's what I want you to do right now. Take out your crayons and color the balls any way that you like. When you're finished I'm going to put every one of them up on the board. So be careful and do a good job."

We all knew how to color, or thought we did, and so were not intimidated by the first task in our education. And for most of us it was our first exotic sniff of ditto fluid. But it wasn't easy. Not for me. Was it true that we could color the balls any color we'd like? Or should we try to make them look like the beach balls that we had actually seen? I wanted to color mine green and black. But I figured that what the teacher wanted was a ball colored like real ones. I traced the pale blue lines with my black crayon, then colored alternate panels red and yellow, smooth and light, all in the same direction, just as my mother had taught me.

The teacher thumbtacked the finished sheets to the bulletin board. "Oh, nice. Very good. Very, very good. Pretty." We felt wonderful. When all the sheets were attached in a long row to the strip of cork which stretched the width of the room above the blackboard, she turned to the class and announced. "These are so good I'm going to give every one of you a star. Standing before each ball she contemplated which star to select. Some papers she awarded green stars, others blue. For a few she selected gold stars.

My paper was at the far end. As she neared it, I became anxious. When she pasted a gold star on my work, I felt very wise for having colored it red and yellow instead of green and black. Thereafter, life for me was that beach ball, red and yellow and rolling downhill faster and faster.

In the fifth grade my class had square dancing twice a week on the school's asphalt playground. The blacktop was covered with basketball courts. Steel backboards and rims without nets towered over irregular lines that were painted in the days when the foul circle and three-second lane really looked like a keyhole. The courts were never used because no one in grade school knew how to play basketball and older kids in the neighborhood would not play on rims without nets.

Every Tuesday and Thursday the boys from all four fifth-grade classes lined up on one side of the blacktop, the girls on the other.

Some teacher turned on "Pomp and Circumstance" and the grand march began. We walked to the pavement's end, made crisp ninety-degree turns, marched toward each other and found our partners at the center. From week to week no one knew whose partner he or she would be. There were good partners like Pamela DeVane and Janice Bandeau, who had already begun to wear bras. We liked to feel the thin straps across their backs as we danced.

But we all lived in terror of the day we would be paired with Booga.

Booga's real name was Karen Mert. She was ugly and fat. Nobody liked her. Booga picked her nose. But that alone did not terrify us. Peter Cross, who was a Holy Roller, picked his nose and no one called him Booga. B. F. Johnson had named Karen that because, as he pointed out, "Karen Mert eats boogers."

Along with the rest, I too said, "Karen Mert eats boogers."

Then B. F. Johnson named her Booga and no one ever called her Karen again. Everyone said, "Booga eats boogers." No one except B. F. Johnson ever actually saw her eat boogers. But it must have been true because everyone said she did.

Booga's presence in the girls' line across from us made the grand march into Russian roulette. Whichever boy had to dance with her was teased until the next square-dancing day, when attention was shifted to someone else.

For weeks I escaped the fate of becoming Booga's square-dancing partner. But then one dismal day "Pomp and Circumstance" brought us together. I was terrified. But I was smart, and quickly fashioned a method to keep the booganess from rubbing off on me. I pulled my hands up inside my long-sleeve shirt, flexing my elbows and tucking my thumbs inside loosely made fists. I felt uncomfortable and must have looked like I was doing an imitation of Frankenstein. But my skin did not touch Booga's and I was saved.

Until a teacher who was not even my own spied my contortion. She was waiting for me outside my classroom after school that day. "Richie Janus," she said sternly.

"Yes ma'am."

"Why did you have your hands in your sleeves during square dancing today?"

"I dunno," I shrugged.

"It was because you were dancing with Karen Mert, wasn't it?"

No, it was because I was dancing with Booga. "Yes ma'am," I said.

"Do you call her names like the others?"

"No ma'am." She fixed me with a hard look. "Not where she can hear," I said.

"Richie, you know better than that. You shouldn't call her names at all. Have you ever thought of how that poor child feels?"

I hadn't. One side of me resented being scolded, argued it was Booga that ate boogers, not me. But another side suddenly understood something easily more frightening than having to square dance with the school outcast. In recognizing Karen Mert's horrible loneliness I was forced to see for the first time my own powerful capacity for evil. I stared around me at the walkways and courtyard of my school. I knew them like the rooms of my own house. But at the moment they seemed like some new place, foreign and hostile.

"I'm disappointed in you, Richie," concluded the teacher who was not even my own. "You're a nice boy, a leader. You're more mature than the other boys in your grade. You should set an example for them. Will you do that from now on?"

"Yes ma'am" I said.

After that all the boys in the fifth grade wore long-sleeve shirts on square-dancing days.

In the eighth grade I cheated on a Latin test. I was forced to do it, because I was afraid that without cheating I might not get a very high grade. This was sound reasoning in the finest tradition of Leo Durocher and Richard Nixon. I was so afraid that I didn't go to school the day the test was given. I got diarrhea instead.

Sickness served me well in the eighth grade. And it has served me well since. Diarrhea has continued to plague me. But I have also contracted every strain of flu, an ulcer it turned out I didn't have, sprained ankles, and a brief but acute case of the heartbreak of psoriasis.

At other times I have been well served by manslaughter. To provide funerals for me to attend coincident with the due dates of papers I couldn't write, or tests I wasn't prepared for, I have killed off all my aunts and uncles, some cousins (usually by suicide—I drove them to it), and my grandparents several times each. I have generally refrained from patricide, matricide, and siblingcide. But in desperate moments I have afflicted the members of my immediate family with automobile accidents, broken limbs, appendicitis, breast lumps, and operable hemorrhoids. In the eighth grade, though, I used diarrhea to stay home and thus avoid not getting a very high grade on my Latin test. But I still had to take the exam, of course, on the day I returned.

My teacher was an attractive, buxom thirty-five-year-old woman named Mrs. Brisket, who wore daring scoop-necked blouses every Wednesday because she belonged to a folk-dancing club that met that day. The puffy-sleeved, low-cut blouses were part of her uniform. Mrs. Brisket's breasts were wonderfully revealed on Wednesdays and the sight of their freckled creaminess never failed to launch me into a fantasy about fondling the breasts of the girl who sat next to me. At the time I had never actually fondled any breasts and didn't know exactly how one went about it. While I rotely conjugated Latin verbs, *amo, amas, amat,* I was off in a reverie thrusting my hands through the armholes of Judy Finas' sleeveless tops.

To make up my Latin test Mrs. Brisket sent me to the lunchroom, as I knew she would, so that I could take the exam undisturbed by the proceedings of the class. In the lunchroom I proceeded to copy all the answers, except those I couldn't find and which probably didn't exist, out of the Latin textbook I had augustly brought with me.

It was a Caesarean performance. By answering Mrs. Brisket's

ten-point bonus question correctly I made 103 percent. Which would have been terrific had not my friend Ronald Demart also made 103 percent. He too had been sick for the Latin test the day before. I don't know what was wrong with him. But whatever he had, it was terminal, and it killed him when the land mine he stepped on in the Mekong Delta blew him to bits.

Mrs. Brisket sent him with me to the cafeteria to take his exam. But Ronald Demart didn't bring his textbook along. When I saw that he was struggling, I offered him my test paper, and he copied all the answers off my sheet. Including those I had made up to the questions whose answers I couldn't find. Since these answers probably didn't exist, the ones I made up were wrong. Conspicuously so. When Mrs. Brisket discovered that my conspicuously wrong answers were identical to those of Ronald Demart, she became suspicious.

"Richie and Ronald," Mrs. Brisket said. "May I see the two of you after class."

"Yes ma'am," we answered.

"You boys made 103 percent on your tests," Mrs. Brisket said as the other members of the class filed from the room. Ronald and I smiled. "But I am concerned that you cheated." We stopped smiling. We looked down, hands in the front pockets of our jeans, lips aquiver, and shifted our weights nervously from one leg to the other.

"I . . . I don't know what happened." I stammered, searching in panic for some lie to acquit us.

"Never mind," Mrs. Brisket said. "I'm going to ignore what has happened this time. You are both nice boys. But this must never happen again. Do you understand?"

"Yes ma'am," we said.

"Ronald you may go. I want to speak to you further, Richie." When Ronald had gone she said to me, "I know what happened on that test. You let Ronald copy your test paper, didn't you?"

I felt like a quarterback when one of his linemen holds a defender to prevent him from being thrown for a loss. I knew that my escape was unjust, but I ran for daylight nonetheless. "Yes ma'am," I replied. I tried to infuse my voice with contrition and reluctance.

"Well, I knew that you were trying to do Ronald a favor. But it's no favor to help someone cheat. Cheaters never gain."

And she was right, of course, because Ronald Demart has since died.

When I was a junior in high school I developed a crush on my world history teacher. The other kids didn't like her, made fun of her mannerisms. Whenever in lecture she came to something that needed to be enclosed in quotation marks, she would raise her arms from the elbow to shoulder height, and with the index and middle fingers of each hand flick in the needed punctuation. And whenever someone asked her a question to which she did not know the answer, she would throw back her head, roll her eyes, and announce, "I really haven't the foggiest."

Almak Acen was a homely woman of Balkan parentage, whose pronounced overbite and tight-skinned face gave her visage a skeletal quality, like that in a child's Halloween mask, which is amusing rather than gruesome. She was short, abnormally thin and loose-jointed, tawny colored with black eyes that gleamed when she looked at me as if we were sharing some private joke. There was a pixieish quality in the herky-jerky strobe-light way she moved her tiny body so that she seemed never to be in motion at all but always to have just arrived.

Almak Acen had been educated at prestigious institutions, culminating with a master's degree in European history from Yale. She had the reputation at my high school of being an excessively hard grader. But I regarded her as absolutely fair. After all, she had given me an A for the first grading period. And more, she had actually made world history both interesting and challenging.

When the second grading period began Mrs. Acen announced to the class, "I am no longer going to award honors to students solely on the basis of superior performance on assigned work." She always referred to an A as honors. "Beginning this term, those of you who aspire to honors must submit a paper on some topic related to our course of study. It must be five to seven pages long, typed, and have its assertions documented by footnotes in the proper form. This is to be regarded as a research paper. Please do not confuse this project with a book report."

I did not confuse the assignment with a book report. When I decided to write a paper on Charles de Gaulle for our unit on France, I checked out *all* the books on de Gaulle in our school library. The shortest of these I read. Afterward I typed up seven pages summarizing what I remembered. Then the tricky part: using the index of the book I had read and the indexes of those I had not, I ran down enough page references to specific points in my paper to provide myself with a set of footnotes.

My conscience bothered me. I knew I was giving the impression that I had drawn material from several sources. On the other hand I saw no need to read any more than one of the books on Charles de Gaulle, since they all contained the same information. My conscience pangs eased when Mrs. Acen graded my paper A.

When the third term was getting under way, Mrs. Acen asked me to see her after school. Though it was an unusually cold day in early December, the stubborn greenery of New Orleans could still be seen through the yellow haze of late afternoon.

"Richie," she began when I entered her classroom.

"I like to be called Rich, ma'am," I said.

"Yes, of course, Rich," she said, smiling with pleasant acquiescence. "I wanted to talk to you about your de Gaulle paper."

Good God. Had she somehow detected that I had forged my footnotes from a bogus bibliography? I started to sweat, beads of perspiration breaking out first on my lower back just above my belt and spreading from there up toward my armpits. What was I going to do?

"Your paper was fine, I want you to understand. You presented your information on de Gaulle in a straightforward manner. And you write very well. You have an eye for dramatic detail. But the paper does not attain the level of sophistication of which you are capable."

Looking past her out the window as she said this, I watched the last rays of the afternoon sun shrink and disappear, merging the school's lawn and the asphalt parking lot behind it into one massive black shadow.

"Yes ma'am," I said, confused. I could just as well have said, No ma'am. Or nothing. I didn't really grasp what it was she was driving at. I wanted her approval. I did the paper for her. She had given me an A. What more was there?

"In your paper on de Gaulle you have provided only a narrative. A narrative, even one as good as this," she laid her hand outstretched on my paper, "is not adequate." She softened her tone, "You'll understand this fully with time, Rich. You see, in this paper you have posed no problems for yourself as an historian." Why *an* historian? Why not *a* historian? Besides I was neither. I was just a kid in high school who admired his teacher and wanted to please her.

"In the paper you will write for the present grading period, I want you to pose such a question or questions and then strive to answer them from your assessment of the historical data. In other words, I want analysis. You're a mature young man with a lot of potential. You're capable of this kind of work right now. I want to see you do it. Do you understand?"

"Yes ma'am," I said. I understood that it was going to be a lot more difficult in the future to get an A in world history.

"Good," she concluded. "I will be willing to help you in any way that I can, Rich. Never hesitate to ask me or stop by after school." I thought she was beautiful, sitting intense in her dark classroom, which she seemed not to notice was growing chilly.

"I won't," I promised as I turned to leave.

"It has grown quite dark during our talk hasn't it?" she said, evidently noticing for the first time. "Could you turn on the lights on your way out?"

"Yes ma'am," I said, but when I got to the door I had trouble locating the switch. I turned back to her for help. She was sitting motionless, staring into the dimness. It had gotten so dark that I could scarcely distinguish the tattered red history textbook from the green dictionary on her desk. She pointed out the switch and I flicked it on, bathing Almak Acen in the strangeness of the fluorescent light. Then I passed through the doorway into the darkened hall.

I thought I was in love with her.

And so I was determined to write for her a sophisticated paper more in line with my capabilities. A paper which would pose some question or questions and suggest answers based upon my unique analysis of the historical data.

I decided to write my paper on Mahatma Gandhi. We were studying India that term in a unit on Asia. My father suggested the idea. He had become a supporter of Martin Luther King and was interested in Gandhi's thinking on the politics of civil disobedience. He offered to buy me a book on Gandhi that he was anxious to read.

One Saturday he took me to the bookstore of the small Baptist college where he taught. We quickly found the Gandhi book. Father lingered to leaf through books by or about Martin Luther King. Neither one of us foresaw that in less than four years both of us would be in Chicago. I with long hair in the streets outside the Democratic National Convention. And he, after having lost his job over his stance on the race issue, with no prospects, in a furnished bachelor apartment without dishes save for one empty ice-cream container from which he drank water and into which he poured his Scotch. And that Martin Luther King would be dead.

To research my paper I checked out all the books on Gandhi, from the school library and from the public library as well. Five or six in all. I didn't read any of them. Instead I read the book that father had bought me.

I posed a question for myself. I figured one was sufficient for an eleventh grader. Was Mahatma Gandhi's leadership crucial to the Indian independence movement? Subscribing to the great-man theory of history, which has since gone out of fashion, I answered yes. Of course, I was careful to argue that only the particular climate of British foreign policy in the post–World War II period would have allowed the movement to succeed, based as it was on the politics of pacifism. In other words, the question I asked, I begged. But the begging comprised an ambitiously long 12 pages. Using the technique I had mastered earlier, I fashioned a set of footnotes.

I titled the paper "Mohandas K. Gandhi: Enigma of the East." Without realizing it I had adopted the common style for academic titles. With colons. Almak Acen loved it.

"This is just what I was looking for," she told me. "It is truly superior work. It is well researched, well organized, and well written. Rich, you have a real future as an historian." And she was right of course. I had a real future as an historian who writes an ambitious twelve-page prospectus but never a dissertation.

Reading about the career of Mahatma Gandhi had an impact on me that transcended my desire to succeed in world history. If my fundamentalist religious training was correct then Gandhi must have gone to hell. I couldn't bear the thought. Not when I considered all the creeps that had probably crowded into heaven on the basis of deathbed conversions.

I brought the issue up for consideration in my Sunday-school class. My teacher had urged us to bring up any matter which we found troubling. Ned Marasmus was a wiry man with an unwieldy shock of brown hair. A big-time building contractor when he wasn't teaching Sunday school, he specialized in erecting entire prefabricated subdivisions into which, among others, black people were not allowed to move. "Don't let Satan get you into a game of one on one," he warned. "Bring your troubles here to the house of the Lord where your brothers in Christ can help you give old Satan the beating of his life."

"Mr. Marasmus," I asked, "do you think that Mahatma Gandhi went to hell?"

"Gandhi? The Indian fella? He wasn't a Christian, was he?"

"No."

"Well, then, Rich, what do you think?"

"I think Gandhi lived a Christlike life."

"But you remember Rich that in John 3:16 the Scripture quotes Jesus as saying, 'Whosoever believeth in me shall not perish, but have everlasting life.'"

I mulled this over a moment and then replied, "Yes sir. But Jesus didn't say whosoever does not believeth in me *shall* perish and have *not* everlasting life." Mr. Marasmus was astounded.

"See here now," he said, biting off each word. "None cometh unto the Father but by *me*. This Gandhi was no Christian. He was a socialist or something. And you better make no mistake about it, Richard Janus, Mahatma Gandhi went to hell. I don't care how he lived or how you think he lived. He went to hell. Do you understand?"

"No sir," I said. "I don't."

But that moment of confrontation with Ned Marasmus was uncharacteristic. It didn't last long enough. It happened too long ago.

I went north to college. I demonstrated against the war, of course. But I never got to find out whether I'd really have gone to jail rather than surrender to the draft.

I majored in history, studied hard, and got good grades. I was praised and encouraged. My senior year I won a fellowship for graduate study. Two years later, when the ligaments in my left ankle gave way and the draft was thwarted, I enrolled at UCLA to study social history.

That was four years ago. In the time since I've been here I've finished my course work, passed my written and oral exams, researched my dissertation. You have rewarded me with a teaching fellowship, for which I am very grateful.

This year I served on the appointments committee. The "search committee," it is generally called. The search committee's mission is to select nominees for vacant positions in the department, of which there are frightfully too few. The nation may or may not be heading for depression, but the university teaching profession is already there. I am one of the depressed.

I was selected as the graduate representative on the search committee because, of all the students considered, I was judged the brightest. And the best. "The most mature of our young scholars."

I felt honored and was eager to serve. I spent all my Christmas vacation reading the doctoral dissertations of this year's hopefuls, documents which, in every case, were intended as the bases for future books. My service on the search committee did entail a bit of sacrifice. I gave up plans to visit back home. Just as I had similar ones the summer prior. And the Christmas before that. In order to spend my vacation time arduously not working on my own dissertation, which I intended as the basis of a future book. Not working on my dissertation is full-time work. If I allowed myself to, I could probably spend the rest of my life doing it.

Working with the search committee gave me the opportunity to gauge the quality of theses which had actually been completed. It provided me with a standard by which to judge my own work. It offered me the chance to sit as nearly equal with men (not women) who had really become university professors and further demonstrate to them my depth and breadth and strength of mind. It allowed me to impress them with my incisiveness and my wit and with my dedication to our mutual craft, which it seems I do not possess.

To my delight I found that the strenuous work of the search committee still enabled me not to work on my own dissertation. And to do so with more ease, far greater efficiency, and considerably less guilt.

And I savored every implication that I was in the processes of becoming, that I was almost, that one day soon I would surely be, "one of us."

Until it frightened me. As I came to understand that becoming "one of us" required that I finish not writing my dissertation and begin immediately not revising it for publication. And after that a whole long life of not churning out suggestive articles, and not embarking on stimulating new research projects which developed naturally from leads uncovered in projects past. I had not yet made it in the movies, nor become a baseball player, but I was just a finished dissertation from becoming "one of us" when I realized that becoming "one of us" required that I become an historian, something I was rather good at, something that had earned me a measure of praise and even more encouragement, but something, finally, I had never wanted to become.

After guiltlessly reading away my Christmas vacation, immersed in the scholarship of bright, mature young men and women who made subtle distinctions on issues I cared not one whit about, I joined the professors for a crucial meeting of our committee. The field of candidates for the year's three vacancies was to be winnowed, and nominees were to be chosen.

I was prepared to make my contribution, for I had been able to identify the strongest candidate for each position. For our regular tenure-ladder appointments these were bright, mature young men (not women) who used the language with greater precision than their competitors, who made the subtlest distinction of issues I cared not one whit about, whose scholarship was the most rigorous. These were men, I determined, like myself.

The candidates the committee rejected were dismissed most often as "pedestrian." For God's sake run, don't walk. For some, however, was reserved the sop "interesting but small; we need a man of scope, of vision." On the other hand a few were rejected as "too broad; the candidate has not demonstrated his abilities to do in-depth scholarship." And for a few the committee offered the commendation "shows potential, but not presently of our caliber." This last was awarded to several candidates who might ultimately emerge as "one of us" whether we liked it or not.

Finally, having selected the best and brightest candidates for each of our regular positions, we set a date for each to come to campus for an interview. We then turned our attention to the task of selecting a nominee for a one-year replacement position in nineteenth-century intellectual history. Richard Boeotian was tenured in the position but had won a Guggenheim Fellowship to finance his stimulating new research in Boston which had developed naturally from leads uncovered in his most recent book, *Bulls in a Chinashop: Fabian Socialism Among the Boston Brahmins*. As you know, Professor Boeotian is hoping that the Guggenheim will pave the way for a new book tentatively titled *Bulls in a Closed Shop: Unionism Among the Boston Brahmins.*

The candidates to replace Professor Boeotian had come down to two, a fifty-four-year-old male Ph.D. who had finished his degree at Vanderbilt in the fifties and a twenty-seven-year-old female Ph.D. who had just finished her degree at Yale. The female candidate had yet to publish. But she had gone to a more prestigious school, was fresher, likely more up-to-date, and female. The male candidate was male; he had published a book a decade ago but nothing since. And he was old.

Professor Boeotian chaired the committee. He opened the discussion. "I think we should go with the girl. She's female. As I am sure all of you realize, we're under rather heavy pressure to hire some more of that persuasion. This position gives us the opportunity to do so without a lasting commitment. In addition, she's fresher, likely more up-to-date, and as I say female. Shall we vote?" I raised my hand. "Yes, Rich. Do you have something to add? I'm glad to see that as our graduate representative you have come to participate and not merely observe. That is just the sort of input we need. Go ahead."

"Well," I said, "I would just like to raise a human consideration, operating on the assumption that despite our different areas of expertise we all hold human concerns in common. Mr. Jobe's credentials are really quite sound. Rather nearly the equal of Ms. Sexton's, in my opinion. If you will bear with me I'd like to advance an argument in behalf of his candidacy. As his cover letter indicates he lost a tenured spot in the late sixties because of personal problems we need not review. He has since been teaching on a succession of temporary appointments. He has a family to support. His oldest child begins college next fall. Mr. Jobe has over twenty years of teaching experience. He desperately needs a job. I grant that Ms. Sexton probably has more scholarly potential because of her age if nothing more. But we are discussing here a one-year replacement position only. The key then is teaching and I suggest we give the job to Mr. Jobe based on his experience. And based upon the fact that he needs the job so much more. You will note that Ms. Sexton has been offered a fellowship next year to revise her dissertation for publication. She won't make much money on the fellowship, of course, but she will have an income. If we don't hire Mr. Jobe, I'm afraid he won't."

"Your analysis of departmental hiring policy is rather negative, Mr. Janus," Boeotian responded indignantly. "And frankly, I thought that young fellows like yourself were sympathetic to women's lib."

"I certainly am in sympathy with the women's movement, but tokenism isn't . . ."

"Look, Rich," Harold Lockhart interrupted with a brisk nod meant to look understanding. "I share your concern for Mr. Jobe, but in matters of hiring, just as in matters of promotion, we simply cannot take personal considerations into account. You'll understand that with time, I suspect."

Ms. Sexton was nominated.

The committee did not meet again until the nominees for the regular positions came to campus to be interviewed. The first to come was MacDonald Ford, the candidate for our position in late-nineteenth-century social history. He was from Harvard and had just turned 29. Like mine, his hair was long. But his was dirty and pushed straight back from his face. There was a studied carelessness about MacDonald Ford. Probably he was too busy to take extra time for grooming, his mind too filled with ponderous reflection on issues I cared not one whit about.

The day of the interview he wore a plaid sport coat and gray trousers. His narrow striped tie had a crooked knot which he hadn't bothered to pull snug against his neck. Had he not been from Harvard, we would perhaps have thought him sloppy. MacDonald Ford was a chain smoker. He lit up even during meals, shrouding himself in a perpetual gray fog. And yet, he impressed us all as completely calm. He had that marvelous Boston accent in which he bantered with wit, thrusted with rapierlike sharpness, parried with chivalry. His voice dripped with tradition and money.

MacDonald Ford impressed us all with his depth and breadth and strength of mind. He answered questions with confidence and occasionally with respectful winsome levity. Questions which neither he, nor anyone, including the asker, understood. Questions designed to display the intelligence of the asker rather than to elicit information from the respondent. And MacDonald Ford had plans for future research projects which developed naturally from leads uncovered in his dissertation. MacDonald Ford was unquestionably "one of us."

"He's one of us," Harold Lockhart proclaimed to the members of the committee when MacDonald Ford's interview was over. "I am thoroughly impressed with the candidate's depth and breadth and strength of mind. Unquestionably he's one of us." This made me uncomfortable. I was not a professor. I had not yet finished not writing my dissertation. "His research is brilliant. He has already published not one but two articles in the *Journal of American History*. And Knopf, no less, has contracted to take his dissertation with only the most minor revisions." MacDonald Ford's thesis was titled *The Blue Movement: An Examination of the Philadelphia Police Force as a Vehicle for Social Mobility, 1880–1890*. "And leads uncovered in this project have suggested to him the stimulating new research needed on Philadelphia firemen. Is there any question that this young man is one of us?" Lockhart's fiery eyes moved from face to face seeking contact with each member of the committee. I stared at my sheaf of notes. I did not know whether his gaze would pass me by or linger on me as it did on the others. I did not want to find out.

Harold Lockhart was an enigma. I suspected him at times of being deliberately inscrutable. A short, balding, nervous man in his midforties, he was aggressively sympathetic to the plight of minorities, poor people, and women. He displayed this concern in his scholarly work, which he termed the history of the inarticulate.

And in his politics, which were Marxist. And in his life-style, which was nonmonogamous. And in his dress, which was the garb of a counterculture that has all but ceased to exist, preserved primarily in the formaldehydic halls of academe.

Harold Lockhart had always been friendly to me, in a reserved professional sort of way. Something about me struck a responsive chord. But like most students I regarded him as distant and somewhat absentminded. Since he was normally reticent, this day's animation was extraordinary. Harold Lockhart was a fidgeter. Time and time again he reached inside his faded jeans and pulled from the pocket a gold watch which he opened with an upward flick of his thumb and closed immediately with a snap. In the intervals between checking his watch Harold Lockhart drummed his fingers. Perhaps he was trying to count the precious seconds he was losing from his research projects. But for the short moment after his speech about MacDonald Ford, he was calm, tranquilized that he had found that rare person who was unquestionably "one of us."

The second scholar to come for an interview was Bryan Jennings. He was the candidate for our position in American Indian history. The committee was not altogether favorably disposed to Bryan Jennings' application despite ultimately deciding to interview him. It was not enthusiastic because Bryan Jennings had gotten his Ph.D. at the University of Nebraska at Omaha. And his dissertation, *James Logan and the Delaware Walking Purchase,* was sought for publication not by Knopf or Norton or Oxford but only by the University of Oklahoma Press, and they were requiring substantial revisions.

I took a special interest in Bryan Jennings' candidacy. He was in my field and thought about issues I cared at least one whit about. He too was young, about my age. He had stylishly long, curly black hair which hid his ears and the temples of his wire-rim glasses, which he seemed to have difficulty keeping properly in place. The day of his interview Bryan Jennings wore a brown corduroy sport coat and plaid pants and his broad striped tie was pulled snug at the neck. Unlike MacDonald Ford, he did not smoke. Unlike MacDonald Ford, his hand shook when he talked, and his voice which contained the slightest hint of a lisp, cracked occasionally when with neither confidence nor wit he sought to answer questions that neither he, nor anyone, including the asker, understood. Sadly, he had not developed a single new research project from leads uncovered in his dissertation. Bryan Jennings failed to impress the committee with his breadth and depth and strength of mind despite the fact that he was the best and brightest of the applicants for our job.

Hence, in the interval between the morning interview and the afternoon committee session I was asked to accompany Bryan Jennings to lunch. Harold Lockhart had taken MacDonald Ford to lunch.

"This is really an exciting place," Bryan Jennings enthused to me over his poor-boy sandwich. "Such a stimulating intellectual community. Such a challenging group of scholars to work with. You know I read that piece Harold Lockhart did for the *William and Mary Quarterly* on the Boston working class. It was such a nice piece. Quite useful for my own work, interestingly. Who better qualified for inclusion among the inarticulate than the American Indian? You must really love it here."

"Of course," I said. Of course. But I had to take the luster off. "There are a lot of bright people here. But I'm not so sure I'd term the place a community. The department is riddled with political divisions and personal jealousies. As David Halberstam might say, the brightest people aren't always the best."

"Of course," Bryan Jennings said. Of course. "But that is true wherever you are. I can't imagine many places I'd rather work than here. This school is at the cutting edge of the important work in social history." Bryan Jennings' glasses had slid down to the end of his nose. He took them off and ran a hand over his face and up through his curly hair. Then looking skyward in an unabashedly prayerful way, he said "This is really the place for me. Among men who are genuinely committed to studying the forgotten man, women, the poor man, Indians, the common man."

Neither of us spoke for a moment after that. Finally I said,

"How did you get into history? I mean, did you grow up planning on becoming an historian?"

"Oh no. When I started college I had no idea what I wanted to do. Just drifted. For a time I thought I might become a male nurse. I would have thought about medicine, but I figured out early on I could never get into medical school."

"Some history professor along the way turn you on?"

"Not at all. I was always a very poor student. My undergraduate professors would be shocked that I'm even being interviewed for a job at UCLA. My senior year in college I read *Black Elk Speaks*. I was fascinated by the world of Indian thought. I had to understand it. I've been trying ever since."

"Why did you choose to do your graduate work at Omaha?"

Bryan Jennings laughed. "Hell, it was the only school I could get into. They don't even have an Indian historian there. I had to learn the field by myself."

"Well, I'd say you've done a pretty good job of it."

"That's nice of you to say. But I imagine that you've far more potential in this profession than I. I envy you."

"You shouldn't," I said. "For more reasons than just one, but for starters I could point out that you're being interviewed for a job you really want today. While I'm just passing the time in the California sun."

"He just isn't one of us," Harold Lockhart said that afternoon when the search committee convened. He reached in his jeans to find the pocket watch, promptly opened it with an upward flick of his thumb, and just as promptly closed it with a snap.

"Well, his thesis shows potential," Richard Boeotian said. "But I was awfully disappointed with his answers to our queries. Sadly, he has not developed a single stimulating new research project from leads uncovered in his dissertation."

"Really, Dick," Charles Mollusk, our diplomatic historian said. "I find his work irredeemably pedestrian. He did his work at Omaha? What kind of training can he have gotten? In my mind, without a doubt, he isn't sound enough for this department."

"He just isn't one of us," Harold Lockhart concluded, drumming his fingers on the table. "And I cannot vote to recommend his appointment. The American Indian field is an important one. But it is a young field. If Bryan Jennings is the best and brightest Ph.D. the field has to offer at the present time, then I think we should wait until the field produces a better one. And I think this very room may contain the man we're looking for." He reached over and drummed his fingers on my knee. "This young gentleman," he continued, meaning me, "*is* one of us. He is at work on a highly promising dissertation on King Philip's War, which for those of you who might not know was not named for a sixteenth-century Spanish monarch, ha ha. I move we award the position to Richard Janus on an interim basis and that once he completes his thesis we consider him for the regular appointment."

But I was not one of them. For though I had not yet found my way from Westwood to the bluffs over the Pacific at the western end of Wilshire, I was not at work on a highly promising dissertation on King Philip's war or anything else.

I could see the darkness outside the windows. Professor Boeotian asked me to wait in the hall while the committee considered Lockhart's proposal. I gathered my blasphemous notes and walked into the abandoned corridor. I walked toward the exit sign at the head of the stairway, opened the door and started down.

I had been at UCLA for four years. In all that time of passing through the Sculpture Garden I had never paused to look at the statues. It was time. I came out of the history building and into the moonlight. For a long time I looked at Francisco Zuñiga's *Desmudo Reclinada*. And then at Henry Lauren's *Esquisse D'Automne*. I liked Jacques Lipchitz' *The Song of Vowels*. My favorites were Gaston Lachaise's *Standing Woman* and Auguste Rodin's *The Walking Man*.

Leaving the Sculpture Garden I boarded the bus to return to my apartment in Santa Monica. Through Westwood and then out Wilshire. Past the Brentwood Twins at Twenty-Sixth Street. *The Sailor Who Fell from Grace with the Sea* was in Cinema One. In Cinema Two was *Bound for Glory*. Past the porno house where *Beyond*

Fulfillment was playing. Past Yale Street. Past Harvard Street and Princeton and Berkeley.

I was swallowed by the fog.

But it is noon now and the fog has lifted. I have found my way to the western end of Wilshire where I sit at a picnic table finishing this note. The fog will return, I know. Perhaps as early as tomorrow. But today, with a single turn of my head I can see from Palos Verdes to Point Dume, from Ocean Boulevard to Catalina and beyond.

Today I say to all of you, no sir. No sir. I will not finish my dissertation. I do not want your job in Indian history. It should go to Bryan Jennings. He deserves it, not I. No sir. Thank you.

The winter sun is throwing a swathe on the green water of the Pacific that extends as far as I can see. Above, sea gulls float, effortlessly, endlessly.

From the fence at the edge of the bluff I can look down on the almost abandoned beach. To the north begins a group of houses for the rich, blocking access to the sea. Just this side is a bike path ending in a loop, beginning its southward course. Beyond some red, white, and blue trash cans starts the vast expanse of sand covered with the footprints of children. Walking aimlessly is a lone black dog. Beyond the row of empty lifeguard stations, where the sand is wet and firm, two figures jog toward each other, become for a moment one, and move forever away. At the water's edge a young man is about to go for a swim.

On the fence there is a faded green sign that reads Notice: Bluff Subject to Slides. Use At Your Own Risk. With that counsel I sit for a moment on a concrete bench. On its back a loving wife has had inscribed:

In the
Evening
Of his life
John P. Kite
Used to

Come each day
To sit in this spot
And
Watch the sun set
Over the
Ocean

In his way Mr. Kite has challenged the world. And in his honor, I must say, no sir, no thank you.

CARL WOOTON

THE AUCTIONEER

Laura played the piano. Her fingers followed the notes in the *Elementary Piano for Adults: Book II,* and the sounds of a Mozart minuet lifted through the open window and down to where I sat on the ground beside the rose bushes. I pulled nut grass from around the Queen Elizabeth—a full, pink rose—and listened to her playing the minuet. It was delicate, balanced, ordered. She played about halfway through it, and her fingers stumbled. She started over. She stumbled again, and I heard the sound of the cover closing over the keys. For a moment I imagined her sitting there, looking at, maybe running her fingers along the grain of the polished wood. I figured she was remembering I had promised nothing would happen to the piano. But she could have been remembering I had made lots of other promises, too.

Laura called, "Mark! Mark!"

I called back, "Out here, in the yard."

As soon as I said it, she was standing in the open window looking out at the yard.

"What time is it?"

I looked at my watch.

"Four-thirty and a little bit," I said.

From *Sun Dog,* V (1984), 58–66. Reprinted by permission.

"He's late," she said.

"I know."

"Where is he?"

"I don't know."

I tried to say it carefully. I didn't want to say it the wrong way, with the wrong tone. That's how most of our arguments started. I'd say something, anything, and she'd hear something I didn't know I was saying. She said I did the same thing to her sometimes.

I said, "He'll be here."

She said, "He promised four o'clock."

"You want to come outside and wait?"

She said, "No," and moved away from the window and did not hear me yell, "Ouch!"

A dark spot formed on my thumb where I had stuck it on a thorn. Roses are not only beautiful. I stood up and squeezed the wound to make it bleed. My legs were stiff from squatting to pull grass and weeds from the flower beds. I walked from the side of the house that sheltered the roses through the shade of the red oak that stood next to the driveway. A car turned the corner, and I looked to see if it was him. It sped past. The telephone rang in the house, and in a minute Laura was standing in the window. I stepped out from behind the tree so she could find me.

"It was him. He called. He said he'll be here in ten minutes."

"Okay," I said.

"Do you want me to make some coffee?"

"If you'd like."

"Do you think I should?"

I said, "It's not necessary."

Another car turned the corner. It wasn't him, and when I looked back to the house, she was gone again from the window. The sun had angled below the roof, and the front yard was all shade. I walked to the end of the driveway and along the street in front of the house. It was not a spectacular house, but it was bigger than any other I had ever lived in. I had liked to stroll the street at night and see the house in shadows from the streetlamp and see the lights in the windows and hear music—even elementary Mozart—coming through the windows. When I was a kid, I would have thought it a spectacular house. The sky was clear, and the air was cool with the sun behind the house and with the hint of the first real front about to come in and drive the heat back across the swamps and into the Gulf, at least for a little while. I walked in front of the house and looked at it and tried not to remember the promises I had made about the house.

Another car turned the corner and moved slowly along the street. There were two men in the car. We were expecting only one, but the passenger pointed toward the mailbox at the street with the name and number—GEORGE 1206—stenciled on it. The driver nodded and turned into the driveway. I couldn't tell whether he saw me or not, until we were shaking hands beside the car.

He said, "You're Mr. George."

"Yes."

"Arthur Romero," he said.

He was tall and thin. He combed his dark hair straight back and he wore a thin moustache. He wore a short-sleeved sport shirt, open at the collar, dark slacks, the old-fashioned kind with pleats in the front and a razor crease all the way down to the shoes. His shoes were wing tips, brown-and-white with the little holes punched in the leather, just like my daddy wore for dressing up in the fifties. His handshake was firmer than it needed to be, and he held it too long, and smiled. I pulled loose from his grip.

Romero pointed across the top of his car and said, "This is my assistant."

A young man—maybe he was twenty—stood on the other side of the car and seemed to be looking at some point ten or twenty feet above my head. I waited for one of them to speak a name, but neither one did.

I said, "Hello."

Romero's assistant answered, "Right!" and stepped toward the front of the car. He carried a clipboard with several sheets of paper held to it. He was blond, and he wore a Superman T-shirt.

We walked up the driveway toward the carport. Romero and I walked in front, and the young man fell in behind us. We went into the house through the utility room and into the kitchen. I took them in that way because my lawyer had said the auctioneer probably would start in the kitchen. The porcelain coffee pot stood in a pan of water set on a low fire on the stove. Laura was not there.

I said, "Excuse me. I'll find my wife."

Neither of them replied, and I went through the house to find Laura. I had supposed she was in the back, in the bedroom or the bathroom. She was not. I came back down the hall and looked in the living room. She was there, sitting in the chair with the cane back and the oak arms that still had a little of the original varnish on them. The chair and a matching sofa were nearly eighty years old, family pieces from Laura's Aunt Emily.

I said, "They're here."

"They?"

"He brought an assistant."

"Oh."

She ran a fingernail along the arm of the chair. It made a thin blond line in the varnish.

I said, "I see you made coffee."

"Yes."

"They're waiting."

"I'm coming. I didn't put out any cups."

"I'll get them," I said.

"Use the blue ones."

"Are you sure?"

"Yes!"

"Okay. They're waiting."

"I'll just be a minute," she said.

The auctioneer and his assistant were still standing in the kitchen. Romero leaned with one hand on the table and looked around. I went to the cabinet where Laura kept the cups.

Romero said, "Lived here long?"

I said, "Six years and a little."

"Nice house."

"We like it."

I took four blue cups from the cabinet. They were mugs, and

Laura hated them. They were painted a glossy blue on the outside and were white on the inside. The blue was wearing off around the rim. The handle barely had room for a finger. She had always said they were ugly. I had never noticed that. I set them in a row on the cabinet and set the spoons and the bowls with the artificial creamer and the sugar beside them. Laura came into the room.

Romero said, "Mrs. George."

He reached out to take her hand, the same he would if she were another man. She held her right hand to his, and the muscles in her face went rigid at the touch.

"This is my assistant," he said.

The blond young man with the Superman T-shirt grinned. Laura stared at him for a moment, as though she wondered how he had come so suddenly to be there. I realized she had not even seen the assistant until Romero mentioned him.

"Well, we might as well get on with it," Romero said.

"Yes. Might as well," I said.

"Let's get on with it," Laura said.

Romero held out a hand toward the assistant. Nothing happened. The assistant was looking out a window into the backyard. Our neighbor's dog was in heat, and she was in our backyard surrounded by a half dozen males. The assistant made a noise and Romero snapped his fingers—crack! crack!—twice. The assistant jerked away from the window, saw Romero's extended hand, and gave him the clipboard.

"Right!" the assistant said.

Romero took the clipboard and turned toward us. He held it to let us see the paper on top. It was a legal-size sheet with lines dividing it into four columns. He pointed to the sheet as he explained his procedures.

"I'm going to make a list of all your possessions that the law says are subject to auction in the bankruptcy."

He looked at us. His face and voice were without expression, like he was doing the one thing that bored him the most.

He said, "That means I do not list the things excluded by the law. We cannot take—"

I felt Laura flinch at *take.* I reached for her arm. I wanted to comfort her, to reassure her. It was going to be all right. She pried at my fingers and removed my hand.

"—dishes, cooking utensils, the stove, refrigerator, or washing machine—although we get the dryer—children's toys, clothes, except luxury items like a fur coat—"

I laughed. The room was getting warm. No one seemed to have heard me.

"—bed linens and other things considered necessary."

Laura said, "What about musical instruments?"

He said, "Whose are they?"

"They're for the children," I said.

The lawyer had explained that nothing belonging to the children could be auctioned.

Romero said, "Where are they?"

I said, "At their grandmother's. We thought it would be easier if they weren't here."

He said, "The instruments. Where are they?"

"Oh," I said.

"In a different room," Laura said.

"So long as they're taking lessons on them, it's all right," Romero said.

I said, "They're taking lessons," and wondered if I was going to have to prove it.

"They're all right, then. If that explains everything, I better get started. I'm going to list things and assign a value to them. The value will be what I believe I can get at the auction. For example, is this the only table and chairs you have?"

I said, "No, there's another set in the dining room."

We maneuvered around the chrome-and-formica table in the kitchen toward the extra-wide space that opened into the dining room. Romero handed the clipboard back to his assistant and stood in the passageway and looked back and forth at the two tables and sets of chairs. The dining room set was made of wood, with a polished walnut finish and ladder-back chairs.

Romero said, "I usually let folks keep the better one. So, I'll call that one table, yellow, twenty dollars, with four matching chairs, five dollars each."

The assistant had produced a ball-point pen from somewhere and wrote on the paper as Romero talked. They moved back into the kitchen. Romero opened a cabinet door, then another. He turned to Laura.

"You have any electrical things, like blenders or mixers?"

Laura pointed toward a cabinet.

"In there," she said, and she crossed over to the other side of the cabinet area and closed the doors Romero had left open.

The kitchen took less than ten minutes, the utility room hardly five. Laura and I followed them into the den. I was sweating. Romero's voice recited what he saw: television, sofa, chair, recliner, lamps. The inflections never varied. The assistant never responded. He just wrote the quantity, the description, and the appraisal in the proper columns.

I watched Laura. A couple of times I thought I saw her bottom lip quiver. I wondered if she had felt the same emotions I felt when the auctioneer's shapeless voice named objects I had hardly noticed before.

When they finished in the den, Laura said, "I dripped some coffee just before you came."

Romero said, "Pardon?"

She said, "Would you like some coffee?"

"Sounds good," he said.

"It's in the kitchen."

And we all went back into the kitchen where the blue cups and the sugar and the artificial creamer were lined up on the counter. The counter was actually a little bar that extended from the wall and divided the working area from the table area. There were four high stools—which Romero had listed—against the counter, but Romero ignored them and stood. The assistant pulled one of the stools toward him until he looked up at Romero's face. He replaced the stool against the counter and stood beside the auctioneer.

Laura poured the coffee, and her hand trembled. The assistant put mounds of sugar and creamer in his coffee. Romero took just a little sugar and sipped. Laura fixed hers and held her cup in both hands to keep her trembling from showing. I burned my tongue.

Romero said, "What happened?"

I looked at him. I looked at Laura. I didn't know whether he was talking to me, or what he was asking about.

He said, "Wasn't there enough business?"

He was talking to me. He wanted to know what happened. I felt sarcastic. I almost asked if he wanted the explanation of how I—we—went bankrupt in twenty-five words or less. *He* wanted to know what happened. Bad management. Mine. Desperation. Good money after bad. Ours and the bank's. My ears rang. I felt flushed.

I said, "Too many mistakes."

My voice came from a distance, like a voice spreading out across water. I looked at the assistant in the Superman T-shirt and wondered if he had ever tried to fly. I would have bet he had. I heard Romero's voice coming back across the counter.

"Too bad," he said.

I agreed with him. He sipped his coffee and seemed to study his cup. He looked at Laura.

"A pretty cup," he said.

"That's all that's left, those four," she said.

"There were eight," I said.

"They were a gift," she said.

Romero sipped again. The assistant took a couple of large swallows, emptying his cup, and set it on the counter.

"Right!" he said.

Romero said, "A pretty cup," and set his on the counter.

It was an ugly cup. Its finger hole wasn't big enough. The blue was too glossy and worn off around the rim. Ugly.

"Guess we should finish," Romero said.

Laura took the cups and put them in the sink. I led the way through the den and down the hall to the bedrooms. Laura did not follow. Romero and his assistant went quickly through the children's bedrooms, listing almost nothing. In our bedroom there were only a couple of lamps and an occasional table that he listed. I looked for Laura as we went from room to room, and I figured she was cleaning up the coffee things. But it didn't take long to wash four ugly blue cups.

Romero said, "Is this all there is?"

I said, "No. There's still the living room."

I wanted to be thorough. The lawyers had warned us to be thorough, to make certain we did not seem to be hiding anything. We could get in a lot of trouble if *they* thought we were hiding anything.

Laura was in the living room. She sat in the center of her Aunt Emily's sofa and put her hands out to the cushions on either side of her. She was angry. The anger shone in her eyes and reddened her face. It made the muscles on the sides of her neck taut and bulging. I had the impulse to go to her, to touch her. I suppose I was thinking I could calm her. But I did not. I stood back.

Romero and his assistant moved to the center of the room and looked around. The auctioneer bent over the woven-cane-back chair and stroked the wood. It was a caress, the touch of a lover who has at last found a value he has been searching for.

He said, "This is old."

I said, "It was her aunt's."

"How old is it?"

"I don't really know," I said.

"It's old," he said.

I thought he didn't believe me, but I told the truth, in a sense. I didn't know exactly when Aunt Emily had bought the sofa and the chair. And I didn't know whether my saying they were *about* eighty years old would increase or decrease their value in the auctioneer's eyes.

Laura said, "Mr. Romero."

"Ma'am?"

I saw it coming. I wanted somehow to reach out and grab her words with my hands and keep them from escaping into the room.

She said, "I want to tell you this set once belonged to my aunt. It isn't very elegant, but it—and that piano—mean more to me than anything else I could ever own. I don't want to lose them."

The auctioneer said, "Talk to your husband, ma'am. He's the one went bankrupt."

There was thunder in the room, thunder and cymbals crashing and heat making sweat pop out on my forehead, and a whirling sensation. Inside my head I heard someone scream—SONOFABITCH—and it took some time to get time started again. When time did start again, I realized I was the only one who heard the scream. Then I looked at Laura and I could not look at Laura. I looked at her Aunt Emily's sofa and chair and at the piano at the other end of the room, and I remembered how many times I had heard her struggle through the little Mozart minuet before she ever got it right. I felt shamed.

Laura said, "Our lawyer told us we would have first chance to buy our things back. Is that right?"

Romero said, "Yes ma'am. Most of your furniture won't bring much at an auction, and if you can come up with the cash and save us the trouble of having to haul your stuff out of here, I can arrange for you to keep everything."

I said, "How much money?"

He said, "I don't know. I'll have to add it up first."

He turned back to his work, and it was soon over. I heard little else but the shapelessness of his voice. He finished the living room, went outside, and listed the garden and lawn tools in the storage shed. I followed him. Laura did not.

On the carport, he said, "You'll hear from me in a day or two about the value assigned to your things."

I said, "How much time will we have to raise the cash?"

He said, "A week, maybe ten days. It's negotiable, if you really think you can get it."

I didn't tell him a friend was ready with the money.

I said, "We'll get it."

We walked to the car, and Romero stopped and looked around again. His eyes went all the way up to the roof line of the house—I wondered if he worked for the bank too—and down across the yard to the rose bushes on the other side.

"Nice roses," he said.

"Thanks," I said.

He offered his hand, and I shook it. It was sticky with sweat.

The assistant looked at me over the top of the car and said, "Right."

In a moment they were gone. The auctioneer and the young man in the Superman T-shirt had gone, and I stood in the driveway and sucked at the pain in the dark spot on my thumb. I didn't want to go back into the house filled with bankrupted promises. Laura was in there. I didn't want not to go back in either. Laura was in there.

She was in the kitchen, standing by the counter, with two of the blue cups in her hands.

She said, "He thought these were pretty."

"He said so."

"They're ugly!"

"They're ugly."

The cups, both at once, fell from her hands and crashed on the floor. Pieces of broken blue-and-white glass spread out in no kind of pattern at all. She picked up the other two and dropped them. I stared at the amount of glass scattered over the kitchen floor. I looked up at her and she was crying, softly crying.

She said, "He shouldn't have said that."

"What's that?"

"He shouldn't have blamed you."

"Oh, that," I said.

I shrugged and made a gesture with my hands to show how I had blown it off. Neither of us believed either the shrug or the gesture.

"It doesn't matter," I said. "It was the truth."

I moved toward her, and the fragments of glass crunched under my feet.

She said, "I wish I hadn't served them any coffee."

"I'm glad you did."

"Why?"

"Because otherwise you might never have broken those ugly cups."

"They were ugly," she said.

"They sure were."

"You noticed? You really noticed?"

I said, "I always thought they were ugly."

We knelt down, surrounded by fragments of blue-and-white glass, and began picking up the pieces.

JAMES KNUDSEN

THERE ARE NO BIRDS IN HOBOKEN

Wendel says things like, "I've forgotten more than you'll ever know," and you believe him. One look at that cracked leather face of his, even when he's smiling, and you know that making it to sixty hasn't been a picnic. He likes to quote Sinatra on the subject: "I've been a puppet, a pauper, a pirate, a poet, a pawn and a king." If this town has produced a success story (and what town hasn't?), Wendel's it. Wendel gives the commencement address at our high school every June; he's an example on the lips of every civics teacher. When I was growing up, I was fed Wendel with my breakfast cereal. "The early bird can make a hundred dollars before breakfast," my mother would chirp. Wendel is supposed to have said this. Wendel is supposed to have said a lot of wise things, but let me tell you, in my recent association with him here at his own Retread Rent-a-Car, the pickings have been slim. People are always asking me for the "inside story" on Wendel, figuring I've been closest in his recent times of crisis, but I guess Wendel has a right to decide who he wants to tell what, and when I think about how bad seeing Wendel like this has made me feel, I'm not sure that the town would be ready for the truth even if I knew it.

I guess you could say I got in on the ground floor at Retread Rent-a-Car. When I saw Wendel's ad, I showed up at five in the morning figuring to be the first in line. Unemployment around here is a way of life, and someone called me anonymously (probably put up to it by my mother) and said in a voice that sounded like somebody's idea of Ben Franklin, "The early bird can get a job before breakfast."

So I was there sitting on a stack of tires when Wendel pulled up in his mauve Continental. "I like your moxie," he called, jumping from the car. "Show me your baccalaureate and the job is yours." Since the job ad had said, "College ed. a plus," I'd brought a photocopy of my diploma, which I unfolded from my back pocket.

Wendel glanced over it, tenderly touching the spot where the gold seal would be on the original. "My doctorate's from the School of Hard Knocks," he chuckled as he thrust his right hand toward mine. "Shake on it, buddy."

When other job hunters began showing up, I was instructed to inform them that the vacancy had been filled. Wendel couldn't bear to do it himself. If they didn't drive up (and most of them didn't, since anywhere in town was within walking distance of anywhere in town), I was to try to rent them something to drive home in. "Impress your friends. Even though you didn't get the job, they'll think you've got a line on something." Though I followed a couple guys to the road jingling a set of keys, no one listened. "You can't succeed," I reminded myself, "unless you're willing to be less than successful." Another example of Wendel's reputed wisdom.

When a sharp-looking redhead emerged from Penny's Powderbox with her hair elaborately tousled and crossed the road carrying a clear vinyl briefcase full of résumés, I was dumbfounded and she got into Wendel's office before I could find my tongue. I could see through the window that Wendel wished he could reconsider my appointment. Finally, he offered her a secretarial position, which she politely declined. When he came outside and offered *me* the secretarial position, I reminded him that we'd shaken on the deal.

"There are no birds in Hoboken," he said as he turned away. I hadn't heard this quote around town yet, so I figured it was newly minted and that the truth and wisdom of it would eventually hit me.

Before I got this job, I was the kind of person who arrives at parties when the keg has turned to foam. I was never the kind to find "neat" apartments, and I was always the kind to buy something expensive and then to see it on sale for half price the following week. That's why it was so incredible to find myself in this job. It was the kind of job that if I had seen someone else doing it, I would have said, "Why can't I find a job like that?" Just to be able to say you worked for Wendel gave you a certain prestige. "Success flakes off" was another quote attributed to Wendel. I knew that in gossip all over town, that chestnut was being applied to me.

I suppose Wendel thought he had it made when he opened this place. None of the cars here is under five years old. Wendel went around the South with one of those car trailers and a mechanic named Toby, who's still on the payroll, picking up cream puffs and anything marked "executive driven" in the want ads. It's actually a good bunch of cars, though Toby tries to look busy with regular vacuuming and windshield washing.

In a town where everyone is surviving from day to day, the rental system must have seemed like a surefire idea. And the fact that the cars aren't hot off the assembly line means people can afford them whenever they're even slightly in the chips. I guess Wendel just forgot there's no place to go. After seven weeks in operation, I can still remember every person who's rented a car from us: Kay Sibley, who sprained her ankle at the Powderbox when she was already late for her son's second wedding, and Don Hervey, who hasn't been seen or heard from since. His wife's lawyer has been threatening to name us as co-respondents in a divorce case. Though the FBI's been called in, it looks like a tax write-off for us. Hervey's probably spray-painted that Nova already. I've been hearing so many nasty things about him I figure some people must be jealous. Of course, there's been lots of rumors recently that Retread Rent-a-Car has turned into Wendel's ticket to financial ruin. Let me make it clear that this piece of news did not originate here. Someone says that housewives are taking turns stationing themselves down by the courthouse waiting to see Wendel come in and file for bankruptcy. Don't they realize that if he does file, he'll more than likely take the town's economy with him? Sometimes I can't figure whose destruction they crave more, their own or someone else's.

It could be that Wendel's on the brink of bankruptcy. That would explain the way he's been hanging around here in his three-piece suit, picking his cuticles. Used to be I could watch TV at my desk or check out the girls entering Penny's Powderbox across the street and wait for them to emerge hours later with new poufs and plastic nails. The sign in the window of the Powderbox says Soap Opera Spoken Here—who says we're not a bilingual country? I keep the TV on so I can learn my share.

Wendel sent me a message when he was here this morning by pulling the shades and snapping off the set. "Isn't there anything you could do?"

I started sharpening pencils, though I was pretty sure the question had larger implications. He had appointed me general manager of Retread Rent-a-Car while on a roll. The Family Wendel's Family Restaurants were still pulling them in, and to judge from the number of women who were suddenly decking out in hats for the grocery even, it was clear that his wife's boutique was doing more than paying the rent. True, his snowmobile showroom was deserted, but then it was the middle of July. What do you expect?

"Isn't there something you could do?" he repeated.

I couldn't believe Mr. I've Forgotten More Than You'll Ever Know was asking me. To be frank, it kind of scared me. I thought about suggesting a new ad campaign or offering discounts to Powerbox customers, but it occurred to me that he had something more specific in mind. "About what?" I asked finally.

"My wife, dammit!"

"What's with her?"

"What's with her, he asks." Wendel turned to an imaginary audience. "She's gone to Las Vegas."

"Oh." I had heard something to that effect.

"She went to the travel agent and says, 'What's a good place to go?' and Fern Whatsername suggests the Las Vegas package. Something involving gambling tokens, three continental breakfasts, and complimentary champagne."

"Sounds fun."

"Dull, friend," Wendel groaned. "Dullwits' capital of the world." He sat down on the edge of my desk. "Get me some coffee."

Though this wasn't in my job description, I did it. Watching TV and the Powderbox girls wasn't in my job description either. "All this time I thought *we* were living in the dullwits' capital of the world. Why didn't you go with her?"

"She didn't ask."

I took this in as I poured some coffee for myself.

"She went with that Fern Whatsername. They got so excited making the plans, the wife said she felt like it was *their* trip and she kept saying how I hated planes and all."

"She right?"

"Yes."

"So let her have a good time."

"She won't come back."

"What makes you think that? *I* wouldn't think that."

Wendel pulled at his tie as if to loosen it and gave me a pained look. "Listen, buddy," he said. "I've forgotten more things than you'll ever know."

Someone in town once came up to Wendel with the bright idea of making some inspirational tapes—tapes that could be put in a vinyl carrying case for traveling salesmen to listen to on their long drives or at night in their motel rooms instead of drinking when they were feeling low. It would also be a great late afternoon pick-me-up for housewives. Wendel said, "No dice." He had no great philosophy of life, and in any case whatever worked for him wouldn't necessarily work for anyone else.

The would-be entrepreneur didn't give up easily. "Look, I'll just turn on the tape and you wing it. Say whatever comes into your head. People will buy it."

"That's right, they probably will, but I've never been interested in those kind of bucks. You just go on home with your tape recorder."

The entrepreneur angrily packed his things into his old high-school gym bag. This was the first idea he'd had in the ten years since graduation, and he slammed the door mumbling all kinds of things.

I suppose a lot of the early rumors about Wendel's alleged selfishness got started there, though I don't know a soul who really believed them. The entrepreneur, to save face with his drinking buddies, had claimed Wendel told him he was already planning to make a set of tapes but actually stole the idea as the words came out of his mouth.

When I asked Wendel about this incident, I was hoping to set the record straight, but he said he couldn't understand why I cared. What difference did it make? "All these years people round here have been saying I've said all kinds of smart things. Maybe I have, and maybe I haven't. Makes no difference. People are always going to believe what they want to believe. No amount of truth is going to stop that."

All of this made sense. I remembered when Wendel addressed my high-school graduation. Like my fellow students, I had really been looking forward to Wendel's words. It was the first time I had actually heard him speak, and I think we all felt that to be in his presence would confer on us something more valuable than a simple diploma. I listened as carefully to his speech as I would have listened to directions for finding buried treasure, but all I heard was this: To be successful, you have to really want something and what you want has to be worthy of your desire. He said it again and again through different anecdotes and parables, but that's all it came down to. It was a boring speech that he'd given dozens of times before.

The audience response was virtual pandemonium. Wendel was interrupted by applause so many times that by the end of the speech the applause was continuous even as he spoke, and I, for one, couldn't hear what he was saying. When he sat down, everyone rose to their feet, whistling and shouting. Mortarboards caromed off the ceiling. Wendel had looked bewildered and slipped out the door at the back of the gym as everyone was busy relocating their chairs and hats. I may have been the only one who saw him go. I think the others figured his disappearance was some kind of miracle, because they let out a communal "a-a-a-ah" that blew down the floral arrangements onstage.

"Wendel meeting payroll this week?" It's Toby calling from the phone in the garage. I imagine him reclining across the back seat of the old Chrysler New Yorker he calls home, his long bare feet comfortably crossed at the ankles.

"Has he missed one yet?"

"No," Toby concedes. "But I got my suspicions."

"Like?"

"Like the fact that he might just chase off to Vegas for that wife of his. Everybody says so."

"This is true, but I think he can manage the payroll, too." I say this because I want to believe it. "Besides, he hates Las Vegas, and if I know him he's still following that redhead who applied for my job."

"Hell, man," says Toby. "You trying to start a scandal? You writing an article about it for the *Midnight Star?* The man's a flirt, but that redhead could never replace his wife. He's got a picture of the wife in his Continental, and I've seen him kiss it. Besides which the redhead came in from out of town and is long gone. You got your brain chewing on the wrong stuff." I'd be impressed with

Toby's loyalty to Wendel if I wasn't just a little suspicious that he was trying to get me to argue and reveal more information. I've seen him across the street flirting with the Powderbox girls; who knows what they might do to get their hands on some information from a source close to Wendel.

Wendel is calling from the Family Wendel's on Sumpter for a report. He sounds a bit desperate, and the tone isn't becoming. "One inquiry by phone," I tell him. "Woman sounded about fifty and wanted to rent something to visit some new shopping center, wherever *it* is, heard the price of the old T-bird and asked the price on the worst car we got."

"And?"

"Then she asked what we had for a dollar fifty."

"Who are these dreamers?" Wendel explodes. "And how did it happen they all settled here?"

"Heard from your wife?"

"You had to ask. Someone from the Powderbox put you up to this?"

"Simple human curiosity."

"You been reading the *Enquirer.* I can tell by your inquiring mind. Listen, pal, I don't care what you tell anyone. I got a postcard today asking for a money order."

"She's having a good time," I suggest.

"To the tune of five thousand dollars."

"You sending it?"

"You bet. She signed off with, 'I might die if you don't.'"

"What do you suppose that means?" I play dumb figuring she's in debt to some shady dealer.

"That's life," Wendel almost croons. "The less said the better."

I don't reveal this latest development to Toby; in fact, I don't tell a soul. I feel like I am doing Wendel a favor, and because of this job, I owe him one. I wonder if the five thousand dollars will be easy for him to pull together. He has to be overextended what with all his investments.

Still I'm surprised later that week to hear from one of the waitresses at Family Wendel's that the restaurant chain will be closing for a two-month vacation. It might make sense if this were winter when people don't get out so much, but it isn't. I saw a big For Sale sign being nailed across the door of Wendel's Snowmobile Showroom when I walked over here this morning. That was enough to make me huddle with Toby over the coffee machine. "What do you bet we'll be a used-car lot by Friday? Damn, I knew this job was too good to last."

"Just scaling down," says Wendel as he barges in from the garage. "The wife just hit me up for another five grand."

I nod to suggest that I understand, but Wendel is having none of this. "Look, sons, if she doesn't think there's plenty of money to come back to, she'll stay on the lam."

"I thought you already were sure that she's not coming back."

"She isn't, but I don't want *her* to know that."

"Huh?" Toby's jaw drops.

"Once she knows she isn't coming back, I won't hear from her anymore. We loved each other, we had it all. It wasn't enough, it never is. Amen."

Toby's jaw seemed locked in the down position.

"It's like everything else, sons, you can't live with it and you can't live without it, and you can't live with it and you can't live without . . ." It was like his tongue was stuck in the groove of some old record.

Two weeks later Wendel's Wife's Boutique is closing with a bang. Hats are going two for the price of one, then six for the price of two. Main Street is a perpetual Easter parade. We probably should be passing around the hat for Wendel, but he's laughing harder than ever. Some say he's laughing all the way to the bank, but they don't see the disintegrating hulk that's been hanging around my desk every day.

He sits here with the TV tuned soundlessly to the endless string of "sex and other problems" shows, as he calls them. If an actor has a sad expression on his face, Wendel sobs again. "So true," he blubbers. "There are no birds in Hoboken."

Toby and I begin puzzling over that one together. "Maybe it's slang," Toby suggests. "Birds are women, Hoboken represents this place. He's just missing his wife."

That's all well and good, but why's he talking in code? The Quotations of Chairman Wendel have always been so simple you can hear school children advising each other with them on the playground. On a summer night you might hear a wife through the open window of a living room egging her husband on to better things with Wendel's words. When they turned to each other and said, "There are no birds in Hoboken," what would they mean? I didn't like the sound of it.

I go into the garage and turn on Toby's TV. The sound track explodes with laughter. Something hilarious has been said or done, and I've just missed it. As usual, I watch for a while, trying to figure out what has happened, but it doesn't work.

Wendel is gone. I don't think anyone in town knows it yet, but he hasn't been in in a week. He wasn't here on payday and a couple of times a day I leave the phone off the hook ringing his house to no answer. I sit at my desk watching as much TV as possible because I know the electricity will soon be turned off and I'll be back on the dole. There must be some quote from Wendel to suit this situation, but for the life of me, I can't think of it.

About lunchtime, I hear the front door open and it's Penny with ham spread on hamburger buns, something she made at home.

"You busy?"

"Not really," I say as I turn the TV to a murmur. I've known Penny all my life, as I've known just about everyone, but this will be the first time we've had lunch. Her hair is a braid-encircled bronze bubble. Large coins that spin in larger hoops pull at her earlobes.

"I'd like to chat," she says. I expect her to hand over one of the sandwiches, but she quickly eats one and takes a territorial bite from the other. "I suppose Wendel's in Vegas by now."

"He's not around?"

"Who are you kidding? When you drive a mauve Continental, people notice when you pass city limits."

"Maybe he's gone out to that new shopping center."

Penny's eyes light up. "Where's that?"

"I don't know. Somebody said there was one."

Penny looks deflated. "Some people will say anything." She finishes up her second "burger" and looks around for something to drink. She spies my coffee cup and grabs it on the way to the water cooler. "I hope he's gone for good. Success went to his head like a bottle of burgundy brew."

I say nothing. I'm tempted to turn the TV up to get her to leave.

"Everyone's been saying it, so why shouldn't I?" Penny asks, as if she's heard my response. "They say he beat his wife and that's why she left. He beat her silly and didn't love her a whit. He wouldn't let her have kids and he slapped her if she mentioned it. They said he decked her when she dragged him into the kids' department at Silver's. I mean, why'd she run off with another woman, that Fern?"

I almost call Toby in to help me fend off this attack, but who can say how he'd react?

"And he was a grafter and a cheat. He set up all these businesses, gives everybody a job, and then closes all the businesses so everybody gets fired and nobody can get her or his hair done or fix their nails nice . . ." One of Penny's bobby pins pops at this point, and her braid uncoils like a snake. This seems to calm her but only for a moment. "Everyone is sick to death of his graduation sermons and these endless bits and pieces and phrases about 'Living the good life isn't enough, you have to feel it'—what the hell is he talking about except putting up a damn smoke screen so he can nearly beat his wife to death and destroy everyone in the town and run off with every cent we might have earned and spent on the finer things."

"I'm overwhelmed," I say. "This is certainly a revelation." I am willing my hand not to raise itself up, grab her braid, and whirl her through the door. "Why don't you write this up for one of the better tabloids? This is quite a story."

"I have half a mind to do that."

"Well, why don't you get Toby to jump-start the other half and get going."

Penny nods at this "encouragement" with a smile. She's glad we see eye to eye. She pins up her braid and turns off the TV so she can check her reflection in the glass. "Well, tomorrow is the following day's yesterday."

I can't tell if she's quoting some bargain-basement Wendelism or is simply vying to take his place. "See you then," I say noncommittally as I close and lock the door behind her.

Then I scoot over and lock the door that leads to the garage. I don't need to hear any more whining from Toby over his paycheck. When I get back to my desk, I stop in the middle of my turn-on-the-set reflex. I sit down thinking about Wendel. I imagine his mauve Continental on a road somewhere, but I'm pretty sure that the road doesn't lead to Las Vegas. Maybe to some other little town, out of reach. I turn on the TV again, with no sound, and there's this man with a stethoscope around his neck staring at some nameless place offscreen. He's been crying or is about to cry, and the words form silently on my lips, "There are no birds in Hoboken."

NANCY RICHARD

ANNIE, LISTENING

It was summer and Saturday, and I didn't have to get up, but the sun shone into my bedroom window and woke me early. Before I was fully awake I had already begun to listen for things, my daddy's snoring, my brother's stereo, my mama in the kitchen. I remembered Daddy was in New Orleans on business, and I figured Ben for once had turned his music off before he fell asleep. But my mama wasn't emptying the dishwasher or perking coffee yet, so I thought it must be too early to get up, even for me.

I had burrowed beneath my pillow to try to go back to sleep when I heard Ben in our bathroom, the toilet flushing, the faucet running. He went to his room, but instead of going back to bed, he went down the hall and into the kitchen. After a minute I heard him in the hall again, then in Mama and Daddy's room. When he came out he stopped outside my door. He called to me to see if I was awake yet. I didn't care then if Ben came in without knocking, but once he started high school, he always knocked first.

I told him to come in. He opened the door just a little, and I could see he was still in his T-shirt and shorts. "Get up," he said. His voice was soft and husky. "Get dressed and meet me in the kitchen." He pulled the door shut and didn't wait for me to say anything.

Ben took me on picnics before he got a girlfriend, and I wondered if he felt bad that he quit and decided to surprise me that morning. I pulled on the jeans I'd thrown on the floor the night before and then took off my nightgown. I looked in the mirror to check my breasts, but they were still pancake flat. Melba Jean Mumpower had started wearing a bra the year before, in fifth grade. When she heard that one of the boys said it was probably stuffed with tissue, she made me go into the bathroom with her to see for myself, sort of as her witness, so I could spread the word that they were real. I did.

I asked Ben once if boys minded. He said not to worry, I'd get some soon enough, and any boy who cared more about that than anything else was a goon anyway. I asked him if his girlfriend had nice ones, and he said he'd never noticed. I told him he was full of baloney, and he punched me, not real hard, like he used to when we wrestled on the floor, but easy, as though I'd suddenly become breakable.

I had to hunt around under the bed for my tennis shoes. I'd kicked them off the night before, after Mama started crying in the middle of Scrabble. She told me she had to be alone and I'd have to go to my room, even if it was only eight o'clock.

That was the year Mama seemed to cry all the time. I'd hear her late at night, when I was supposed to be asleep. And it got that nearly every afternoon when I came home from school she was in her room with the door shut. I'd call to her to tell her I was home, and I'd stand and listen till she washed her face and let me in. Mama went to the hospital the week before school let out for the summer.

She'd been home only a few days, mostly sitting in the kitchen real quiet for hours, staring at the window with the blinds closed. I figured if she was in a better mood, I'd ask if I could take the whole bag of Oreos on the picnic. I found my shoes and a shirt I thought I'd left at Melba Jean's. I was putting them on when Ben came to the door.

"Hurry," he said.

"I am," I said. "I couldn't find my shoes. Are we going on a picnic?"

"No," he said. He came into my room and stood at the foot of my bed. Then he took a cigarette from his shirt pocket and lit it. When Ben started smoking, Mama told him he couldn't do it in the house 'cause it'd be a bad influence on me.

"You're not supposed to do that in the house," I told him. "Mama will take the car away from you again. And if we're not going on a picnic, why'd you make me get up?"

"She's not here," he said.

"She'll smell the smoke when she gets back," I said, and I lay across my bed. "When Melba Jean and I just *lit* one of her sister's in here with the door shut Mama smelled it all the way from the kitchen."

"You know where she is?"

"Probably the grocery store or something."

"No, Annie, she's not at the grocery store." He breathed a blue stream of smoke toward the ceiling and didn't look at me.

"What is this, twenty questions? Okay, where is Mama?"

"I don't know." He went into the bathroom and flushed his cigarette down the toilet. When he came back he sat beside me on the bed. "When I got up I found a note in the kitchen. She's gone. She left."

I sat up. "What do you mean gone? Where? What does the note say?"

"It says that she can't live with us anymore."

"You're lying," I told him. "That's a mean, stupid joke, Ben, and it's not funny. There's no note, you're making it up, and if you don't stop, I'll tell, I'll tell Mama when she gets back from the store and Daddy when he gets back from his trip, and I'll tell you smoked in the house!"

"Stop hitting me, Annie," he said and got up. "I'm not lying. Here's the note if you want to see." He held it out for me, a long envelope, the kind the bills came in. Mama's handwriting was on the back.

I crumpled up the note and threw it at my reflection in the mirror over my dresser. It bounced to the floor and landed on my knapsack. "You must think I'm real dumb, Ben. Cut it out, you're not funny." I watched the envelope start to unfold. One corner opened up and I could see the note inside. She'd used one of my felt-tip pens, the green one.

Ben took me by the shoulders. He was short for sixteen, and I was tall for my age, so I could look him nearly square in the eyes, and I knew he wasn't lying. "I wouldn't kid you about that," he said. "We have to go look for her. She didn't take the car. We'll drive around town."

He started off down the hall ahead of me before I could think of anything to say. When we got to the kitchen he took the car keys off the hook next to the telephone.

"Call Daddy," I said, but my voice was so small I didn't think he'd heard me. He was already standing on the back steps. "Ben, call Daddy," I said again.

He answered without turning around, just kept walking toward the car. "I tried. He's checked out of the motel." He got inside and reached over and unlocked my door. "There's a comb in the glove box," he said. "Your hair's a mess."

I found a rubber band in my pocket and pulled my hair back and tied it up. My stomach hurt, and I felt like yelling, but my voice was real small again. "How do we know where to look?"

He started the car and backed out of the driveway. "I don't know," he answered. "She didn't take her purse or pack a bag. I don't know where to start, Annie. What are some places you two used to go?"

I heard Ben talking, but the words didn't make any sense, and when I tried to think hard enough to figure it out, my head hurt, too. It probably wasn't really happening anyway, I thought, and if this was a dream I'd call Melba Jean first thing when I woke up. She'd just hoot.

"Annie." Ben touched my shoulder. "Annie, please, you have to help."

"We went to the supermarket, the bank, the post office, the gas station, the cleaners, the library. I don't know, Ben. We didn't go anywhere that was anywhere."

He lit another cigarette. "Okay. It's okay. We'll just start by driving through downtown." He turned on the radio then turned it off again. "What about the park?"

I shook my head, but I didn't look at him. "Not lately." I was watching my side of the road, looking down every street we crossed, but there weren't many people out yet that morning and nobody who looked like my mama.

"When?"

"What?"

"When was the last time you went to the park?"

"Before she went to the hospital the first time, when she used to run." Mama wore jogging suits all the time then, even on days when she didn't run. On my eleventh birthday she took me shopping, and we bought green ones just alike. The last time we went to the park I ran with her, but I couldn't keep up.

"Which park, Annie?"

"The one with the track."

"The park on the river?"

We stopped at a red light, and I watched for it to change. I knew without turning my head that Ben was looking at me.

"Annie," he said, "the park on the river?"

I nodded. "It's no use going there," I said when he turned the car south. "Mama said she'd never run there this time of year. It's too steamy on the water, and since they cleared out half the trees to build up the levee, half the track's always in the sun." If Ben had heard anything I'd said, I couldn't tell. "She isn't at the river, Ben, you're just wasting time, but go ahead if you want to. What do I know? You never listen to anything I say anyway." We'd gone three more blocks, and I'd forgot I was supposed to be watching my side of the road.

Ben turned on the air-conditioner. It was barely nine o'clock, but he was sweating already, and I felt bad that I'd yelled at him. "Ben?"

"Yes."

"My stomach hurts."

"Are you hungry?"

"No."

"Do you have to throw up?"

"No, it just hurts."

"Maybe because you're scared." He reached over and tugged at my ponytail. "It'll be okay. We'll find her, or she'll show up at home."

I could see the bridge ahead. "Are you?"

"Scared? Yes," he said, "a little."

"Because of the pills?"

"Yes, mainly because of that."

"She promised not to do it again," I said, watching the bridge.

"I know. They let her come home too soon." He steered the car over to the right lane so we could take the first street past the foot of the bridge, the one to the park.

I looked down at the water. It was low and muddy. "I forgot to check for them," I said.

"I did," he said, "after I found the note. They're all in her purse."

"I never heard the door," I said. Ben and Daddy were always hard sleepers, but that was one of the ways I was like my mama. "I sleep real light, Ben, and I never heard the door or anything."

"Even you have to sleep sometime," he said. "If she wanted to leave, Annie, she'd have been extra quiet." He turned onto the street that led to the park. "It's not your fault." He looked over at me. "Are you listening?"

We drove through the park entrance, Ben looking to the left toward the woods and hiking trails. On my side were the picnic tables and playground equipment, and a hundred yards or so beyond the road were the tracks and the levee. Almost every table was taken, and I saw children running from swings to merry-go-round to slides, running, I remember, all the time, jumping from wherever they were with feet in motion, it seemed, never stopping. And yelling, calling one another, their mothers, with look how high I am, how fast I go, how loud I scream, the mothers waving, the fathers cleaning barbecue grills, unloading lawn chairs and blankets, ice chests, frisbees. But there was no one who looked like my mama.

Ben eased the car over the speed bumps, letting it creep over and down, sometimes letting it stop, never taking his eyes off the woods, forgetting to smoke. He pulled over to the left, onto a narrow clamshell parking strip, and stopped. "I'm going to take one of the trails," he said, "and make my way to the other end of the track. You walk around out here by the levee, maybe walk along the track for a while, and I'll meet you back here."

We got out of the car, and I watched my brother until he disappeared around a bend in the trail past the oak tree with the swinging vine. I wondered if he'd remembered as he walked past it that I used to swing from it and that once I'd lost my grip and sailed right at him, but instead of jumping out of the way, he'd caught me, or at least tried. We both ended up on the ground, and he sprained his shoulder.

I crossed the road to the playground and watched. When the children could get far enough away from their mothers, they ran to the levee, clambered to the top, rolled down giggling and shoving, then back up again. I was watching one of them, a boy of ten or so, running along the levee, parallel with a runner on the track below him, a girl, I thought, no, a small thin woman. He might have been racing with her, the runner who was my mama.

My first impulse was to go after Ben, but instead I ran through the picnic area, made my way between the monkey bars and the tunnel slide, and reached the track about fifty yards behind her. And I kept running, too fast at first, then slowing my pace to match hers, not wanting to catch up, not wanting her to see me. I ran to keep her in view, her hair tied back like mine but more to the side so it bounced against her shoulder, the back of her green shirt dark with sweat, her arms working, her knees brought high. The boy on the levee dropped back, stopped, and threw himself onto the ground, one arm shielding his eyes from the sun, his chest heaving. Mama ran, an easy trot I recognized from all those mornings watching her run, an easing-up before the cool-down, but this time not stopping. It was a kind of pushing-forward, toward something she could see but I couldn't.

I envied Ben the cool woods, wished I'd been the one to wander around among the quiet trees, not the one to have found her. If she saw me would she run faster, stop and cry, or maybe pretend nothing had happened, that she hadn't run away from us? Maybe the note was a mistake, I thought. That must be it: she just got real sad and wrote the note without thinking, but when she tried to call us at home to tell us that she was sorry, that she didn't mean it, we were already gone.

She ran toward the woods, where the track wound among the oaks and Chinese tallows, through the tangle of blackberry vines and wild violets. I picked up my pace, pounded the track past the children swinging, the mothers sunning, moved close enough behind her that I could hear her breathing, the rhythm steady, her lungs sucking each gulp of air with a gasp.

Then she turned her head and saw me, and what I read in my mama's face was not the relief I looked for, not guilt, or even sadness, but fear. And I was sorry, sorry that I'd found her, that the fact of my existence as her daughter would compel me to beg her to return. I longed for the dark woods, for Ben to take over.

She seemed to run faster then, but I must have dropped back, too, for she disappeared as quickly as she had turned her head, a moment of recognition, of fear, and then she rounded a shaded curve through the trees and was gone. I stopped to catch my breath and tried to run but couldn't, so I walked. I followed the track into the woods, picturing my mama just ahead of me, just around the next curve, listening for the sound of the cinders beneath her feet, trying to separate it from the noise of the children behind me, from the sound of my own breathing.

And then I saw her. She had seen me first, for when I looked at her, she was already watching me, leaning against an oak tree, her arms hanging at her sides.

"Nothing helps," she said, more to herself than to me. She dropped down to the ground and sat with her knees drawn up, her arms resting across them.

I sat in the middle of the track, facing her.

"Not the pills or the running. Nothing."

"Mama, are you okay?" My chest ached, I could hear my blood in my ears, and I was afraid I might be sick.

"Did you see that boy back there?" she asked me.

I nodded.

"He wanted to race, said he could beat me, no sweat." She covered her face with her hands for a moment and pushed her hair away from her forehead. Her face was still perfectly dry. Her shirt stuck to her in big, damp patches, but her face was dry. Then she looked at me again. "He didn't, did he?"

"Didn't what, Mama?" I could barely hear her over the rushing in my ears, like the sea in a conch shell, only louder.

"Catch up with me, not once, did he? Were you watching? Did he ever keep up with me, Annie?"

"No," I lied, "he never could."

She smiled a little, a small, quick sort of half-grin, and then it was gone. "Well," she said softly, "I guess that's something." She rested her forehead on her arms, and we sat there for what seemed a long time, without saying anything. When she finally looked up she rested her chin on her arm and stared at the ground between us.

I picked up a stick and began to draw in the dirt at my feet. I poked holes and shoved cinders around into little piles.

"Melba Jean thinks her big sister might be pregnant," I said. "Her mama said Belinda isn't that kind of girl. She's just precocious. We looked it up and Melba Jean said she doesn't think that's the right word."

I glanced at Mama, but she didn't seem to have heard me. She hadn't moved, except for the angle of her head. Her eyes followed the blackbirds and jays as they moved from tree to tree. They made such a racket it was the first time I'd thought of the woods as noisy. Even the voices of the children from the playground had become distant, drowned out by the cawing from above us.

I lost track of time. I couldn't guess how long we'd sat there, and I hoped Ben would find us soon. "Mama," I said, "are you mad at me?"

She opened her mouth, but if she said anything, all I could hear was a tiny sound from way down in her throat.

"If you're not mad at me, then tell me what to do," I said. My bottom was sore from sitting on the cinders. I started to get up, but she flinched, as though she'd forgot I was there and I'd surprised her. "It's okay," I said. "I'll stay here till you feel better."

I still believed then, that morning in the summer before I turned twelve, that if I waited a little while longer, my mama would get up, come home with us, and everything would be as it had been. "Just tell me what to do," I pleaded, "and come home, and everything will be okay."

She straightened and leaned back against the trunk of the oak and tilted her head, her face toward the sunlight that broke through the clearing in the trees. Then she closed her eyes, and if I had blinked in that moment, I might have missed it, the shaking of her head in a single, brief movement from right to left and back again. And then it was over. In that moment I knew there would be nothing I could do, not then, not ever, that would make it all okay. I was her daughter, and she would have to come home, but she would never believe it could be okay.

I picked up every twig I could reach and snapped them all into eight or ten pieces, and I started throwing them, in every direction but hers. "I know my room's a mess, but I'll clean it up soon as we get home, and I'll help with the dishes before you ask, and I won't ever fail a social-studies test again."

When she finally opened her eyes and turned her head toward me, I scooped up one of the piles of cinders and tossed it up into the air right over my head. But she just sat there, looking at me but not seeing me, a red cloud of dust settling all over me and getting into my eyes, and I thought she didn't even care. I'd felt like yelling all morning since Ben showed me her note, and my stomach hurt with keeping it down, and I couldn't anymore. "Stop it!" I picked up another pile of cinders and threw them at her.

She turned her head and covered her eyes. "Annie, please."

But I hurled another handful. "Stop it, Mama! Stop this right now and come home. I'll do anything you say. I'll be perfect. But you have to get better now!" Then my face was all wet, and when I wiped it on my shirt sleeve it left muddy red streaks. "We don't have to play Scrabble every Friday night," I said. "We can do whatever you want."

I heard footsteps running through the woods, then Ben calling my name. Mama stood when she heard him, but she didn't even brush cinders out of her hair or off her clothes. When she looked at me again she was crying, and when Ben came through the trees behind me she covered her face and shook her head again, but hard that time.

"I'm sorry," she said. "I don't know how to be your mother. I keep getting it wrong."

Ben asked me if I was all right, then he went over and hugged her. Mama didn't hug him back; she kept her face covered and cried the hardest I ever heard her.

"Shhh," Ben said. "Hush, Mama. It's okay. It'll be okay."

Daddy was home when we got there. He took Mama back to the hospital that afternoon.

Since it was summer and Ben and I were at home all the time, we took care of things while Daddy went to work. If he had to go to New Orleans on business and Ben wanted to go out with his girlfriend, I stayed at Melba Jean's. Her sister wasn't pregnant after all, and Melba Jean said it was to her mama's praying the credit was due, not to Belinda's good sense.

Every Wednesday night we went to visit Mama. That was family night, when there was Ping-Pong or bingo, sometimes a movie. Then we'd go home, the three of us, but I could never fall asleep till past midnight. After Daddy and Ben went to bed I'd walk through the house, check the lock on the back door, turn off Ben's stereo, and sit up and read in my bed. I listened for Daddy's snoring till it got loud enough to wake him and he'd turn over and go back to sleep. Sometimes I got up and turned Ben's stereo back on.

After two months they let Mama spend Saturdays at home. One Saturday morning just before school started we picked her up, and when we got home I told Mama I had to talk to her in private, without Ben and Daddy around. So we went into my room. I'd been keeping it pretty straight; we didn't even have to clear the bed before we sat down.

"Can we go shopping?" I asked her. She'd begun to look as I'd remembered her, crinkly around the eyes and soft. She'd started wearing makeup again.

"They won't let me drive yet, Annie," she said. "I'm sure your daddy would take you."

"No," I said. "He can't take me to do this." I never meant to cry over it, but once it started, I couldn't stop. "I want a bra like Melba Jean's," I said. "It's white lace and has a tiny pink rose in the middle."

Then Mama looked like she was going to cry, but instead she hugged me and said I could have a dozen of them if I wanted, in every color they came in. So Daddy took us to the mall, and after we sent him to the hardware department, Mama and I spent an hour in lingerie. She bought me three of them, two whites and a pink. I wore the pink one home.

Ben must have known where we were, 'cause when we got home he whistled at me. I told him he'd better never forget to knock before he came into my room, and if he so much as teased me one time, I'd hate him forever. Then I called Melba Jean.

The weekend after Mama came home from the hospital that fall Melba Jean asked me to come over to spend the night.

"I can't," I said. "I have to be here."

We decided she'd come over instead. Mama played Scrabble with us for a little while. Then she said she was tired, kissed us good-night, and went to her room.

Melba Jean got up to shut the door like we always did when she came over.

"No," I said. "Leave it open, in case my mama needs something."

We found the Oreos and took them to my room. I let Melba Jean get ready for bed first. While she was in the bathroom I looked in on Mama. She was asleep, and I shut her door real easy, till the lock clicked. I told Melba Jean I wasn't sleepy yet, so I finished the last chapter of my library book. And for a long time after Melba Jean fell asleep and I turned out the light, I lay there, listening.

ALBERT BELISLE DAVIS

THE MISSISSIPPIMAN'S SON

There's a one-room net shop on the eastern levee of Bayou Grand Caillou. In summer the windows on all four walls are open to let in the breezes. When the breeze is from the east or west, the room fills with mosquitoes because the marsh is to the east and west. In fall the smoke from burning sugarcane blows in from the north. In winter only the window on the southern wall is open, but it's open at all times. A bare bulb on the end of a wire hanging down center-ceiling glares night and day through every season except spring. No one knows where Calin, the retired oysterman who lives in the net shop, goes in spring.

Calin is blind and smells of his nets, of bottom mud and salt and shrimp, because he sleeps on his nets. He doesn't make nets but rather repairs old ones. He never takes a net from the bottom of the pile in the shop. He mends the first net on top, and so there are nets that have been in the pile for years. There's a joke among the people of Dulac, the nearest village, that the nets at the bottom of Calin's pile calcify into fossil-like cells. The pressure of Calin's sleep pushes the cells into the boards on the floor. Now after years the floor itself is black shell. The saying "He lost his net to Calin's floor" is a way of reporting that a fisherman is lost at sea.

The town north of Dulac is like a crippled netman's palm. From it five bayous reach out at the Gulf: Chinese Bayou, the two Caillous, the Mondebon, and Bayou DuPetit. To the bayou Cajuns, all strangers who speak French are from another bayou; all strangers who do not speak French, whether or not they have a French accent, are from town. Calin speaks French with an accent that no one in the villages can place. In his English there are some words only educated townspeople know. Everywhere, Calin is a stranger.

Calin sings or tells stories while he mends his nets. He calls his shorter pieces—his songs and small histories—*petites lunettes,* little eyeglasses. Long stories—narratives that sometimes take him several days to tell—he calls *entrelacs noires,* black knots within knots. During a story he will look up as though he has seen the bulb burning above him. His eyes, milky blue, roll up behind his lids. For a moment Calin becomes a character in his story. The character speaks through Calin. This is the only time Calin's hands stop moving. When the character leaves him, the hands begin knotting the black twine again, palm up and then palm down with the help of the forked netman's stick. Some say he is possessed, but they have not seen the smile that comes over Calin's face after each soliloquy.

To most, Calin is an oddity, to some an embarrassment. To the most imaginative along the bayous, he is captivating, a singer, a storyteller nonpareil. The saying "His hair is twine for Calin's net" identifies a person as an idle daydreamer.

My hair is twine for Calin's net, but I don't think he'll believe that of me anymore.

I first heard about Calin in a Dulac bar. After many days and many beers, I got five men who were faithful listeners to let me accompany them to Calin's shop. As they and I approached, I could see the room was going dark.

"I thought you said the bulb is always on," I said.

"It is," one of them answered. "Calin knows there's one more set of feet crunching on the shells."

I told them I would wait outside until they got permission from Calin for me to join them inside. All five men laughed at this. The only way to get in, they said, was to go in. They were certain Calin had heard my voice and was already sizing me up. They also said that once inside I shouldn't worry if Calin didn't speak. The silent treatment had happened to all of them, but the day would come when he would speak again.

The sun had set by the time we were all seated. I could barely make out the form of the old man on his pile. The only sound in the room was the whack of my palm against my skin as I killed mosquitoes lighting on my neck and cheek. After Calin fell asleep on the pile, we left, and at the bar over another beer, the five men told me I'd have to learn to be still. It took me two days, but I did learn. Mosquitoes go for motion. Absolute stillness is the best repellent.

After I learned to be still, Calin still didn't speak for a week or so. Then one night, he said to me from the darkness, "You are the Mississippiman's son."

"I'll be a son of a bitch," one of the five said.

"You are a son of a bitch," another answered him. "It don't take a Calin to deduction that." Then to me, "Go 'head. Talk to the old man. He's placed your voice and your smell."

"My father's from Mississippi," I said. "He worked down here for a while once. Made some friends at the university in Thibodaux. He sent me to school there. I quit for a job in the oil fields."

"Ain't no more oil fields," one of the five said. "How you place him, Calin?"

"He sounds, him, like his daddy, a man we all know more than well. But he has a few more words about him than his daddy, the twenty-seven words a daddy-bought education pays for. And he smells, him, like his daddy's smell. Like Biloxi. Like sand that's been stolen from someplace else and spilled on the beach by the Army Corps of Engineers."

The five men laughted, but not Calin. "You break promises?" he asked me.

"No more, no less than you coonasses," I said. "But I might be less of a man when it comes to mosquitoes."

"I want you to promise me you'll resist the temptation to make my words permanent. I don't mind if you use your memory."

"I don't make promises if I'm not sure I'll be able to keep them."

"As long as you're not sure, that's still a promise. If you know you'll break a promise when you make it, that's a lie. A lie comes somewhere after a promise. Try your best not to get the two confused the way your daddy did."

"Promise him," one of the men said. "Promise him and we're in business again."

"Go ahead," another said.

"Yes," Calin said, "a chance at promise." I heard his laugh for the first time then, low in his skinny throat. "Like the fallen priest said about the trinity—women, whiskey, and grace—*Take it when you can get it*."

I promised.

Over beers in the bar that night Calin first talked to me, I learned that my father had a reputation on the five bayous because of the documentary he'd filmed about the people he called Cajuns. Everyone in the bar that night decided I could drink with them anyhow. *Bad genes ain't impossible to overcome.*

I didn't tell anyone that my father had made enough money doing the documentary to buy his beachside house, or that his last words to me—in a letter he'd written and mailed the night before the hurricane and tidal wave—were, "There's a gold mine down there, son. A cheap tape recorder'll get you a grant. A grant will get you a book. A book, movie rights. A gold mine in stories, son. Don't end up like the rest of your mama's family or your brothers—drinking, belching, fucking, wishing."

It's easy for me to remember that next morning, a hangover, winter. We stood outside the southern window, six of us. Through the open window, we saw Calin asleep on the black pile. Under the bulb, lit again and swinging in a wind, his fingers, gnarled as cypress knees, were burrowing down into the nets as though making and discovering channels through the countless layers of cells.

We watched until he woke. He sat up. His eyes rolled back as he faced the sun through the east window. We heard Calin say: "On Chinese Bayou they are good at nothing but at death and curses, at love and at dreams."

You might have guessed by now. This isn't just an introduction. This is a sketch of a broken promise and the lie that came somewhere after.

At first I trusted memory. Calin began with short Chinese Bayou love songs, graffiti, epitaphs. Then the *petites lunettes* became short histories, and I became scared the words would all be gone forever. I was sincerely worried that these words of his, haunting at times, were as much prey to the four breezes as the mosquitoes had been to my murdering palms.

One day, I stole a pad and pencil from the diner next door to the bar. As soon as I left the bar after a session in the net shop, I wrote as fast as I could everything that I remembered Calin having said. When it got to the point that I didn't trust my memory and the pad, I borrowed my first tape recorder—a bulky job, a squeaky job—from a friend of my father's who taught at the university. Calin heard the whir of the wheels immediately, and after a day of silence, my five companions threw the machine into a *trenasse,* a trapper's ditch. It took some persuading to convince them that I had lost my head because of bad genes, and I promised that my senses had returned.

I told my father's friend about Calin. I was worried now that Calin would begin a long story, one of his *entrelacs noires,* and that the story would also be lost. My father's friend upheld the conviction of my concern, agreeing that the loss would be, as he put it, excessive.

The grant came next. With that came the microphone the size of a barroom matchbox, the wireless-remote tape recorder. And everything tumbled down from there to my success: the first edition of this book, the movie rights, this new edition of the book.

Before I said good-bye, I tried to tell Calin that I wasn't going to take any credit. History would hold his words forever, his art.

"The lowest lie," he said, "a liar's lie to himself. And two of your twenty-seven junior-college words—history and art—are the lowest goddamned excuses for broken promises."

For whatever it's worth, here is one of Calin's *entrelacs noires*. This is what Calin said. These are the people he became.

Listen.

Calin

His name is Adrian, and he says his name as we would say it, Ahdree-ann.

We have all seen him standing behind the thick moss-green glass as we sit on the hoods of our cars waiting for the boats to pass. And though it is our right to raise our fists to curse the man who keeps us waiting one boat too long, we have all hesitated before raising our arms to this man.

Behind that same glass other men have looked like shadows, toys of the light. With the setting sun behind him, this man forestalls that part of dusk that meets his presence.

And what of the combination lock on the outside of the bridge house door, of the sheriff's car that comes once every week with food?

One who swears he has gotten close enough to the bridge house to know, told me that the face of the bridgetender is not covered with flesh as we recognize it. From this I am sure will come another marsh creature legend for midnight crab boils.

In truth, his face is awful, but not frightening. What skin there is seemed stretched tight over the bones and pasted to itself along lines that run from the corners of his lips over the cheeks to the corners of his eyes. The skin shines like white waxed paper, except along the joining lines, which are pink and blue and dull.

He has a missing ear and keeps the lobe of remaining roostercomb flesh covered by a wave of black hair from his temple. The other ear is covered also, also with a coarse wave.

Adrian grew up in Chackbay, north of here, but not so north as to be not south Louisiana. He was handsome, big, and fatherless. Like us, his earliest memory was of being lifted up to kiss the forehead of a dead relative.

From outward appearance, he was what we here call a loudmouth coonass. He could not be ignored, made and sought enemies with delight, and because he was young and death was far-far down the road, had no fear, just as an animal without a predator has no fear.

Because he held a grudge for sleep, he took his waking moments in a big way, took each breath violently, as though claiming it for himself. He treated all he encountered, marsh and people, as an extension of his breathing.

Besides shaking fists at bridgetenders, we claim another right, and in this regard Adrian was no different. Our women are ours. Adian went about this with a somewhat grander sweep, too—charming women, having women, long before they caught and reclaimed their breath.

If we speak of ambitious plans, we always finish with the words "If God says the same." Even those of us who are not sure we believe say it, maybe for insurance, maybe out of habit, maybe out of connection to those who have said it before us. It is good for all to say. It is a humbling force.

Before he encountered a humbling force, Adrian had lived for fifteen years, to the day.

On his fifteenth birthday his great-aunt T-Chant Sue was trying to put a curse on Looloo, the owner of the barroom next door to her house. A crowd had gathered long before she limped out of her house at noon—when the shells on the barroom parking lot blazed their whitest—with a box of salt under her arm, a cypress cane in her hand.

"White on white," she said, starting a trail of salt to the front corner of the parking lot.

That was when Adrian staggered from her house with a red tin can hidden in his hand. Everyone laughed as Adrian, drunk at fifteen, sprinkled black pepper over her salt.

"Ah-dree-ann!" she screamed. "You have broken God's accords. Accordingly, you must be cursed. God damns you. Monsieur Death is your godfather. You mother should have pinched your head off the day you were born."

She poured the rest of the salt over Adrian as he curled up under the pecan tree in the front yard and called a truce with sleep.

When he woke, pushing sleep off him with a start an hour later, the crowd was still in place, and quiet. They had realized what it would take Adrian another day to realize. His great-aunt had cursed him in leechtime, that time in a dry fall in the swamp when water congeals in the pools in low places under the trees and everywhere leeches abound.

The people in the Chackbay believe the days of leechtime to be the lowest days for the soul. Those things that suck at the soul feast during leechtime. No one in Chackbay gets married in leechtime. If someone dies during leechtime, he gets the last sacrament twice. If someone is born during leechtime, his godparents just shake their heads. There is no hope.

Adrian had been born in leechtime, but this had made no difference in the actions of his life. He never gave it mind. He was that strong.

He also never gave mind to church or spells. But from the day his great-aunt cursed him, he no longer had to search for the trouble he relished.

There is a joke along Chinese Bayou, maybe we have all heard—each new misfortune is fatter and stinkier than its siblings. This gross family, or so they say, we carry in an airtight plastic sack.

They also say that there is a day when all the burdens of a life combine to what is called a "greatest weight." And on that day the sack must be put down and opened. The strongest among us carry the most for the longest, but for them the day is called the Day of Heroic Smells.

That day did not come for Adrian until many years later, on October 20, 1976.

We all remember that day for another reason, a reason we found out about as soon as we ourselves pushed off sleep and listened to the news on the radio or listened as we saw it on the television.

Those of us who could see to read and could read, read it this way in the morning paper from New Orleans: "The death toll from the collision of the Norwegian tanker and a ferry near Luling early Wednesday morning could reach 100 or more. . . . Nightfall ended the attempt to bring more bodies up from the Mississippi. During the daylight hours 18 persons were hauled alive from the water. Twenty-two bodies were recovered. . . . Sunrise had just begun to illuminate the river when the tanker *Frosta* 'loomed up' with its whistle screeching at the side of the ferry and plowed into the 125-foot *George Prince.*"

For Adrian, the morning of that October 20 began like an Easter.

He woke with the same feeling he had had before T-Chant Sue cursed him, that there was no motion until he woke, that each waking motion was his to make, that motions became a scheme of his design.

When he threw open the door to his Chinese Bayou camp, he had not as yet buttoned his shirt. The cold air slapped at the flesh of his chest. He jumped off the porch, leaping at the cold, with his Eisenhower jacket in one hand and a loose-leaf notebook in the other.

Owing no back rent, he was leaving Yen's Marina with a new boat and trailer. He was going fishing with a friend. He had finally rid himself of the *fille de joie,* his wife Sara.

Sara had left during the night, taking everything she owned with her, but she had left behind on the bed the orange binder she had been writing in since their first day in Mondebon Parish. Adrian was sure she had left it for him to read. And if that was her wish, he would dispense with her wish, one page at a time, into the wind.

Adrian took the shell road out of the marsh on his way to Louisiana 57, the highway on the high levee of Chinese Bayou that would take him out of the marsh and north to the town.

On his right, he could see the shrimpboats, the commercial tugs and barges, wharfed in Chinese Bayou. Highway 57 followed the bayou, wound with it, and there was no stoplight or stop sign the entire fifteen miles to town. There was only one bridge before he got to the highway, the bridge over Chinese Bayou.

That morning there were no boats waiting for the bridge, not a mast or net anywhere. Adrian laughed at his good luck, but before he could get his hand to his throat to feel the vibration of his laugh, the barricade started down.

He stepped out of the truck with the notebook. As he walked, the village water tower rose slowly over the turtleback of the bridge grating.

Leaning on the barricade, he watched the sunrise, a clear fisherman's sunrise. He saw a hook-brass sun on a line of sky stretched tight as blue monofilament, but he still did not see a boat. All he saw was a faint yellow light at the far curve in Chinese Bayou.

"It's got to be a mile away," he yelled at the bridgetender. "Turn around and face me. You might as well be deaf. You won't last as long as the others the rate you're going. Goddamn."

Cars lined up past the east barricade. A man and a boy sitting on the hood of the lead car shook a fist at the bridge house.

To Adrian, the two trawl booms in Chinese Bayou were tapered like legs above the horizon. The yellow light grew and gleamed in in a loin of net. Sara would have called that Adrian's lurid imagination.

After the barricade started up, as Adrian was reaching for a shell to sail at the bridge house, he saw a woman walking toward him on the road shoulder. She had a willow branch in one hand and a plate covered with aluminum foil in the other.

With her hair black enough to flare purple at the edges, she had to be an Indian from Lower Chinese Bayou. With his eyes on that purple edging flare, Adrian opened Sara's notebook. He ripped out the last pages and, without seeing they had been written to him, threw the white leaves to the wind.

Adrian

The boat settled, leveled to plane. Simon settled to reading the green book. He marked his pages with Ecclesiastes.

I settled to the sound of the buzz and to speed. It would take less than fifteen minutes to reach the lake.

When I stood up to steer the boat, my eyes watered and the wind swept the cold tears back along my temples. I laughed and called out to Simon, but he went on reading.

The buzz of the big Merc was loud enough to come in over the buzz in my ears. It must have been a beautiful piece of noise.

"Simon!"

Easing back on the throttle, I turned the wheel right. The wake lifted the stern and carried the boat, and I used the wave to coast toward the canal. At the end of the canal, I saw Lake Des Allemands.

"Look, Mon!"

"You're shouting."

"Will you answer one thing for me?" I asked.

I pressed the button and killed the idling motor. I waited until all the waves had washed into the swamp.

"Is it quiet here, Mon?"

"Yeah, Adrian, only we make a noise."

I closed my eyes and nodded my head, yes. We had finally made it. I smoothed my hair back behind my ears.

"You know how to get to the Company Canal?" Simon asked.

"My father used to take me duck hunting there when he was overseer."

"Let's fish it."

"We'd have to go all the way back past the landing. It would be better to fish the lake. Have you been reading about fish in that book of yours?"

"About one fish. One big fish. A manatee."

That was the first time I had ever seen the word, *man-a-tee.*

"A big fish, Mon? Well, why didn't you say that? Let's go get the bastard." I pressed the ignition. "But answer one other thing for me. What kind of a deal you make with Virgil?"

"We're going to get the Overseer."

A fence blocked our entrance to the canal. Simon walked to the back of the boat, stumbling once from the shove of a wave on the side of the hull. He flipped the tabs from two cans of Dixie and threw one to me.

Simon drank, smiled. "Come on, Ah-dree-ann. There's something going on in that canal. A few fishermen told Virgil that it's enchanted."

"What isn't enchanted to the people around here, Mon?"

"They've seen something in there. One of them saw an elephant grazing on the hyacinth." Simon grinned. "Another said it was a skin diver formed over into a creature."

"And what isn't a creature around here?" I laughed. "Tell me, Mon. What do you think it is?"

"Me? Without no doubts, I know."

Simon put his can down. With his hands, he drew the curves and bulges of a woman.

"A mermaid," he said.

"Are you promising me eyes in the water?"

We laughed.

"Come on, Ah-dree-ann."

"Just how much do you want to get into the Company Canal, Mon?"

"Badly, badly."

I could not remember Simon ever wanting anything badly.

"Then damn the Overseer and his fence," I said.

Simon lifted his can. "To us. And to our expedition, a glimpse of sleek skin in water."

I looked past the fence to the canal. "The devil's built himself a straight ditch," I said, but Simon, back to his book, did not hear.

Rat cypress grew tall on both sides of the canal. The water hyacinth had begun to brown and die and sink in the bayou, but in the canal, protected from the wind by the cypress, it flourished. It would be hell getting a boat through that green.

I went to work on the gate lock with a monkey wrench from my tool chest. After the lock snapped open, I threw it and the wrench into the bayou. Full throttle, I plowed into the hyacinth.

I weaved the boat left, and I weaved the boat right, no more than a foot at a time, through the dense mat. I felt the motor straining through the superstructure. I smelled the smoke from burning engine oil.

I smelled the Odor all around.

I saw a clearing ahead, a black circle in the green. Simon closed the book and climbed through the windshield break up to the bow. Lying on his stomach, he passed his head under the chrome railing and extended his trunk until his face was out over the water.

The bow penetrated the black. Simon raised his arm.

"Cut the motor, Adrian, cut it."

"What now, Mon?"

"Just quiet."

Simon took the gaff hook from its place on the metal fishing rack. He lifted his sweater and wiped the varnished pole and the brass hook. After tying one end of the nylon rope through the eye at the opposite end of the pole, he stood up and took swings at imaginary intruders in the boat.

On one swing, he struck the windshield and the pole fell to the deck. I bent over to pick it up, but he pulled it away.

"No, Adrian."

I slid the minnow bucket close to my feet. Inside, the shiners were still. When I dabbed my hand into the water, they swam.

I trapped one fish, a wriggling speck of silver and transparent blue, between my fingers, and I hooked it through the eyes. One of the eyes remained impaled, a minute black bead, on the end of the point, but the hook was alive with jerks and twitches and slapping of the wounded silver against my finger. I dropped the line over the side, and I faced the bow to watch Simon.

He set the gaff hook down. He crossed his legs as he stood and sipped his beer, and he stared down at the water. Now and then, he cocked his ear to a disturbance.

I reached for the book Simon had left on the seat.

"No, Adrian."

I handed him the book. He laid it at his feet.

"You want me to keep my vision small, Mon?"

"Just quiet."

Simon heard something. His eyes were on a patch of hyacinth that had broken off the mass ahead. The patch floated toward the boat.

Simon's mouth twisted in anger. He reached for the book. Without opening it, he threw it down.

He took a swing at the hyacinth. "Goddamn, goddamn, goddamn," he said, shredding leaf bits from the hook.

"Why are you upset, Mon?"

"I can't hear you."

"Mon . . ."

"I said I can't hear you. You think I'm lying? You're talking too low."

"Come on, Mon. What the hell's the matter?"

"The book's wrong."

"You should know better than to learn to fish from a book. It's like learning about women from a book, from pictures on a page. You put your nose close and sniff and you smell ink on paper. If you aren't careful you'll get hard up for the smell of ink on paper."

Simon did not laugh. He fanned the pages of his book without looking inside.

"It's all scientific," he said. "But the timing's all wrong. All wrong, damn it."

Simon paced the length of the boat, one side and then the other, peering over both sides and the stern.

"Do you want me to help?" I asked.

"Just quiet."

"I can help if you tell me what it is you're looking for."

"I'm looking for a swell of the water."

"You want me to go on the bow and look out for you?" I asked. "I think I know a swell when I see one."

"It'll come up quick, soon. You got to tell me quick if you see something."

I stood on the bow with my hands at my sides, watching water. Behind me, Simon walked the port and stern and starboard, his ear to the water.

In a few minutes, I saw a swell in the center of the hyacinth patch. I saw a skullcap, and eyes. A woman's eyes?

After the hyacinth settled, I called to Simon. He ran to the bow. With the book, he took a one-arm swing, just missing my face with the end of the pole.

"Goddamn to hell, Adrian!"

I heard my name over the buzz.

"I said quick, Adrian. Don't you know quick, Adrian?"

"It was a skin diver, Mon. A woman skin diver."

"It ain't no goddamn skin diver."

I smiled. "A mermaid then?"

"Not a mermaid. A mammal. Genus *Trichecus*."

I smiled again. "Tricky cuss?"

Simon shook the book in front of my face. "It's all in here. In this green book. It's all scientific. I'm going to get it. It's mine, Adrian. Do you hear? I want that goddamn animal."

Standing on the bow again, I tried to be patient. I saw it once more, saw it when it was just a single moving stem on a single cluster over the port side where Simon was watching.

"There, Mon."

We both saw the eyes this time, small, dark, and the strange lips. The skin was brown-gray, folded and thick and smooth.

"Now, Mon!"

Simon's swing was graceful, but he hit nothing.

"The damn book says fifteen minutes," he said. "That wasn't no fifteen minutes."

"It's feeding on the broken patches of hyacinth. Watch that one."

"Quiet, please, just quiet. Let me think."

Simon got on the bow to watch the patch. I watched Simon.

As soon as the pole went up, I pressed the ignition, pushed the throttle full forward. The bow reared.

Simon flew over the windshield onto the deck near his seat. I felt a bump under the hull before the pin in the motor foot sheared and the boat stopped dead.

By the time I cut the motor, Simon had recovered. He cursed me until he saw the agitation in the water. I had gotten this animal, this manatee, with one stroke of my stainless-steel prop.

"Quick, Mon!"

Simon stepped up on the port side, balanced himself, but the animal had disappeared. Simon swung at the hyacinth anyway. It was a great, mad arch.

I saw spurts of red on the green. "For the love of . . . Mon, you got it . . ."

Simon lost his balance. He tried to fall back with a squat, but a sudden tug from the rope brought him up into his stance again. The pole slipped through his hands.

"Mon!"

Simon tightened his hold on the rope. His body angled back, stiff and straight. He stopped the pull.

Balanced at that tilt, he looked at me. He laughed.

"Eee-yah!" Simon yelled.

"That's it, Mon, goddamn it, hot-hot damn . . ."

"Eee-Yah!" Simon yelled again, his eyes still on me, as he whipped forward over the side.

There were no splashes anywhere, just swells, swells again and again, mounds of water rising, rounding, falling, but no fish or fin or sweater or shoe. I called out Simon's name three, four times until I caught sight of the top of his head capped with mud and stem and root. I watched his mouth for a word, but he sank.

Simon made it to the shallows with the rope in his hands. He crawled for the swamp. At the edge of the swamp, five or six feet to his right, the manatee was up, was rolling.

Simon fell forward, exhausted, sucking in air. He got up, spit water and words, but I could not understand. He fell.

The manatee dragged him. Simon coiled the rope around his elbow and shoulder and dug into the mud with his feet. Again, he fell forward.

"I don't want to touch it, Adrian."

Simon's arms were pinned between two cypress knees. He looked for me.

"Ah-dree-ann. Ah-dree-ann . . ."

I jumped in, swam until I found bottom. I freed Simon's hands and arms and dove at the moving mud.

I wrapped my arms around the manatee at midsection and fell to my side. I tried to lift it out of the water and mud and get to my knees, but the manatee, as long as I was tall, weighed several of me.

I squeezed. The guts gave like cotton stuff. I shifted my weight, circled until my shoulder was where my hands had been, and my hands were in the motor wound.

The manatee was a backboned thing. I felt the bone in my hands. On my hands, the flesh in the wound was warm.

I worked on the wound and the bone with my shoulder. I slid my face up, and my arms, over the smooth, cool skin until my cheek was behind the head. I slid down again until my face pressed into the soft belly and my hands were deep in the gash.

I squeezed. I felt a snap. I slid up again and lifted.

The bone gave with another snap against my knee. Long after the struggling stopped and the muscles relaxed, I slid and lifted and squeezed.

With my face in the belly, my hand in the wound, I pushed the animal through the mud into the swamp. I rolled away to breathe.

The air was brittle and cold deep in my lungs. Deep in my lungs were the gases, methane and sulphur, the fight had released from the swamp.

I opened my eyes. I saw white sky and rat cypress.

Simon sat on the flat top of a cypress stump. He shivered and wiped black mud from his face and sweater.

He pointed to me and laughed. "Nigger Jom . . ."

I kept my eyes on Simon's mouth. I tried to guess what he would say next. The words formed slowly, between a laugh and a breath, but I knew.

"We did it," he said. "We did it, did it, did it."

I crawled to him. I trembled from the cold.

At his feet, I sat on my calves in the mud. "You knew what we just did, Mon? Look at that thing. Look at that goddamn thing."

The manatee was another mud mound in the swamp. The mud rose and fell as the manatee breathed. I saw the oozing red, vivid over the black where the hook had pierced, and I saw an eye, ivory-colored, weak, and covered with mucus.

The eye never blinked. Only the strange mouth moved. The cleft upper lip opened and closed like mandibles over the lower lip bristles.

Simon shook, laughed. "I feel . . ."

"Go on, Mon. Say it. I know what you're going to say. I know."

"I feel . . ."

"You feel good, don't you?"

"In the Bible . . ."

"You feel alive."

"In the Bible, Adrian, bowels move. That means strong emotion. That means to feel something so deep in your gut, a grinding. I never . . . My bowels move from all this, Ah-dree-ann, you understand? I feel it deep, a grinding in my guts."

"Yes," I said.

I sat shivering, waiting for Simon to speak again. When he laughed, I laughed, and the spasms ruled us awhile. We had no control, and we let it pass.

"But, Ah-dree-ann. My bowels, Ah-dree-ann. They need to move in all ways."

Simon walked to a cypress tree and pulled his pants down and leaned against the trunk. I laughed for a long while. When that stopped and there was just the pain in my throat, there remained the thought of man's need to stoop at such a time.

I watched Simon go through the same stages. His eyes watered like mine and washed the mud from under his eyes. I looked at the red underwear at his ankles in the mud and at his white skin, and I laughed again, laughed into and past pain and thought.

There was something Sah-rah would have called *delightful* about it, something that would never come again. I felt a sweep of sadness in my last, uncontrollable shiver, and I sat back to let it pass.

Simon stopped laughing. He walked to me and kneeled in the mud. Reaching out, he touched each of my shoulders.

I felt the sadness again, and I shivered.

"Ah-dree-ann," he said.

My name was all he could say. Taking his hands away, he looked down in the mud.

"Ah-dree-ann, I'm sorry."

I inhaled to find the scent of cedar in his sweater. I smelled the swamp, the Odor.

I looked at the manatee to find the taking-in and the letting-out of a breath, but some time ago the manatee had died, its eyes still open, its many-parted mouth open, but still.

Simon tapped my leg. I kept my eyes on the dead flesh.

Simon put his head in front of mine. The mud around his lips had dried to the cracks and creases of his speech.

At times, when I had been learning to read lips, when my mind dived into the quiet below the buzz and my eyes stayed above, it was as though I heard words before a mouth moved.

Out of the terrible silence below the buzz came the name, and then on Simon's mouth it formed—*Sah-rah.*

"Me and Sara," he said. "Me and Sara."

CONTRIBUTORS

PATRICK ANDREWS, employed as a product specialist dealing with control valves, is also a part-time marketing student at the University of New Orleans. His poetry has been published in *Ellipsis*. He resides in Metairie with his wife and son.

FREDERICK BARTON, a native New Orleanian, is the author of two novels, *The El Cholo Feeling Passes* and *Courting Pandemonium*. Educated at Valparaiso University, the University of California at Los Angeles, and the Writers' Workshop at the University of Iowa, he is a recent winner of the Louisiana Arts Council Fellowship Award in literature and has received nine awards from the New Orleans Press Club for his film criticism in the newsweekly *Gambit*. He has taught English at the University of New Orleans since 1979.

JOHN WILLIAM CORRINGTON was from Shreveport. At his death, in 1988, he was working on a short novel entitled *The Prison Gods* and editing material in one of the volumes of *The Collected Works of Eric Voegelin*, which are being published by Louisiana State University Press. *The Collected Stories of John William Corrington* has recently appeared.

ALBERT BELISLE DAVIS received an M.A. degree in creative writing from Colorado State University. His novel *Leechtime*, published by Louisiana State University Press in 1989, won the 1984 Deep South Writers Conference novel competition. Davis, who teaches at Nicholls State University, lives and writes on Bayou Terrebonne, in Terrebonne Parish.

André Dubus was born in Lake Charles and grew up in Lafayette, where he attended Cathedral School. He has published two novels and six collections of stories, as well as a book of essays. He has had two Guggenheim grants for fiction and two National Endowment for the Arts grants for fiction. He recently received the Jean Stein Award from the Academy of Arts and Letters and a John D. and Catherine T. MacArthur Foundation Fellowship.

Ernest Gaines, born in Oscar, has lived most of his adult life in California, although he now spends part of each year in Lafayette, where he is writer in residence at the University of Southwestern Louisiana. He is the author of seven books of fiction, including *Catherine Carmier* and *The Autobiography of Miss Jane Pittman,* a filmed adaptation of which was presented by CBS. His most recent novel is *A Gathering of Old Men,* and it has also aired in a filmed presentation by CBS.

Elton Glaser, born in New Orleans, spent part of his childhood in Slidell. He has a B.A. and M.A. in English from the University of New Orleans, and an M.F.A. from the University of California at Irvine. Primarily a poet, he has published two full-length collections of poetry, *Relics* and *Tropical Depressions,* the latter of which won the first Iowa Poetry Prize awarded. Glaser's short fiction has appeared in several magazines, including the *North Dakota Quarterly* and the *Barataria Review.* The recipient of fellowships from the National Endowment for the Arts and from the Ohio Arts Council, he is now professor of English at the University of Akron.

Shirley Ann Grau was born in New Orleans, grew up in Alabama and Massachusetts, and now lives in New Orleans. She has published eight books in addition to a large number of short stories and travel pieces. Currently at work on a novel, she has received various awards, including the Pulitzer Prize for fiction.

MARTHA LACY HALL served for a number of years as managing editor at Louisiana State University Press. She has published short fiction in the *Southern Review*, the *Sewanee Review*, the *New Orleans Review*, the *Virginia Quarterly*, and other journals. *Music Lesson*, a collection of her short stories, appeared in 1984, and *The Apple-Green Triumph and Other Stories* was published by Louisiana State University Press in 1990. She lives in Baton Rouge.

DEV HATHAWAY is a former editor of the *Black Warrior Review*. His stories and poems have appeared in the *Carolina Quarterly*, *Crazyhorse*, the *Missouri Review*, *Shenandoah*, and other journals. "The Goose and the Thorn" will be included in a collection of his short fiction, *The Widow's Boy*.

JAMES KNUDSEN has taught at the University of New Orleans for the past eleven years. "There Are No Birds in Hoboken" is his first story to be published in the Deep South. Other stories by him have appeared in numerous literary magazines, including the *Denver Quarterly*, the *Kansas Quarterly*, the *Sonora Review*, *Puerto del Sol*, *Four Quarters*, the *Pacific Review*, the *North Dakota Quarterly*, and *Intro*. He has also published two novels for young adults, *Just Friends* and *Playing Favorites*. He is at work on a novel for adults called *Mid-City*.

DAVID MADDEN has written most of his thirty books since coming to Louisiana in 1968. His several works of fiction include *The Suicide's Wife*, *Bijou*, *Pleasure Dome*, *On the Big Wind*, *Cassandra Singing*, *The Beautiful Greed*, and the collection of stories *The Shadow Knows*. He has just completed a Civil War novel called *Sharpshooter*. He has also published an impressive body of nonfiction. Since his move to the state, he has been writer in residence at Louisiana State University.

William Mills has published nine books, including the novel *Those Who Blink,* the collection of poetry *The Meaning of Coyotes,* and the collection of short stories *I Know a Place,* as well as *Bears and Men: A Gathering,* a work of nonfiction with color photographs, and *The Stillness in Moving Things: The World of Howard Nemerov.* His latest book is *The Arkansas: An American River.* He has read and lectured in Hungary, Russia, Latvia, Lithuania, Turkey, and Finland, and at the American Academy in Rome. He has directed the poetry workshops at Oklahoma State University and has served as poetry editor of the *Cimarron Review.*

Stella Nesanovich holds a Ph.D. in English from Louisiana State University and is associate professor of English at McNeese State University. During the summers of 1985 and 1986, she was a fellow at the Virginia Center for the Creative Arts, where she worked on fiction. She has published stories in the *Southern Review* and *New Dog.* She has also written essays and reviews for a number of publications, including the *Southern Review,* the *New York Times Book Review,* the Houston *Chronicle,* and the Charlotte *Observer.*

Walker Percy, born in Alabama, made his home in the years before his death, in 1990, on the edge of Bogue Falaya, a bayou just above Lake Pontchartrain. After graduating from the University of North Carolina, he attended the College of Physicians and Surgeons of Columbia University. His first novel, *The Moviegoer,* won the National Book Award in 1962. He was the author of one work of nonfiction, *The Message in the Bottle,* and several novels, including *Love in the Ruins, The Second Coming,* and *Lancelot.* The last work he published was *The Thanatos Syndrome.*

Nancy Richard, a native of Lafayette, currently lives in North Carolina, where she is enrolled in the M.F.A. program in creative writing at the University of North Carolina at Greensboro. An earlier story, "What Goes Around Comes Around," appeared in the literary review *Caesura,* published at Auburn University.

JOHN S. TARLTON, born in Shreveport, now lives in Baton Rouge with his wife and young son. Portions of a soon-to-be-completed novel, of which "Piccadilly" forms a part, have appeared in the *Crescent Review*, the *Southwestern Review*, the *Albany Review*, the *Uncommon Reader*, and *Mississippi Arts and Letters*.

JAMES H. WILSON, a native of Baton Rouge and a graduate of Louisiana State University and Tulane University, is professor emeritus of English at the University of Southwestern Louisiana. During World War II, he completed thirty-five combat missions as a member of a B-24 heavy bombardment group of the Fifteenth Air Force stationed in Italy. He has published scholarly books, articles, and one play. For the academic year 1988–1989 he was awarded a Fulbright lectureship to China in American literature. He lives in Lafayette with his wife, Jacqueline, the mother of their nine children.

CARL WOOTON is a short-story writer and critic whose work has appeared in the *Hudson Review*, the *Literary Review*, the *Georgia Review*, the *Midwest Quarterly*, *Callaloo*, *Forum*, *Sun Dog*, and other magazines. The editorial staff of the *Hudson Review* has called him one of the "most promising new writers in the country." He is working on more stories and a novel. In collaboration with the folklorist Marcia Gaudet, he has completed a study of Ernest Gaines that was recently published by Louisiana State University Press. He lives in Lafayette.